ALEXANDER CARMICHEAL
CARMINA GADELICA, VOL. I & II

ALEXANDER CARMICHEAL
CARMINA GADELICA, VOL. I & II

Carmina Gadelica

Vol. I & II

By Alexander Carmicheal

CONTENTS

INTRODUCTION

THIS work consists of old lore collected during the last forty-four years. It forms a small part of a large mass of oral literature written down from the recital of men and women throughout the Highlands and Islands of Scotland, from Arran to Caithness, from Perth to St Kilda.

The greater portion of the collection has been made in the Western Isles, variously called 'Eileana Bride,' Hebrid Isles, Outer Hebrides, Outer Isles, 'Eilean Fada,' 'Innis Fada,' Long Island, and anciently 'Iniscead,' 'Innis Cat.' Isle of the Cat, Isle of the Catey. Probably the Catey were the people who gave the name 'Cataibh,' Cat Country, to Sutherland, and 'Caitnis,' Cat Ness, to Caithness.

The Long Island is composed of a series of islands, separately known as Barra, South Uist, Benbecula, North Uist, and Harris and Lewis. This chain is one hundred and nineteen miles in length, varying from a few yards to twenty-five miles in width. Viewed from the summit of its highest link, the Long Island chain resembles a huge artificial kite stretched along the green Atlantic Ocean, Lewis forming the body, the disjointed tail trending away in the blue haze and terminating in Bearnarey of Barra.

This long series of islands is evidently the backbone of a large island, perhaps of a great continent, that extended westward beyond the Isle of the Nuns, beyond the Isle of the Monks, beyond the Isle of St Flann, beyond the Isle of St Kilda, beyond the Isle of Rockal, probably beyond the storied Isle of Rocabarraidh, and possibly beyond the historic Isle of Atlantis.

This backbone is now disarticulated like the vertebra of some huge fossil fish, each section having a life of its own. These joints are separated by rills and channels varying from a few feet to eight miles in width.

The Atlantic rushes through these straits and narrows into the Minch, and the Minch rushes through the straits and narrows into the Atlantic, four times every twenty-four hours. The constant rushing to and fro of these mighty waters is very striking. Many of the countless islands comprising the Outer Hebrides are indented with arms of the sea studded with rocks and islands dividing and ramifying into endless mazes, giving in some cases a coast-line of over four hundred miles within their one-mile entrance. No mind could conceive, no imagination could realise, the disorderly distribution of land and water that is to be seen in those Outer Islands, where mountain and moor, sand and peat, rock and morass, reef and shoal, fresh-water lake and salt-water loch, in wildest confusion strive for mastery. Viewing this bewildering scene from the summit of Ruaival in Benbecula, Professor Blackie exclaimed:--

O God-forsaken, God-detested land!
Of bogs and blasts, of moors and mists and rain;
Where ducks with men contest the doubtful strand,
And shirts when washed are straightway soiled again! [*1]

The formation of the Long Island is Laurentian gneiss, with some outcrops of Cambrian at Aoi, Lewis, and four examples of trap at Lochmaddy, Uist. The rocks everywhere show ice action, being smoothed and polished, grooved and striated from hill to sea--the grooves and striae lying east and west or thereby.

There are no trees in the Long Island except some at Rodail, Harris, and a few at Stornoway, Lewis. The wind and spray of the Atlantic are inimical to trees under present climatic conditions. There are evidences, however, that there were trees in historic and prehistoric times.

It is said that a prince of Lewis forsook a Norse princess and married a native girl. The princess vowed by Odin, Thor, and Frea, and by all the other gods and goddesses of her fathers, to avenge the insult, and she sent her witch to burn the woods of Lewis. The tradition of the burning of these woods is countenanced by the presence of charred trees in peat-moss in many places. It is on record that a Norse prince married a native Barra girl, but whether or not this was the prince of Lewis is uncertain. There are many evidences that the sea has gained upon the land in the Long Island. In the shore and in the sea, peat-moss, tree-roots, sessile reeds, stone dykes, dwellings and temples may be seen, while pieces of moss, trees and masonry have been brought up from time to time by hooks and anchors in from ten to twenty fathoms of water. I do not know anything more touching yet more fascinating than these submerged memorials of bygone times and of bygone men.

Immense stretches of sandy plains run along the Atlantic border of the Outer Hebrides. These long reaches of sessile sand are locally called machairs--plains. They are singularly bleak, barren, and shelterless in winter, giving rise to the saying:--

'Is luath fear na droch mhnatha
Air a mhachair Uibhistich.'

Fast goes the man of the thriftless wife
Upon the machair of Uist.

The inference is that the man is ill clad. In summer, however, these 'machairs' are green and grassy, comforting to the foot, pleasing to the eye, and deliciously fragrant, being covered with strongly aromatic plants and flowers.

But the charm of these islands lies in their people--goodly to see, brave to endure, and pleasing to know.

The population of the Long Island is about forty-four thousand. Of these, about forty-four families occupy two-thirds of the whole land, the crofters, cottars, and the poor who exist upon the poor, being confined to the remaining third. These are crowded upon one another like sheep in a pen:--

Na biasta mar ag itheadh nam biasta beag,
Na biasta beag a deanamh mar dh'fhaodas iad.'

The big beasts eating the little beasts,
The little beasts doing as best they may.

There are no intermediate farms, no gradation holdings, to which the industrious crofter might aspire, and become a benefit to himself, an example to his neighbour, and a lever to his country.

The people of the Outer Isles, like the people of the Highlands and Islands generally, are simple and law-abiding, common crime being rare and serious crime unknown among them. They are good to the poor, kind to the stranger, and courteous to all. During all the years that I lived and travelled among them, night and day, I never met with incivility, never with rudeness, never with vulgarity, never with aught but courtesy. I never entered a house without the inmates offering me food or apologising for their want of it. I never was asked for charity in the West, a striking contrast to my experience in England, where I was frequently asked for food, for drink, for money, and that by persons whose incomes would have been wealth to the poor men and women of the West. After long experience of his tenants, the late Mr John Gordon said:--'The Uist people are born gentlemen-- Nature's noblemen.'

Gaelic oral literature was widely diffused, greatly abundant, and excellent in quality--in the opinion of scholars, unsurpassed by anything similar in the ancient classics of Greece or Rome.

Many causes contributed towards these attainments--the crofting system, the social customs, and the evening 'ceilidh.' In a crofting community the people work in unison in the field during the day, and discuss together in the house at night. This meeting is called 'ceilidh'--a word that throbs the heart of the Highlander wherever he be. The 'ceilidh' is a literary entertainment where stories and tales, poems and ballads, are rehearsed and recited, and songs are sung, conundrums are put, proverbs are quoted, and many other literary matters are related and discussed. This institution is admirably adapted to cultivate the heads and to warm the hearts of an intelligent, generous people. Let me briefly describe the 'ceilidh' as I have seen it.

In a crofting townland there are several story-tellers who recite the oral literature of their predecessors. The story-tellers of the Highlands are as varied in their subjects as are literary men and women elsewhere. One is a historian narrating events simply and concisely; another is a historian with a bias, colouring his narrative according to his leanings. One is an inventor, building fiction upon fact, mingling his materials, and investing the whole with the charm of novelty and the halo of romance. Another is a reciter of heroic poems and ballads, bringing the different characters before the mind as clearly as the sculptor brings the figure before the eye. One gives the songs of the chief poets, with interesting accounts of their authors, while another, generally a woman, sings, to weird airs, beautiful old songs, some of them Arthurian. There are various other narrators, singers, and speakers, but I have never heard aught that should not be said nor sung.

The romance school has the largest following, and I go there, joining others on the way. The house of the story-teller is already full, and it is difficult to get inside and away from the cold wind and soft sleet without. But with that politeness native to the people, the stranger is pressed to come forward and occupy the seat vacated for him beside the houseman. The house is roomy and clean, if homely, with its bright peat fire in the middle of the floor. There are many present--men and women, boys and girls. All the women are seated, and most of the men. Girls are crouched between the knees of fathers or brothers or friends, while boys are perched wherever--boy-like--they can climb.

The houseman is twisting twigs of heather into ropes to hold down thatch, a neighbour crofter is twining quicken roots into cords to tie cows, while another is plaiting bent grass into baskets to hold meal.

'Ith aran, sniamh murari,
Is bi thu am bliadhn mar him thu'n uraidh.'

Eat bread and twist bent,
And thou this year shalt be as thou wert last.

The housewife is spinning, a daughter is carding, another daughter is teazing, while a third daughter, supposed to be working, is away in the background conversing in low whispers with the son of a neighbouring crofter. Neighbour wives and neighbour daughters are knitting, sewing, or embroidering, The conversation is general: the local news, the weather, the price of cattle, these leading up to higher themes--the clearing of the glens (a sore subject), the war, the parliament, the effects of the sun upon the earth and the moon upon the tides. The speaker is eagerly listened to, and is urged to tell more. But he pleads that he came to hear and not to speak, saying:--

'A chiad sgial air fear an taighe,
Sgial gu la air an aoidh.'

The first story from the host,
Story till day from the guest.

The stranger asks the houseman to tell a story, and after a pause the man complies. The tale is full of incident, action, and pathos. It is told simply yet graphically, and at times dramatically--compelling the undivided attention of the listener. At the pathetic scenes and distressful events the bosoms of the women may be seen to heave and their silent tears to fall. Truth overcomes craft, skill conquers strength, and bravery is rewarded. Occasionally a momentary excitement occurs when heat and sleep overpower a boy and he tumbles down among the people below, to be trounced out and sent home. When the story is ended it is discussed and commented upon, and the different characters praised or blamed according to their merits and the views of the critics.

If not late, proverbs, riddles, conundrums, and songs follow. Some of the tales, however, are long, occupying a night or even several nights in recital. 'Sgeul Coise Cein,' the story of the foot of Clan, for example, was in twenty-four parts, each part occupying a night in telling. The story is mentioned by Macnicol in his Remarks on Johnson's Tour.

The hut of Hector Macisaac, Ceannlangavat, South Uist, stood in a peat-moss. The walls were of 'riasg,' turf, and the thatch of 'cuilc,' reeds, to the grief of the occupants, who looked upon the reed as banned, because it was used on Calvary to convey the sponge with the vinegar. The hut was about fifteen feet long, ten feet broad, and five feet high. There was nothing in it that the vilest thief in the lowest slum would condescend to steal. It were strange if the inmates of this turf hut in the peat-morass had been other than ailing. Hector Macisaac and his wife were the only occupants, their daughter being at service trying to prolong existence in' her parents. Both had been highly endowed physically, and were still endowed mentally, though now advanced in years. The wife knew many secular runes, sacred hymns, and fairy songs; while the husband had numerous heroic tales, poems, and ballads.

I had visited these people before, and in September 1871 Iain E. Campbell of Islay and I went to see them. Hector Macisaac, the unlettered cottar who knew no language but his own, who came into contact with no one but those of his own class, his neighbours of the peat-bog, and who had never been out of his native island, was as polite and well-mannered and courteous as Iain Campbell, the learned barrister, the world-wide traveller, and the honoured guest of every court in Europe. Both were at ease and at home with one another, there being neither servility on the one side nor condescension on the other.

The stories and poems which Hector Macisaac went over during our visits to him would have filled several volumes. Mr Campbell now and then put a leading question which brought out the story-teller's marvellous memory and extensive knowledge of folklore.

It was similar with blind old Hector Macleod, cottar, Lianacuithe, South Uist, and with old Roderick Macneill, cottar, Miunghlaidh, Barra. Each of those men repeated stories and poems, tales and ballads, that would have filled many books. Yet neither of them told more than a small part of what he knew. None of the three men knew any letters, nor any language but Gaelic, nor had ever been out of his native island. All expressed regret in well-chosen words that they had not a better place in which to receive their visitors, and all thanked them in polite terms for coming to see them and for taking an interest in their decried and derided old lore. And all were courteous as the courtier. During his visit to us, Mr Campbell expressed to my wife and to myself his admiration of these and other men with whom we had come in contact. He said that in no other race had he observed so many noble traits and high qualities as in the unlettered, untravelled, unspoiled Highlander.

In 1860, 1861, and 1862, I took down much folk-lore from Kenneth Morrison, cottar, Trithion, Skye. Kenneth Morrison had been a mason, but was now old, blind, and poor. Though wholly unlettered, he was highly intelligent. He mentioned the names of many old men in the extensive but now desolate parish of Minngnis, who had been famous story-tellers in his boyhood--men who had been born in the first decade of the eighteenth century. Several of these, he said, could recite stories and poems during many nights in succession--some of the tales requiring several nights to relate. He repeated fragments of many of these. Some of them were pieces of poems and stories published by Macpherson, Smith, the Stewarts, the MacCallums, the Campbells, and others.

Kenneth Morrison told me that the old men, from whom he heard the poems and stories, said that they had heard them from old men in their boyhood. That would carry these old men back to the first half of the seventeenth century. Certainly they could not have learnt their stories or poems from books, for neither stories nor poems were printed in their time, and even had they been, those men could not have read them.

Gaelic oral literature has been disappearing during the last three centuries. It is now becoming meagre in quantity, inferior in quality, and greatly isolated.

Several causes have contributed towards this decadence--principally the Reformation, the Risings, the evictions, the Disruption, the schools, and the spirit of the age. Converts in religion, in politics, or in aught else, are apt to be intemperate in speech and rash in action. The Reformation movement condemned the beliefs and cults tolerated and assimilated by the Celtic Church and the Latin Church. Nor did sculpture and architecture escape their intemperate zeal. The risings harried and harassed the people, while the evictions impoverished, dispirited, and scattered them over the world. Ignorant school-teaching and clerical narrowness have been painfully detrimental to the expressive language, wholesome literature, manly sports, and interesting amusements of the Highland people. Innumerable examples occur.

A young lady said:--'When we came to Islay I was sent to the parish school to obtain a proper grounding in arithmetic. I was charmed with the schoolgirls and their Gaelic songs. But the schoolmaster--an alien like myself--denounced Gaelic speech and Gaelic songs. On getting out of school one evening the girls resumed a song they had been singing the previous evening. I joined willingly, if timidly, my knowledge of Gaelic being small. The schoolmaster heard us, however, and called us back. He punished us till the blood trickled from our fingers, although we were big girls, with the dawn of womanhood upon us. The thought of that scene thrills me with indignation.'

I was taking down a story from a man, describing how twin giants detached a huge stone from the parent rock, and how the two carried the enormous block of many tons upon their broad shoulders to lay it over a deep gully in order that their white-maned steeds might cross. Their enemy, however, came upon them in the night-time when thus engaged, and threw a magic mist around them, lessening their strength and causing them to fail beneath their burden. In the midst of the graphic description the grandson of the narrator, himself an aspirant teacher, called out tone: of superior authority, 'Grandfather, the teacher says that you ought to be placed upon the stool for your lying Gaelic stories.' The old man stopped and gasped in pained surprise. It required time and sympathy to soothe his feelings and to obtain the rest of the tale, which was wise, beautiful, and poetic, for the big, strong giants were Frost and Ice, and their subtle enemy was Thaw. The enormous stone torn from the parent rock is called 'Clach Mhor Leum nan Caorach,' the big stone of the leap of the sheep. Truly 'a little learning is a dangerous thing'! This myth was afterwards appreciated by the Royal Society of Edinburgh.

After many failures, and after going far to reach him, I induced a man to come to the lee of a knoll to tell me a tale. We were well into the spirit of the story when two men from the hill passed us. The story-teller hesitated, then stopped, saying that he would be reproved by his family, bantered by his friends, and censured by his minister. The story, so inauspiciously interrupted and never resumed, was the famous 'Sgeul Coise Cein,' already mentioned.

Having made many attempts, I at last succeeded in getting a shepherd to come to me, in order to be away from his surroundings. The man travelled fifty-five miles, eight of these being across a stormy strait of the Atlantic. We had reached the middle of a tale when the sheriff of the district came to call on me in my rooms. [paragraph continues] The reciter fled, and after going more than a mile on his way home he met a man who asked him why he looked so scared, and why without his bonnet. The shepherd discovered that he had left his bonnet, his plaid, and his staff behind him in his flight. The remaining half of that fine story, as well as much other valuable Gaelic lore, died with the shepherd in Australia.

Ministers of Lewis used to say that the people of Lewis were little better than pagans till the Reformation, perhaps till the Disruption. If they were not, they have atoned since, being now the most rigid Christians in the British Isles.

When Dr William Forbes Skene was preparing the third volume of Celtic Scotland, he asked me to write him a paper on the native system of holding the land, tilling the soil, and apportioning the stock in the Outer Hebrides. Being less familiar with Lewis than with the other portions of the Long Island, I visited Lewis again. It was with extreme difficulty that I could obtain any information on the subject of my inquiry, because it related to the foolish past rather than to the sedate present, to the secular affairs rather than to the religious life of the people. When I asked about old customs and old modes of working, I was answered, 'Good man, old things are passed away, all things are become new'; for the people of Lewis, like the people of the Highlands and Islands generally, carry the Scriptures in their minds and apply them in their speech as no other people do. It was extremely disconcerting to be met in this manner on a mission so desirable.

During my quest I went into a house near Ness. The house was clean and comfortable if plain and unpretending, most things in it being home-made. There were three girls in the house, young, comely, and shy, and four women, middle-aged, handsome, and picturesque in their homespun gowns and high-crowned mutches. Three of the women had been to the moorland pastures with their cattle, and had turned in here to rest on their way home.

'Hail to the house and household,' said I, greeting the inmates in the salutation of our fathers. 'Hail to you, kindly stranger,' replied the housewife. 'Come forward and take this seat. If it be not ill-mannered, may we ask whence you have come to-day? You are tired and travel-stained, and probably hungry?' 'I have come from Gress,' said I, 'round by Tolasta to the south, and Tolasta to the north, taking a look at the ruins of the Church of St Aula, at Gress, and at the ruins of the fort of Dunothail, and then across the moorland.' 'May the Possessor keep you in His own keeping, good man! You left early and have travelled far, and must be hungry.' With this the woman raised her eyes towards her daughters standing demurely silent, and motionless as Greek statues, in the background. In a moment the three fair girls became active and animated. One ran to the stack and brought in an armful of hard, black peats, another ran to the well and brought in a pail of clear spring water, while the third quickly spread a cloth, white as snow, upon the table in the inner room. The three neighbour women rose to leave, and I rose to do the same. 'Where are you going, good man?' asked the housewife in injured surprise, moving between me and the door. 'You must not go till you eat a bit and drink a sip. That indeed would be a reproach to us that we would not soon get over. These slips of lassies and I would not hear the end of it from the men at the sea, were we to allow a wayfarer to go from our door hungry, thirsty, and weary. No! no! you must not go till you eat a bite. Food will be ready presently, and in the meantime you will bathe your feet and dry your stockings, which are wet after coming through the marshes of the moorland.' Then the woman went down upon her knees, and washed and dried the feet of the stranger as gently and tenderly as a mother would those of her child. 'We have no stockings to suit the kilt,' said the woman in a tone of evident regret, 'but here is a pair of stockings of the houseman's which he has never had on, and perhaps you would put them on till your own are dry.'

One of the girls had already washed out my stockings, and they were presently drying before the bright fire on the middle of the floor. I deprecated all this trouble, but to no purpose. In an incredibly short time I was asked to go 'ben' and break bread.

Through the pressure of the housewife and of myself the other three women had resumed their seats, uneasily it is true. But immediately before food was announced the three women rose together and quietly walked away, no urging detaining them.

The table was laden with wholesome food sufficient for several persons, There were fried herrings and boiled turbot fresh from the sea, and eggs fresh from the yard. There were fresh butter and salt butter, wheaten scones, barley bannocks, and oat cakes, with excellent tea, and cream. The woman apologised that she had no 'aran coinnich'--moss bread, that is, loaf bread--and no biscuits, they being simple crofter people far away from the big town.

'This,' said I, taking my seat, looks like the table for a "reiteach," betrothal, rather than for one man. Have you betrothals in Lewis?' I asked, turning my eyes towards the other room where we had left the three comely maidens. 'Oh, indeed, yes, the Lewis people are very good at marrying. Foolish young creatures, they often marry before they know their responsibilities or realise their difficulties,' and her eyes followed mine in the direction of her own young daughters. 'I suppose there is much fun and rejoicing at your marriages--music, dancing, singing, and, merry-making of many kinds?' 'Oh, indeed, no, our weddings are now quiet and becoming, not the foolish things they were in my young days. In my memory weddings were great events, with singing and piping, dancing and amusements all night through, and generally for two and three nights in succession. Indeed, the feast of the "bord breid," kertch table, was almost as great as the feast of the marriage table, all the young men and maidens struggling to get to it, On the morning after the marriage the mother of the bride, and failing her the mother of the bridegroom, placed the "breid tri chearnach," three-cornered kertch, on the head of the bride before she rose from her bed. And the mother did this "all ainm na Teoire Beannaichte," in name of the Sacred Three, under whose guidance the young wife was to walk. Then the bride arose and her maidens dressed her, and she came forth with the "breid beannach," pointed kertch, on her head, and all the people present saluted her and shook hands with her, and the bards sang songs to her, and recited "rannaghail mhora," great rigmaroles, and there was much rejoicing and merrymaking all day long and all night through. "Gu dearbh mar a b'e fleadh na bord breid a b'fhearr, chan e gearr bu mheasa"--Indeed, if the feast of the kertch table was not better, it was not a whit worse.

'There were many sad things done then, for those were the days of foolish doings and of foolish people. Perhaps, on the day of the Lord, when they came out of church, if indeed they went into church, the young men would go to throw the stone, or to toss the cabar, or to play shinty, or to run races, or to race horses on the strand, the young maidens looking on the while, ay, and the old men and women.' 'And have you no music, no singing, no dancing now at your marriages?' 'May the Possessor keep you! I see that you are a stranger in Lewis, or you would not ask such a question,' the woman exclaimed with grief and surprise in her tone. 'It is long since we abandoned those foolish ways in Ness, and, indeed, throughout Lewis. In my young days there was hardly a house in Ness in which there was not one or two or three who could play the pipe, or the fiddle, or the trump. And I have heard it said that there were men, and women too, who could play things they called harps, and lyres, and bellow-pipes, but I do not know what those things were.' 'And why were those discontinued?' 'A blessed change came over the place and the people,' the woman replied in earnestness, 'and the good men and the good ministers who arose did away with the songs and the stories, the music and the dancing, the sports and the games, that were perverting the minds and ruining the souls of the people, leading them to folly and stumbling.' 'But how did the people themselves come to discard their sports and pastimes?' 'Oh, the good ministers and the good elders preached against them and went among the people, and besought them to forsake their follies and to return to wisdom. They made the people break and burn their pipes and fiddles. If there was a foolish man here and there who demurred, the good ministers and the good elders themselves broke and burnt their instruments, saying:--

"Is fearr an teine beag a gharas la beag na sithe,
Na'n teine mor a loisgeas la mor na feirge."

Better is the small fire that warms on the little day of peace,
Than the big fire that burns on the great day of wrath.

[paragraph continues] The people have forsaken their follies and their Sabbath-breaking, and there is no pipe, no fiddle here now,' said the woman in evident satisfaction. 'And what have you now instead of the racing, the stone-throwing, and the cabar-tossing, the song, the pipe, and the dance?' 'Oh, we have now the blessed Bible preached and explained to us faithfully and earnestly, if we sinful people would only walk in the right path and use our opportunities.'

'But what have you at your weddings? How do you pass the time?' 'Oh! the carles are on one side of the house talking of their crops and their nowt, and mayhap of the days when they were young and when things were different. And the young men are on the other side of the house talking about boats, and sailing, and militia, and naval reserve, perhaps of their own strength, and of many foolish matters besides.

'And where are the girls? What are they doing?' 'Oh, they, silly things! are in the "culaist," back-house, perhaps trying to croon over some foolish song under their breath, perhaps trying to amble through some awkward steps of dancing on the points of their toes, or, shame to tell, perhaps speaking of what dress this or that girl had on at this or that marriage, or worse still, what hat this girl or that girl had on on the Day of the Lord, perhaps even no the Day of the Holy Communion, showing that their minds were on the vain things of the world instead of on the wise things of salvation.'

'But why are the girls in the "culaist"? What do they fear?'

'May the Good Being keep you, good man! They are in the "culaist" for concealment, "ages eagal am beatha agus am bais orra gun cluinnear no gum faicear iad"--and the fear of their life and of their death upon them, that they may be heard or seen should the good elder happen to be passing the way.' 'And should he, what then?' 'Oh, the elder will tell the minister, and the good minister will scold them from the pulpit, mentioning the girls by name. But the girls have a blanket on the door and another blanket on the window to deafen the sound and to obscure the light.'

'Do the young maidens allow the young men to join them in the "culaist"?' 'Indeed, truth to tell, the maidens would be glad enough to admit the young men were it not the fear of exposure. But the young men are so loud of voice, and so heavy of foot, and make so much noise, that they would betray the retreat of the girls, who would get rebuked, while the young men would escape. The girls would then be ashamed and downcast, and would not lift a head for a year and a day after their well-deserved scolding. They suffer most, for, sad to say, the young men are becoming less afraid of being admonished than they used to be.'

'And do the people have spirits at their marriages?' 'Oh yes, the minister is not so hard as that upon them at all. He does not interfere with them in that way unless they take too much, and talk loudly and quarrel. Then he is grieved and angry, and scolds them severely. Occasionally, indeed, some of the carles have a nice "frogan," liveliness, upon them and are very happy together. But oh, they never quarrel, nor fight, nor get angry with one another. They are always nice to one another and civil to all around them.'

'Perhaps were the minister to allow the people less drink and more music and dancing, singing and merry-making, they would enjoy it as much. I am sure the young girls would sing better, and dance better, with the help of the young men. And the young men themselves would be less loud of voice and less heavy of heel, among the maidens. Perhaps the happiness of the old people too, would be none the less real nor less lasting at seeing the joyousness of the young people.'

To this the woman promptly and loyally replied: 'The man of the Lord is untiring in work and unfailing in example for our good, and in guiding us to our heavenly home, constantly reminding us of the littleness of time and the greatness of eternity, and he knows best, and we must do our best to follow his counsel and to imitate his example.'

A famous violin-player died in the island of Eigg a few years ago. He was known for his old style playing and his old-world airs which died with him. A preacher denounced him, saying:--'Tha thu shios an sin cul na comhla, a dhuine thruaigh le do chiabhan liath, a cluich do sheann fhiodhla, le laimh fhuair a mach agus le teine an diabhoil a steach'--Thou art down there behind the door, thou miserable man with thy grey hair, playing thine old fiddle with the cold hand without, and the devil's fire within. His family pressed the man to burn his fiddle and never to play again. A pedlar came round and offered ten shillings for the violin. The instrument had been made by a pupil of Stradivarius, and was famed for its tone. 'Cha b'e idir an rud a fhuaradh na dail a ghoirtich mo chridhe cho cruaidh ach an dealachadh lithe! an dealachadh rithe! agus gun tug mi fhein a bho a b'fhearr am buaile m'athar air a son, an uair a bha mi og'--It was not at all the thing that was got for it that grieved my heart so sorely, but the parting with it! the parting with it! and that I myself gave the best cow in my father's fold for it when I was young. The voice of the old man faltered and a tear fell. He was never again seen to smile.

The reciters of religious lore were more rare and more reticent than the reciters of secular lore. Men and women whom I knew had hymns and incantations, but I did not know of this in time. The fragments recalled by their families, like the fragments of Greek or Etruscan vases, indicated the originals.

Before dictating, the reciter went over the tale or poem, the writer making mental notes the while. This was helpful when, in the slow process of dictating, the narrator lost his thread and omitted passages. The poems were generally intoned in a low recitative manner, rising and falling in slow modulated cadences charming to hear but difficult to follow.

The music of the hymns had a distinct individuality, in some respects resembling and in many respects differing from the old Gregorian chants of the Church. I greatly regret that I was not able to record this peculiar and beautiful music, probably the music of the old Celtic Church.

Perhaps no people had a fuller ritual of song and story, of secular rite and religious ceremony, than the Highlanders. Mirth and music, song and dance, tale and poem, pervaded their lives, as electricity pervades the air. Religion, pagan or Christian, or both combined, permeated everything--blending and shading into one another like the iridescent colours of the rainbow. The people were sympathetic and synthetic, unable to see and careless to know where the secular began and the religious ended-- an admirable union of elements in life for those who have lived it so truly and intensely as the Celtic races everywhere have done, and none more truly or more intensely than the ill-understood and so-called illiterate Highlanders of Scotland.

If this work does nothing else, it affords incontestable proof that the Northern Celts were endowed, as Renan justly claims for Celts everywhere, with 'profound feeling and adorable delicacy' in their religious instincts. [*1]

The Celtic missionaries allowed the pagan stock to stand, grafting their Christian cult thereon. Hence the blending of the pagan and the Christian religions in these poems, which to many minds will constitute their chief charm. Gaelic lore is full of this blending and grafting--nor are they confined to the literature of the people, but extend indeed to their music, sculpture, and architecture. At Rodail, Harris, is a cruciform church of the thirteenth century. The church abuts upon a broad square tower of no great height. The tower is called 'Tur Chliamain,' tower of Clement, 'Cliaman Mor Rodail,' Great Clement of Rodail. Tradition says that the tower is older than the church, and the masonry confirms the tradition.

There are sculptures within the church of much originality of design and of great beauty of execution, but the sculptures without are still more original and interesting. Round the sides of the square tower are the figures of birds and beasts, reptiles and fishes, and of men and women representing phallic worship. Here pagan cult joins with Christian faith, the East with the West, the past with the present. The traveller from India to Scotland can here see, on the cold, sterile rocks of Harris, the petrified symbols of a faith left living behind him on the hot, fertile plains of Hindustan. He can thus in his own person bridge over a space of eight thousand miles and a period of two thousand years.

There are observances and expressions current in the West which savour of the East, such as sun, moon, star, and fire worship, once prevalent, nor yet obsolete.

Highland divinities are full of life and action, local colour and individuality. These divinities filled the hearts and minds of the people of the Highlands, as their deities filled the hearts and minds of the people of Greece and Rome. The subject of these genii of the Highlands ought to be investigated and compared with those of other lands. Even yet, on the verge of disappearance, they would yield interesting results. Though loving their haunts and tenacious of their habitats, the genii of the Highlands are disappearing before the spirit of modernism, as the Red Indian, once bold and courageous, disappears before the white man. Once intrusive, they are now become timid as the mullet of the sea, the shrew of the grass, or the swift of the air--a glimpse, a glint, and gone for ever. They are startled at the crack of the rifle, the whistle of the steamer, the shriek of the train, and the click of the telegraph. Their homes are invaded and their repose is disturbed, so that they find no rest for their weary feet nor sleep for their heavy eyes; and their native land, so full of their love, so congenial to their hearts, will all too soon know them no more. Let an attempt be made even yet to preserve their memories ere they disappear for ever.

Whatever be the value of this work, it is genuine folk-lore, taken down from the lips of men and women, no part being copied from books. It is the product of far-away thinking, come down on the long stream of time. Who the thinkers and whence the stream, who can tell? Some of the hymns may have been composed within the cloistered cells of Derry and Iona, and some of the incantations among the cromlechs of Stonehenge and the standing-stones of Callarnis. These poems were composed by the learned, but they have not come down through the learned, but through the unlearned--not through the lettered few, but through the unlettered many--through the crofters and cottars, the herdsmen and shepherds, of the Highlands and Islands.

Although these compositions have been rescued chiefly among Roman Catholics and in the islands, they have been equally common among Protestants and on the mainland.

From one to ten versions have been taken down, differing more or less. It has been difficult to select. Some examples of these variants are given. Several poems and many notes are wholly withheld, while a few of the poems and all the notes have been abbreviated for want of space.

I had the privilege of being acquainted with Iain F. Campbell of Islay during a quarter of a century, and I have followed his counsel and imitated his example in giving the words and in recording the names of the reciters. Some localisms are given for the sake of [paragraph continues] Gaelic scholars. Hence the same word may be spelt in different ways through the influence of assonance and other characteristics of Gaelic compositions.

With each succeeding generation Gaelic speech becomes more limited and Gaelic phraseology more obscure. Both reciter and writer felt this when words and phrases occurred which neither knew. These have been rendered tentatively or left untranslated. I can only hope that in the near or distant future some competent scholar may compare these gleanings of mine with Celtic writings at home and abroad, and that light may be shed upon what is to me obscure.

I have tried to translate literally yet satisfactorily, but I am painfully conscious of failure. Although in decay, these poems are in verse of a high order, with metre, rhythm, assonance, alliteration, and every quality to please the ear and to instruct the mind, The translation lacks these and the simple dignity, the charming grace, and the passionate devotion of the original.

I see faults that I would willingly mend, but it is easier to point to blemishes than to avoid them--

'Is furasda dh'an fhear eisdeachd
Beum a thoir dh'an fhear labhairt.'

It is easy for the listening roan
To give taunt to the speaking man.

Again and again I laid down my self-imposed task, feeling unable to render the intense power and supreme beauty of the original Gaelic into adequate English. But I resumed under the inspiring influence of my wife, to whose unfailing sympathy and cultured ear this work owes much.

My daughter has transcribed the manuscripts and corrected the proofs for press, and has acted as amanuensis throughout; while my three sons have helped in various ways.

The Celtic letters in the work have been copied by my wife from Celtic MSS., chiefly in the Advocates' Library. This has been a task of extreme difficulty, needing great skill and patient care owing to the defaced condition of the originals. The letters have been prepared for the engraver with feeling and insight by Mr John Athel Lovegrove, of H.M. Ordnance Survey.

The Rev. Father Allan Macdonald, Eriskey, South Uist, generously placed at my disposal a collection of religious folk-lore made by himself. For this I am very grateful though unable to use the manuscript, having so much material of my own.

Mr John Henry Dixon, Inveran, Lochmaree, offered to publish the work at his own expense. That I have not availed myself of his generous appreciation does not lessen my gratitude for Mr Dixon's characteristic liberality.

The portrait is the friendly work and generous gift of Mr W. Skeoch Cumming, and is inserted at the request of friends outside my family.

My dear friend Mr George Henderson, M.A. Edin., Ph.D. Leipsic, B.Litt. Oxon., has helped and encouraged me throughout.

These, and the many others whose names I am unable to mention through want of space, I ask to accept my warm, abiding thanks.

Three sacrifices have been made--the sacrifice of time, the sacrifice of toil, and the sacrifice of means. These I do not regret. I have three regrets--that I had not been earlier collecting, that I have not been more diligent in collecting, and that I am not better qualified to treat what I have collected.

These notes and poems have been an education to me. And so have been the men and women reciters from whose dictation I wrote them down. They are almost all dead now, leaving no successors. With reverent hand and grateful heart I place this stone upon the cairn of those who composed and of those who transmitted the work.

ALEXANDER CARMICHAEL.

EDINBURGH,
St Michael's Day, 1899.

Footnotes

ACHAINE

INVOCATIONS

RANN ROMH URNUIGH

RUNE BEFORE PRAYER

OLD people in the Isles sing this or some other short hymn before prayer. Sometimes the hymn and the prayer are intoned in low tremulous unmeasured cadences like the moving and moaning, the soughing and the sighing, of the ever-murmuring sea on their own wild shores.

They generally retire to a closet, to an outhouse, to the lee of a knoll, or to the shelter of a dell, that they may not be seen nor heard of men. I have known men and women of eighty, ninety, and a hundred years of age continue the practice of their lives in going from one to two miles to the seashore to join their voices with the voicing, of the waves and their praises with the praises of the ceaseless sea.

TA mi lubadh mo ghlun
An suil an Athar a chruthaich mi,
An suil an Mhic a cheannaich mi,
An suil an Spioraid a ghlanaich mi,
Le caird agus caoimh.
Tre t'Aon Unga fein a Dhe,
Tabhair duinn tachar 'n ar teinn,
Gaol De,
Gradh De,
Gair De,
Gais De,
Gras De,
Sgath De,
Is toil De,
Dheanamh air talamh nan Tre,
Mar to ainghlich is naoimhich
A toighe air neamh.
Gach duar agus soillse,
Gach la agus oidhche,
Gach uair ann an caoimhe,
Thoir duinn do ghne.

I AM bending my knee
In the eye of the Father who created me,
In the eye of the Son who purchased me,
In the eye of the Spirit who cleansed me,

In friendship and affection.
Through Thine own Anointed One, O God,
Bestow upon us fullness in our need,
Love towards God,
The affection of God,
The smile of God,
The wisdom of God,
The grace of God,
The fear of God,
And the will of God
To do on the world of the Three,
As angels and saints
Do in heaven;
Each shade and light,
Each day and night,
Each time in kindness,
Give Thou us Thy Spirit.

DIA LIOM A LAIGHE

GOD WITH ME LYING DOWN

THIS poem was taken down in 1866 from Mary Macrae, Harris. She came from Kintail when young, with Alexander Macrae, whose mother was one of the celebrated ten daughters of Macleod of Rararsay, mentioned by Johnson and Boswell. Mary Macrae was rather under than over middle height, but strongly and symmetrically formed. She often walked with companions, after the work of the day was done, distances of ten and fifteen miles to a dance, and after dancing all night walked back again to the work of the morning fresh and vigorous as if nothing unusual had occurred. She was a faithful servant and an admirable worker, and danced at her leisure and carolled at her work like 'Fosgag Moire,' Our Lady's lark, above her.

The people of Harris had been greatly given to old lore and to the old ways of their fathers, reciting and singing, dancing and merry-making; but a reaction occurred, and Mary Macrae's old-world ways were abjured and condemned.

'The bigots of an iron time
Had called her simple art a crime.'

But Mary Macrae heeded not, and went on in her own way, singing her songs and ballads, intoning her hymns and incantations, and chanting her own 'port-a-bial,' mouth music, and dancing to her own shadow when nothing better was available.

I love to think of this brave kindly woman, with her strong Highland characteristics and her proud Highland spirit. She was a true type of a grand people gone never to return.

DIA liom a laighe,

2

Dia liom ag eirigh,
Dia liom anus gach rath soluis,
Is gun mi rath son as aonais,
Gun non rath as aonais.

Criosda liom a cadal,
Criosda liom a dusgadh,
Criosda liom a caithris,
Gach la agus oidhche,
Gach aon la is oidhche.

Dia liom a comhnadh
Domhnach liom a riaghladh,
Spiorad liom a treoradh,
Gu soir agus siorruidh,
Soir agus siorruidh, Amen.
Triath nan triath, Amen.

GOD with me lying down,
God with me rising up,
God with me in each ray of light,
Nor I a ray of joy without Him,
Nor one ray without Him.

Christ with me sleeping,
Christ with me waking,
Christ with me watching,
Every day and night,
Each day and night.

God with me protecting,
The Lord with me directing,
The Spirit with me strengthening,
For ever and for evermore,
Ever and evermore, Amen.
Chief of chiefs, Amen.

ORA NAM BUADH

THE INVOCATION OF THE GRACES

DUNCAN MACLELLAN, crofter, Carnan, South Uist, heard this poem from Catherine Macaulay in the early years of this century. When the crofters along the east side of South Uist were removed, many of the more frail and aged left behind became houseless and homeless, moving among and existing upon the crofters left remaining along the west side of the island.

Among these was Catherine Macaulay. Her people went to Cape Breton. She came from Mol-a-deas, adjoining Corradale, where Prince Charlie lived for several weeks when hiding in South Uist after Culloden. Catherine Macaulay had seen the Prince several times, and had many reminiscences of him and of his movements among the people of the district, who entertained him to their best when much in need, and who shielded him to their utmost when sorely harassed.

Catherine Macaulay was greatly gifted in speaking, and was marvellously endowed with a memory for old tales and hymns, runes and incantations, and for unwritten literature and traditions of many kinds.

She wandered about from house to house, and from townland to townland, warmly welcomed and cordially received wherever she went, and remained in each place longer or shorter according to the population and the season, and as the people could spare the time to hear her. The description which Duncan Maclellan gave of Catherine Macaulay, and of the people who crowded his father's house to hear her night after night, and week after week, and of the discussions that followed her recitations, were realistic and instructive. Being then but a child he could not follow the meaning of this lore, but he thought many times since that much of it must have been about the wild beliefs and practices of his people of the long long ago, and perhaps not so long ago either. Many of the poems and stories were long and weird, and he could only remember fragments, which came up to him as he lay awake, thinking of the present and the past. and of the contrast between the two, even in his own time.

I heard versions of this poem in other islands and in districts of the mainland, and in November 1888 John Gregorson Campbell, minister of Tiree, sent me a fragment taken down from Margaret Macdonald, Tiree. The poem must therefore have been widely known. in Tiree the poem was addressed to boys and girls, in Uist to young men and maidens. Probably it was composed to a maiden on her marriage. The phrase 'cala dhonn,' brown swan, would indicate that the girl was young--not yet a white swan.

IONNLAIME do bhasa
Ann am frasa fiona,
Ann an liu nan lasa,
Ann an seachda siona,
Ann an subh craobh,
Ann am bainne meala,
Is cuirime na naoi buaidhean glana caon,
Ann do ghruaidhean caomha geala,
Buaidh cruth,
Buaidh guth,
Buaidh rath,
Buaidh math,
Buaidh chnoc,
Buaidh bhochd,

I BATHE thy palms
In showers of wine,
In the lustral fire,

In the seven elements,
In the juice of the rasps,
In the milk of honey,
And I place the nine pure choice graces
In thy fair fond face,
The grace of form,
The grace of voice,
The grace of fortune,
The grace of goodness,
The grace of wisdom,
The grace of charity,

Buaidh na rogha finne,
Buaidh na fior eireachdais,
Buaidh an deagh labhraidh.

Is dubh am bail ud thall,
Is dubh na daoine th'ann,
Is tu an eala dhonn,
Ta dol a steach 'n an ceann.
Ta an cridhe fo do chonn,
Ta an teanga fo do bhonn,
'S a chaoidh cha chan iad bonn
Facail is oil leat.

Is dubhar thu ri teas,
Is seasgar thu ri fuachd,
Is suilean thu dha'n dall,
Is crann dh' an deoraidh thruagh,
Is eilean thu air muir,
Is cuisil thu air tir,
Is fuaran thu am fasach,
Is slaint dha'n ti tha tinn.

Is tu gleus na Mnatha Sithe,
Is tu beus na Bride bithe,
Is tu creud na Moire mine,
Is tu gniomh na mnatha Greig,
Is tu sgeimh na h-Eimir aluinn,
Is tu mein na Dearshul agha,
Is tu meanm na Meabha laidir,
Is tu taladh Binne-bheul.

Is tu sonas gach ni eibhinn,
Is tu solus gath na greine,

The grace of choice maidenliness,
The grace of whole-souled loveliness,
The grace of goodly speech.

Dark is yonder town,
Dark are those therein,
Thou art the brown swan,
Going in among them.
Their hearts are under thy control,
Their tongues are beneath thy sole,
Nor will they ever utter a word
To give thee offence.

A shade art thou in the heat,
A shelter art thou in the cold,
Eyes art thou to the blind,
A staff art thou to the pilgrim,
An island art thou at sea,
A fortress art thou on land,
A well art thou in the desert,
Health art thou to the ailing.

Thine is the skill of the Fairy Woman,
Thine is the virtue of Bride the calm,
Thine is the faith of Mary the mild,
Thine is the tact of the woman of Greece,
Thine is the beauty of Emir the lovely,
Thine is the tenderness of Darthula delightful,
Thine is the courage of Maebh the strong,
Thine is the charm of Binne-bheul.

Thou art the joy of all joyous things,
Thou art the light of the beam of the sun,

Is tu dorus flath na feile,
Is tu corra reul an iuil,
Is tu ceum feidh nan ardu,
Is tu ceum steud nam blaru,
Is tu seimh eal an t-snamhu,
Is tu ailleagan gach run.

Cruth aluinn an Domhnuich
Ann do ghnuis ghlain,
An cruth is ailinde
Bha air talamh.

An trath is fearr 's an latha duit,
An la is fearr 's an t-seachdain duit,
An t-seachdain is fearr 's a bhliadhna duit,
A bhliadhn is fearr an domhan Mhic De duit.

Thainig Peadail 's thainig Pol,
Thainig Seumas 's thainig Eoin,
Thainig Muiril is Muir Oigh,
Thainig Uiril uile chorr,
Thainig Airil aill nan og,
Thainig Gabriel fadh na h-Oigh,
Thainig Raphail flath nan seod,
'S thainig Micheal mil air sloigh,
Thainig 's Iosa Criosda ciuin,
Thainig 's Spiorad fior an iuil,
Thainig 's Righ nan righ air stiuir,
A bhaireadh duit-se graidh is ruin,
A bhaireadh duit-se graidh is ruin.

Thou art the door of the chief of hospitality,
Thou art the surpassing star of guidance,
Thou art the step of the deer of the hill,
Thou art the step of the steed of the plain,
Thou art the grace of the swan of swimming,
Thou art the loveliness of all lovely desires.

The lovely likeness of the Lord
Is in thy pure face,
The loveliest likeness that
Was upon earth.

The best hour of the day be thine,
The best day of the week be thine,
The best week of the year be thine,
The best year in the Son of God's domain be thine.

Peter has come and Paul has come,
James has come and John has come,
Muriel and Mary Virgin have come,
Uriel the all-beneficent has come,
Ariel the beauteousness of the young has come,
Gabriel the seer of the Virgin has come,
Raphael the prince of the valiant has come,
And Michael the chief of the hosts has come,
And Jesus Christ the mild has come,
And the Spirit of true guidance has come,

And the King of kings has come on the helm,
To bestow on thee their affection and their love,
To bestow on thee their affection and their love.

ACHANAIDH CHOITCHEANN

A GENERAL SUPPLICATION

DHE, eisd ri m' urnuigh,
Lub rium do chluas,
Leig m' achan agus m' urnuigh.
T' ionnsuidh a suas.
Thig, a Righ na glorach
Da m' chomhnadh a nuas,
A Righ na bith 's na trocair,
Le comhnadh an Uain,
A Mhic na Muire Oighe
Da m' chomhnadh le buadh,
A Mhic na Muire mine
Is finne-ghile snuadh.

GOD, listen to my prayer,
Bend to me Thine ear,
Let my supplications and my prayers
Ascend to Thee upwards,
Come, Thou King of Glory,
To protect me down,
Thou King of life and mercy
With the aid of the Lamb.
Thou Son of Mary Virgin
To protect me with power,
Thou Son of the lovely Mary
Of purest fairest beauty.

DHE BI MAILLE RUINN

GOD BE WITH US

THE three poems which follow were obtained from Dr Donald Munro Morrison in 1889, a few days before he died. Dr Morrison heard them from an old man known as 'Coinneach Saor'--Kenneth the Carpenter--and his wife, at Obbe, Harris. These aged people were habitually practising quaint religious ceremonies and singing curious religious poems to peculiar music, evidently ancient. In childhood Dr Morrison lived much with this couple, and in manhood recorded much of their old lore and music. These however he noted in characters and notations of his own invention which he did not live to render intelligible to others. This is extremely regrettable, as Dr Morrison's wonderfully wide, accurate, and scientific attainments, deep knowledge of Gaelic, of music, and of acoustics, were only surpassed by his native modesty of mind and tender benevolence of heart. He was a distinguished medallist in several subjects at the University of Edinburgh.

A Gaelic proverb says: 'Theid dualchas an aghaidh nan creag'--Heredity will go against the rocks. Dr Morrison was descended from the famous hereditary brehons of the Isles. These Morrisons have been celebrated throughout the centuries for their wit, poetry, music, philosophy, medicine and science, for their independence of mind and sobriety of judgment, and for their benevolence of heart and unfailing hospitality.

DHE bi maille ruinn
Air an la an diugh,
Amen.
[Dhe bi maille ruinn
Air an oidhche nochd,
Amen.]
Ruinn agus leinn
Air an la an diugh,
Amen.
[Ruinn agus leinn
Air an oidhche nochd,
Amen.]
Tha e soilleir duinn ri leirsinn,
Bho thaine sinn chon an t-saoghail,
Gu robh sinn toillteanach air t' fhearg.
Amen.
O t' fhearg fein
A Dhe nan dul,
Amen.
Tabhair mathanas duinn,
Amen.

GOD be with us
On this Thy day,
Amen.
[God be with us
On this Thy night,
Amen.]
To us and with us,
On this Thy day,
Amen.
[To us and with us,
On this Thy night,
Amen.]
It is clear to be seen of us,
Since we came into the world,
That we have deserved Thy wrath,

Amen.
O Thine own wrath,
Thou God of all,
Amen.
Grant us forgiveness,
Amen.

Tabhair mathanas duinn,
Amen.
Tabhair duinn do mhathanas fein
A Dhe mheinich nan dul,
Amen.
Ni sam bith is dona duinn,
No thogas fianuis 'n ar n-aghaidh
Far am faide am bi sinn,
Suabharaich thus oirnn e,
Duabharaich thus oirnn e,
Fuadaich fein uainn e,
Agus ruaig as ar cridheachan,
Duthainn, suthainn, sior,
Duthainn, suthainn, sior.
Amen.

Grant us forgiveness,
Amen.
Grant to us Thine own forgiveness,
Thou merciful God of all,
Amen.
Anything that is evil to us,
Or that may witness against us
Where we shall longest be,
Illume it to us,
Obscure it to us,
Banish it from us,
Root it out of our hearts,
Ever, evermore, everlastingly.
Ever, evermore, everlastingly.
Amen.

IOS, A MHIC MUIRE

JESU, THOU SON OF MARY

IOS, a Mhic Muire
Dean trocair oirnn,
Amen.

Ios, a Mhic Muire
Dean siochain ruinne,
Amen.
Ruinn agus leinn
Far am faide am bi sinn,
Amen.
Bi mu thus ar slighe,
Bi mu chrich ar saoghail,
Amen.
Bi aig mosgladh ar beatha,
'S aig dubhradh ar laithean,
Amen.
Bi ruinn agus leinn
A Dhe mheinich nan dul,
Amen.
Coisrig sinn
Cor agus crann,
A Re nan re,
A Dhe nan dul,
Amen.
Coisrig sinn
Coir agus cuid,
A Re nan re,
A Dhe nan dul,
Amen.

JESU, Thou Son of Mary,
Have mercy upon us,
Amen.
Jesu, Thou Son of Mary,
Make peace with us,
Amen.
Oh, with us and for us
Where we shall longest be,
Amen.
Be about the morning of our course,
Be about the closing of our life, [world
Amen.
Be at the dawning of our life,
And oh! at the dark'ning of our day,
Amen.
Be for us and with us,
Merciful God of all,
Amen.
Consecrate us
Condition and lot,

Thou King of kings,
Thou God of all,
Amen.
Consecrate us
Rights and means,
Thou King of kings,
Thou God of all,
Amen.

Coisrig sinn
Cri agus ere,
A Re nan re,
A Dhe nan dul,
Amen.
Gach cri agus cre,
Gach la dhuit fein.
Gach oidhche nan reir,
A Re nan re,
A Dhe nan dul,
Amen.

Consecrate us
Heart and body,
Thou King of kings,
Thou God of all,
Amen.
Each heart and body,
Each day to Thyself,
Each night accordingly,
Thou King of kings,
Thou God of all,
Amen.

ATHAIR NAOMHA NA GLOIR

HOLY FATHER OF GLORY

BUIDHEACHAS duit, Athair Naomha na Gloir,
Athair chaomha bhith-bheo, bhith-threin,
Thaobh gach foghair, gach fabhair, gach foir,
Tha thu bairigeadh oirnne 'n ar feum;
Ge b'e freasdal thig oirnn mar do chlann,
'N ar cuibhrionn, 'n ar crann, 'n ar ceum,
Tabhair 'na chuideachd dhuinn soirbhis do laimh
Agus suilbhireachd saibhir do bheuil.

Ta sinn ciontach is truaillidh, a Dhe,
Ann an Spiorad, an cre, is an corp,
Ann an smuain, am focal, am beus,
Tha sinn cruaidh 'na do leirsinn 's an olc.
Cuir-sa tabhachd do ghraidh dhuinn an ceill.
Bi leum thairis thar sleibhtean ar lochd,
Is nigh sinn am fior-fhuil na reit
Mar chanach an t-sleibh, mar leuig an loch.

An slighe chorraich choitchinn ar gairm,
Biodh i soirbh no doirbh do ar feoil,
Biodh i soilleir no doilleir ri seirm,
Do threorachadh foirfe biodh oirnn.
Bi 'n ad sgeith dhuinn bho chuilbh an fhir-cheilg,
Bho'n chreach-cheilgneach ta le dheilg air ar toir,
Is anns gach run gheobh ar curam r'a dheilbh,
Bi-sa fein air ar failm is aig ar sgod.

THANKS be to Thee, Holy Father of Glory,
Father kind, ever-loving, ever-powerful,
Because of all the abundance, favour, and deliverance
That Thou bestowest upon us in our need.
Whatever providence befalls us as thy children,
In our portion, in our lot, in our path,
Give to us with it the rich gifts of Thine hand
And the joyous blessing of Thy mouth.

We are guilty and polluted, O God,
In spirit, in heart, and in flesh,
In thought, in word, in act,
We are hard in Thy sight in sin.
Put Thou forth to us the power of Thy love,
Be thou leaping over the mountains of our transgressions,
And wash us in the true blood of conciliation,
Like the down of the mountain, like the lily of the lake.

In the steep common path of our calling,
Be it easy or uneasy to our flesh,
Be it bright or dark for us to follow,
Thine own perfect guidance be upon us.
Be Thou a shield to us from the wiles of the deceiver,
From the arch-destroyer with his arrows pursuing us,
And in each secret thought our minds get to weave,
Be Thou Thyself on our helm and at our sheet.

Ged bhiodh madruich is gadruich gar sgaradh bho'n chro,

Biodh Aoghar crodha na gloir air ar sgath.
Ge be cuis no cion-fath no cion-sgeoil
Bhios gu leireadh no leoin thoir 'n ar dail,
No bheir fianuis 'n ar n-aghaidh fa-dheoidh,
Taobh thall abhuinn mhor an dubh-sgail,
O duabharaich thusa sin oirnn,
Is as ar cridhe dean fhogradh gu brath.

Nis dh' an Athair a chruthaich gach creubh,
Nis dh' an Mhac a phaigh eirig a shloigh,
Nis dh' an Spiorad an Comhfhurtair treun:--
Bi d' ar dion is d' ar seun bho gach leon,
Bi mu thus is mu dheireadh ar reis,
Bi toir dhuinn a bhi seinn ann an gloir,
Ann an sith, ann am fois, ann an reit,
Far nach silear an deur, far nach eugar ni 's mo.
Far nach silear an deur, far nach eugar ni 's mo.

Though dogs and thieves would reive us from the fold,
Be Thou the valiant Shepherd of glory near us.
Whatever matter or cause or propensity,
That would bring to us grief, or pains, or wounds,
Or that would bear witness against us at the last,
On the other side of the great river of dark shadows,
Oh! do Thou obscure it from our eyes,
And from our hearts drive it for ever.

Now to the Father who created each creature,
Now to the Son who paid ransom for His people,
Now to the Holy Spirit, Comforter of might:--
Shield and sain us from every wound;
Be about the beginning and end of our race,
Be giving us to sing in glory,
In peace, in rest, in reconciliation,
Where no tear shall be shed, where death comes no more.
Where no tear shall be shed, where death comes no more.

UIRNIGH

A PRAYER

A DHIA,
Ann mo ghniamh,
Ann mo bhriathar,
Ann mo mhiann,
Ann mo chiall,

Ann an riarachd mo chail,
Ann mo shuain,
Ann mo bhruail,
Ann mo chluain,
Ann mo smuain,
Ann mo chridh agus m'anam a ghnath,
Biodh an Oigh bheannaichte, Moire,
Agus Ogan geallaidh na glorach a tamh,
O ann mo chridh agus m'anam a ghnath,
Biodh an Oigh bheannaichte, Moire,
Agus Ogan cubhraidh na glorach a tamh.

O God,
In my deeds,
In my words,
In my wishes,
In my reason,
And in the fulfilling of my desires,
In my sleep,
In my dreams,
In my repose.
In my thoughts,
In my heart and soul always,
May the blessed Virgin Mary,
And the promised Branch of Glory dwell,
Oh! in my heart and soul always,
May the blessed Virgin Mary,
And the fragrant Branch of Glory dwell.

DUAN NA MUTHAIRN

RUNE OF THE 'MUTHAIRN'

A RIGH na gile,
A Righ na greine,
A Righ na rinne,
A Righ na reula,
A Righ na cruinne,
A Righ na speura,
Is aluinn do ghnuis,
A lub eibhinn.

Da lub shioda
Shios ri d' leasraich
Mhinich, chraicich;
Usgannan buidhe

Agus dolach
As gach sath dhiubh

THOU King of the moon,
Thou King of the sun,
Thou King of the planets,
Thou King of the stars,
Thou King of the globe,
Thou King of the sky,
Oh! lovely Thy countenance,
Thou beauteous Beam.

Two loops of silk
Down by thy limbs,
Smooth-skinned;
Yellow jewels
And a handful
Out of every stock of them.

BEANNAICH, A THRIATH NAM FLATH FIAL

BLESS, O CHIEF OF GENEROUS CHIEFS

BEANNAICH, a Thriath nam flath fial,
Mi fein 's gach sion a ta na m' choir,
Beannaich mi 'n am uile ghniomh,
Dean mi tearuinte ri m' bheo,
Dean mi tearuinte ri m' bheo.

Bho gach gruagach is ban-sith,
Bho gach mi-run agus bron,
Bho gach glaistig is ban-nigh,
Gach luch-sith agus luch-feoir,
Gach luch-sith agus luch-feoir.

Bho gach fuath bhiodh feadh nam beann
Bho gach greann bhiodh teann d' am thoir,
Bho gach uruisg measg nan gleann,
Teasruig mi gu ceann mo lo,
Teasruig mi gu ceann mo lo.

BLESS, O Chief of generous chiefs,
Myself and everything anear me,
Bless me in all my actions,
Make Thou me safe for ever,
Make Thou me safe for ever.

From every brownie and ban-shee,
From every evil wish and sorrow,
From every nymph and water-wraith,
From every fairy-mouse and grass-mouse,
From every fairy-mouse and grass-mouse.

From every troll among the hills,
From every siren hard pressing me,
From every ghoul within the glens,
Oh! save me till the end of my day.
Oh! save me till the end of my day.

SOLUS-IUIL NA SIORRUIDHEACHD

THE GUIDING LIGHT OF ETERNITY

DHE, thug mis a fois na h-oidhch an raoir
Chon solus aoibh an la an diugh,
Bi da mo thoir bho sholus ur an la an diugh,
Chon solus iul na siorruidheachd,
O! bho sholus ur an la an diugh,
Gu solus iul na siorruidheachd.

O GOD, who broughtst me from the rest of last night
Unto the joyous light of this day,
Be Thou bringing me from the new light of this day
Unto the guiding light of eternity.
Oh! from the new light of this day
Unto the guiding light of eternity.

ACHANAIDH GRAIS

A PRAYER FOR GRACE

TA mi lubadh mo ghlun
An suil an Athar a chruthaich mi,
An suil a Mhic a cheannaich mi,
An suil a Spioraid a ghlanaich mi,
Le gradh agus run.

Doirt a nuas oirnn a flathas
Trocair shuairce do mhathas;
Fhir tha 'n uachdar na Cathair,
Dean-sa fathamas ruinn.

Tabhair duinn, a Shlan'ear Aigh,
Eagal De, gaol De, agus gradh,
Is toil De dheanamh air talamh gach re,
Mar ni ainghlich is naoimhich air neamh;
Gach la agus oidhche thoir duinn do sheimh,
Gach la agus oidhche thoir duinn do sheimh.

I AM bending my knee
In the eye of the Father who created me,
In the eye of the Son who died for me,
In the eye of the Spirit who cleansed me,
In love and desire.

Pour down upon us from heaven
The rich blessing of Thy forgiveness;
Thou who art uppermost in the City,
Be Thou patient with us.

Grant to us, Thou Saviour of Glory,
The fear of God, the love of God, and His affection,
And the will of God to do on earth at all times
As angels and saints do in heaven;
Each day and night give us Thy peace.
Each day and night give us Thy peace.

ACHANAIDH COMHNADH

PRAYER FOR PROTECTION

BHO is tu is Buachiaill thar an treuid
Iomain fein shin do chleidh 's do chaimir,
Seun sinn fo do bhrot riomhach reidh;
A Sgeith dhidinn, dion ri 'r mairionn.

Bi-sa do chlaidheamh cruaidh, cosgarra,
Chon sinne dhion a irinn arrais,
Bho fhigeirich is bho fheadaine frinne fuara,
'S bho dheathach ruadh an aigeil.

M' anam an urrachd an Ard Righ,
Micheil murrach an comhdhail m' anama.

As Thou art the Shepherd over the flock
Tend Thou us to the cot and the fold,
Sain us beneath Thine own glorious mantle;
Thou Shield of protection, guard us for ever,

Be Thou a hard triumphant slave
To shield us securely from wicked hell,
From the fiends and from the stieve snell gullies,
And from the lurid smoke of the abyss.

Be my soul in the trustance of the High King,
Be Michael the powerful meeting my soul.

EOSAI BU CHOIR A MHOLADH

JESU WHO OUGHT TO BE PRAISED

THE reciter said that this poem was composed by a woman in Harris. She was afflicted with leprosy, and was removed from the community on the upland to dwell alone on the sea-shore, where she lived on the plants of the plains and on the shell-fish of the strand. The woman bathed herself in the liquid in which she had boiled the plants and shell-fish. All her sores became healed and her flesh became new--probably as the result of the action of the plants and shell-fish. Leprosy was common everywhere in mediaeval times. In Shetland the disease continued till towards the end of last century. Communities erected lazar-houses to safeguard themselves from persons afflicted with leprosy. Liberton, now a suburb of Edinburgh, derives its name from a lazaretto having been established there.

The shrine of St James of Compostello in Spain was famous for the cure of leprosy. Crowds of leper pilgrims from the whole of Christendom resorted to this shrine, and many of them were healed to the glory of the Saint and the enrichment of his shrine. In their gratitude, pilgrims offered costly oblations of silks and satins, of raiments and vestments, of silver and gold, of pearls and precious stones, till the shrine of St James of Compostello became famous throughout the world. The bay of Compostello was famed for fish and shell-fish, and the leper pilgrims who came to pray at the altar of the Saint and to bestow gifts at his shrine were fed on those and were healed--according to the belief of the period, by the miraculous intervention of the Saint. As the palm was the badge of the pilgrims to Jerusalem, the scallop-shell was the badge of the pilgrims to Compostello:--

'My sandal shoon and scallop-shell.'

BU cho fus a dh' Iosa
An crann crion uradh
'S an crann ur a chrionadh,
Nam b'e run a dheanadh.
Eosai! Eosai! Eosai!
Eosai! bu choir a mholadh.

Ni bheil lus an lar
Nach bheil lan d'a thoradh,
Ni bheil cruth an traigh
Nach bheil lan d'a shonas.
Eosai! Eosai! Eosai!

Eosai! bu choir a mholadh.

Ni bheil creubh am fairge,
Ni bheil dearg an abhuinn,

IT were as easy for Jesu
To renew the withered tree
As to wither the new
Were it His will so to do.
Jesu! Jesu! Jesu!
Jesu! meet it were to praise Him.

There is no plant in the ground
But is full of His virtue,
There is no form in the strand
But is full of His blessing.
Jesu! Jesu! Jesu!
Jesu! meet it were to praise Him.

There is no life in the sea,
There is no creature in the river,

Ni bheil cail an fhailbhe,
Nach bheil dearbh d'a mhaitheas.
Eosai! Eosai! Eosai!
Eosai bu choir a mholadh.

Ni bheil ian air sgeith
Ni bheil reul an adhar,
Ni bheil sian fo'n ghrein.
Nach tog sgeul d'a mhaitheas.
Eosai! Eosai! Eosai!
Eosai bu choir a mholadh.

There is naught in the firmament,
But proclaims His goodness.
Jesu! Jesu! Jesu!
Jesu! meet it were to praise Him.

There is no bird on the wing,
There is no star in the sky,
There is nothing beneath the sun,
But proclaims His goodness.
Jesu! Jesu! Jesu!
Jesu! meet it were to praise Him.

CARRAIG NAN AL

THE ROCK OF ROCKS

THE old man from whom this piece was taken down said that in his boyhood innumerable hymns and fragments of hymns of this nature were common throughout the isles of Barra. When strangers began to come in they derided the old people and their old lore and their old ways, and the younger generations neglected the ways of their fathers, alike the questionably and the unquestionably good.

AIR Carraig nan al,
Sith Pheadail is Phail,
Sheumais is Eoin na baigh,
Is na lan ionraic Oigh,
Na lan ionraic Oigh.

Sith Athar an aigh,
Sith Chriosda na pais,
Sith Spiorad nan gras,
Duinn fein is do 'n al ta og,
Duinn fein is do 'n al ta og.

ON the Rock of rocks,
The peace of Peter and Paul,
Of James and John the beloved,
And of the pure perfect Virgin,
The pure perfect Virgin.

The peace of the Father of joy,
The peace of the Christ of pasch,
The peace of the Spirit of grace,
To ourselves and to our children,
Ourselves and our children.

SORCHAR NAN REUL

THE LIGHTENER OF THE STARS

FEUCH Sorchar nan reul
Air corbha nan neul,
Agus ceolradh nan speur
Ri luaidh dha.

Tighinn le caithrim a nuas
Bho an Athair tha shuas,
Clar agus farcha nan duan
Ri seirm dha.

Chriosd, a chomairc mo ruin
Corn nach togainn do chliu!
Ainglich is naomhaich chiuil
Ri luaidh dhut.

A Mhic Mhoire nam buadh,
Is fire finne-ghile snuadh,
Liom bu shon a bhi an cluan
Do shaoibhreis.

A Chriosda mo chaoimhe,
A Chriosda Chro-naoimhe,
Bithim gach la agus oidhche
Ri luaidh ort.

BEHOLD the Lightener of the stars
On the crests of the clouds,
And the choralists of the sky
Lauding Him.

Coming down with acclaim
From the Father above,
Harp and lyre of song
Sounding to Him.

Christ, Thou refuge of my love,
Why should not I raise Thy fame!
Angels and saints melodious
Singing to Thee.

Thou Son of the Mary of graces,
Of exceeding white purity of beauty,
Joy were it to me to be in the fields
Of Thy riches.

O Christ my beloved,
O Christ of the Holy Blood,
By day and by night
I praise Thee.

CROIS NAN NAOMH AGUS NAN AINGEAL

THE CROSS OF THE SAINTS AND THE ANGELS

CROIS nan naomh agus nan aingeal liom

Bho fhrois m' aodain gu faobhar mo bhonn.

* * * * * *

A Mhicheil mhil, a Mhoire ghlorach,
A Bhride mhin nan dualan orach,
Dionaibh mi 's a cholunn bhronach,
Dionadh tri mi air sligh via corach.
O! tri mi air sligh na corach.

Dionaibh mi 's a choich-anama bhochd,
Dionaibh mi 's mi cho diblidh nochd,
Dionaibh mi air sligh gun lochd,
Dionadh tri air mo thi a nochd.
O! tri air mo thi a nochd.

THE cross of the saints and of the angels with me
From the top of my face to the edge of my soles.

* * * * * *

O Michael mild, O Mary of glory,
O gentle Bride of the locks of gold,
Preserve ye me in the weakly body,
The three preserve me on the just path.
Oh! three preserve me on the just path.

Preserve ye me in the soul-shrine poor,
Preserve ye me, and I so weak and naked,
Preserve ye me without offence on the way,
The preservation of the three upon me to-night.
Oh! the three to shield me to-night.

AN T-AINGHEAL DIONA

THE GUARDIAN ANGEL

AINGHIL Dhe a fhuair mo churam
Bho Athair cumh na trocaireachd,
Ciobaireachd caon cro nan naomh
Dheanamh dha mo thaobh a nochd;

Fuad uam gach buar is cunnart
Cuart mi air cuan na dobhachd,
Anns a chunglait, chaimleit, chumhan,
Cum mo churach fein an comhnuidh.

Bi 'na do lasair leith romham,
Bi 'na do reuil iuil tharam,
Bi 'na do ro reidh fotham,
Is 'na do chiobair caomh mo dheoghann,
An diugh, an nochd agus gu suthann.

Tha mi sgith is mi air m' aineol,
Treoraich mi do thir nan aingheal;
Liom is tim a bhi dol dachaidh
Do chuirt Chriosd, do shith nam flathas.

THOU angel of God who hast charge of me
From the dear Father of mercifulness,
The shepherding kind of the fold of the saints
To make round about me this night;

Drive from me every temptation and danger,
Surround me on the sea of unrighteousness,
And in the narrows, crooks, and straits,
Keep thou my coracle, keep it always.

Be thou a bright flame before me,
Be thou a guiding star above me,
Be thou a smooth path below me,
And be a kindly shepherd behind me,
To-day, to-night, and for ever.

I am tired and I a stranger,
Lead thou me to the land of angels;
For me it is time to go home
To the court of Christ, to the peace of heaven.

RUIN

DESIRES

LABHRAM gach la a reir do cheartais,
Gach la taisbim do smachd, a Dhe;
Labhram gach la a reir do reachd-sa,
Gach la is oidhche bithim toigh riut fein.

Gach la cunntam fath do throcair,
Toirim gach la dha do nosda speis;
Gach la tionnsgam fein dhut oran,
Teillim gach la do ghloir, a Dhe.

Beirim gach la gaol dhut, Iosa,
Gach oidhche nithim da reir;
Gach la 's oidhche, duar is soillse,
Luaidhim do chaoibhneas dhomh, a Dhe.

MAY I speak each day according to Thy justice,
Each day may I show Thy chastening, O God;
May I speak each day according to Thy wisdom,
Each day and night may I be at peace with Thee.

Each day may I count the causes of Thy mercy,
May I each day give heed to Thy laws;
Each day may I compose to Thee a song,
May I harp each day Thy praise, O God.

May I each day give love to Thee, Jesu,
Each night may I do the same;
Each day and night, dark and light,
May I laud Thy goodness to me, O God.

ORA CEARTAIS

INVOCATION FOR JUSTICE

PROVERBS anent law and justice abound in Gaelic, as:--'Is cam agus is direach an lagh':--Crooked and straight is the law. Bheir buidire breith ach co bheir ceartas?'--A witling may give judgment, but who will give justice? 'Colach ri ceart a mhadaidh-ruaidh, lugach, liugach, lamalach'--Like the justice of the fox, crooked, cunning, corrupt.

The administration of law and justice throughout the Highlands and Islands before the abolition of heritable jurisdictions was inadequate--men being too often appointed to administer justice not from their fitness but from their influence. Probably the feeling of distrust engendered by this absence of even-handed justice evoked these poems from the consciousness of the people and led them to appeal their cause to a Higher Court.

The litigant went at morning dawn to a place where three streams met. And as the rising sun gilded the mountain crests, the man placed his two palms edgeways together and filled them with water from the junction of the streams. Dipping his face into this improvised basin, he fervently repeated the prayer, after which he made his way to the court, feeling strong in the justice of his cause. On entering the court and on looking round the room, the applicant for justice mentally, sometimes in an undertone, said

'Dhe, seun an teach
Bho steidh gu fraigh;
M' fheart os cinn gach neach,

Feart gach neach fo m' thraigh.'

God sain the house
From site to summit;
My word above every person,
The word of every person below my foot.

The ceremonies observed in saying these prayers for justice, like those observed on many similar occasions, are symbolic. The bathing represents purification; the junction of three streams, the union of the Three Persons of the Godhead; and the spreading rays of the morning sun, divine grace. The deer is symbolic of wariness, the horse of strength, the serpent of wisdom, and the king of dignity.

IONNLAIDH mise m' aodann
'S na naodh gatha greine,
Mar a dh' ionnlaid Moire a Mac
Am bainne brat na breine.

Gaol a bhi 'na m' aodann,
Caomh a bhi 'na m' ghnuis,
Caora meala 'na mo theanga,
M' anail mar an tuis.

Is dubh am bail ud thall,
Is dubh daoine th' ann;
Is mis an eala bhan,
Banruinn os an ceann.

Falbhaidh mi an ainme Dhe,
An riochd feidh, an riochd each,
An riochd nathrach, an riochd righ:
Is treasa liom fin na le gach neach.

I WILL wash my face
In the nine rays of the sun,
As Mary washed her Son
In the rich fermented milk.

Love be in my countenance,
Benevolence in my mind,
Dew of honey in my tongue,
My breath as the incense.

Black is yonder town,
Black are those therein,
I am the white swan,
Queen above them.

I will travel in the name of God,
In likeness of deer, in likeness of horse,
In likeness of serpent, in likeness of king:
Stronger will it be with me than with all persons.

ORA CEARTAIS

INVOCATION FOR JUSTICE

DHE, tha mi liuthail m' aodainn,
Anns na naodh gatha greine,
Mar a liuthail Moire a Mac,
Am bainne brac breine.

Meilc a bhi 'na m' aodann,
Maon a bhi 'na m' ghnuis,
Mire meala 'na mo theanga,
M' anail mar an tuis.

Is dubh an taigh ud thall,
Is duibhe daoine a th' ann;
Is mis an eala bhan,
Banruinn os an ceann.

Falbhaidh mi an ainme Dhia,
An riochd fiadh, an riochd each,
An riochd nathar, an riochd righ,
Is cathar mi na gach neach.

GOD, I am bathing my face
In the nine rays of the sun,
As Mary bathed her Son
In generous milk fermented.

Sweetness be in my face,
Riches be in my countenance,
Comb-honey be in my tongue,
My breath as the incense.

Black is yonder house,
Blacker men therein;
I am the white swan,
Queen over them.

I will go in the name of God,

In likeness of deer, in likeness of horse,
In likeness of serpent, in likeness of king,
More victorious am I than all persons.

ORA BUAIDH

PRAYER FOR VICTORY

IONNLAIDH mi m' aodann
'S na naoi gatha greine,
Mar a dh' ionnlaid Moir a Mac,
Am bainne bragh na breine.

Mil a bhi 'na m' bheul,
Seirc a bhi 'na m' aodann;
An gaol thug Moire dha Mac
Bhi an cridhe gach cairc domhsa.

Gum bu suileach, cluasach, briathrach Dia,
Da m' riarachadh, is da m' neartachadh;
Gum bu dall, bodhar, balbh, sion sior,
Mo luchd tair is mo luchd taimhlis.

Teanga Chalum-chille 'na mo cheann,
Agall Chalum-chille 'na mo chainn;
Foisneachd Mhic bhuadhaich nan gras
Dhol thugam-sa an lathair sluaigh.

I BATHE my face
In the nine rays of the sun,
As Mary bathed her Son
In the rich fermented milk.

Honey be in my mouth,
Affection be in my face;
The love that Mary gave her Son
Be in the heart of all flesh for me.

All-seeing, all-hearing, all-inspiring may God be,
To satisfy and to strengthen me;
Blind, deaf, and dumb, ever, ever be
My contemners and my mockers,

The tongue of Columba in my head,
The eloquence of Columba in my speech;
The composure of the Victorious Son of grace

Be mine in presence of the multitude.

AN LIUTHAIL

THE LUSTRATION

TA mi liuthail m' aodainn
An caora caon na greine,
Mar a liuthail Moire Criosd
Am bainne miamh na h-Eiphit.

Meilc bhi 'na mo bhial,
Ciall bhi 'na mo chainn,
An gaol thug Moire mhin dha Mac
Bhi an cridhe gach mire dhomhsa.

Gradh Chriosd am chom,
Cruth Chriosd am chomhnadh,
Chan 'eil am muir no 'm fonn
Na bheir buaidh air Righ an Domhnuich.

Bas Bhride mu m' mhuineal,
Bas Mhuire mu m' bhraghad,
Bas Mhicheil dha m' liuthail,
Bas Chriosda dha m' thearnadh.

Doigh eile--
Bith a bhith 'na m' bheul,
Ceil a bhith 'na m' chainn,
Blas na sile 'na mo bhile
Gon an till mi nall.

I AM bathing my face
In the mild rays of the sun,
As Mary bathed Christ
In the rich milk of Egypt.

Sweetness be in my mouth,
Wisdom be in my speech,
The love the fair Mary gave her Son
Be in the heart of all flesh for me.

The love of Christ in my breast,
The form of Christ protecting me,
There is not in sea nor on land
That can overcome the King of the Lord's Day.

The hand of Bride about my neck,
The hand of Mary about my breast,
The hand of Michael laving me,
The hand of Christ saving me.

Variant--
Force in my mouth,
Sense be in my speech,
The taste of nectar on my lips,
Till I return hither.

ORA BOISILIDH

BATHING PRAYER

THIS poem was taken down at Creagorry, Benbecula, on the 16th of December 1872, from Janet Campbell, nurse, Lochskiport, South Uist. The reciter had many beautiful songs and lullabies of the nursery, and many instructive sayings and fables of the animal world. These she sang and told in the most pleasing and natural manner, to the delight of her listeners. Birds and beasts, reptiles and insects, whales and fishes talked and acted through her in the most amusing manner, and in the most idiomatic Gaelic. Her stories had a charm for children, and it was delightful to see a small cluster of little ones pressing round the narrator, all eyes, all ears, all mouth, and all attention, listening to what the bear said to the bee, the fox to the lamb, the harrier to the hen, the serpent to the pipet, the whale to the herring, and the brown otter of the stream to the silvery grilse of the current. Those fair young heads, now, alas! widely apart, probably remember some of the stories heard at Janet Campbell's knee better than those they afterwards heard in more formal schools.

BOISILEAG air th' aois,
Boisileag air th' fhas,
Boisileag air th' ugan,
Tuilim air a chail.

Air do chuid an chugan dhut,
Gruidhim agus cal;
Air do chuid an ghabhail dhut,
Meal is bainne blath.

Air do chuid an chomaidh dhut,
Omhan agus ais;
Air do chuid an chobhartaich
Le bogha agus gais.

Air do chuid an uidheam dhut,
Uibhean buidhe Chasg;
Air do chuid an chuileagan,

M' ulaidh agus m' agh.

Air do chuid an chuilm dhut,
Uilim agus can;
Air do chuid an chuilidh dhut
Cuisilin mo ghraidh.

A PALMFUL for thine age,
A palmful for thy growth,
A palmful for thy throat,
A flood for thine appetite.

For thy share of the dainty,
Crowdie and kail;
For thy share of the taking,
Honey and warm milk.

For thy share of the supping,
Whisked whey and milk-product;
For thy share of the spoil,
With bow and with spear.

For thy share of the preparation,
The yellow eggs of Easter;
For thy share of the treat,
My treasure and my joy,

For thy share of the feast
With gifts and with tribute;
For thy share of the treasure,
Pulset of my love.

Air do chuid an fhaghaid dhut,
Ri aghaidh Beinn-a-cheo;
Air do chuid an fhiadhach dhut,
Is riaghladh air sloigh.

Air do chuid an luchairt,
An curtaibh nan righ;
Air do chuid a fhlathas dhut,
Le mhathas is le shith.

A chuid nach fas 's a chumhanaich,
Gum fas 's an dubha-thrath;
A chuid nach fas 's an oidhche dhiot,
Air dhruim a mheadhon la.

Tri baslach
Nan Tri run,
Dha do chumhn
Bho gach tnu,
Suil agus bas;
Baslach Ti nan dul
Baslach Chriosda chumh,
Baslach Spiorad numh,
Tri-un
Nan gras.

For thy share of the chase
Up the face of the Beinn-a-cheo;
For thy share of the hunting
And the ruling over hosts.

For thy share of palaces,
In the courts of kings;
For thy share of Paradise
With its goodness and its peace.

The part of thee that does not grow at dawn,
May it grow at eventide;
The part of thee that does not grow at night,
May it grow at ridge of middle-day.

The three palmfuls
Of the Secret Three,
To preserve thee
From every envy,
Evil eye and death;
The palmful of the God of Life,
The palmful of the Christ of Love,
The palmful of the Spirit of Peace,
Triune
Of Grace.

DHE STIUIR MI

GOD GUIDE ME

DHE stiuir mi le d' ghliocas,
Dhe smachd mi le d' cheartas,
Dhe foir mi le d' throcair,
Dhe comh'n mi le d' chumhachd.

Dhe lion mi le d' lanachd,
Dhe dion mi le d' sgaileachd,
Dhe lion mi le d' ghrasachd,
Air sgath do Mhic Unga.

Iosa Criosda a shiol Dhaibhidh,
Fear-tathaich an teampuill,
Uan-iobairt a gharaidh,
A bhasaich air mo shon.

GOD guide me with Thy wisdom,
God chastise me with Thy justice,
God help me with Thy mercy,
God protect me with Thy strength.

God fill me with Thy fullness,
God shield me with Thy shade,
God fill me with Thy grace,
For the sake of Thine Anointed Son.

Jesu Christ of the seed of David,
Visiting One of the Temple,
Sacrificial Lamb of the Garden,
Who died for me.

BEANNACHADH CADAIL

SLEEP BLESSING

THE night prayers of the people are numerous. They are called by various names, as: 'Beannachadh Beinge'--Bench-Blessing, 'Beannachadh Bobhstair'--Bolster Blessing, 'Beannachadh Cluasaig'--Pillow Blessing, 'Beannachadh Cuaiche'--Couch Blessing, 'Coich Chuaiche'--Couch Shrining, 'Altachadh Cadail'--Sleep Prayer; and other terms. Many of these prayers are become mere fragments and phrases, supplemented by the people according to their wants and wishes at the time.

It is touching and instructive to hear these simple old men and women in their lowly homes addressing, as they say themselves, 'Dia mor nan dui, Athair nan uile bheo,' the great God of life, the Father of all living. They press upon Him their needs and their desires fully and familiarly, but with all the awe and deference due to the Great Chief whom they wish to approach and to attract, and whose forgiveness and aid they would secure. And all this in language so homely yet so eloquent, so simple yet so dignified, that the impressiveness could not be greater in proudest fane.

BIODH do lamh dheas, a Dhe, fo mo cheann,
Biodh do shoills, a Spioraid, os mo chionn,
Is biodh crois nan naodh aingeal tharam sios,

Bho mhullach mo chinn gu iochdar mo bhonn,
Bho mhullach mo chinn gu iochdar mo bhonn.

O Ios gun lochd, a cheusadh gort
Fo bhinn nan olc a sgiursadh Thu,
A liuthad olc a rinn mo chorp!
Nach urr' mi nochd a chunntachadh,
Nach urr' mi nochd a chunntachadh.

A Righ na fola firinnich,
Na dibir mi a d' mhuinntireas,
Na tagair orm mo mhi-cheartan,
Is na dichuimhnich a d' chunntadh mi,
Na dichuimhnich a d' chunntadh mi.

Crois Mhoir is Mhicheil, bhi tharam ann an sith,
M' anam a bhi am firinn, gun mhi-run am chom,
M' anam a bhi an sith aig Sorchair na frithe,
Micheal crodhal an codhail m' anama,
Moch agus anmoch, la agus oidhche. Amen.

BE Thy right hand, O God, under my head,
Be Thy light, O Spirit, over me shining.
And be the cross of the nine angels over me down,
From the crown of my head to the soles of my feet,
From the crown of my head to the soles of my feet.

O Jesu without offence, crucified cruelly,
Under ban of the wicked Thou wert scourged,
The many evils done of me in the body!
That I cannot this night enumerate,
That I cannot this night enumerate.

O Thou King of the blood of truth,
Cast me not from Thy covenant,
Exact not from me for my transgressions,
Nor omit me in Thy numbering,
Nor omit me in Thy numbering.

Be the cross of Mary and of Michael over me in peace,
Be my soul dwelling in truth, be my heart free of guile,
Be my soul in peace with thee, Brightness of the mountains.
Valiant Michael, meet thou my soul,
Morn and eve, day and night. May it be so.

THIGEAM AN DIUGH

COME I THIS DAY

THIGEAM an diugh 'an t-Athair,
Thigeam an diugh 'an Mhac,
Thigeam 'an Spiorad neartor naomh;
Thigeam an diugh le Dia,
Thigeam an diugh le Criosd,
Thigeam le Spiorad iocshlaint chaomh.

Dia, agus Spiorad, agus Ios,
Bho mhullach mo chinn,
Gu iochdar mo bhonn;
Thigeam le mo chliu,
Falbham le mo theasd,
Thigeam thugad, Iosa--
Iosa, dean mo leasd.

COME I this day to the Father,
Come I this day to the Son,
Come I to the Holy Spirit powerful;
Come I this day with God,
Come I this day with Christ,
Come I with the Spirit of kindly balm,

God, and Spirit, and Jesus,
From the crown of my head
To the soles of my feet;
Come I with my reputation,
Come I with my testimony,
Come I to Thee, Jesu--
Jesu, shelter me.

AN ACHANAIDH ANAMA

THE SOUL PLAINT

O IOS, a nochd,
Aghair nam bochd,
Cholann gun lochd,
Dh' fhuilinn gu gort,
Fo bhinn nan olc,
'S a cheusadh.

Saor mi bho olc,
Saor mi bho lochd,

Caomhain mo chorp,
Naomhaich mi nochd,
O Ios, a nochd,
'S na treig mi.

Bairig domh neart,
Aghair nam feart,
Stiuir mi 'na d' cheart,
Stiuir mi 'na d' neart,
O Ios, 'na d' neart
Gleidh mi.

O JESU! to-night,
Thou Shepherd of the poor,
Thou sinless person
Who didst suffer full sore,
By ban of the wicked,
And wast crucified.

Save me from evil,
Save me from harm,
Save Thou my body,
Sanctify me to-night,
O Jesu! to-night,
Nor leave me.

Endow me with strength,
Thou Herdsman of might.
Guide me aright,
Guide me in Thy strength,
O Jesu! in Thy strength
Preserve me.

URNUIGH CHADAIL

SLEEPING PRAYER

TA mi cur m' anama 's mo chorp
Air do chomaraig a nochd, a Dhe,
Air do chomaraig, Iosa Criosda,
Air do chomaraig, a Spioraid na firinne reidh,
An Triuir a sheasadh mo chuis,
Is nach cuireadh an cul rium fein.

Thus, Athair, tha caomh agus ceart,
Thus, a Mhic, thug air peacadh buaidh,

Thus, a Spioraid Naoimhe nam feart,
Da mo ghleidheadh an nochd o thruaigh;
An Triuir a dheanadh mo cheart
Mo ghleidheadh an nochd 's gach uair.

I AM placing my soul and my body
On Thy sanctuary this night, O God,
On Thy sanctuary, O Jesus Christ,
On Thy sanctuary, O Spirit of perfect truth,
The Three who would defend my cause,
Nor turn Their backs upon me.

Thou, Father, who art kind and just,
Thou, Son, who didst overcome death,
Thou, Holy Spirit of power,
Be keeping me this night from harm;
The Three who would justify me
Keeping me this night and always.

TIUBHRADH NAN TRI

THE GIFTS OF THE THREE

SPIORAID, tiubhair dhomh do phailteas,
Athair, tiubhair dhomh do ghliocas,
Mhic, tiubhair dhomh na m' airceas,
Iosa fo fhasga do sgeith.

Laigheam sios a nochd,
Le Trithinn mo neart,
Le Athair, le Iosa,
Le Spiorad nam feart.

SPIRIT, give me of Thine abundance,
Father, give me of Thy wisdom,
Son, give me in my need,
Jesus beneath the shelter of Thy shield.

I lie down to-night,
With the Triune of my strength,
With the Father, with Jesus,
With the Spirit of might.

URNUIGH CHADAIL

SLEEP PRAYER

O IOS gun lochd,
A Righ nam bochd,
A chiosadh gort
Fo bhinn nan olc,
Dion-s, an nochd,
Bho Iudas mi.

M' anam air do laimh, a Chriosda,
A Righ na Cathrach Neomh,
Is tu cheannaich m' anam, Iosa,
Is tu dh' iobair beatha dhomh.

Teasruig mi air sgath mo sprochd,
Air sgath do phais, do lot is t' fhala fein,
Is tabhair tearuint mi an nochd
Am fochar Cathair De.

O JESU without sin,
King of the poor,
Who wert sorely subdued
Under ban of the wicked,
Shield Thou me this night
From Judas.

My soul on Thine own arm, O Christ,
Thou the King of the City of Heaven,
Thou it was who bought'st my soul, O Jesu,
Thou it was who didst sacrifice Thy life for me.

Protect Thou me because of my sorrow,
For the sake of Thy passion, Thy wounds, and Thine own blood,
And take me in safety to-night
Near to the City of God.

BEANNACHD TAIMH

RESTING BLESSING

AN ainm an Tighearn Iosa,
Agus Spiorad iocshlain aigh,
An ainm Athar Israil,
Sinim sios gu tamh.

Ma tha musal na dusal,
Na run air bith dhomh 'n dan,

38

Dhia fuasgail orm is cuartaich orm,
Is fuadaich uam mo namh.

An ainm Athar priseil,
Is Spiorad iocshlain aigh,
An ainm Tighearn Iosa,
Sinim sios gu tamh.
* * * *
Dhia, cobhair mi is cuartaich mi,
O 'n uair 's gu uair mo bhais.

IN name of the Lord Jesus,
And of the Spirit of healing balm,
In name of the Father of Israel,
I lay me down to rest.

If there be evil threat or quirk,
Or covert act intent on me,
God free me and encompass me,
And drive from me mine enemy.

In name of the Father precious,
And of the Spirit of healing balm,
In name of the Lord Jesus,
I lay me down to rest.
* * * *
God, help me and encompass me,
From this hour till the hour of my death.

COISRIG CADAIL

SLEEP CONSECRATION

LUIGHIM sios an nochd
Le Muire min 's le Mac,
Le Micheal finn-gheal,
'S le Bride fo brat.

Luighim sios le Dia,
Is luighidh Dia lium,
Cha luigh mi sios le Briain.
'S cha luigh Briain lium.

A Dhe nam bochd,
Foir orm an nochd,
Na treig mi tort,

A t' ionndastaigh.

Aig meid nan lot
A reub mi ort,
Cha leir 'omh nochd
An cunntachadh.

A Righ na fola firinnich,
Na dichuimhn mi 'na d' thuinneachadh,
Na tagair mi 's 'na mi cheartan,
Na dibir mi 'na d' chruinneachadh.
O 'na d' chruinneachadh!

I LIE down to-night
With fair Mary and with her Son,
With pure-white Michael,
And with Bride beneath her mantle.

I lie down with God,
And God will lie down with me,
I will not lie down with Satan,
Nor shall Satan lie down with me.

O God of the poor,
Help me this night,
Omit me not entirely
From Thy treasure-house.

For the many wounds
That I inflicted on Thee,
I cannot this night
Enumerate them.

Thou King of the blood of truth,
Do not forget me in Thy dwelling-place,
Do not exact from me for my transgressions,
Do not omit me in Thine ingathering.
In Thine ingathering.

BEANNACHADH LEAPA

BED BLESSING

LAIGHIM sios an nochd mar is coir
An cluanas Chriosda Mac Oigh nan cleachd,
An cluanas Athair aigh na gloir,

An cluanas Spioraid foir nam feart.

Laighim sios an nochd le Dia,
Is laighidh Dia an nochd a sios liom,
Cha laigh mi sios an nochd le olc, 's cha dean
Ole no fhiamh laighe liom.

Laighim sios an nochd le Spiorad Naomh,
Is laighidh Spiorad Naomh an nochd a sios liom,
Laighim sios le Teoiridh mo chaoimh,
Is laighidh Teoiridh mo chaoimh a sios liom.

I AM lying down to-night as beseems
In the fellowship of Christ, son of the Virgin of ringlets.
In the fellowship of the gracious Father of glory,
In the fellowship of the Spirit of powerful aid.

I am lying down to-night with God,
And God to-night will lie down with me,
I will not lie down to-night with sin, nor shall
Sin nor sin's shadow lie down with me.

I am lying down to-night with the Holy Spirit,
And the Holy Spirit this night will lie down with me,
I will lie down this night with the Three of my love,
And the Three of my love will lie down with me.

AN URNUIGH CHADAIL

THE SLEEP PRAYER

THA mis a nis a dol dh' an chadal,
Gu mu slan a dhuisgeas mi;
Ma 's a bas domh anns a bhas chadail,
Gun ann air do ghairdean fein
A Dhe nan gras a dhuisgeas mi;
O air do ghairdean gradhach fein,
A Dhe nan gras a dhuisgeas mi!

M' anam air do laimh dheis, a Dhe,
A Re nan neamha neomh;
Is tu fein a cheannaich mi le t'fhuil,
Is tu thug do bheatha air mo shon,
Comraig mis an nochd, a Dhe,
Is na h-eireadh dhomh beud no cron.

Am feadh bhios a cholann a tamh 's a chadal,
Biodh an t-anam a snamh an sgath nam flathas,
Micheal cra-gheal an dail an anama,
Moch agus amnoch, oidhche agus latha,
Moch agus anmoch, oidhche agus latha.
Amen.

I AM now going into the sleep,
Be it that I in health shall waken;
If death be to me in the death-sleep,
Be it that on Thine own arm,
O God of Grace, I in peace shall waken;
Be it on Thine own beloved arm,
O God of Grace, that I in peace shall waken.

Be my soul on Thy right hand, O God,
Thou King of the heaven of heavens;
Thou it was who bought'st me with Thy blood,
Thou it was who gavest Thy life for me,
Encompass Thou me this night, O God,
That no harm, no evil shall me befall.

Whilst the body is dwelling in the sleep,
The soul is soaring in the shadow of heaven,
Be the red-white Michael meeting the soul,
Early and late, night and day,
Early and late, night and day.
Amen.

COISRIG CADAIL

SLEEP CONSECRATION

TA mise laighe nochd
Le Athair, le Mac,
Le Spiorad na firinn,
Ta 'm dhion o gach lochd.

Cha laigh mi le olc,
Cha laigh olc liom,
Ach laighidh mi le Dia,
Is laighidh Dia liom.

Dia agus Criosd agus Spiorad naomh,
Is crois nan naodh aingeal fionn,
Da m' dhion mar Thri is mar Aon,

Bho chlar mhullach m'aodainn gu faobhar mo bhonn.

A Righ na greine agus na gloire,
Ios a Mhic na h-Oighe cubhra,
Gleidh-sa sinn a glinn nan diar,
Is a taigh nan diamha dubhra,
Gleidh sinn a glinn nan diar,
Is a taigh nan diamha dubhra.

I AM lying down to-night,
With Father, with Son,
With the Spirit of Truth,
Who shield me from harm.

I will not lie with evil,
Nor shall evil lie with me,
But I will lie down with God,
And God will lie down with me.

God and Christ and Spirit Holy,
And the cross of the nine white angels,
Be protecting me as Three and as One,
From the top tablet of my face to the soles of my feet.

Thou King of the sun and of glory,
Thou Jesu, Son of the Virgin fragrant,
Keep Thou us from the glen of tears,
And from the house of grief and gloom,
Keep us from the glen of tears,
From the house of grief and gloom.

BEANNACHADH LEAPA

BED BLESSING

LAIGHIM sios an nochd,
Le Moire mhin is le Mac,
Le Mathair mo Righ,
Tha da m' dhion o gach lochd.

Cha laigh mi leis an olc,
Cha laigh an t' olc liom,
Ach laighidh mi le Dia,
Is laighidh Dia liom.

Dia agus Moire agus Micheal caon,

Agus crois nan naodh aingeal fionn
Da m' dhion mar Thri is mar Aon,
Bho chlar m' aodainn gu faobhar mo bhuinn.

Guidheam Peadail, guidheam Pol,
Guidheam Moir Oigh, guidheam am Mac,
Guidheam an da Ostal dochaidh deug
Mo ghleidheadh bho bheud 's bho lochd;
O gun mi a dhol eug a nochd,
Gun mi a dhol eug a nochd!

A Dhia, agus a Mhoire na glorach,
Ios, a Mhic na h-Oighe cubhraidh,
Siantaibh sinn bho phiantaibh siorruidh,
'S bho theine diantaidh dubhraidh,
Sinn bho phiantaidh siorruidh,
'S bho theine diantaidh dubhraidh.

I AM lying down to-night,
With Mary mild and with her Son,
With the Mother of my King,
Who is shielding me from harm.

I will not lie down with evil,
Nor shall evil lie down with me,
But I will lie down with God,
And God will lie down with me.

God and Mary and Michael kindly
And the cross of the nine angels fair,
Be shielding me as Three and as One,
From the brow of my face to the edge of my soles.

I beseech Peter, I beseech Paul,
I beseech Mary, I beseech the Son,
I beseech the trustful Apostles twelve
To preserve me from hurt and harm;
O from dying to-night,
From dying to-night!

O God! O Mary of Glory!
O Jesu! Son of the Virgin fragrant,
Sain Ye us from the pains everlasting,
And from the fire fierce and murky,
From the pains everlasting,
And from the fire fierce and murky!

A CHOICH ANAMA

THE SOUL SHRINE

THE Soul Shrine is sung by the people as they retire to rest. They say that the angels of heaven guard them in sleep and shield them from harm. Should any untoward event occur to themselves or to their flocks, they avow that the cause was the deadness of their hearts, the coldness of their faith, and the fewness of their prayers.

DHE tabhair aithne da t' ainghle beannaichte,
Caim a chumail air an staing-sa nochd,
Comachadh crabhaidh, tabhaidh, teannachaidh,
Chumas a choich anama-sa bho lochd.

Teasruig a Dhe an t-ardrach seo a nochd,
Iad fein 's an cuid 's an cliu,
Tar iad o eug, o ghabhadh, o lochd,
'S o thoradh na farmaid 's na mi-ruin.

Tabhair duinn, a Dhe na fois,
Taingealachd an cois ar call,
Bhi coimhlionadh do lagh a bhos,
'S to fein a mhealtuinn thall.

GOD, give charge to Thy blessed angels,
To keep guard around this stead to-night,
A band sacred, strong, and steadfast,
That will shield this soul-shrine from harm.

Safeguard Thou, God, this household to-night,
Themselves and their means and their fame,
Deliver them from death, from distress, from harm,
From the fruits of envy and of enmity.

Give Thou to us, O God of peace,
Thankfulness despite our loss,
To obey Thy statutes here below,
And to enjoy Thyself above.

COICH-ANAMA

SOUL-SHRINE

AINGHIL Dhe, a fhuair mo churam,
Bho Athair cubhraidh na trocaireachd,

45

Cuartachadh caon na Cro-Naoimhe
A dheanamh air mo choich-anam a nochd,
O air mo choich-anam a nochd.

Fuadaich uam gach cuar is cunnart,
Cuartaich mi air cuan na corach,
Iarram thu dheanamh solus ur romham,
O ainghil aoibh-ghil, air an oidhche nochd,
O ainghil aoibh-ghil, air an oidhche nochd.

Bi fein a d' reuil-iuil os mo chionn,
Sorchair orm gach foirche is fonn,
Stiuir mo bharc air bharr an liuinn,
Chon cala tamh an samhchair thonn,
Chon cala tamh an samhchair thonn.

THOU angel of God who hast charge of me
From the fragrant Father of mercifulness,
The gentle encompassing of the Sacred Heart
To make round my soul-shrine this night,
Oh, round my soul-shrine this night.

Ward from me every distress and danger,
Encompass my course over the ocean of truth,
I pray thee, place thy pure light before me,
O bright beauteous angel on this very night,
Bright beauteous angel on this very night.

Be Thyself the guiding star above me,
Illume Thou to me every reef and shoal,
Pilot my barque on the crest of the wave,
To the restful haven of the waveless sea,
Oh, the restful haven of the waveless sea.

LAIGHIM AM LEABAIDH

I LIE IN MY BED

LAIGHIM am leabaidh,
Mar a laighinn 's an uaigh,
Do ruighe ri m' mhuineal,
Mhic Mhuire nam buadh.

Bidh ainghlean da m' fhaire
'S mi am laighe an suain,
'S bidh ainghlean da m' chaithris

'S mi 'n cadal na h-uaigh.

Bidh Uiril ri m' chasan,
Bidh Airil ri m' chul,
Bidh Gabrail ri m' bhathais,
'S bidh Rafal ri m' thubh.

Bidh Micheal le m' anam
Sgiath dhaingean mo ruin!
'S bidh an Leighe Mac Moire,
Cur na seile ri m' shuil,
'S bidh an Leighe Mac Moire,
Cur na seile ri m' shuil!

I LIE in my bed
As I would lie in the grave,
Thine arm beneath my neck,
Thou Son of Mary victorious.

Angels shall watch me
And I lying in slumber,
And angels shall guard me
In the sleep of the grave.

shall be at my feet,
Ariel shall be at my back,
Gabriel shall be at my head,
And Raphael shall be at my side.

Michael shall be with my soul,
The strong shield of my love!
And the Physician Son of Mary
Shall put the salve to mine eye,
The Physician Son of Mary
Shall put the salve to mine eye!

URNUIGH MADUINN

MORNING PRAYER

TAING dhut Iosda Criosda,
Thug mis a nios o 'n oidhche 'n raoir
Chon solas soillse an la 'n diugh,
Chon sonas siorruidh a chosnadh dha m' anam,
An cion na fal a dhoirt thu dhomh.

Cliu dhut fein a Dhe gu brath,
An sgath gach agh a bhairig thu orm--
Mo bhiadh, mo bhriathar, mo ghniomh, mo chail,
* * * * * *

'S tha mi griosad ort
Mo dhion bho'n olc,
Mo dhion bho lochd,
Mo shian an nochd
'S mi iosal bochd,
O Dhia nam bochd!
O Chriosd nan lot!
Thoir ciall dhomh 'n cois do ghrais.

Gun coraich an Ti Naomha mi,
Gun comhnaich air muir 's air tir mi,
'S gun treoraich o ir gu ir mi
Chon sith na Cathair Shiorruiche,
Sith na Cathair Shiorruiche.

THANKS be to Thee, Jesus Christ,
Who brought'st me up from last night,
To the gladsome light of this day,
To win everlasting life for my soul,
Through the blood Thou didst shed for me.

Praise be to Thee, O God, for ever,
For the blessings Thou didst bestow on me--
My food, my speech, my work, my health,
* * * * * *

And I beseech Thee
To shield me from sin,
To shield me from ill,
To sain me this night,
And I low and poor,
O God of the poor!
O Christ of the wounds!
Give me wisdom along with Thy grace.

May the Holy One claim me,
And protect me on sea and on land,
And lead me on from step to step,
To the peace of the Everlasting City,
The peace of the Everlasting City!

AN TIONNSGANN

THE DEDICATION

TAING dhuit, a Dhe
Thug mise bho 'n de
Gu tos an diugh,
Chum solas siorruidh
A chosnadh dha m' chre
Le feum maith.
'S air son gach tiodhlac sith
A dh'iobair thu dhomh,
Mo smuaine, mo bhriathra,
Mo ghniamha, mo thoil,
Tha mi tionnsgann duit.
Tha mi 'g urnuigh riut,
Tha mi griasad ort,
Mo chumail bho lochd,
Mo chomhnadh an nochd,
Air sgath do lot,
Le oifreil do ghrais.

THANKS to Thee, God,
Who brought'st me from yesterday
To the beginning of to-day,
Everlasting joy
To earn for my soul
With good intent.
And for every gift of peace
Thou bestowest on me,
My thoughts, my words,
My deeds, my desires
I dedicate to Thee.
I supplicate Thee,
I beseech Thee,
To keep me from offence,
And to shield me to-night,
For the sake of Thy wounds
With Thine offering of grace.

ACHANAIDH TAIMH

A RESTING PRAYER

DHE, teasruig an tigh, an teine, 's an tan,
Gach aon ta gabhail tamh an seo an nochd.

49

Teasruig mi fein 's mo chroilean graidh,
Is gleidh sinn bho lamh 's bho lochd;
Gleidh sinn bho namh an nochd,
Air sgath Mhic Mhuire Mhathar
'S an ait-s 's gach ait a bheil an tamh an nochd,
Air an oidhche nochd 's gach aon oidhche,
An oidhche nochd 's gach aon oidhche.

GOD shield the house, the fire, the kine,
Every one who dwells herein to-night.
Shield myself and my beloved group,
Preserve us from violence and from harm;
Preserve us from foes this night,
For the sake of the Son of the Mary Mother,
In this place, and in every place wherein they dwell to-night,
On this night and on every night,
This night and every night.

TEISREADH TAIGHE

HOUSE PROTECTING

DHE, beannaich an ce 's na bheil ann,
Dhe, beannaich mo cheile is mo chlann,
Dhe, beannaich an re a ta 'na m' cheann,
Is beannaich, a Dhe, laimhseachadh mo laimh;
An am domh eirigh 's a mhaduinn mhoich,
Is laighe air leabaidh anamoich,
Beannaich m' eirigh 's a mhaduinn mhoich,
Is mo laighe air leabaidh anamoich.

Dhe, teasruig an teach 's an t-ardrach,
Dhe, coistrig a chlann mhathrach,
Dhe, cuartaich an spreidh 's an t-alach;
Bi-sa fein na'n deigh 's da'n taladh,
Duair dhireas ni ri frith 's ri fruan,
Duair shineas mi a sios an suan,
Duair dhireas ni ri frith 's ri fruan,
Duair shineas mi an sith gu suan.

GOD, bless the world and all that is therein.
God, bless my spouse and my children,
God, bless the eye that is in my head,
And bless, O God, the handling of my hand;
What time I rise in the morning early,
What time I lie down late in bed,

Bless my rising in the morning early,
And my lying down late in bed.

God, protect the house, and the household,
God, consecrate the children of the motherhood,
God, encompass the flocks and the young;
Be Thou after them and tending them,
What time the flocks ascend hill and wold,
What time I lie down to sleep,
What time the flocks ascend hill and wold,
What time I lie down in peace to sleep.

BEANNACHADH TAIGHE

BLESSING OF HOUSE

DHE, beannaich an taigh,
Bho steidh gu staidh,
Bho chrann gu fraigh,
Bho cheann gu saidh,
Bho dhronn gu traigh,
Bho sgonn gu sgaith,
Eadar bhonn agus bhraighe,
Bhonn agus bhraighe.

GOD bless the house,
From site to stay,
From beam to wall,
From end to end,
From ridge to basement,
From balk to roof-tree,
From found to summit,
Found and summit.

CO DHA DHIOLAS MI CIOS

TO WHOM SHALL I OFFER OBLATION

CO dha dhiolas mi cios
An ainm Mhicheil o'n aird?
Thugam deachamh dhe m' ni,
Dh' an Diobarach Aigh.

Air sgath na chunna mi,
Do shith is d'a bhaigh,
Tog m' anam riut, a Mhic De,

Na treig mi gu brath.

Cuimhnich orm anns an t-sliabh,
Fo do sgiath dean-sa mo sgail;
Charra na firinn na dibir mi'n cian
B'e mo mhiann bhi gu siorruidh na d' dhail.

Tabhair domh trusgan bainnse,
Biodh ainghlean a cainnt rium 's gach cas,
Biodh ostail naomha da m' dhion,
Moire mhin is thus, Iosa nan gras,
Moire mhin is thus, Iosa nan gras.

To whom shall I offer oblation
In name of Michael on high?
I will give tithe of my means
To the forsaken illustrious One.

Because of all that I have seen,
Of His peace and of His mercy,
Lift Thou my soul to Thee, O Son of God,
Nor leave me ever.

Remember me in the mountain,
Under Thy wing shield Thou me;
Rock of truth, do not forsake me,
My wish it were ever to be near Thee.

Give to me the wedding garment,
Be angels conversing with me in every need,
Be the holy apostles protecting me,
The fair Mary and Thou, Jesu of grace,
The fair Mary and Thou, Jesu of grace.

EARNA MHOIRE

HAIL, MARY

FAILT, a Mhoire! failt, a Mhoire!
Righinn nan gras, Mathair na trocair;
Failt, a Mhoire, air mhodh gun choimeas,
Geil ar slainte, fath ar solais.

Riut tha sinne, dh' oidhch 's a latha,
Sliochd seachranach Adhamh is Eubha,
Togail ar guth 's ag achan,

An gul 's an gal 's an deura.

Tabhair duinn, a Fhreimh an aigh,
O 's tu copan nan grasa fial,
Creid Eoin, is Pheaid, is Phail,
Le sgeith Airil an aird nan nial.

Deoin dhuinn, a gheug dhonn,
Aros ann am Fonn na sith,
Tamh o ghabhadh 's o anradh thonn,
Fo sgath toraidh do bhronn, Ios.

HAIL, Mary! hail, Mary!
Queen of grace, Mother of mercy;
Hail, Mary, in manner surpassing,
Fount of our health, source of our joy.

To thee we, night and day,
Erring children of Adam and Eve,
Lift our voice in supplication,
In groans and grief and tears.

Bestow upon us, thou Root of gladness,
Since thou art the cup of generous graces,
The faith of John, and Peter, and Paul,
With the wings of Ariel on the heights of the clouds.

Vouchsafe to us, thou golden branch,
A mansion in the Realm of peace,
Rest from the perils and stress of waves,
Beneath the shade of the fruit of thy womb, Jesu.

FAILTE A MHOIRE

HAIL TO THEE, MARY

FAILTE dhuit, a Mhoire Mhathair!
Tha thu lan dhe na grasan caomh,
Tha 'n Tighearna Dia maille riut a ghnath.
Beannaicht thu, Mhairi, am measg nam mnai,
Beannaicht toradh do bhronn, Iosa,
Beannaicht thu, Righinn an ais;
A Naomh Mhoire, a Mhathair Iosa,
Guidh air mo shon-sa, peacach truagh,
Nis agus aig uair mo bhais,
Nis agus aig uair mo bhais!

HAIL to thee, Mary, Mother!
Thou art full of loving grace,
The Lord God is always with thee,
Blessed art thou Mary among women,
Blessed is the fruit of thy womb, Jesus,
Blessed art thou, Queen of grace;
Thou holy Mary, thou Mother of Jesus,
Plead for me a miserable sinner,
Now and at the hour of death,
Now and at the hour of death!

AN CATH NACH TAINIG

THE BATTLE TO COME

IOSA Mhic Mhoire eighim air th' ainm,
Is air ainm Eoin ostail ghradhaich,
Is air ainm gach naoimh 's an domhan dearg,
Mo thearmad 's a chath nach tainig,
Mo thearmad 's a chath nach tainig.

Duair theid am beul a dhunadh,
Duair theid an t-suil a dhruideadh,
Duair sguireas an anail da struladh,
Duair sguireas an cridhe da bhuille,
Sguireas an cridhe de bhuille.

Duair theid am Breitheamh dh' an chathair,
Is a theid an tagradh a shuidheach,
Iosa Mhic Mhoire cobhair air m' anam,
A Mhicheil mhin gobh ri mo shiubhal.
Iosa Mhic Mhoire cobhair air m' anam!
A Mhicheil mhin gobh ri mo shiubhal!

JESUS, Thou Son of Mary, I call on Thy name,
And on the name of John the apostle beloved,
And on the names of all the saints in the red domain,
To shield me in the battle to come,
To shield me in the battle to come.

When the mouth shall be closed,
When the eye shall be shut,
When the breath shall cease to rattle,
When the heart shall cease to throb,
When the heart shall cease to throb.

When the Judge shall take the throne,
And when the cause is fully pleaded,
O Jesu, Son of Mary, shield Thou my soul,
O Michael fair, acknowledge my departure.
O Jesu, Son of Mary, shield Thou my soul!
O Michael fair, receive my departure!

AM BEANNACHADH BAISTIDH

THE BAPTISM BLESSING

IT is known that a form of baptism prevailed among the Celts previous to the introduction of Christianity, as forms of baptism prevail among pagan people now. Whenever possible the Celtic Church christianized existing ceremonies and days of special observance, grafting the new on the old, as at a later day Augustine did in southern Britain. Immediately after its birth the nurse or other person present drops three drops of water on the forehead of the child. The first drop is in the name of the Father, representing wisdom; the second drop is in the name of the Son, representing peace; the third drop is in the name of the Spirit, representing purity. If the child be a male the name 'Maol-domhnuich,' if a female the name 'Griadach,' is applied to it temporarily. 'Maol-domhnuich' means tonsured of the Lord, and 'Griadach' is rendered Gertrude. When the child is ecclesiastically baptized--generally at the end of eight days--the temporary is superseded by the permanent name. This lay baptism is recognised by the Presbyterian, the Anglican; the Latin, and the Greek Churches. If the child were not thus baptized it would need to be carefully guarded lest the fairies should spirit it away before the ecclesiastical baptism took place, when their power over it ceased. The lay baptism also ensured that in the event of death the child should be buried in consecrated ground.

THI, tha comhnadh nan ard,
Tiur do bheannachd 'na thrath,
Cuimhnich-s' leanabh mo chri,
An Ainm Athar na sith;
Trath chuireas sagart an Righ
Air uisge na brigh,
Builich da beannachd nan Tri
Ta lionadh nan ard.
Beannachd nan Tri
Ta lionadh nan ard.

Crath nuas air do ghras,
Tabh dha feart agus fas,
Tabh dha trein agus treoir,
Tabh dha seilbh agus coir,
Rian agus ciall gun gho,
Gliocas aingeal r'a lo,
Chum's gun seas e gun sgeo
'Na d' lathair.

Gun seas e gun sgeo
'Na d' lathair.

THOU Being who inhabitest the heights
Imprint Thy blessing betimes,
Remember Thou the child of my body,
In Name of the Father of peace;
When the priest of the King
On him puts the water of meaning,
Grant him the blessing of the Three
Who fill the heights.
The blessing of the Three
Who fill the heights.

Sprinkle down upon him Thy grace,
Give Thou to him virtue and growth,
Give Thou to him strength and guidance,
Give Thou to him flocks and possessions,
Sense and reason void of guile,
Angel wisdom in his day,
That he may stand without reproach
In Thy presence.
He may stand without reproach
In Thy presence.

AN TREORAICH ANAMA

THE SOUL LEADING

DEATH blessings vary in words but not in spirit. These death blessings are known by various names, as: 'Beannachadh Bais,' Death Blessing, 'Treoraich Anama,' Soul Leading, 'Fois Anama,' Soul Peace, and other names familiar to the people.

The soul peace is intoned, not necessarily by a cleric, over the dying, and the man or the woman who says it is called 'anam-chara,' soul-friend. He or she is held in special affection by the friends of the dying person ever after. The soul peace is slowly sung--all present earnestly joining the soul-friend in beseeching the Three Persons of the Godhead and all the saints of heaven to receive the departing soul of earth. During the prayer the soul-friend, makes the sign of the cross with the right thumb over the lips of the dying.

The scene is touching and striking in the extreme, and the man or woman is not to be envied who could witness unmoved the distress of these lovable people of the West taking leave of those who are near and dear to them in their pilgrimage, as they say, of crossing 'abhuinn dubh a bhais'--the black river of death; 'cuan mor na duibhre'--the great ocean of darkness; and 'beanntaibh na bith-bhuantachd'--the mountains of eternity. The scene may be in a lowly cot begrimed with smoke and black with age, but the heart is not less warm, the tear is not less bitter, and the parting is not less distressful, than in the court of the noble or in the palace of royalty.

'Nowhere beats the Heart so kindly
As beneath the tart plaid.'--AYTON.

According to the old people:--

'Duair a bheir an duine suas an ospag chithear an t-anam air cleas meall soluis ag eirigh a suas anns na neoil. Theirear an uair sin:--

Tha 'n t-anam truagh a nis fo sgaoil
An taobh a muigh dh' an chaim;
A Chriosd chaoimh nam beannachd saor
Cuartaich mo ghaol 'na aim.'

When a person gives up the ghost the soul is seen ascending like a bright ball of light into the clouds. Then it is said:--

The poor soul is now set free
Outside the soul-shrine;
O kindly Christ of the free blessings.
Encompass Thou my love in time.

AN t-anam-s' air do laimh, a Chriosda,
A nigh na Cathrach Neomh.
Amen.
Bho is tus, a Chriosd, a cheannaich an t-anam-s',
Biodh a-shith air do theannal fein.
Amen.
Is biodh Micheal mil, and righ nan aingeal,
A reiteach an rathaid romh 'n anam-s', a Dhe.
Amen.
O Micheal mil an sith riut, anaim,
Is a reiteach dhuit rathaid gu flathas Mhic De.
Amen.

BE this soul on Thine arm, O Christ,
Thou King of the City of Heaven..
Amen.
Since Thou, O Christ, it was who bought'st this soul,
Be its peace on Thine own keeping.
Amen.
And may the strong Michael, high king of the angels,
Be preparing the path before this soul, O God.
Amen.

Oh! the strong Michael in peace with thee, soul,
And preparing for thee the way to the kingdom of the Son of God.
Amen.

AM BEANNACHADH BAIS

THE DEATH BLESSING

DHIA, na diobair a bhean a d' mhuinntireas, [fear
Agus a liuth olc a rinn a corp,
Nach urr i nochd a chunntachas;
A liuth olc a rinn a corp,
Nach urr i nochd a chunntachas.

An t-anam-s' air do laimh, a Chriosda,
A Righ na Cathrach Naomh.
Bho's tu, a Chriosda, cheannaich an t-anam,
An am tomhas na meidhe,
An am tobhar na breithe,
Biodh e nis air do dheas laimh fein,
O air do dheas laimh fein,

Is biodh Naomh Micheal, righ nan aingeal,
Tighinn an codhail an anama,
Is ga threorachadh dachaidh
Gu flathas Mhic De.
Naomh Micheal, ard righ nan aingeal,
Tighinn an codhail an anama,
Is ga threorachadh dachaidh
Gu flathas Mhic De

GOD, omit not this woman from Thy covenant, [man
And the many evils which she in the body committed,
That she cannot this night enumerate.
The many evils that she in the body committed,
That she cannot this night enumerate.

Be this soul on Thine own arm, O Christ,
Thou King of the City of Heaven,
And since Thine it was, O Christ, to buy the soul,
At the time of the balancing of the beam,
At the time of the bringing in the judgment,
Be it now on Thine own right hand,
Oh! on Thine own right hand.

And be the holy Michael, king of angels,

Coming to meet the soul,
And leading it home
To the heaven of the Son of God.
The Holy Michael, high king of angels,
Coming to meet the soul,
And leading it home
To the heaven of the Son of God.

FOIS ANAMA

SOUL PEACE

O 'S tus a Chriosd a cheannaich an t-anam--
Ri linn dioladh na beatha,
Ri linn bruchdadh na falluis,
Ri linn iobar na creadha,
Ri linn dortadh na fala,
Ri linn cothrom na meidhe,
Ri linn sgathadh na h-anal,
Ri linn tabhar na breithe,
Biodh a shith air do theannal fein;
Iosa Criosda Mhic Moire mine,
Biodh a shith air do theannal fein,
O Ios! air do theannal fein.

Is bitheadh Micheal geal caomh,
Ard righ nan aingeal naomh,
An cinnseal an anama ghaoil,
Ga dhion dh'an Triu barra-chaon,
O! dh'an Triu barra-chaon.

SINCE Thou Christ it was who didst buy the soul---
At the time of yielding the life,
At the time of pouring the sweat,
At the time of offering the clay,
At the time of shedding the blood,
At the time of balancing the beam,
At the time of severing the breath,
At the time of delivering the judgment,
Be its peace upon Thine own ingathering;
Jesus Christ Son of gentle Mary,
Be its peace upon Thine own ingathering,
O Jesus! upon Thine own ingathering.

And may Michael white kindly,
High king of the holy angels,

Take possession of the beloved soul,
And shield it home to the Three of surpassing love,
Oh! to the Three of surpassing love.

A GHEALACH UR

THE NEW MOON

THIS little prayer is said by old men and women in the islands of Barra. When they first see the new moon they make their obeisance to it as to a great chief. The women curtsey gracefully and the men bow low, raising their bonnets reverently. The bow of the men is peculiar, partaking somewhat of the curtsey of the women, the left knee being bent and the right drawn forward towards the middle of the left leg in a curious but not inelegant manner.

The fragment of moon-worship is now a matter of custom rather than of belief, although it exists over the whole British Isles.

In Cornwall the people nod to the new moon and turn silver in their pockets. In Edinburgh cultured men and women turn the rings on their fingers and make their wishes. A young English lady told the writer that she had always been in the habit of bowing to the new moon, till she had been bribed out of it by her father, a clergyman, putting money in her pocket lest her lunar worship should compromise him with his bishop. She naively confessed, however, that among the free mountains of Loch Etive she reverted to the good customs of her fathers, from which she derived great satisfaction!

AN ainm Spiorad Naomh nan gras,
An ainm Athar na, Cathrach aigh,
An ainm Iosa thug dhinn am bas,
O! an ainm na Tri tha d' ar dion 's gach cas,
Ma's math a fhuair thu sinn an nochd,
Seachd fearr gum fag thu sinn gun lochd,
A Ghealach gheal nan trath,
A Ghealach gheal nan trath.

IN name of the Holy Spirit of grace,
In name of the Father of the City of peace,
In name of Jesus who took death off us,
Oh! in name of the Three who shield us in every need,
If well thou hast found us to-night,
Seven times better mayest thou leave us without harm,
Thou bright white Moon of the seasons,
Bright white Moon of the seasons.

The following versification is by Mr John Henry Dixon, Inveran:--

In name of the Father Almighty,
In name of the Glorious Son,

In name of the Holy Spirit,
By grace of the Three-in-One.

If to-night, O moon, thou hast found us
In peaceful, happy rest,

May thy laving lustre leave us
Seven times still more blest.

O moon so fair,
May it be so,
As seasons come,
And seasons go.

II

AIMSIRE

SEASONS

NUALL NOLLAIG

CHRISTMAS HAIL

CHRISTMAS chants were numerous and their recital common throughout Scotland. They are now disappearing with the customs they accompanied. Where they still linger their recital is relegated to boys. Formerly on Christmas Eve bands of young men went about from house to house and from townland to townland chanting Christmas songs. The band was called 'goisearan,' guisers, 'firduan,' song men, 'gillean Nollaig,' Christmas lads, 'nuallairean,' rejoicers, and other names. The 'rejoicers' wore long white shirts for surplices, and very tall white hats for mitres, in which they made a picturesque appearance as they moved along singing their loudest. Sometimes they went about as one band, sometimes in sections of twos and threes. When they entered a dwelling they took possession of a child, if there was one in the house. In the absence of a child, a lay figure was improvised. The child was called 'Crist, Cristean'--Christ, Little Christ. The assumed Christ was placed on a skin, and carried three times round the fire, sunwise, by the 'ceannsnaodh'--head of the band, the song men singing the Christmas Hail. The skin on which the symbolic Christ was carried was that of a white male lamb without spot or blemish and consecrated to this service. The skin was called 'uilim.' Homage and offerings and much rejoicing were made to the symbolic Christ. The people of the house gave the guisers bread, butter, crowdie, and other eatables, on which they afterwards feasted.

The three poems which follow were taken down from Angus Gunn, Ness, Lewis, then over eighty-four years of age. Angus Gunn had been a strong man physically and was still a strong man mentally. He had lived for many years in the island of North Roney, and gave a graphic description of it, and of his life there. He had much oral lore which he told with great dramatic power. The following tale is one of those related by him:--'Ronan came to Lewis to convert the people to the Christian faith. He built himself a prayer-house at Eorabay. But the people were bad and they would not give him peace. The men quarrelled about everything, and the women quarrelled about nothing, and Ronan was distressed and could not say his prayers for their clamour. He prayed to be removed from the people of Eorabay, and immediately an angel came and told him to go down to the "laimirig," natural landing-rock, where the "cionaran-cro," cragen was waiting him. Ronan arose and hurried down to the sea-shore shaking the dust of Eorabay off his feet, and taking nothing but his "pollaire," satchel, containing the Book, on his breast. And there, stretched along the rock, was the great "cionaran-cro," his great eyes shining like two stars of night. Ronan sat on the back of the "cionaran-cro," and it flew with him over the sea, usually wild as the mountains, now smooth as the plains, and in the twinkling of two eyes reached the remote isle of the ocean. Ronan landed on the island, and that was the land full of "nathair bheumnaich, gribh inich, nathair nimhe, agus leomhain bheucaich"--biting adders, taloned griffins, poisonous snakes, and roaring lions. All the beasts of the island fled before the holy Ronan and rushed backwards over the rocks into the sea. And that is how the rocks of the island of Roney are grooved and scratched and lined with the claws and the nails of the unholy creatures. The good Ronan built himself a prayer-house in the island where he could say his prayers in peace.'

Roney is a small, precipitous island in the North Atlantic, sixty miles from the Butt of Lewis and sixty miles from Cape Wrath, forming the apex of a triangle between the two promontories. It is inaccessible except in a smooth sea, which is rare there. The rocks of Roney are much striated. The island is now uninhabited. St Ronan lived in the end of the seventh century.

HO Ri, ho Ri,
Beannaicht e, beannaicht e,
Ho Ri, ho Ri,
Beannaicht e, thainig 's an am,
Ho Ri, ho Ri,
Beannaicht an tigh 's na bheil ann,
Ho Ri, ho Ri,
Eadar chuall, is chlach, is chrann,
Ho Ri, ho Ri,
Iomair do Dhia, eadar bhrat is aodach,

HAIL to the King, hail to the King,
Blessed is He, blessed is He,
Hail to the King, hail to the King,
Blessed is He who has come betimes,
Hail to the King, hail to the King,
Blessed be the house and all therein,
Hail to the King, hail to the King,
'Twixt stock and stone and stave,
Hail to the King, hail to the King,
Consign it to God from corslet to cover,

Slainte dhaoine gun robh ann,
Ho Ri, ho Ri,
Beannaicht e, beannaicht e,
Ho Ri, ho Hi,
Beannaicht e, beannaicht e,
Ho Ri, ho Ri,
Gum bu buan mu'n tulach sibh,
Ho Ri, ho Ri,
Gum bu slan mu'n teallach sibh,
Ho Ri, ho Ri,
Gum bu liuth crann 's an tigh,
Daoine tamh 's a' bhunntair,
Ho Ri, ho Ri,
Beannaicht e, beannaicht e,
Ho Ri, ho Ri,
Beannaicht e, beannaicht e.

Ho Ri, ho Ri,

Nochd oichdhe Nollaige moire,
Ho Ri, ho Ri,
Beannaicht e, beannaicht e,
Ho Ri, ho Ri,
Rugadh Mac na Moir Oighe,
Ho Ri, ho Ri,
Beannaicht e, beannaicht e,
Ho Ri, ho Ri,
Rainig a bhonnaibh an lar,
Ho Ri, ho Ri,
Beannaicht e, beannaicht e,
Ho Ri, ho Ri,
Shoillsich grian nam beann ard,
Ho Ri, ho Ri,
Beannaicht e, beannaicht e.

Be the health of men therein,
Hail to the King, hail to the King,
Blessed is He, blessed is He,
Hail to the King, hail to the King,
Blessed is He, blessed is He,
Hail to the King, hail to the King,
Lasting round the house be ye,
Hail to the King, hail to the King,
Healthy round the hearth be ye,
Hail to the King, hail to the King,
Many be the stakes in the house,
And men dwelling on the foundation,
Hail to the King, hail to the King,
Blessed is He, blessed is He,
Hail to the King, hail to the King,
Blessed is He, blessed is He.

Hail to the King, hail to the King,
This night is the eve of the great Nativity,
Hail to the King, hail to the King,
Blessed is He, blessed is He,
Hail to the King, hail to the King,
Born is the Son of Mary the Virgin,
Hail to the King, hail to the King,
Blessed is He, blessed is He,
Hail to the King, hail to the King,
The soles of His feet have reached the earth,
Hail to the King, hail to the King,
Blessed is He, blessed is He,
Hail to the King, hail to the King,

Illumined the sun the mountains high,
Hail to the King, hail to the King,
Blessed is He, blessed is He.

Shoillsich fearann, shoillsich fonn,
Ho Ri, ho Ri,
Beannaicht e, beannaicht e,
Ho Ri, ho Ri,
Chualas an tonn air an traigh,
Ho Ri, ho Ri,
Beannaicht e, beannaicht e,
Beannaicht e, beannaicht e,
Ho Ri, ho Ri,
Beannaicht an Righ,
Gun tus, gun chrich,
Gu suthainn, gu sior,
Gach linn gu brath.

Shone the earth, shone the land,
Hail to the King, hail to the King,
Blessed is He, is He,
Hail to the King, hail to the King,
Heard was the wave upon the strand,
Hail to the King, hail to the King,
Blessed is He, blessed is He,
Blessed is He, blessed is He,
Hail to the King, hail to the King,
Blessed the King,
Without beginning, without end,
To everlasting, to eternity,
To all ages, to all time.

DUAN NOLLAIG

CHRISTMAS CAROL

HOIRE! hoire! beannaicht e! beannaicht e!
Hoire! hoire! beannaicht e! beannaicht e!
Hoire! hoire! beannaicht e'n Righ dh' am bi sinn a' seinn,
Ho! ro! biodh aoibh!

Nochd oidhche Nollaige moire,
Rugadh Mac na Moir Oighe,
Rainig a bhonnaibh an lar,
Mac nam buadh a nuas o'n ard,
Dhealraich neamh is cruinne dha,

Ho! ro! biodh aoibh!

Seimh saoghal dha, sona neamh dha,
Feuch rainig a bhonn an lar,
Fodhail Righ dha, failt Uain dha,
Righ nam buadh, Uan nan agh,
Shoillsich cluan agus cuanta dha,
Ho! ro! biodh aoibh!

Shoillsich frith dha, shoillsich fonn dha,
Nuall nan tonn le fonn nan tragh,
Ag innse dhuinne gun d' rugadh Criosda
Mac Righ nan righ a tir na slaint;
Shoillsich grian nam beannaibh ard dha,
Ho! ro! biodh aoibh!

Shoillsich ce dha is cruinne comhla,
Dh' fhosgail De an Domhnaich Dorus;
A Mhic Mhuir Oighe greas ga'm chomhnadh,
A Chriosd an dochais, a Chomhla 'n t-sonais,
Oradh Ghreine shleibh is mhonaidh,
Ho! ro! biodh aoibh!

HAIL King! hail King! blessed is He! blessed is He!
Hail King! hail King! blessed is He! blessed is He!
Hail King! hail King! blessed is He, the King of whom we sing,
All hail! let there be joy!

This night is the eve of the great Nativity,
Born is the Son of Mary the Virgin,
The soles of His feet have reached the earth,
The Son of glory down from on high,
Heaven and earth glowed to Him,
All hail! let there be joy!

The peace of earth to Him, the joy of heaven to Him,
Behold His feet have reached the world;
The homage of a King be His, the welcome of a Lamb be His,
King all victorious, Lamb all glorious,
Earth and ocean illumed to Him,
All hail! let there be joy!

The mountains glowed to Him, the plains glowed to Him,
The voice of the waves with the song of the strand,
Announcing to us that Christ is born,
Son of the King of kings from the land of salvation;

Shone the sun on the mountains high to Him,
All hail! let there be joy!

Shone to Him the earth and sphere together,
God the Lord has opened a Door;
Son of Mary Virgin, hasten Thou to help me,
Thou Christ of hope, Thou Door of joy,
Golden Sun of hill and mountain,
All hail! let there be joy!

DUAN NOLLAIG

CHRISTMAS CHANT

HOIRE! hoire! beannaicht e! beannaicht e!
Hoire! hoire! beannaicht e! beannaicht e!
Ho! hi! beannaicht an Righ!
Ho! hi! biodh aoibh.

Buaidh biodh air an tulaich seo,
Na chualas leibh 's na chunnas leibh,
Air na leaca loma loinnear lair,
'S air na clacha corrach cuimir clair,
Hoire! hoire! beannaicht e! beannaicht e!

Beannaich an taigh 's na bheil ann,
Eadar chuaill is chlach is chrann
Imir do Dhia eadar bhrat is aodach,
Slainte dhaoine gun robh ann,
Hoire! hoire! beannaicht e! beannaicht e!

Gu mu buan mu'n tulach sibh,
Gu mu slan mu'n teallach sibh,
Gu mu liuth dul 's ceann sguilb 's an aros,
Daoine tamh 's a bhunntair,
Hoire! hoire! beannaicht e! beannaicht e!

HAIL King! hail King! blessed is He! blessed is He!
Hail King! hail King! blessed is He! blessed is He!
Ho, hail! blessed the King!
Ho, hi! let there be joy!

Prosperity be upon this dwelling,
On all that ye have heard and seen,
On the bare bright floor flags,
On the shapely standing stone staves,

Hail King! hail King! blessed is He! blessed is He!

Bless this house and all that it contains,
From rafter and stone and beam;
Deliver it to God from pall to cover,
Be the healing of men therein,
Hail King! hail King! blessed is He! blessed is He!

Be ye in lasting possession of the house,
Be ye healthy about the hearth,
Many be the ties and stakes in the homestead,
People dwelling on this foundation,
Hail King! hail King! blessed is He! blessed is He!

Iobair dh 'an Ti eadar bhonn agus bhrat,
Eadar chuaill agus chlach agus chrann;
Iobair a ris eadar shlat agus aodach,
Slanadh shaoghal a dhaoine th' ann,
Hoire! hoire! beannaicht e! beannaicht e!
Hoire! hoire! beannaicht e! beannaicht e!
Ho, hi, beannaicht an Righ,
Ho, hi, biodh aoibh!

Beannaicht an Righ,
Gun tus gun chrich,
Gu suth, gu sior,
Gach linn gu brath,
Ho! hi! biodh aoibh!

Offer to the Being from found to cover,
Include stave and stone and beam;
Offer again both rods and cloth,
Be health to the people therein,
Hail King! hail King! blessed is He! blessed is He!
Hail King! hail King! blessed is He! blessed is He!
Ho, hail! blessed the King!
Let there be joy!

Blessed the King,
Without beginning, without ending,
To everlasting, to eternity,
Every generation for aye,
Ho! hi! let there be joy!

HEIRE BANNAG

69

HEY THE GIFT

THESE carols were sung by a band of men who went about from house to house in the townland. The band selected a leader for their singing and for their actions throughout the night. This leader was called 'fear-duan,' song-man, and the others were called 'fir-fuinn,' chorus-men. When they had sung their carols at a house, two or three bannocks were handed out to them through a window.

The song-man got half of every bannock so received, and the other half went to the chorus-men.

HEIRE Bannag, hoire Bannag,
Heire Bannag, air a bheo.

Chaidh Muire mhin gheal air a glun,
Is e Righ nan dul a bha 'na h-uchd.

Taobh an t-sorcain, taobh an t-searcain,
Buailtear boicionn air an spar.

'G innse duinn gun do rugadh Criosd,
Righ nan righ, a tir na slaint.

Chi mi tulach, chi mi traigh,
Chi mi ullaim air an t-snamh.

Chi mi ainghlean air an luinn,
Tighinn le cimh is cairdeas duinn.

HEY the Gift, ho the Gift,
Hey the Gift on the living.

The fair Mary went upon her knee,
It was the King of glory who was on her breast.

The side of the sack (?) the side of the sark (?)
The hide is struck upon the spar.

To tell to us that Christ is born,
The King of kings of the land of salvation.

I see the hills, I see the strand,
I see the host upon the wing.

I see angels on clouds, [waves
Coming with speech and friendship to us.

HEIRE BANNAG, HOIRE BANNAG

HEY THE GIFT, HO THE GIFT

[p. `4`]

HEIRE Bannag, hoire Bannag,
Heire Bannag, air a bheo.

Mac na niula, Mac na neula,
Mac na runna, Mac na reula,
Heire Bannag, etc.

Mac na dile, Mac na deire,
Mac na spire, Mac na speura,
Heire Bannag, etc.

Mac na lasa, Mac na leusa,
Mac na cruinne, Mac na ce,
Heire Bannag, etc.

Mac nan dula, Mac nan neamha,
Mac na gile, Mac na greine,
Heire Bannag, etc.

Mac Moire na De-meine,
Is Mac De tus gach sgeula,
Heire Bannag, etc.

HEY the Gift, ho the Gift,
Hey the Gift, on the living.

Son of the dawn, Son of the clouds,
Son of the planet, Son of the star,
Hey the Gift, etc.

Son of the rain, Son of the dew,
Son of the welkin, Son of the sky,
Hey the Gift, etc.

Son of the flame, Son of the light,
Son of the sphere, Son of the globe,
Hey the Gift, etc.

Son of the elements, Son of the heavens,
Son of the moon, Son of the sun,
Hey the Gift, etc.

Son of Mary of the God-mind,
And the Son of God first of all news,
Hey the Gift, etc.

BANNAG NAM BUADH

THE GIFT OF POWER

IS mise Bannag, is mise Bochd,
Is mise Fear na h-oidhche nochd.

Is mise Mac De anns an dorus,
Di-luain air thuaradh nam bannag.

Is uasal Bride mhin-gheal air a glun,
Is uasal High nan dul 'na h-uchd.

Mac na gile, Mac na greine,
Mac Moire mor na De-meine,

Crois air gach guala dheis,
Mis is dorus, fosgail thusa.

Is leir 'omh tulach, is leir 'omh traigh,
Is leir 'omh ainghlean tighinn air snamh.

Is leir 'omh calaman, cuimir, caon,
Tighinn le caomh is cairdeas duinn.

I AM the Gift, I am the Poor,
I am the Man of this night.

I am the Son of God in the door,
On Monday seeking the gifts.

Noble is Bride the gentle fair on her knee,
Noble the King of glory on her breast.

Son of the moon, Son of the sung
Great Son of Mary of God-like mind.

A cross on each right shoulder,
I am in the door, open thou.

I see the hills, I see the strand,

I see angels heralding on high.

I see the dove shapely, benign,
Coming with kindness and friendship to us.

AN OIGH AGUS AN LEANABH

THE VIRGIN AND CHILD

CHUNNACAS an Oigh a teachd,
Criosda gu h-og 'na h-uchd.

A Mhoir Oighe, agus a Mhic,
Beannaich an taigh agus a luchd.

Beannaich am biadh, beannaich am bord,
Beannaich an dias, an triall 's an stor.

An trath bha oirnn an raithe gann,
Is tu fein, Oighe, bu mhathair dhuinn.

Is gil thu na ghealach earra-gheal
Ag eirigh air an tulaich.

Is gil thu na ghrian cheit-ghil,
Fo eibhneas subhach.

Bho nach faod am bard fuireach,
Cuiribh uilim 's a bhalg le beannachd.

Mise gille Mhic De an cois an doruis,
A uchd De, eirich fein is fosgail domh e.

BEHOLD the Virgin approaching,
Christ so young on her breast.

O Mary Virgin! and O Holy Son!
Bless ye the house and all therein,

Bless ye the food, bless ye the board,
Bless ye the corn, the flock and the store.

What time to us the quarter was scarce,
It is thou thyself, Virgin, who wast mother to us.

Thou art brighter than the waxing moon

Rising over the mountains.

Thou art brighter than the summer sun,
Under his fullness of joy.

Since the bard must not tarry,
Place ye alms in the bag with a blessing.

Servant am I of God the Son on the threshold,
For the sake of God, arise thyself and open to me.

RUGADH BUACHAILLE NAN TREUD

THE SHEPHERD OF THE FLOCK WAS BORN

OIDHCHE sin a dhealraich an reult,
Rugadh Buachaille nan treud,
Le Oigh nan ceudaibh beus,
Moire Mhathar.

An Trianaid shiorruidh r'a taobh,
Ann am frasach fuar, faoin.
Thig 's thoir deachamh de d' mhaoin,
Dh' an t-Slan-Fhear.

An cobhrach, ciochrach, caomh,
Gun aon dachaidh fo 'n t-saoghal,
Am Fogaran naomha, maoth,
'Manul!

A thri ainglibh nam buadh,
Thigibh, thigibh a nuas;
Do Chriosd an t-sluaigh
Thugaibh failte.

Pogaibh a bhasa,
Tioramaichibh a chasa
Le falt bhur cinn;
'S O! Thi na cruinne,
'S Iosa, Mhicheil, Mhuire,
Na fagaibh sinn.

THAT night the star shone
Was born the Shepherd of the Flock,
Of the Virgin of the hundred charms;
The Mary Mother.

The Trinity eternal by her side,
In the manger cold and lowly.
Come and give tithes of thy means
To the Healing Man.

The foam-white breastling beloved,
Without one home in the world,
The tender holy Babe forth driven,
Immanuel!

Ye three angels of power,
Come ye, come ye down;
To the Christ of the people
Give ye salutation.

Kiss ye His hands,
Dry ye His feet
With the hair of your heads;
And O! Thou world-pervading God,
And Ye, Jesu, Michael, Mary,
Do not Ye forsake us.

CALLUINN A BHUILG

HOGMANAY OF THE SACK

CALLUINEN HO!--This rune is still repeated in the Isles. Rarely, however, do two persons recite it alike. This renders it difficult to decide the right form of the words.

The walls of the old houses in the West are very thick--from five to eight feet. There are no gables, the walls being of uniform height throughout. The roof of the house being raised from the inner edge of the wall, a broad terrace is left on the outside. Two or three stones project from the wall at the door, forming steps. On these the inmates ascend for purposes of thatching and securing the roof in time of storm.

The 'gillean Callaig' carollers or Hogmanay lads perambulate the townland at night. One man is enveloped in the hard hide of a bull with the horns and hoofs still attached. When the men come to a house they ascend the wall and run round sunwise, the man in the hide shaking the horns and hoofs, and the other men striking the hard hide with sticks. The appearance of the man in the hide is gruesome, while the din made is terrific. Having descended and recited their runes at the door, the Hogmanay men are admitted and treated to the best in the house. The performance seems to be symbolic, but of what it is not easy to say, unless of laying an evil spirit. That the rite is heathen and ancient is evident.

CALLIUINN a bhuilg,

Calluinn a bhuilg,
Buail am boicionn,
Buail am boicionn.
Calluinn a bhuilg,
Calluinn a bhuilg,
Buail an craicionn,
Buail an craicionn.
Calluinn a bhuilg,
Calluinn a bhuilg,
Sios e! suas e!
Buail am boicionn.
Calluinn a bhuilg,
Calluinn a bhuilg,
Sios e! suas e!
Buail an craicionn.
Calluinn a bhuilg,
Calluinn a bhuilg.

HOGMANAY of the sack,
Hogmanay of the sack,
Strike the hide,
Strike the hide.
Hogmanay of the sack,
Hogmanay of the sack,
Beat the skin,
Beat the skin.
Hogmanay of the sack,
Hogmanay of the sack,
Down with it! up with it!
Strike the hide.
Hogmanay of the sack,
Hogmanay of the sack,
Down with it! up with it!
Beat the skin.
Hogmanay of the sack,
Hogmanay of the sack.

CAIRIOLL CALLAIG

HOGMANAY CAROL

NIS tha mis air tighinn dh' ur duthaich
A dh' urachadh dhuibh na Callaig;
Cha leig mi leas a dhol ga innse,
Bha i ann ri linn ar seanar.

76

Dirim ris an ardorus,
Teurnam ris an starsach,
Mo dhuan a ghabhail doigheil,
Modhail, moineil, maineil.

Caisean Callaig 'na mo phoca,
Is mor an ceo thig as an ealachd.
* * * *

Gheibh fear an taighe 'na dhorn e,
Cuiridh e shron anns an teallach;
Theid e deiseil air na paisdean,
Seachd ar air bean an taighe.

Bean an taighe is i is fhiach e,
Lamh a riarach oirnn na Callaig,
Sochair bheag a bhlath an t-samhraidh,
Tha mi 'n geall air leis an arain.

Tabhair duinn ma dh' fhaodas,
Mar a faod na cum maill oirnn,
Mise gille Mhic De 's an dorus,
Eirich fein is fosgail domh e.

I AM now come to your country,
To renew to you the Hogmanay,
I need not tell you of it,
It was in the time of our forefathers.

I ascend by the door lintel,
I descend by the doorstep,
I will sing my song becomingly,
Mannerly, slowly, mindfully.

The Hogmanay skin is in my pocket,
Great will be the smoke from it presently.
* * * *

The house-man will get it in his hand,
He will place its nose in the fire;
He will go sunwards round the babes,
And for seven verities round the housewife.

The housewife it is she who deserves it,
The hand to dispense to us the Hogmanay,
A small gift of the bloom of summer,

Much I wish it with the bread.

Give it to us if it be possible,
If you may not, do not detain us;
I am the servant of God's Son at the door,
Arise thyself and open to me.

DUAN CALLAIG

THE SONG OF HOGMANAY

NIST o thaine sinn dh' an duthaich,
Dh' urachadh dhuibh na Callaig,
Cha ruig uine dhuinn bhi 'g innse,
Bha i ann ri linn ar seanar.

A direadh ri tobht an taighe,
A teurnadh aig an dorus,
Mo dhuan a ghabhail modhail,
Mar b' eol domh aig a Challaig.

Caisein Callaig 'na mo phocaid,
Is mor an ceo thig as an fhear ud,
Chan 'eil aon a gheobh de aile,
Nach bi gu brath de fallain.

Gheobh fear an taighe 'na dhorn e,
Cuiridh e shron anns an teallach;
Theid e deiseil air na paisdean,
Is seachd araid bean an taighe.

Gheobh a bhean e, is i 's t-fhiach e,
Lamh a riarachadh na Callaig,
Lamh a bhairig cais is im duinn,
Lamh gun spiocaireachd, gun ghainne.

Now since we came to the country
To renew to you the Hogmanay,
Time will not allow us to explain,
It has been since the age of our fathers.

Ascending the wall of the house,
Descending at the door,
My carol to say modestly,
As becomes me at the Hogmanay.

The Hogmanay skin is in my pocket,
Great the fume that will come from that;
No one who shall inhale its odour,
But shall be for ever from it healthy.

The house-man will get it in his grasp,
He will put its point in the fire;
He will go sunwise round the children,
And very specially round the goodwife.

The wife will get it, she it is who deserves it,
The hand to distribute the Hogmanay,
The hand to bestow upon us cheese and butter,
The hand without niggardliness, without meanness.

Bho 'n ta tart air tighinn an duthaich,
Is nach bi duil againn ri annas,
Rud beag a shugh an t-samhraidh,
B' annsa leinn e leis an aran.

Mur bheil sin againn ri fhaotainn,
Ma dh' fhaodas tu, na cum maill oirnn;
Mise gille Mhic De air Chollaig,
Eirich fein is fosgail dorus,
Callain seo! Callain seo!

Since drought has come upon the land,
And that we do not expect rarity,
A little of the substance of the summer,
Would we desire with the bread.

If that we are not to have it,
If thou mayest, do not detain us;
I am the servant of God's Son on Hogmanay,
Arise thyself and open the door.
Hogmanay here! Hogmanay here!

OIDHCHE CHALLAIG

HOGMANAY

THAINE sinne chon an doruis,
Feuch am feairrde sinn an turas,
Dh' innis a mhnathan coir a bhaile,
Gur e maireach La Cullaig.

79

WE are come to the door,
To see if we be the better of our visit,
To tell the generous women of the townland
That to-morrow is Calendae Day.

After being entertained the guisers go sunwise round the fire singing--

Gum beannaicheadh Dia an t-ardrach,
Eadar chlach, is chuaille, is chrann,
Eadar bhithe, bhliochd, is aodach,
Slainte dhaoin bhi daonnan ann,

May God bless the dwelling,
Each stone, and beam, and stave,
All food, and drink, and clothing,
May health of men he always there.

Should the guisers be inhospitably treated, they file round the fire withershins and walk out, and raise a cairn in or near the door, called 'carnan mollachd,' cairn of malison, 'carnan cronachd,' scaith cairn.

They tramp loudly, shaking the dust of the place off their feet, and intoning with a deep voice the following and other maledictions:--

Mallachd Dhe is Challaig oirbh,
'S cronachd chlaimhein chiuchaich,
Fioinn, fithich agus fiolair,
'S cronachd sionnaich liugaich.

Cronachd chon is chat oirbh,
Thorc is bhroc is bhrugha,
Mhaghain mais 's mhadaidh-alla,
'S cronachd thaghain tutaidh.

The malison of God and of Hogmanay be on you,
And the scath of the plaintive buzzard,
Of the hen-harrier, of the raven, of the eagle,
And the scath of the sneaking fox.

The scath of the dog and of the cat be on you,
Of the boar, of the badger, and of the 'brugha,'
Of the hipped bear and of the wild wolf,
And the scath of the foul foumart.

BEANNACHADH BLIADHNA UIR

THE BLESSING OF THE NEW YEAR

THIS poem was repeated the first thing on the first day of the year. It was common throughout the Highlands and Islands. The writer has heard versions of it in many places.

DHE, beannaich dhomh an la ur,
Nach do thuradh dhomh roimhe riamh;
Is ann gu beannachadh do ghnuis,
Thug thu 'n uine seo dhomh, a Dhia.

Beannaich thusa dhomh mo shuil,
Beannaicheadh mo shuil na chi;
Beannaichidh mise mo nabaidh,
Beannaicheadh mo nabaidh mi.

Dhe tabhair dhomh-sa cridhe glan,
Na leig a seall do shula mi;
Beannaich dhomh mo ghin 's mo bhean,
'S beannaich domh mo nearc 's mo ni.

GOD, bless to me the new day,
Never vouchsafed to me before;
It is to bless Thine own presence
Thou hast given me this time, O God.

Bless Thou to me mine eye,
May mine eye bless all it sees;
I will bless my neighbour,
May my neighbour bless me.

God, give me a clean heart,
Let me not from sight of Thine eye;
Bless to me my children and my wife,
And bless to me my means and my cattle.

CRIOSDA CLEIREACH OS AR CIONN

CHRIST THE PRIEST ABOVE US

CRIOSDA Cleireach os ar cionn,
Dh' orduich Ti nan dul do gach dull a t'ann.
Criosda Cleireach os ar cionn.

Nochd oidhch a chrochaidh chruaidh,
Crann cruaidh ris na chrochadh Criosd.
Criosda Cleireach os ar cionn.

Is uasal Bannag, is uasal Bochd,
Is uasal Fear na h-oidhche nochd.
Criosda Cleireach os ar cionn.

Is i Bride mhin chaidh air a glun,
Is e Righ nan dul a ta 'na h-uchd,
Criosda Cleireach os ar cionn.

Chluinn mi tulach, chluinn mi traigh,
Chluinn mi ainghlean air an t-snamh,
Criosda Cleireach os ar cionn.

Chluinn mi Cairbre cuimir, cruinn,
Tighinn cluimh le cairdeas duinn.
Criosda Cleireach os ar cionn.

Is ioma tionailt air an tulaich,
Gun farmad duine ri cheile.
Criosda Cleireach os ar cionn.

Is mise gille Mic De is an dorus,
Eirich fein is fosgail domh e.
Criosda Cleireach os ar cionn.

CHRIST the Priest above us,
Ordained of God for all living.
Christ the Priest above us.

To-night, the night of the cross of agony,
The cross of anguish to which Christ was crucified.
Christ the Priest above us.

Noble the Gift! noble the Poor!
Noble the Man of this night.
Christ the Priest above us.

It was Bride the fair who went on her knee,
It is the King of glory who is in her lap.
Christ the Priest above us.

I hear the hills, I hear the seas,
I hear the angels heralding to earth
Christ the Priest above us.

I hear Cairbre of the shapely, rounded limbs,
Coming softly in friendship to us.

Christ the Priest above us.

Great the assemblage upon this knoll,
Without the envy of man to another.
Christ the Priest above us.

I am servant of God the Son at the door,
Oh! arise thou thyself and open to me.
Christ the Priest above us.

LA CHALUIM-CHILLE

THE DAY OF ST COLUMBA

DIARDAOIN, Didaoirn--the day between the fasts--Thursday, was St Columba's Day--Diardaoin Chaluim-chille, St Columba's Thursday--and through him the day of many important events in the economy of the people. It was a lucky day for all enterprises--for warping thread, for beginning a pilgrimage, or any other undertaking. On Thursday eve the mother of a family made a bere, rye, or oaten cake into which she put a small silver coin. The cake was toasted before a fire of rowan, yew, oak, or other sacred wood. On the morning of Thursday the father took a keen-cutting knife and cut the cake into as many sections as there were children in the family, all the sections being equal. All the pieces were then placed in a 'ciosan'--a beehive basket--and each child blindfold drew a piece of cake from the basket in name of the Father, Son, and Spirit. The child who got the coin got the crop of lambs for the year. This was called 'sealbh uan'--lamb luck. Sometimes it was arranged that the person who got the coin got a certain number of the lambs, and the others the rest of the lambs among them. Each child had a separate mark, and there was much emulation as to who had most lambs, the best lambs, and who took best care of the lambs.

Maunday Thursday is called in Uist 'Diardaoin a brochain,' Gruel Thursday, and in Iona 'Diardaoin a brochain mhoir,' Great Gruel Thursday. On this day people in maritime districts made offerings of mead, ale, or gruel to the god of the sea. As the day merged from Wednesday to Thursday a man walked to the waist into the sea and poured out whatever offering had been prepared, chanting:--

'A Dhe na mara,
Cuir todhar 's an tarruinn
Chon tachair an talaimh,
Chon bailcidh dhuinn biaidh.'

O God of the sea,
Put weed in the drawing wave
To enrich the ground,
To shower on us food.

Those behind the offerer took up the chant and wafted it along the sea-shore on the midnight air, the darkness of night and the rolling of the waves making the scene weird and impressive. In 1860 the writer conversed in Iona with a middle-aged man whose father, when young, had taken part in this ceremony. In Lewis the custom was continued till this century. It shows the tolerant spirit of the Columban Church and the tenacity of popular belief, that such a practice should have been in vogue so recently.

The only exception to the luck of Thursday was when Beltane fell on that day.

"D uair is Ciadaoineach an t-Samhain
Is iarganach fir an domhain,
Ach 's meirg is mathair dh' an mhac bhaoth
'D uair is Daorn dh' an Bhealltain.'

When the Wednesday is Hallowmas
Restless are the men of the universe;
But woe the mother of the foolish son
When Thursday is the Beltane.

DAORN Chalum-chille chaoimh
La chur chaorach air seilbh,
La chur ba air a laogh,
La chur aodach an deilbh.

La chur churach air sal,
La chur gais chon a meirgh,
La chon breith, la chon bais,
La chon ardu a sheilg.

La chur ghearran an eill,
La chur feudail air raon,
La chur urnuigh chon feum,
La m' eudail an Daorn.
La m' eudail an Daorn.

THURSDAY of Columba benign,
Day to send sheep on prosperity,
Day to send cow on calf,
Day to put the web in the warp.

Day to put coracle on the brine,
Day to place the staff to the flag,
Day to bear, day to die,
Day to hunt the heights.

Day to put horses in harness,
Day to send herds to pasture,
Day to make prayer efficacious,
Day of my beloved, the Thursday,

Day of my beloved, the Thursday.

SLOINNTIREACHD BHRIDE

THE Genealogy of Bride was current among people who had a latent belief in its efficacy. Other hymns to Bride were sung on her festival, but nothing now remains except the names and fragments of the words. The names are curious and suggestive, as: 'Ora Bhride,' Prayer of Bride, 'Lorg Bhride,' Staff of Bride, 'Luireach Bhride,' Lorica of Bride, 'Lorig Bhride,' Mantle of Bride, 'Brot Bhride,' Corslet of Bride, and others. La Feill Bhride, St Bridget's Day, is the first of February, new style, or the thirteenth according to the old style, which is still much in use in the Highlands. It was a day of great rejoicing and jubilation in olden times, and gave rise to innumerable sayings, as:--

'Feill na Bride, feis na finne.'

'Bride binn nam bas ban.'

'A Bhride chaoin cheanail,
Is caoimh liom anail do bheoil,
'D uair reidhinn air m' aineol
Bu to fein ceann eisdeachd mo sgeoil.'

Feast of the Bride, feast of the maiden.

Melodious Bride of the fair palms.

Thou Bride fair charming,
Pleasant to me the breath of thy mouth,
When I would go among strangers
'Thou thyself wert the hearer of my tale.

There are many legends and customs connected with Bride. Some of these seem inconsistent with one another, and with the character of the Saint of Kildare. These seeming inconsistencies arise from the fact that there were several Brides, Christian and pre-Christian, whose personalities have become confused in the course of centuries--the attributes of all being now popularly ascribed to one. Bride is said to preside over fire, over art, over all beauty, 'fo cheabhar agus fo chuan,' beneath the sky and beneath the sea. And man being the highest type of ideal beauty, Bride presides at his birth and dedicates him to the Trinity. She is the Mary and the Juno of the Gael. She is much spoken of in connection with Mary,--generally in relation to the birth of Christ. She was the aid-woman of the Mother of Nazareth in the lowly stable, and she is the aid-woman of the mothers of Uist in their humble homes.

It is said that Bride was the daughter of poor pious parents, and the serving-maid in the inn of Bethlehem. Great drought occurred in the land, and the master of the hostel went away with his cart to procure water from afar, leaving with Bride 'faircil buirn agus breacag arain,' a stoup of water and a bannock of bread to sustain her till his return. The man left injunctions with Bride not to give food or drink to any one, as he had left only enough for herself, and not to give shelter to any one against his return.

As Bride was working in the house two strangers came to the door. The man was old, with brown hair and grey beard, and the woman was young and beautiful, with oval face, straight nose, blue eyes, red lips, small ears, and golden brown hair, which fell below her waist. They asked the serving-maid for a place to rest, for they were footsore and weary, for food to satisfy their hunger, and for water to quench their thirst. Bride could not give them shelter, but she gave them of her own bannock and of her own stoup of water, of which they partook at the door; and having thanked Bride the strangers went their way, while Bride gazed wistfully and sorrowfully after them. She saw that the sickness of life was on the young woman of the lovely face, and her heart was sore that she had not the power to give them shade from the heat of the sun, and cover from the cold of the dew. When Bride returned into the house in the darkening of the twilight, what was stranger to her to see than that the bannock of bread was whole, and the stoup of water full, as they had been before! She did not know under the land of the world what she would say or what she would do. The food and the water of which she herself had given them, and had seen them partake, without a bit or a drop lacking from them! When she recovered from her wonderment Bride went out to look after the two who had gone their way, but she could see no more of them. But she saw a brilliant golden light over the stable door, and knowing that it was not 'dreag a bhais,' a meteor of death, she went into the stable and was in time to aid and minister to the Virgin Mother, and to receive the Child into her arms, for the strangers were Joseph and Mary, and the child was Jesus Christ, the Son of God, come to earth, and born in the stable of the hostel of Bethlehem. "D uair a rugadh an leanabh chuir Bride tri braona burna fuarain fioir-uisge air clar a bhathais ann an ainm De, ann an ainm Iosa, ann an ainm Spioraid.' When the Child was born Bride put three drops of water from the spring of pure water on the tablet of His forehead, in name of God, in name of Jesus, in name of Spirit. When the master of the inn was returning home, and ascending the hill on which his house stood, he heard the murmuring music of a stream flowing past his house, and he saw the light of a bright star above his stable door. He knew from these signs that the Messiah was come and that Christ was born, 'oir bha e ann an dailgneachd nan daoine gum beirte Iosa Criosda Mac De ann am Betlehem, baile Dhaibhidh'--for it was in the seership of the people that Jesus Christ, the Son of God, would be born in Bethlehem, the town of David. And the man rejoiced with exceeding joy at the fulfilment of the prophecy, and he went to the stable and worshipped the new Christ, whose infant cradle was the manger of the horses.

Thus Bride is called 'ban-chuideachaidh Moire,' the aid-woman of Mary. In this connection, and in consequence thereof, she is called 'Muime Chriosda,' foster-mother of Christ; 'Bana-ghoistidh Mhic De,' the god-mother of the Son of God; 'Bana-ghoistidh Iosda Criosda nam bane agus nam beannachd,' god-mother of Jesus Christ of the bindings and blessings. Christ again is called 'Dalta Bride,' the foster-son of Bride; 'Dalta Bride bith nam beannachd,' the foster-son of Bride of the blessings; 'Daltan Bride,' little fosterling of Bride, a term of endearment.

John the beloved is called Dalta Moire,' foster-son of Mary, and 'Comhdhalta Chriosda,' the foster-brother, literally co-foster, of Christ. Fostership among the Highlanders was a peculiarly close and tender tie, more close and more tender even than blood. There are many proverbs on the subject, as, 'Fuil gu fichead, comhdhaltas gu ceud,' blood to the twentieth, fostership to the hundredth degree. A church in Islay is called 'Cill Daltain,' the Church of the Fosterling.

When a woman is in labour, the midwife or the woman next her in importance goes to the door of the house, and standing on the 'fad-buinn,' sole-sod, doorstep, with her hands on the jambs, softly beseeches Bride to come:

'Bhride! Bhride! thig a steach,
Tha do bheatha deanta,
Tabhair cobhair dha na bhean,
'S tabh an gein dh'an Triana.'

Bride! Bride! come in,
Thy welcome is truly made,
Give thou relief to the woman,
And give the conception to the Trinity.

When things go well, it indicates that Bride is present and is friendly to the family; and when they go ill, that she is absent and offended. Following the action of Bride at the birth of Christ, the aid-woman dedicates the child to the Trinity by letting three drops of clear cold water fall on the tablet of his forehead. (See page <page 114>.)

The aid-woman was held in reverence by all nations. Juno was worshipped with greater honour than any other deity of ancient Rome, and the Pharaohs paid tribute to the aid-women of Egypt. Perhaps, however, appreciation of the aid-woman was never more touchingly indicated than in the reply of two beautiful maidens of St Kilda to John Macdonald, the kindly humorist, and the unsurpassed seaman and pilot of Admiral Otter of the West Coast Survey: 'O ghradhanan an domhain agus an t-saoghail, carson a Righ na gile 's na greine! nach 'eal sibh a posadh is sibh cho briagh?' 'A ghaol nan daona, ciamar a phosas sinne? nach do chaochail a bheanghluin!' 'Oh! ye loves of the domain and of the universe, why, King of the moon and of the sun! are ye not marrying and ye so beautiful?' 'Oh! thou love of men, how can we marry? has not the knee-wife died!'

On Bride's Eve the girls of the townland fashion a sheaf of corn into the likeness of a woman. They dress and deck the figure with shining shells, sparkling crystals, primroses, snowdrops, and any greenery they may obtain. In the mild climate of the Outer Hebrides several species of plants continue in flower during winter, unless the season be exceptionally severe. The gales of March are there the destroyers of plant-life. A specially bright shell or crystal is placed over the heart of the figure. This is called 'reul-iuil Bride,' the guiding star of Bride, and typifies the star over the stable door of Bethlehem, which led Bride to the infant Christ. The girls call the figure 'Bride,' 'Brideag,' Bride, Little Bride, and carry it in procession, singing the song of 'Bride bhoidheach oigh nam mile beus,' Beauteous Bride, virgin of a thousand charms. The 'banal Bride,' Bride maiden band, are clad in white, and have their hair down, symbolising purity and youth. They visit every house, and every person is expected to give a gift to Bride and to make obeisance to her. The gift may be a shell, a spar, a crystal, a flower, or a bit of greenery to decorate the person of Bride. Mothers, however, give 'bonnach Bride,' a Bride bannock, 'cabag Bride,' a Bride cheese, or 'rolag Bride,' a Bride roll of butter. Having made the round of the place the girls go to a house to make the 'feis Bride,' Bride feast. They bar the door and secure the windows of the house, and set Bride where she may see and be seen of all. Presently the young men of the community come humbly asking permission to honour Bride. After some parleying they are admitted and make obeisance to her.

Much dancing and singing, fun and frolic, are indulged in by the young men and maidens during the night. As the grey dawn of the Day of Bride breaks they form a circle and sing the hymn of 'Bride bhoidheach muime chorr Chriosda,' Beauteous Bride, choice foster-mother of Christ. They then distribute fuidheal na feisde,' the fragments of the feast--practically the whole, for they have partaken very sparingly, in order to have the more to give--among the poor women of the place.

A similar practice prevails in Ireland. There the churn staff, not the corn sheaf, is fashioned into the form of a woman, and called 'Brideog,' little Bride. The girls come clad in their best, and the girl who has the prettiest dress gives it to Brideog. An ornament something like a Maltese cross is affixed to the breast of the figure. The ornament is composed of straw, beautifully and artistically interlaced by the deft fingers of the maidens of Bride. It is called 'rionnag Brideog,' the star of little Bride. Pins, needles, bits of stone, bits of straw, and other things are given to Bride as gifts, and food by the mothers.

Customs assume the complexion of their surroundings, as fishes, birds, and beasts assimilate the colours of their habitats. The seas of the 'Garbh Chriocha,' Rough Bounds in which the cult of Bride has longest lived, abound in beautiful iridescent shells, and the mountains in bright sparkling stones, and these are utilised to adorn the ikon of Bride. In other districts where the figure of Bride is made, there are no shining shells, no brilliant crystals, and the girls decorate the image with artistically interlaced straw.

The older women are also busy on the Eve of Bride, and great preparations are made to celebrate her Day, which is the first day of spring. They make an oblong basket in the shape of a cradle, which they call 'leaba Bride,' the bed of Bride. It is embellished with much care. Then they take a choice sheaf of corn, generally oats, and fashion it into the form of a woman. They deck this ikon with gay ribbons from the loom, sparkling shells from the sea, and bright stones from the hill. All the sunny sheltered valleys around are searched for primroses, daisies, and other flowers that open their eyes in the morning of the year. This lay figure is called Bride, 'dealbh Bride,' the ikon of Bride. When it is dressed and decorated with all the tenderness and loving care the women can lavish upon it, one woman goes to the door of the house, and standing on the step with her hands on the jambs, calls softly into the darkness, 'Tha leaba Bride deiseal,' Bride's bed is ready. To this a ready woman behind replies, 'Thigeadh Bride steach, is e beatha Bride,' Let Bride come in, Bride is welcome. The woman at the door again addresses Bride, 'A Bhride! Bhride thig a stench, tha do leaba deanta. Gleidh an teach dh'an Triana,' Bride! Bride, come thou in, thy bed is made. Preserve the house for the Trinity. The women then place the ikon of Bride with great ceremony in the bed they have so carefully prepared for it. They place a small straight white wand (the bark being peeled off) beside the figure. This wand is variously called 'slatag Bride,' the little rod of Bride, 'slachdan Bride,' the little wand of Bride, and 'barrag Bride,' the birch of Bride. The wand is generally of birch, broom, bramble, white willow, or other sacred wood, 'crossed' or banned wood being carefully avoided. A similar rod was given to the kings of Ireland at their coronation, and to the Lords of the Isles at their instatement. It was straight to typify justice, and white to signify peace and purity--bloodshed was not to be needlessly caused. The women then level the ashes on the hearth, smoothing and dusting them over carefully. Occasionally the ashes, surrounded by a roll of cloth, are placed on a board to safeguard them against disturbance from draughts or other contingencies. In the early morning the family closely scan the ashes. If they find the marks of the wand of Bride they rejoice, but if they find 'long Bride,' the footprint of Bride, their joy is very great, for this is a sign that Bride was present with them during the night, and is favourable to them, and that there is increase in family, in flock, and in field during the coming year. Should there be no marks on the ashes, and no traces of Bride's presence, the family are dejected. It is to them a sign that she is offended, and will not hear their call. To propitiate her and gain her ear the family offer oblations and burn incense. The oblation generally is a cockerel, some say a pullet, buried alive near the junction of three streams, and the incense is burnt on the hearth when the family retire for the night.

In the Highlands and Islands St Bride's Day was also called 'La Cath Choileach,' Da y of Cock-fighting. The boys brought cocks to the school to fight. The most successful cock was called 'coileach buadha,' victor cock, and its proud owner was elected king of the school for the year. A defeated bird was called 'fuidse,' craven, 'coileach fuidse,' craven cock. All the defeated, maimed, and killed cocks were the perquisites of the schoolmaster. In the Lowlands 'La Coinnle,' Candlemas Day, was the day thus observed. It is said in Ireland that Bride walked before Mary with a lighted candle in each hand when she went up to the Temple for purification. The winds were strong on the Temple heights, and the tapers were unprotected, yet they did not flicker nor fail. From this incident Bride is called 'Bride boillsge,' Bride of brightness. This day is occasionally called 'La Fheill Bride nan Coinnle,' the Feast Day of Bride of the Candles, but more generally 'La Fheill Moire nan Coinnle,' the Feast Day of Mary of the Candles--Candlemas Day.

The serpent is supposed to emerge from its hollow among the hills on St Bride's Day, and a propitiatory hymn was sung to it. Only one verse of this hymn has been obtained, apparently the first. It differs in different localities:--

'Moch maduinn Bhride,
Thig an nimhir as an toll,
Cha bhoin mise ris an nimhir,
Cha bhoin an nimhir rium.'

Early on Bride's morn
The serpent shall come from the hole,
I will not molest the serpent,
Nor will the serpent molest me.

Other versions say:--

La Feill na Bride,
Thig nighean Imhir as a chnoc,
Cha bhean mise do nighean
'S cha dean i mo lochd.' [Imhir,

'La Fheill Bride brisgeanach
Thig an ceann de in chaiteanach,
Thig nighean Iomhair as an tom
Le fonn feadalaich.'

'Thig an nathair as an toll
La donn Bride,
Ged robh tri traighean dh' an
Air leachd an lair.' [t-sneachd

The Feast Day of the Bride,
The daughter of Ivor shall come from the knoll,
I will not touch the daughter of Ivor,
Nor shall she harm me.

On the Feast Day of Bride,
The head will come off the 'caiteanach,'
The daughter of Ivor will come from the knoll
With tuneful whistling.

The serpent will come from the hole
On the brown Day of Bride,
Though there should be three feet of snow
On the flat surface of the ground.

The 'daughter of Ivor' is the serpent; and it is said that the serpent will not sting a descendant of Ivor, he having made 'tabhar agus tuis,' offering and incense, to it, thereby securing immunity from its sting for himself and his seed for ever.

'La Bride nam brig ban
Thig an rigen ran a tom,
Cha bhoin mise ris an rigen ran,
'S cha bhoin an rigen ran rium.'

On the day of Bride of the white hills
The noble queen will come from the knoll,
I will not molest the noble queen,
Nor will the noble queen molest me.

These lines would seem to point to serpent-worship. One of the most curious customs of Bride's Day was the pounding of the serpent in effigy. The following scene was described to the writer by one who was present:--'I was one of several guests in the hospitable house of Mr John Tolmie of Uignis, Skye. One of my fellow-guests was Mrs Macleod, widow of Major Macleod of Stein, and daughter of Flora Macdonald. Mrs Macleod was known among her friends as "Major Ann." She combined the warmest of hearts with the sternest of manners, and was the admiration of old and young for her wit, wisdom, and generosity. When told that her son had fallen in a duel with the celebrated Glengarry-- the Ivor MacIvor of Waverley--she exclaimed, "Math thu fein mo ghiullan! math thu fein mo ghiullan! gaol geal do mhathar fein! Is fearr bias saoidh na gras daoidh; cha bhasaich an gaisgeach ach an aon turas, ach an gealtair iomadaidh uair!"--"Good thou art my son! good thou art my son! thou the white love of thine own mother! Better the hero's death than the craven's life; the brave dies but once, the coward many times." In a company of noblemen and gentlemen at Dunvegan Castle, Mrs Macleod, then in her 88th year, danced the reel of Tulloch and other reels, jigs, and strathspeys as lightly as a girl in her teens. Wherever she was, all strove to show Mrs Macleod attention and to express the honour in which she was held. She accepted all these honours and attentions with grace and dignity, and without any trace of vanity or self-consciousness. One morning at breakfast at Uignis some one remarked that this was the Day of Bride. "The Day of Bride," repeated Mrs Macleod meditatively, and with a dignified bow of apology rose from the table. All watched her movements with eager curiosity. Mrs Macleod went to the fireside and took up the tongs and a bit of peat and walked out to the doorstep. She then took off her stocking and put the peat into it, and pounded it with the tongs. And as she pounded the peat on the step, she intoned a "rann," rune, only one verse of which I can remember:--

"An diugh La Bride,
Thig an righinn as an tom,
Cha bhean mise ris an righinn,
Cha bhean an righinn rium."

This is the day of Bride,
The queen will come from the mound,
I will not touch the queen,
Nor will the queen touch me.

'Having pounded the peat and replaced her stocking, Mrs Macleod returned to the table, apologising for her remissness in not remembering the Day earlier in the morning. I could not make out whether Mrs Macleod was serious or acting, for she was a consummate actress and the delight of young and old. Many curious ceremonies and traditions in connection with Bride were told that morning, but I do not remember them.'

The pounding in the stocking of the peat representing the serpent would indicate destruction rather than worship, perhaps the bruising of the serpent's head. Probably, however, the ceremony is older, and designed to symbolise something now lost.

Gaelic lore is full of sayings about serpents. These indicate close observation. 'Tha cluas nathrach aige,'--he has the ear of a serpent (he hears keenly but does not speak); 'Tha a bhana-bhuitseach lubach mar an nathair,'--the witch-woman is crooked as the serpent; 'Is e an t-iorball is neo-chronail dhiot, cleas na nathrach nimhe,'--the tail is the least harmful of thee, the trick of the serpent venomous.

'Ge min do chraicionn
Is nimheil gath do bheuil;
Tha thu mar an nathair lachdann,
Gabh do rathad fein.'

'Bean na maise te neo-fhialaidh,
'S i lan do na briathra blath,
Tha, i mar an nathair riabhach,
'S gath na spiocaireachd na dail.'

Though smooth be thy skin,
Venomous is the sting of by mouth;
Thou art like the dun serpent,
Take thine own road.

The beauteous woman, ungenerous,
And she full of warm words,
Is like the brindled serpent,
And the sting of greed is in her.

The people of old practised early retiring, early rising, and diligent working:--

'Suipeir is soillse Oidhch Fheill Bride,
Cadal is soillse Oidhch Fheill Paruig.'

Supper and light the Night of St Bride,
Sleep and light the Night of St Patrick.

The dandelion is called 'bearnan Bride,' the little notched of Bride, in allusion to the serrated edge of the petal. The linnet is called 'bigein Bride,' little bird of Bride. In Lismore the oyster-catcher is called 'gille Bride,' page of Bride:--

'Gille Bride bochd,
Gu de bhigil a th' ort?

Poor page of Bride,
What cheeping ails thee?

In Uist the oyster-catcher is called 'Bridein,' bird of Bride. There was once an oyster-catcher in Uist, and he was so elated with his own growing riches that he thought he would like to go and see something of the great world around him. He went away, leaving his three beautiful, olive-brown, blotched black-and-grey eggs in the rough shingle among the stones of the seashore. Shortly after he left the grey crow came hopping round to see what was doing in the place. In her peering she saw the three eggs of the oyster-catcher in the hollow among the rocks, and she thought she would like to try the taste of one of them, as a variant upon the refuse of land and shore. So she drove her strong bill through the broad end of an egg, and seizing it by the shell, carried it up to the mossy holm adjoining. The quality of the egg was so pleasing to the grey crow that she went back for the second, and then for the third egg. The grey crow was taking the last suck of the last egg when the oyster-catcher was heard returning with his usual fuss and flurry and hurry-scurry. He looked at his nest, but there were no eggs there--no, not one, and the oyster-catcher knew not what to do or say. He flew about to and fro, hither and thither in great distress, crying out in the bitterness of his heart, 'Co dh' ol na h-uibhean? Co dh' ol na h-uibhean? Cha chuala mi riamh a leithid! Cha chuala mi riamh a leithid!' Who drank the eggs? Who drank the eggs? I never heard the like! I never heard the like! The grey crow listened now on this side and now on that, and gave two more precautionary wipes to her already well-wiped bill in the fringy, friendly moss, then looked up with much affected innocence and called out in deeply sympathetic tones, 'Cha chuala na sinne sinn fhein sin, ged is sine is sine 's an aite,' No, nor heard we ourselves that, though we are older in the place.

Bride is said to preside over the different seasons of the year and to bestow their functions upon them according to their respective needs. Some call January 'am mios marbh,' the dead month, some December, while some apply the terms, 'na tri miosa marbh,' the three dead months, 'an raithe marbh,' the dead quarter, and 'raithe marbh na bliadhna,' the dead quarter of the year, to the winter months when nature is asleep. Bride with her white wand is said to breathe life into the mouth of the dead Winter and to bring him to open his eyes to the tears and the smiles, the sighs and the laughter of Spring. The venom of the cold is said to tremble for its safety on Bride's Day and to flee for its life on Patrick's Day. There is a saying:--

'Chuir Bride miar 's an abhuinn
La na Feill Bride
Is dh' fhalbh mathair ghuir an fhuachd,
Is nigh i basan anns an abhuinn
La na Feill Padruig
Is dh' fhalbh mathair ghin an fhuachd.'

Bride put her finger in the river
On the Feast Day of Bride
And away went the hatching mother of the cold,
And she bathed her palms in the river
On the Feast Day of Patrick
And away went the conception mother of the cold,

Another version says:--

'Chuir Brighid a bas ann,
Chuir Moire a cas ann,
Chuir Padruig a chiach fhuar ann.' (?)

Bride put her palm in it,
Mary per her foot in it,
Patrick put the cold stone in it,

alluding to the decrease in cold as the year advances. In illustration of this is-- 'Chuir Moire meoirean anns an uisge La Fheili Bride is thug i neimh as, 's La Fheill Padruig nigh i lamhan ann 's dh' fhalbh am fuachd uil as,' Mary put her fingers in the water on Bride's Feast Day and the venom went out of it, and on Patrick's Feast Day she bathed her hands in it and all the cold went out of it,

Poems narrating the events of the seasons were current. That mentioning the occurrences of Spring begins:--

'La Bride breith an earraich
Thig an dearrais as an tom,

Theirear "tri-bhliadhnaich" ri aighean,
Bheirear gearrain chon nam fonn.'

The Day of Bride, the birthday of Spring,
The serpent emerges from the knoll,
'Three-years-olds' is applied to heifers,
Garrons are taken to the fields.

In Uist the flocks are counted and dedicated to Bride on her Day.

'La Fheill Bride boidheach
Cunntar spreidh air mointeach.
Cuirear fitheach chon na nide,
'S cuirear rithis rocais.'

On the Feast Day of beautiful Bride
The flocks are counted on the moor.
The raven goes to prepare the nest,
And again goes the rook.

Nead air Bhrighit, ugh air Inid, ian air Chasg,
Mar a bith aig an fhitheach bithidh am bas.'

Nest at Brigit, egg at Shrove, chick at Easter,
If the raven has not he has death.

The raven is the first bird to nest, closely followed by the mallard and the rook. It is affirmed that--

'Co fad 's a theid a ghaoth 's an dorus
La na Feill Bride,
Theid an cathadh anns an dorus
La na Feill Paruig.'

As far as the wind shall enter the door
On the Feast Day of Bride,
The snow shall enter the door
On the Feast Day of Patrick.

In Barra, lots are cast for the 'iolachan iasgaich,' fishing-banks, on Bride's Day. These fishing-banks of the sea are as well known and as accurately defined by the fishermen of Barra as are the qualities and boundaries of their crofts on land, and they apportion them with equal care. Having ascertained among themselves the number of boats going to the long-line fishing, the people divide the banks accordingly. All go to church on St Bride's Day. After reciting the virtues and blessings of Bride, and the examples to be drawn from her life, the priest reminds his hearers that the great God who made the land and all thereon, also made the sea and all therein, and that 'murachan na mara agus tachar na tire,' 'cuilidh Chaluim agus cuilidh Mhoire,' the wealth of sea and the plenty of land, the treasury of

Columba and the treasury of Mary, are His gift to them that follow Him and call upon His name, on rocky hill or on crested wave. The priest urges upon them to avoid disputes and quarrels over their fishing, to remember the dangers of the deep and the precariousness of life, and in their fishing to remember the poor, the widow and the orphan, now left to the fatherhood of God and to the care of His people. Having come out of church, the men cast lots for the fishing-banks at the church door. After this, they disperse to their homes, all talking loudly and discussing their luck or unluck in the drawing of the lots. A stranger would be apt to think that the people were quarrelling. But it is not so. The simultaneous talking is their habit, and the loudness of their speaking is the necessity of their living among the noise of winds and waves, whether on sea or on shore. Like the people of St Kilda, the people of Barra are warmly attached to one another, the joy of one and the grief of another being the joy and grief of all.

The same practice of casting lots for their fishing-banks prevails among the fisher-folks of the Lofodin Islands, Norway.

From these traditional observations, it will be seen that Bride and her services are near to the hearts and lives of the people. In some phases of her character she is much more to them than Mary is.

Dedications to Bride are common throughout Great Britain and Ireland.

[pp. <page 174>-5

SLOINNTIREACHD BHRIDE

GENEALOGY OF BRIDE

SLOINNEADH na Ban-naomh Bride,
Lasair dhealrach oir, muime chorr Chriosda.
Bride nighinn Dughaill duinn,
Mhic Aoidh, mhic Airt, nitric Cuinn,
Mhic Crearair, mhic Cis, mhic Carmaig, mhic Carruinn.

Gach la agus gach oidhche
Ni mi sloinntireachd air Bride,
Cha mharbhar mi, cha spuillear mi,
Cha charcar mi, cha chiurar mi,
Cha mhu dh' fhagas Criosd an dearmad mi.

Cha loisg teine, grian, no gealach mi,
Cha bhath luin, li, no sala mi,
Cha reub saighid sithich, no sibhich mi,
Is mi fo chomaraig mo Naomh Muire
Is i mo chaomh mhuime Bride.

THE genealogy of the holy maiden Bride,
Radiant flame of gold, noble foster-mother of Christ,

Bride the daughter of Dugall the brown,
Son of Aodh, son of Art, son of Conn,
Son of Crearar, son of Cis, son of Carina, son of Carruin.

Every day and every night
That I say the genealogy of Bride,
I shall not be killed, I shall not be harried,
I shall not be put in cell, I shall not be, wounded,
Neither shall Christ leave me in forgetfulness.

No fire, no sun, no moon shall burn me,
No lake, no water, nor sea shall drown mc,
No arrow of fairy nor dart of fay shall wound me,
And I under the protection of my Holy Mary,
And my gentle foster-mother is my beloved Bride.

BRIDE BAN-CHOBHAIR

BRIDE THE AID-WOMAN

THAINIG thugam cobhair,
Moire gheal is Bride;
Mar a rug Anna Moire,
Mar a rug Moire Criosda,
Mar a rug Eile Eoin Baistidh
Gun mhar-bhith dha dhi,
Cuidich thusa mise 'm asaid,
Cuidich mi a Bhride!

Mar a gheineadh Criosd am Moire
Comhliont air gach laimh,
Cobhair thusa mise, mhoime,
An gein a thoir bho 'n chnaimh;
'S mar a chomhn thu Oigh an t-solais,
Gun or, gun odh, gun ni,
Comhn orm-sa, 's mor m' othrais,
Comhn orm a Bhride!

THERE came to me assistance,
Mary fair and Bride;
As Anna bore Mary,
As Mary bore Christ,
As Eile bore John the Baptist
Without flaw in him,
Aid thou me in mine unbearing,
Aid me, O Bride!

As Christ was conceived of Mary
Full perfect on every hand,
Assist thou me, foster-mother,
The conception to bring from the bone;
And as thou didst aid the Virgin of joy,
Without gold, without corn, without kine,
Aid thou me, great is my sickness,
Aid me, O Bride!

MANUS MO RUIN

MAGNUS OF MY LOVE

MAGNUS was descended from Malcolm Canmore, King of the Scots. Earl Magnus and his half-brother Earl Hakon ruled the Northern Isles, and while they were in agreement with one another there was peace and plenty within those isles. But dissensions arose. Magnus was eminently handsome, beneficent, and beloved. Hakon was lacking in these qualities, and he became morose and jealous of his brother.

The two brothers met at the Thingstead in Lent, Hakon being there for offensive, and Magnus for defensive, purposes. Wisdom prevailed, however, and war was averted. To confirm the peace Hakon invited Magnus to meet him in Pasch week in the church of Egilsey, the brothers agreeing to limit their retinue to two warships each. Magnus observed the agreement and came with two ships, but Hakon brought eight, with their full complement of armed men.

His people wished to defend Magnus, but he refused to allow the spilling of blood, or the perilling of souls. Magnus submitted to his brother three proposals. First, that he should go to his relative, the King of the Scots, and never return; second, that he should go to Rome or to Jerusalem and never return; or third, that he would submit to be maimed, gouged, or slain. Hakon spurned all the proposals save the last, and Magnus was put to death on the 14th of April, 1115, to the great grief of his people.

The place where Magnus was slain had been a rough, sterile moor of heath and moss, but immediately Magnus was put to death the moor became a smiling grassy plain, and there issued a heavenly light and a sweet odour from the holy ground.

Those who were in peril prayed to Magnus and were rescued, and those who were sick came to his grave and were healed. Pilgrims flocked to his tomb to keep vigil at his shrine, and be cured of their leprosy of body or of soul,

St Magnus had three burials--the first in the island of Egilsey where he was slain, and the second at the intercession of his mother, Thora, in Christ Church in the island of Birsa. During imminent peril at sea Earl Rognovald prayed to Magnus for deliverance, and vowed that he would build a minster to his memory more beautiful than any church in those lands. The prayer was heard, and Rognovald built and endowed, to the memory of the holy Magnus, the cathedral church of Kirkwall. Thither the relics of the saint were brought and interred, and the cathedral became the resort of pilgrims who sought the aid of St Magnus.

At the battle of Anglesea, between Magnus Barefoot, his brother Ireland, his cousin Haco, and the Earls of Chester and Shrewsbury, Magnus recited the Psalter during the conflict. The victory of his northern kinsmen was attributed to the holy Magnus.

A MHANUIS mo ruin,
Is to dheanadh dhuinn iul,
A chuirp chubhraidh nan dul,
Cuimhnich oirnn.

Cuimhnich a naoimh nam buadh,
A chomraig 's a chomhn an sluagh,
Cobhair oirnne 'n ar truaigh,
'S na treig sinn.

Tog ar seilbh mach ri leirg,
Casg coin ghioirr is coin dheirg,
Cum uainn fuath, fath, feirg,
Agus foirne.

O MAGNUS of my love,
Thou it is who would'st us guide,
Thou fragrant body of grace,
Remember us.

Remember us, thou Saint of power,
Who didst encompass and protect the people,
Succour thou us in our distress,
Nor forsake us.

Lift our flocks to the hills,
Quell the wolf and the fox,
Ward from us spectre, giant, fury,
And oppression.

Cuartaich tan agus buar,
Cuartaich caor agus uan;
Cum uap an fhamh-bhual,
'S an luch-fheoir.

Crath an druchd o'n speur air crodh,
Thoir fas air feur, deis, agus snodh,
Dubhrach, lus-feidh, ceis, meacan-dogh,
Agus neoinean.

O Mhanuis nan glonn,
Air bharca nan sonn,
Air bharra nan tonn,
Air sala no fonn,
Comhn agus gleidh sinn.

Surround cows and herds,
Surround sheep and lambs;
Keep from them the water-vole,
And the field-vole.

Sprinkle dew from the sky upon kine,
Give growth to grass, and corn, and sap to plants,
Water-cress, deer's-grass, 'ceis,' burdock,
And daisy.

O Magnus of fame,
On the barque of the heroes,
On the crests of the waves,
On the sea, on the land,
Aid and preserve us.

AM BEANNACHADH BEALLTAIN

THE BELTANE BLESSING

BEALLTAIN, Beltane, is the first day of May. On May Day all the fires of the district were extinguished and 'tein eigin,' need-fire, produced on the knoll. This fire was divided in two, and people and cattle rushed through for purification and safeguarding against 'ealtraigh agus dosgaidh,' mischance and murrain, during the year. The people obtained fires for their homes from this need-fire. The practice of producing the need-fire came down in the Highlands and Islands to the first quarter of this century. The writer found traces of it in such distant places as Arran, Dist, and Sutherland. In 1895 a woman in Arran said that in the time of her father the people made the need-fire on the knoll, and then rushed home and brought out their 'creatairean,' creatures, and put them round the fire to safeguard them, 'bho 'n bhana bhuitsich mhoir Nic-creafain,' from the arch-witch Crawford.

The ordeal of passing through the fires gave rise to a proverb which I heard used by an old man in Lewis in 1873:--'A Mhoire! mhicean, bu dora dhomhsa sin a dheanamh dhuit na dhol eadar dha theine mhoir Bheaill,' Ah Mary! sonnie, it were worse for me to do that for thee, than to pass between the two great fires of Beall.

BEANNAICH, a Thrianailt fhioir nach gann,
Mi fein, mo cheile agus mo chlann,
Mo chlann mhaoth 's am mathair chaomh 'n an ceann,

Air chlar chubhr nan raon, air airidh chaon nam beann,
Air chlar chubhr nan raon, air airidh chaon nam beann.

Gach ni na m' fhardaich, no to 'na m' shealbh,
Gach buar is barr, gach tan is tealbh,
Bho Oidhche Shamhna chon Oidhche Bheallt,
Piseach maith, agus beannachd mallt,
Bho mhuir, gu muir, agus bun gach allt,
Bho thonn gu tonn, agus bonn gach steallt.

Tri Pears a gabhail sealbh anns gach ni 'na m' stor,
An Trianailt dhearbha da m' dhion le coir;
O m' anam riaraich am briathra Phoil,
Is dion mo chiallain fo sgiath do ghloir,
Dion mo chiallain fo sgiath do ghloir.

Beannaich gach ni, agus gach aon,
Ta 's an teaghlach bheag ri m' thaobh;

BLESS, O Threefold true and bountiful,
Myself, my spouse, and my children,
My tender children and their beloved mother at their head.
On the fragrant plain, on the gay mountain sheiling,
On the fragrant plain, on the gay mountain sheiling.

Everything within my dwelling or in my possession,
All kine and crops, all flocks and corn,
From Hallow Eve to Beltane Eve,
With goodly progress and gentle blessing,
From sea to sea, and every river mouth,
From wave to wave, and base of waterfall.

Be the Three Persons taking possession of all to me belonging,
Be the sure Trinity protecting me in truth;
Oh! satisfy my soul in the words of Paul,
And shield my loved ones beneath the wing of Thy glory,
Shield my loved ones beneath the wing of Thy glory.

Bless everything and every one,
Of this little household by my side;

Cuir Crois Chriosd oirnn le buaidh baigh,
Gun am faic sinn tir an aigh,
Gun am faic sinn tir an aigh.

Trath threigeas buar am buabhal bho,

Trath threigeas cuanal an cual chro,
Trath dh' eireas ceigich ri beinn a cheo,
Treoir na Trianaid bhi triall 'n an coir,
O treoir na Trianaid bhi triall 'n an coir.

A Thi a chruthaich mi air tus,
Eisd is fritheil rium aig lubadh glun,
Moch is anamoch mar is iul,
A d' lathair fein a Dhe nan dui,
A d' lathair fein a Dhe nan dui.

Place the cross of Christ on us with the power of love,
Till we see the land of joy,
Till we see the land of joy,

What time the kine shall forsake the stalls,
What time the sheep shall forsake the folds,
What time the goats shall ascend to the mount of mist,
May the tending of the Triune follow them,
May the tending of the Triune follow them.

Thou Being who didst create me at the beginning,
Listen and attend me as I bend the knee to Thee,
Morning and evening as is becoming in me,
In Thine own presence, O God of life,
In Thine own presence, O God of life.

AM BEANNACHD BEALLTAIN

THE BELTANE BLESSING

A MHOIRE, a mhathair nan naomh,
Beannaich an t-al 's an crodh-laoigh;
Na leig fuath no foirne, 'n ar gaoith,
Fuadaich oirnne doigh nan daoi.

Cum do shuil gach Luan is Mart,
Air crodh-laoigh's air aighean dair;
Iomachair leinn o bheinn gu sal,
Tionail fein an treud 's an t-al.

Gach Ciadaon agus Daorn bi leo,
Biodh do lamh chaon a chaoidh 'n an coir;
Cuallaich buar d'am buabhal bho,
Cuallaich cuanal d'an cual chro.

Gach Aona bi-sa, a Naoimh, 'n an ceann,
Treoraich caoraich a aodann bheann,
Le 'n al beag ba as an deigh,
Cuartaich 'ad le cuartachd Dhe.

Gach Sathurna bith leo mar chach,
Tabhair gobhair a steach le 'n al,
Gach meann is maos gu taobh sal,
Is Lioc a h-Eigir gu h-ard,
Le biolair uaine shuas m'a barr.

Treoir na Trianailt d' ar dian 's gach cas,
Treoir Chriosda le shith 's le Phais,
Treoir an Spioraid, Ligh na slaint,
Is Athar priseil, Righ nan gras.

MARY, thou mother of saints,
Bless our flocks and bearing kine;
Hate nor scath let not come near us,
Drive from us the ways of the wicked.

Keep thine eye every Monday and Tuesday
On the bearing kine and the pairing queys;
Accompany us from hill to sea,
Gather thyself the sheep and their progeny.

Every Wednesday and Thursday be with them,
Be thy gracious hand always about them;
Tend the cows down to their stalls,
Tend the sheep down to their folds!

Every Friday be thou, O Saint, at their head,
Lead the sheep from the face of the bens,
With their innocent little lambs following them,
Encompass them with God's encompassing.

Every Saturday be likewise with them,
Bring the goats in with their young,
Every kid and goat to the sea side,
And from the Rock of Aegir on high,
With tresses green about its summit.

The strength of the Triune be our shield in distress,
The strength of Christ, His peace and His Pasch,
The strength of the Spirit, Physician of health,
And of the precious Father, the King of grace.

* * * *

'S gach naomh eile bha nan deigh
'S a choisinn suamhnas rioghachd De.

Beannaich sinn fein agus ar cloinn,
Beannaich gach creubh a thig o'r loinn,
Beannaich am fear sin air an sloinn,
Beannaich a Dhe, an te a rug o'n bhroinn.

Gach naomhachd, beannachd agus buaidh,
Bhi 'g aomadh leinn gach am 's gach uair,
An ainm Trithinn Naomha shuas,
Athar, Mic, is Spiorad buan.

Crois Chriosd bhi d' ar dion a nuas,
Crois Chriosd bhi d' ar dion a suas,
Chriosd bhi d' ar dion mu 'r cuart,
Gabhail beannachd Bealltain uainn,
Gabhail beannachd Bealltain uainn.

* * * *

And of every other saint who succeeded them
And who earned the repose of the kingdom of God.

Bless ourselves and our children,
Bless every one who shall come from our loins,
Bless him whose name we bear,
Bless, O God, her from whose womb we came.

Every holiness, blessing and power,
Be yielded to us every time and every hour,
In name of the Holy Threefold above,
Father, Son, and Spirit everlasting.

Be the Cross of Christ to shield us downward,
Be the Cross of Christ to shield us upward,
Be the Cross of Christ to shield us roundward,
Accepting our Beltane blessing from us,
Accepting our Beltane blessing from us.

LAOIDH AN TRIALL

ON the first day of May the people of the crofter townland are up betimes and busy as bees about to swarm. This is the day of migrating, 'bho baffle gu beinn,' from townland to moorland, from the winter homestead to the summer sheiling. The summer of their joy is come, the summer of the sheiling, the song, the pipe, and the dance, when the people ascend the hill to the clustered bothies, overlooking the distant sea from among the fronded ferns and fragrant heather, where neighbour meets neighbour, and lover meets lover. All the families of the townland bring their different flocks together at a particular place and drive the whole away. This miscellaneous herd is called 'triall,' procession, and is composed of horses, cattle, sheep. and goats. In the triall' the sheep lead; the cattle follow according to their ages; then come the goats, and finally the horses, with creels slung across their backs laden with domestic gear of various kinds. The men carry burdens of spades, sticks, pins, ropes, and other things that may be needed to repair their summer huts, while the women carry bedding, meal, and dairy utensils. About their waists the women wear a cord of wool, or a belt of leather called 'crios-feile,' kilt girdle, underneath which their skirts are drawn up and fastened, to enable them to 'walk the moor with greater ease. These crofter women appear like Leezie Lindsay in the old song--

'She kilted her coats of green satin,
And she kilted them up to the knee.'

[paragraph continues] When the people meet, they greet each other with great cordiality, as if they had not seen one another for months or even years, instead of probably only a few days before. There are endless noises in the herd: sheep bleat for their lambs, lambs for their mothers, cows low for their calves, and the calves respond, mares neigh for their foals, and foals whinny in reply to their dams as they lightly skip and scamper, curveting in and out, little dreaming of coming work and hard fare. The men give directions, several at a time; the women knit their stockings and sing their songs, walking free and erect as if there were no burdens on their backs or on their hearts, nor any sin or sorrow in the world so far as they are concerned. Ranged along on either side of the procession are barefooted, bareheaded comely girls and sturdy boys, and sagacious dogs who every now and then, and every here and there, have a neck-and-neck race with some perverse young beast, unwillingly driven from his home, for, unlike his elders, the animal does not know or does not remember the pleasures of the heathery knoll, the grassy dell or fronded glen, and the joyous freedom of the summer sheiling. All who meet them on the way bless the 'triall,' and invoke upon it a good day, much luck and prosperity, and the safe shepherding of the Son of Mary on man and beast. [paragraph continues] When the grazing ground is reached, the loads are laid down, the huts repaired, fires kindled and food made ready. The people bring forward their stock, each man his own, and count them into the fold. The herdsman of the townland and one or two more men stand within the gateway and count the flocks as they enter. Each crofter is restricted in his stock on the common grazing of the townland. He may, however, vary the number and the ages of the species and thus equalise a deficit in one species by an excess in another. Should a man have a 'barr-suma,' oversoum, he may arrange with a man who has a 'di-suma,' undersoum, or with the townland at large, for his extra stock. Every facility is given to a man in straits, the consideration of these intelligent crofting people towards one another being most pleasing. The grazing arrangements of the people, complex to a stranger, but simple to themselves, show an intimate knowledge of animal and pastoral life. Having seen to their flocks and to the repairing of their huts, the people resort to their sheiling feast. This feast consists principally of a male lamb, without spot or blemish, killed that day. Formerly this lamb was sacrificed, now it is eaten. The feast is shared with friends and neighbours; all wish each other luck and prosperity, with increase in their flocks:

'Ann an coir gach fireach

Piseach crodh na h-airidh.'

Beside each knoll
The progeny of the sheiling cows.

[paragraph continues] The frugal feast being finished and the remains divided among the dogs, who are not the least interested or interesting actors in the day's proceedings, every head is uncovered and every knee is bent as they invoke on man and beast the 'shepherding of Abraham, of Isaac, and of Jacob.'

Protestantism prevails in Lewis, Harris, and North Uist, and the people confine their invocations to the Trinity:--

'Feuch air fear coimhead Israil
Codal chan aom no suain.'

The Shepherd that keeps Israel
He slumbers not nor sleeps.

[paragraph continues] Roman Catholicism prevails in Benbecula, South Uist, and Barra, and in their dedicatory hymn the people of these islands invoke, besides the Trinity, St Michael of the three-cornered shield and flaming sword, patron of their horses; St Columba of the holy deeds, guardian of their cattle; Bride of the clustering hair, the foster-mother of Christ; and the golden-haired Virgin, mother of the White Lamb.

As the people intone their prayers on the lonely hill-side, literally in the wilderness, the music of their evensong floats over glen and dell, loch and stream, and is echoed from corrie and cliff till it is lost on the soft evening air.

[pp. <page 192>-3

LAOIDH AN TRIALL

HYMN OF THE PROCESSION

MHICHEIL mhil nan steud geala,
Choisinn cios air Dragon fala,
Ghaol Dia 's pian Mhic Muire,
Sgaoil do sgiath oirnn, dion sinn uile,
Sgaoil do sgiath oirnn, dion sinn uile.

Mhoire ghradhach! Mhathair Uain ghil,
Cobhair oirnne ghlan Oigh na h-uaisleachd,
Bhride bhuaidheach, bhuachaille nan treud,
Cum ar cuallach, cuartaich sinn le cheil,
Cum ar cuallach, cuartaich sinn le cheil.

A Chaluim-chille, chairdeil, chaoimh,
An ainm Athar, is Mic, is Spiorad Naoimh,
Trid na Trithinn, trid na Triaid
Comaraig sinn fein, gleidh ar triall,
Comaraig sinn fein, gleidh ar triall.

Athair! a Mhic! a Spioraid Naoimh!
Biodh an Trithinn leinn a la 's a dh' oidhche,
'S air machair loim no air roinn nam beann
Bidh an Trithinn leinn 's bidh a lamh mu 'r ceann,
Bidh an Trithinn leinn 's bidh a lamh mu 'r ceann!

IASGAIREAN BHARRAIDH--
Athair! a Mhic! a Spioraid Naoimh!
Bi-sa, Thrithinn, leinn a la 's a dh' oidhche,
'S air chul nan tonn no air thaobh nam beann
Bidh ar Mathair leinn 's bidh a lamh fo 'r ceann,
'S air chul nan tonn no air thaobh nam beann
Bidh ar Mathair leinn 's bidh a lamh fo 'r ceann!

VALIANT Michael of the white steeds,
Who subdued the Dragon of blood,
For love of God, for pains of Mary's Son,
Spread thy wing over us, shield us all,
Spread thy wing over us, shield us all.

Mary beloved! Mother of the White Lamb,
Shield, oh shield us, pure Virgin of nobleness,
And Bride the beauteous, shepherdess of the flocks.
Safeguard thou our cattle, surround us together,
Safeguard thou our cattle, surround us together.

And Columba, beneficent, benign,
In name of Father, and of Son, and of Spirit Holy,
Through the Three-in-One, through the Trinity,
Encompass thou ourselves, shield our procession,
Encompass thou ourselves, shield our procession.

O Father! O Son! O Spirit Holy!
Be the Triune with us day and night,
On the machair plain or on the mountain ridge
Be the Triune with us and His arm around our head,
Be the Triune with us and His arm around our head.

BARRA FISHERMEN--

O Father! O Son! O Spirit Holy!
Be thou, Three-One, with us day and night,
And on the back of the wave as on the mountain side
Our Mother shall be with us with her arm under our head.
And on the back of the wave as on the mountain side
Our Mother shall be with us with her arm under our head.

LA FEILL MOIRE

THE FEAST DAY OF MARY

THE Feast Day of Mary the Great is the 15th day of August. Early in the morning of this day the people go into their fields and pluck ears of corn, generally here, to make the 'Moilean Moire.' These ears are laid on a rock exposed to the sun, to dry. When dry, they are husked in the hand, winnowed in a fan, ground in a quern, kneaded on a sheep-skin, and formed into a bannock, which is called 'Moilean Moire,' the fatling of Mary. The bannock is toasted before a fire of fagots of rowan, or some other sacred wood. Then the husbandman breaks the bannock and gives a bit to his wife and to each of his children, in order according to their ages, and the family raise the 'Iolach Mhoire Mhathar,' the Paean of Mary Mother who promised to shield them, and who did and will shield them from scath till the day of death. While singing thus, the family walk sunwise round the fire, the father leading, the mother following, and the children following according to age.

After going round the fire, the man puts the embers of the fagot-fire, with bits of old iron, into a pot, which he carries sunwise round the outside of his house, sometimes round his steadings and his fields, and his flocks gathered in for the purpose. He is followed without as within by his household, all singing the praise of Mary Mother the while.

The scene is striking and picturesque, the family being arrayed in their brightest and singing their best.

LA feill Moire cubhr,
Mathair Buachaille nan treud,
Bhuain mi beum dhe'n toradh ur,
Chruadhaich mi e caon ri grein,
Shuath mi e gu geur dhe 'n rusg
Le mo bhasa fein.

Mheil mi e air brath Di-aoine,
Dh' fhuin mi e air cra na caoire,
Bhruich mi e ri aine caorain,
S' phairtich mi e'n dail mo dhaoine.

Chaidh mi deiseil m' ardrach,
An ainm Mhoire Mhathar,
A gheall mo ghleidheadh,
A rinn mo ghleidheadh,

A ni mo ghleidheadh,
Ann an sith, ann an ni,
Ann am fireantas cridh,

ON the feast day of Mary the fragrant,
Mother of the Shepherd of the flocks,
I cut me a handful of the new corn,
I dried it gently in the sun,
I rubbed it sharply from the husk
With mine own palms.

I ground it in a quern on Friday,
I baked it on a fan of sheep-skin,
I toasted it to a fire of rowan,
And I shared it round my people.

I went sunways round my dwelling,
In name of the Mary Mother,
Who promised to preserve me,
Who did preserve me,
And who will preserve me,
In peace, in flocks,
In righteousness of heart,

Ann an gniomh, ann an gradh,
Ann am brigh, ann am baigh,
Air sgath do Phais.
A Chriosd a ghrais
Gu la mo bhais
Gu brath nach treig mi!
O gu la mo bhais
Gu brath nach treig mi!

In labour, in love,
In wisdom, in mercy,
For the sake of Thy Passion.
Thou Christ of grace
Who till the day of my death
Wilt never forsake me!
Oh, till the day of my death
Wilt never forsake me!

MICHEAL NAM BUAIDH

ST MICHAEL IS spoken of as 'brian Michael,' god Michael.

'Bu tu gaisgeach na misnich
Dol air astar na fiosachd,
Is tu nach siubhladh air criplich,
Ghabh thu steud briain Micheil,
E gun chabstar na shliopan,
Thu mharcachd air iteig,
Leum thu thairis air fiosrachadh Naduir.'

Thou wert the warrior of courage
Going on the journey of prophecy,
Thou wouldst not travel on a cripple,
Thou didst take the steed of the god Michael,
He was without bit in his mouth,
Thou didst ride him on the wing,
Thou didst leap over the knowledge of Nature.

St Michael is the Neptune of the Gael. He is the patron saint of the sea, and of maritime lands, of boats and boatmen, of horses and horsemen throughout the West. As patron saint of the sea St Michael had temples dedicated to him round the coast wherever Celts were situated. Examples of these are Mount St Michael in Brittany and in Cornwall, and Aird Michael in South and in North List, and elsewhere. Probably Milton had this phase of St Michael's character in view. As patron saint of the land St Michael is represented riding a milk-white steed, a three-pronged spear in his right hand and a three-cornered shield in his left. The shield is inscribed 'Quis ut Deus,' a literal translation of the Hebrew Mi-cha-el. Britannia is substituted for the archangel on sea and St George on land.

On the 29th of September a festival in honour of St Michael is held throughout the Western Coasts and Isles. This is much the most imposing pageant and much the most popular demonstration of the Celtic year. Many causes conduce to this--causes which move the minds and the hearts of the people to their utmost tension. To the young the Day is a day of promise, to the old a day of fulfilment, to the aged a day of retrospect. It is a day when pagan cult and Christian doctrine meet and mingle like the lights and shadows on their own Highland hills.

The Eve of St Michael is the eve of bringing in the carrots, of baking the struan,' of killing the lamb, of stealing the horses. The Day of St Michael is the Day of the early mass, the day of the sacrificial lamb, the day of the oblation 'struan,' the day of the distribution of the lamb, the day of the distribution of the 'struan,' the day of the pilgrimage to the burial-ground of their fathers, the day of the burial-ground service, the day of the burial-ground circuiting, the day of giving and receiving the carrots with their wishes and acknowledgments, and the day of the 'oda'--the athletics of the men and the racing of the horses And the Night of Michael is the night of the dance and the song, of the merry-making, of the love-making, and of the love-gifts.

Several weeks previously the people begin to speak of St Michael's Day, and to prepare for Si Michael's Festival. 'Those concerned count whose turn it will be to guard the crops on St Michael's Day and to circuit the townland on St Michael's Night. The young men upon whom these duties fall arrange with old men to take their place on these occasions. As the time approaches the interest intensifies, culminating among the old in much bustle, and among the young in keen excitement.

Three plants which the people call carrots grow in Gist--the 'daucus carota,' the 'daucus maritimus,' and the 'conium.' The 'daucus carota' is the original of the cultivated carrot. The 'daucus maritimus is a long slender carrot, much like the parsnip in appearance and in flavour, and is rare in the British Isles. The 'corium,' hemlock, resembles the carrot, for which it is occasionally mistaken. It is hard, acrid, and poisonous.

Some days before the festival of St Michael the women and girls go to the fields and plains of the townland to procure carrots. The afternoon of the Sunday immediately preceding St Michael's Day is specially devoted to this purpose, and on this account is known as 'Domhnach Curran'--Carrot Sunday. When the soil is soft and friable, the carrots can be pulled out of the ground without digging. When, however, the soil is hard, a space is dug to give the hand access to the root. This space is made in the form of an equal-sided triangle, technically called 'torcan,' diminutive of 'tore,' a cleft. The instrument used is a small mattock of three prongs, called 'tri-meurach,' three-fingered, 'sliopag.' 'sliobhag.' The three-sided 'torcan' is meant to typify the three-sided shield, and the three-fingered 'sliopag,' the trident of St Michael, and possibly each to symbolise the Trinity. The many brightly-clad figures moving to and fro, in and out, like the figures in a kaleidoscope, are singularly pretty and picturesque. Each woman intones a rune to her own tune and time irrespective of those around her. The following fragment was intoned to me in a soft, subdued voice by a woman who had gathered carrots eighty years previously:--

'Torcan torrach, torrach, torrach,
Sonas Curran corr orm,
Michael mil a bhi dha, m' chonuil,
Bride gheal dha m' chonradh.

Piseach linn gash piseach,
Piseach dha mo bhroinn,
Piseach linn nach piseach,
Piseach dha mu chloinn.'

Cleft fruitful, fruitful, fruitful,
Joy of carrots surpassing upon me,
Michael the brave endowing me,
Bride the fair be aiding me.

Progeny pre-eminent over every progeny,
Progeny on my womb,
Progeny pre-eminent over every progeny,
Progeny on my progeny.

Should a woman find a forked carrot, she breaks out into a more exultant strain that brings her neighbours round to see and to admire her luck,

'Fhorca shona, shona, shona,
Fhorca churran mor orm,

Conuil curran corr orm
Sonas curran mor dhomh.'

Fork joyful, joyful, joyful,
Fork of great carrot to me,
Endowment of carrot surpassing upon me,
Joy of great carrot to me.

There is much rivalry among the women who shall have most and best carrots. They carry the carrots in a bag slung from the waist, called 'crioslachan,' little girdle, from 'crios,' a girdle. When the 'earrasaid' was worn, the carrots were carried in its ample folds. The women wash the carrots and tie them up in small bunches, each of which contains a 'glac,' handful, The bunches are tied with three-ply thread, generally scarlet, and put in pits near the houses and covered with sand till required.

The people do not retire to rest on the Eve of St Michael. The women are engaged all night on baking 'struan,' on household matters, and on matters personal to themselves and to others, while the men are out and in watching their horses in the fields and stables. It is permissible on this night to appropriate a horse, wherever found and by whatever means, on which to make the pilgrimage and to perform the circuiting.

'Meirle eich na Feill Michell,
Meirle nach do dhiteadh riamb.'

Theft of horse of the Feast of Michael,
Theft that never was condemned.

The people act upon this ancient privilege and steal horses without compunction, owners and stealers watching and outwitting and circumventing one another. It is obligatory to leave one horse with the owner to carry himself and his wife on the pilgrimage and to make the circuiting, but this may be the worst horse in the townland. No apology is offered or expected for this appropriation provided the horse be returned uninjured; and even if it be injured, no adequate redress is obtained. The Eve of St Michael is thus known as 'feasgar faire nan steud,' the evening of watching the steeds; 'feasgar furachaidh nan each,' the evening of guarding the horses; 'oidhche crothaidh nan capull,' the night of penning the mares; 'oidhche glasadh nan each,' the night of locking the horses--hence also 'glasadh na Feill Micheil,' the locking of the Feast of Michael. A male lamb, without spot or blemish, is slain. This lamb is called 'Uan Michell,' the Michael Lamb.

A cake called 'struan Micheil' is made of all the cereals grown on the farm during the year. It represents the fruits of the field, as the lamb represents the fruits of the flocks. Oats, bere, and rye are the only cereals grown in the Isles. These are fanned on the floor, ground in the quern, and their meal in equal parts used in the struan. The struan should contain a peck of meal, and should be baked on 'uinicinn,' a lamb-skin. The meal is moistened with sheen's milk, the sheep being deemed the most sacred animal. For this purpose the ewes are retained in milk till St Michael's Eve, after which they are allowed to remain in the hill and to run dry. The struan is baked by the eldest daughter of the family, guided by her mother, and assisted by her eager sisters. As she moistens the meal with the milk the girl softly says--

'Ruth agus rath an treo,
Run Mhicheil, dion an Teor.'

Progeny and prosperity of family,
Mystery of Michael, protection of Trinity.

A 'leac struain,' struan flag, brought by the young men of the family from the moorland during the day, is securely set on edge before the fire, and the 'struan' is set on edge against it. The fire should be of 'crionach caon,' sacred fagots, such as the fagots of the oak, the rowan, the bramble, and others. The blackthorn, wild fig, trembling aspen, and other 'crossed' wood are avoided. As the 'struan' gains consistency, three successive layers of a batter of cream, eggs, and butter are laid on each side alternately. The batter ought to be put on with three tail feathers of a cockerel of the year, but in Uist this is generally done with 'badan murain,' a small bunch of bent-grass. This cake is called 'struan treo,' family struan; 'struan mor,' large struan, and 'struan comachaidh,' communal struan, Small struans are made for individual members of the family by mothers, daughters, sisters, and trusted servants. These are known as 'struain beag,' little struans; 'struain cloinne,' children's struans, and by the names of those for whom they are made. If a member of the family be absent or dead, a struan is made in his or her name. This struan is shared among the family and special friends of the absent one in his or her name, or given to the poor who have no corn of their own. In mixing the meal of the individual struan, the woman kneading it mentions the name of the person for whom it is being made.

'Ruth agus rath Dhomhnuill,
Run Mhicheil, dion an Domhnaich.'

Progeny and prosperity to Donald,
Mystery of Michael, shielding of the Lord.

The individual struans of a family are uniform in size but irregular in form, some being three-cornered, symbolic of the Trinity; some five, symbolic of the Trinity, with Mary and Joseph added; some seven, symbolic of the seven mysteries; some nine, symbolic of the nine archangels; and some round, symbolic of eternity. Various ingredients are introduced into the small struans, as cranberries, bilberries, brambleberries, carrayway seed, and wild honey. Those who make them and those for whom they are made vie with their friends who shall have the best and most varied ingredients. Many cautions are given to her who is making the struan to take exceptional care of it. Ills and evils innumerable would befall herself and her house should any mishap occur to the struan. Should it break before being fired, it betokens ill to the girl baking it; if after being fired and before being used, to the household. Were the struan flag to fall and the struan with it, the omen is full of evil augury to the family. A broken struan is not used. The 'fallaid,' dry meal remaining on the baking-board after the struan is made, is put into a 'mogan,' footless stocking, and dusted over the flocks on the following day--being the Day of Michael--to bring them 'piseach agus pailteas agus pronntachd,' progeny and plenty and prosperity, and to ward from them 'suileachd agus ealtraidh agus dosgaidh,' evil-eye, mischance, and murrain. Occasionally the 'fallaid' is preserved for a year and a day before being used.

On the morning of the Feast of Michael all within reach go to early mass. [paragraph continues] They take their struans with them to church to be blessed of the 'pears eaglais,' priest. At this festal service the priest exhorts the people to praise their guardian angel Michael for his leading and their Father God for His corn and wool, fruits of the field and fruits of the flocks, which He has bestowed on them, while the foodless and the fatherless among them are commended to the fatherhood of God and to the care of His people.

On returning from mass the people take the 'biadh Micheil,' Michael food, 'biadh maidne Micheil,' Michael morning food. The father of the family places the struan 'air bord co gile ri cailc na fuinn no ri sneachda nam beann'--on a board as white as the chalk of the rock or the snow of the hill. He then takes

'Sgian gheur, ghlan.
Gun smal, gun scour,
Gun sal, gun sur,
Gun mhur, gun mheirg,'

A knife keen, true,
Without stain, without dust,
Without smear, without flaw,
Without grime, without rust.

and having made the sign of the cross of Christ on the tablet of his face, the man cuts the struan into small sections, retaining in the parts the form of the whole. And he cuts up the lamb into small pieces. He places the board with the bread and the flesh on the centre of the table. Then the family, standing round, and holding a bit of struan in the left hand and a piece of lamb in the right, raise the 'Iolach Michell,' triumphal song of Michael, in praise of Michael, who guards and guides them, and in praise of God, who gives them food and clothing, health, and blessing withal. The man and his wife put struan into one 'coisan,' beehive basket, and lamb into another, and go out to distribute them among the poor of the neighbourhood who have no fruits nor flocks themselves. Nor is this all. 'Ta e iumachaidh gun toireadh gach tuathanach anns a bhaile La na Feill Michell peic mine, ceathramh struain, ceathramh uanail, ceathramh caise agus platar ime dha na buichd, agus dha na deoiridh, agus dha na diolacha-deirce truagha, agus dha na diblidh agus dha na dilleachdain gun chli, gun treoir, cruthaichte ann an cruth an Athar shiorriudh. Agus tha an duine a toir so seachad air mhiodh Mhicheil mar nasga deirce do Dhia treun nan dul a thug dha ni agus ciob, ith agus iodh, buaidh agus pais, fas agus cinneas a chum agus gu'm bi e roimh anam diblidh truagh an trath theid e null. Agus togaidh na buichd agus na deoiridh agus na diolacha-deirce truagha, agus na dilleachdain gun chli, gun treoir, agus togaidh na truaghain an Iolach Micheil a toir cliu agus moladh do Mhicheil min-gheal nam buadh agus do'n Athair uile-bheannaichte, uile-chumhachdach, a beannachadh an duine agus na mnatha 'n am mic agus 'n an nighean 'n an cuid 'n an cliu 'n an crannachar 'n an ni agus 'n an ciob, ann an toradh an tan agus ann an toradh an talamhan, Is iad so am muinntir ris an canair "na feara fiala," "na feara cneasda," agus "na, mnathan matha" "Da mnathan coire," a to deanamh comhnadh agus trocair air na boichd, agus air na deoiridh, air na diblidh, agus air na dimbidh, air na diolacha-deirce truagha agus air na dilleachdain gun chli, gun treoir, gun chul-tacsa, gun lorg bhrollaich, gun sgora-cuil, cruthaichte ann an cruth an Athar uile-chruthachaidh. Agus tha ainglean gile-ghil De agus an cas ri barracha biod, an suil ri bunnacha bachd, an cluas ri fonnacha fuinn, an sgiathan a sgaireanaich an colann a critheanaich a feitheamh ri fios a chur mu'n ghniomh le buille dhe 'n sgeith a chon Righ na Cathair shiorruidh.'

It is proper that every husbandman in the townland should give, on the day of the St Michael Feast, a peck of meal, a quarter of struan, a quarter of lamb, a quarter of cheese, and a platter of butter to the poor and forlorn, to the despised and dejected, to the alms-deserving, and to the orphans without pith, without power, formed in the image of the Father everlasting. And the man is giving this on the beam of Michael as an offering to the great God of the elements who gave him cattle and sheep, bread and corn, power and peace, growth and prosperity, that it may be before his abject, contrite soul when it goes thither. And the miserable, the poor, the tearful, the alms-deserving helpless ones, and the orphan, will raise the triumphal song of Michael, giving fame and laud to Michael, the fair hero of power, and to the Father all-blessed and powerful, blessing the man and the woman in their sons and in their daughters, in their means, fame, and lot, in their cattle, and in their sheep, in the produce of their herds, and in the produce of their lands. 'These are the people who are called "the humane men," "the compassionate men," and "the good women," "the generous women," who are taking mercy and compassion on the poor, and on the tearful, on the dejected and the despised, on the miserable alms-deserving, and on the orphans without pith, without power, without support, without breast-staff, without leaning-rod, formed in the image of the Father all-creative. And the surpassingly white angels of God, with their foot on tiptoe, their eye on the horizon, their ear on the ground, their wings flapping, their bodies trembling, are waiting to send announcement of the deed with a beat of their wings to the King of the throne everlasting.'

After the father and mother have distributed their gifts to the poor, the family mount their horses and set out on their pilgrimage to perform the circuiting of St Michael's burying-ground. None remain at home save the very old and the very young, to whom is assigned for the day the duty of tending the sheep, herding the cattle, and guarding the corn. The husband and wife ride on one horse, with probably a boy astride before the father and a girl sideways beside the mother, filling up the measure of the horse's capacity. A girl sits 'culag' behind her brother, or occasionally behind the brother of another girl, with her arm round him to steady her. A little girl sits 'bialag' in front of a brother, with his hand lovingly round her waist, while with his other hand he guides the horse. A little brother sits 'culag' behind his elder brother, with his two arms round him. The people of the different hills, glens, islands, and townlands join the procession on the way, and all travel along together, the crowded cavalcade gaily clad in stuffs and stripes and tartans whose fineness of texture and brilliancy of colouring are charming to see, is impossible to describe. The air is full of salutations and cordialities. Even the whinnying, neighing, restive horses seem to know and to feel that this is the Day of their patron saint the holy archangel.

'Micheal mil nan steuda geala
Choisin cios air dragon fala.'

The valiant Michael of the white steeds
Who subdued the dragon of blood.

On reaching their destination the people crowd into and round the simple prayer-house. The doors and windows of the little oratory are open, and the people kneeling without join those kneeling within in earnest supplication that all may go well with them for the day. And commending themselves and their horses to the leading of the valiant, glorious archangel of the cornered shield and flaming sword, the people remount their horses to make 'cuartachadh a chlaidh,' the circuiting of the burial ground. The great crowd starts from the east and follows the course of the sun in the name of God, in the name of Christ, in the name of Spirit. The priest leads the way riding on a white horse, his grey hair and white robe waving in the autumn breeze. Should there be more than one priest present they ride abreast. Should there be higher dignitaries they ride in front of, or between the priests. The people follow in a column from two to ten abreast. Those on horseback follow immediately behind the priest, those on foot behind these. The fathers of the different townlands are stationed at intervals on either side of the procession, to maintain regularity and to guard against accidents. All are imbued with a befitting reverence for the solemnity of the proceedings and of the occasion. Families, friends, and neighbours try to keep together in the processional circuiting. As they move from left to right the people raise the 'Iolach Micheil,' song of Michael the victorious, whose sword is keen to smite, and whose arm is strong to save. At the end of the circuit the 'culag' gives to her 'bialag,' 'glac churran,' a handful of carrots, saying:--

'Ruth agus rath air do iaighe 's eirigh.'

Progeny and prosperity on thy lying and rising.

The 'bialag' acknowledges the gift in one of the many phrases common on the occasion:--

'Piseach agus pais air an lamh a thug.
Por agus pais dha mo ghradh a thug.
Piseach agus pailteas gun an airc na d'chomhnuidh.
Banas agus brioghas dha mo nighinn duinn.
Baireas agus buaidh dha mo luaidh a thug.'

Progeny and peace on the hand that gave.
Issue and peace on my love who gave.
Progeny and plenty without scarcity in thy dwelling.
Wifehood and motherhood on my brown maid,
Endowment and prosperity to my love who gave.

Greetings, courtesies, and gifts are exchanged among the people, many of whom have not met since they met at the circuiting. The most prized courtesy, however, is a 'culag' round the burial-ground, and the most prized gift is a carrot with its customary wishes and acknowledgments. Those who have no horses readily obtain them to make the circuiting, the consideration of those who have for those who have not being native and habitual.

Having performed the professional pilgrimage round the graves of their fathers, the people hasten to the 'oda'--the scene of the athletics of the men and the racing of the horses. The games and races excite much interest. The riders in the races ride without bonnet, without shoes, clothed only in a shirt and 'triubhais bheag,' small trews like football trousers. All ride without saddle, some without bridle, guiding and driving their horses with 'steamhag chaol chruaidh,' a hard slender tangle in each hand. Occasionally girls compete with one another and sometimes with men. They sit on either side as may be most convenient in mounting. They have no saddle, and how they retain their seat is inconceivable. Some circuiting goes on all day, principally among the old and the young--the old teaching the young the mysteries of the circuiting and the customs of the olden times. Here and there young men and maidens ride about and wander away, converting the sandy knolls and grassy dells of the fragrant 'machair' into Arcadian plains and Eden groves.

On the night of St Michael a 'cuideachd,' ball, is held in every townland. The leading piper selects the place for the ball, generally the house of largest size and of evenest floor. Every man present contributes a sixpence, or its equivalent in farm produce, usually in grain, towards paying the piper if he be a married man; if not, he accepts nothing. Several pipers, fiddlers, and players of other instruments relieve one another during the night. The small bets won at the 'oda' during the day are spent at the ball during the night, no one being allowed to retain his luck.

The women put their bunches of carrots into white linen bags with the mark of the owner. Having filled their 'crioslachain,' they leave the bags in some house convenient to the 'taigh dannsa,' dance-house. As their 'crioslachain' become empty during the night they replenish them from the 'falachain,' hidden store. When a woman comes into the dance-house after refilling her 'crioslachain,' she announces her entrance with a rhyme, the refrain of which is--

"S ann agam fein a bhiodh na currain,
Ga be co bhuinneadh bhuam iad.'

"S ann agam fein a bhiodh an ulaidh.
Ge be 'n curaidh bheireadh bhuam e.'

It is I myself that have the carrots,
Whoever he be that would win them from me.

It is I myself that have the treasure,
Whoso the hero could take them from me.

At the circuiting by day and at the ball at night, youths and maidens exchange simple gifts in token of good feeling. The girls give the men bonnets, hose, garters, cravats, purses, plaids, and other things of their own making, and the men give the girls brooches of silver, brass, bronze, or copper, knives, scissors, snoods, combs, mirrors, and various other things. Some of these gifts are mentioned in the following verses:--

'NA GEALLAIDH

'Thug mo leannan dhomh sgian bheag
A ghearradh am meangan goid,
A ghearradh am bog 's an cruaidh,
Saoghal buan dh' an laimh a thug.

Gheall mo leannan dhomh-sa stiom
Gheall, agus braiste 's cir,
'S gheall mise coinneamh ris

Am bun a phris mu'n eireadh grian.

Gheall mo leannan dhomh-sa sgathan
Anns am faicinn m'aille fein,
Gheall, agus breid is fainne,
Agus clarsach bhinn nan teud.

Gheall e sid dhomh 's buaile bha,
Agus falaire nan steud,
Agus birlinn bheannach bhan,
Readhadh slan thar chuan nam beud,

Mile beannachd, mile buaidh
Dha mo luaidh a dh'fhalbh an de,
Thug e dhomh-sa 'n gealladh buan,
Gum b'e Bhnachaill-san Mac Dhe.

THE PROMISES

My lover gave to me a knife
That would cut the sapling withe,
That would cut the soft and hard,
Long live the hand that gave.

My lover promised me a snood,
Ay, and a brooch and comb,
And I promised, by the wood,
To meet him at rise of sun.

My lover promised me a mirror
That my beauty I might see,
Yes, and a coif and ring,
And a dulcet harp of chords.

He vowed me those and a fold of kine,
And a palfrey of the steeds,
And a barge, pinnacled white,
That would safely cross the perilous seas.

A thousand blessings, a thousand victories
To my lover who left me yestreen,
He gave to me the promise lasting,
Be his Shepherd God's own Son.

The song and the dance, the mirth and the merriment, are continued all night, many curious scenes being acted, and many curious dances performed, some of them in character. These scenes and dances are indicative of far-away times, perhaps of far-away climes., They are evidently symbolic. One dance is called 'Cailleach an Dudain,' carlin of the mill-dust. This is a curious character-dance. The writer got it performed for him several times.

It is danced by a man and a woman. The man has a rod in his right hand, variously called 'slachdan druidheachd,' druidic wand, 'slachdan geasachd,' magic wand. The man and the woman gesticulate and attitudinise before one another, dancing round and round, in and out, crossing and recrossing, changing and exchanging places. The man flourishes the wand over his own head and over the head of the woman, whom he touches with the wand, and who falls down, as if dead, at his feet. He bemoans his dead 'carlin,' dancing and gesticulating round her body. He then lifts up her left hand, and looking into the palm, breathes upon it, and touches it with the wand. Immediately the limp hand becomes alive and moves from side to side and up and down. The man rejoices, and dances round the figure on the floor. And having done the same to the right hand, and to the left and right foot in succession, they also become alive and move. But although the limbs are living, the body is still inert. The man kneels over the woman and breathes into her mouth and touches her heart with the wand. The woman comes to life and springs up, confronting the man. Then the two dance vigorously and joyously as in the first part. The tune varies with the varying phases of the dance. It is played by a piper or a fiddler, or sung as a 'port-a-bial,' mouth tune, by a looker-on, or by the performers themselves. The air is quaint and irregular, and the words are curious and archaic.

In his West Highland Tales, Iain P. Campbell of Islay mentions that he saw 'cailleach an dudain' danced in the house of Lord Stanley of Alderley. He does not say by whom it was danced, but probably it was by the gifted narrator himself. In October 1871, Mr Campbell spent some time with the writer and his wife in Uist. When driving him to Lochmaddy, at the conclusion of his stay, I mentioned that there were two famous dancers of 'cailleach an dudain' at Clachan-a-ghluip. We went to their bothy, but they were away. The neighbours told us that they were in the direction of Lochmaddy. When we reached there we went in search of them, but were unsuccessful. Some hours afterwards, as I was coming up from the shore after seeing Mr Campbell on board the packet for Dunvegan, I saw the two women racing down the hill, their long hair and short dresses flying wildly in the wind. They had heard that we had been inquiring for them. But it was too late. The packet, with Mr Campbell on board, was already hoisting her sails and heaving her anchor.

Another dance is called 'cath nan coileach,' the combat of the cocks; another, 'turraban nan tunnag,' waddling of the ducks; another, 'ruidhleadh nan coileach dubha,' reeling of the black-cocks; another, 'cath nan curaidh,' contest of the warriors, where a Celtic Saul slays his thousands, and a Celtic David his tens of thousands. Many dances now lost were danced at the St Michael ball, while those that still remain were danced with much more artistic complexity. The sword-dance was performed in eight sections instead of in four, as now. The reel of Tulloch was danced in eight figures with side issues, while 'seann triubhas' contained much more acting than it does now. Many beautiful and curious songs, now lost, were sung at these balls.

The young people who have individual 'struans' give and receive and share them the night through, till sleep overcomes all.

Chiefs and chieftains, tacksmen and tenants, men and women, old and young, rich and poor, mingle in the pilgrimage, in the service, in the circuiting, in the games and races, in the dancing and the merry-making. The granddame of eighty and the granddaughter of eight, the grandsire of ninety and the grandson of nine, all take much interest in the festival of St Michael. The old and the young who do not go to the ball entertain one another at their homes, exchanging 'struans' and carrots and homely gifts in token of friendship and neighbourliness. The pilgrimage, the service, the circuiting, and the games and races of the 'oda,' once so popular in the Western Isles, are now become obsolete. The last circuiting with service was performed in South Uist in 1820. It took place as usual round Cladh Mhicheil, the burial-ground of Michael, near the centre of the island. The last great 'oda' in North Uist was in 1866, and took place on the customary spot, 'Traigh Mhoire,' the strand of Mary, on the west side of the island.

'Ach dh'fhalbh sud uile mar bhruadar,
Mar bhriseadh builgean air uachdar nan tonn.'

But all that has gone like a vision,
Like the breaking of a bubble on the surface of the sea.

The Michael lamb is sometimes slain, the Michael 'struan' is sometimes baked, and the carrots are occasionally gathered, but the people can give no account of their significance. Probably the lamb and the 'struan' represented the first-fruits of the flock and the fields, the circuiting and the sun-warding, ancestor-worship and sun-worship, and the carrots of the west the mandrakes of the east, 'given in the time of the wheat-harvest.'

The wives of husbandmen carried 'struans' to the castles of the chiefs, and to the houses of the gentlemen in their neighbourhood, as marks of good-will. This was one of the many links in the social chain which bound chief and clansmen, proprietor and tenant together. In the past the chiefs and gentlemen and their families joined the people in their festivals, games and dances, secular amusements and religious observances, joys and sorrows, to the great good of all and to the stability of society. In the present, as a rule, the proprietors and gentlemen of the Highlands and Islands are at the best but temporary residents, if so much, and generally strangers in blood and speech, feeling and sympathy, more prone to criticise than to help, to scoff than to sympathise. As a result, the observances of the people have fallen into disuse, to the loss of the spiritual life of the country, and of the patriotic life of the nation.

Throughout the Highlands and Islands special cakes were made on the first day of the quarter. As in the ease of the 'struan,' a large cake was made for the family and smaller cakes for individual members. So far as can now be ascertained, these cakes were round in form. They were named after their dedications. That baked for the first day of spring was called 'bonnach Bride,' bannock of Bride; that for the first day of summer, 'bonnach Bealltain,' Beltane bannock; that for the first day of autumn, 'bonnach Lunastain, Lammas bannock; and that for the first day of winter, 'bonnach Samhthain,' Hallowtide bannock. The names of the individual cakes were rendered into diminutives to distinguish them from the family cake, while the sex of the person for whom they were intended was indicated by the termination, as 'Bridean,' masculine diminutive, 'Brideag,' feminine diminutive, after Bride; 'Bealltan,' 'Bealltag,' after Beltane; 'Luinean,' 'Luineag,' after Lammas; and 'Samhnan,' 'Samhnag,' after Hallowmas. The people repaired to the fields, glens, and corries to eat their quarter cakes. When eating them, they threw a piece over each shoulder alternately, saying: 'Here to thee, wolf, spare my sheep; there to thee, fox, spare my lambs; here to thee, eagle, spare my goats; there to thee, raven, spare my kids: here to thee, marten, spare my fowls; there to thee, harrier, spare my chickens.'

As may be seen from some of the poems, the duty of conveying the souls of the good to the abode of bliss is assigned to Michael. When the soul has parted from the body and is being weighed, the archangel of heaven and the archangel of hell preside at the beam, the former watching that the latter does not put 'cruidhean laimhe na spuir coise an coir na meidhe,' claw of hand nor talon of foot near the beam. Michael and all the archangels and angels of heaven sing songs of joy when the good in the soul outweighs the bad, while the devil howls as he retreats.

MICHEAL NAM BUADH

MICHAEL, THE VICTORIOUS

MHICHEIL nam buadh,
Char tam fo d' dhion,
A Mhicheil nan steud geal,
'S nan leug lanna liomh,
Fhir bhuadhaich an dreagain,
Bi fein ri mo chul,
Fhir-chuartach nan speura,
Fhir-feachd Righ nan dul,
A Mhicheil nam buadh,
M' uaill agus m'
A Mhicheil nam buadh,
Suamhnas mo shul.

THOU Michael the victorious,
I make my circuit under thy shield,
Thou Michael of the white steed,
And of the bright brilliant blades,
Conqueror of the dragon,
Be thou at my back,
Thou ranger of the heavens,
Thou warrior of the King of all,
O Michael the victorious,
My pride and my guide,
O Michael the victorious,
The glory of mine eye.

Deanam an cuarta
An cluanas mo naomh,
Air machair, air cluan domh,
Air fuar-bheanna fraoch;
Ged shiubhlam an cuan
'S an cruaidh cruinne-ce

Cha deifir domh gu sior
'S mi fo dhidionn do sgeith;
A Mhicheal nam buadh,
M' ailleagan ere,
A Mhicheil nam buadh,
Buachaille De.

Tri Naomh na Gloire
Bhith 'n comhnuidh rium reidh,
Ri n' eachraidh, ri m' lochraidh,
Ri cioba cloimh an treud.
Am barr ta fas air raona
No caonachadh an raoid,
Air machair no air mointeach,
An toit, an torr, no an cruach.
Gach ni tha'n aird no'n iosal,
Gach insridh agus buar,
'S le Trithinn naomh na gloire,
Agus Micheal corr nam buadh.

I make my circuit
In the fellowship of my saint,
On the machair, on the meadow,
On the cold heathery hill;
Though I should travel ocean
And the hard globe of the world
No harm can e'er befall me
'Neath the shelter of thy shield;
O Michael the victorious,
Jewel of my heart,
O Michael the victorious,
God's shepherd thou art.

Be the sacred Three of Glory
Aye at peace with me,
With my horses, with my cattle,
With my woolly sheep in flocks.
With the crops growing in the field
Or ripening in the sheaf,
On the machair, on the moor,
In cole, in heap, or stack.
Every thing on high or low,
Every furnishing and flock,
Belong to the holy Triune of glory,
And to Michael the victorious.

AN BEANNACHADH STRUAIN

THE BLESSING OF THE 'STRUAN'

GACH min tha fo m' chleibh,
Theid am measgadh le cheil,
An ainm Mhic De,
Thug fas daibh.

Bainn is uibheann is im,
Sochair mhath ar cuid fhin,
Cha bhi gainne 'n ar tir,
No 'n ar fardaich,

An ainm Mhicheil mo luaidh,
Dh' f hag againn a bhuaidh,
Le beannachd an Uain,
'S a Mhathar.

Umhlaich sinn aig do stol,
Biodh do chumraig fein oirnn,
Cum uainn fuath, fath, foirn,
Agus gleidh sinn.

Coisrig toradh ar tir,
Bairig sonas is sith,
An ainm an Athar an Righ,
'S nan tri ostal gradhach.

Bearnan bride, creamh min,
Lus-mor, glasrach is slim,
Na tri ghroigeanan-cinn,
Is lus Mairi.

EACH meal beneath my roof, [wattle
They will all be mixed together,
In name of God the Son,
Who gave them growth.

Milk, and eggs, and butter,
The good produce of our own flock,
There shall be no dearth in our land,
Nor in our dwelling.

In name of Michael of my love,
Who bequeathed to us the power,

With the blessing of the Lamb,
And of His Mother.

Humble us at thy footstool,
Be thine own sanctuary around us,
Ward from us spectre, sprite, oppression,
And preserve us.

Consecrate the produce of our land,
Bestow prosperity and peace,
In name of the Father the King,
And of the three beloved apostles.

Dandelion, smooth garlic,
Foxglove, woad, and butterwort,
The three carle-doddies,
And marigold.

Cailpeach ghlas air a buain,
Seachd-mhiarach, seachd uair,
Iubhar-beinne, fraoch ruadh,
Agus madar.

Cuiream uisge orr gu lair,
An ainm usga Mhic De,
An ainm Mhuire na fail,
Agus Phadruig.

D'uair shuidheas sinn sios
Gu gabhail ar biadh,
Cratham an ainme Dhia
Air na paisdean.

Gray 'cailpeach' plucked,
The seven-pronged seven times,
The mountain yew, ruddy heath,
And madder.

I will put water on them all,
In precious name of the Son of God,
In name of Mary the generous,
And of Patrick.

When we shall sit down
To take our food,
I will sprinkle in the name of God

On the children.

DUAN AN DOMHNUICH

THE POEM OF THE LORD'S DAY

THIS poem was obtained from Janet Currie, Staonabrig, South Uist, a descendant of the Mac Mhuirichs (corrupted into Currie) of Staoligearry, the famous poet-historians to the Clanranalds. She was a tall, strong, dark-haired, ruddy-complexioned woman, with a clear, sonorous voice. Her language was remarkably fluent and copious, though many of her words and phrases, being obsolete, were unintelligible to the stranger. I took down versions of the poem from several other persons, but they are all more or less corrupt and obscure. Poems similar to this can be traced back to the eighth century.

DUAN an Domhnuich, a Dhe ghil,
Firinn fo neart Chriosd a chomhnuidh.

Di-domhnuich rugadh Muire,
Mathair Chriosd an or-fhuilt bhuidhe,
Di-domhnuich rugadh Criosda
Mar onair dhaoine.

Di-domhnuich, an seachdamh latha,
Dh' orduich Dia gu fois a ghabhail,
Gu cumail na beath-maireannaich,
Gun feum a thoir a damh no duine,
No a creubh mar dheonaich Muire,
Gun sniamh snath sioda no strol,
Gun fuaigheal, gun ghreiseadh ni's mo,
Gun churachd, gun chliathadh, gun bhuain,
Gun iomaradh, gun iomairt, gun iasgaireachd,
Gun dol a mach dh' an t-sliabh sheilg,
Gun snaitheadh deilgne Di-domhnuich,
Gun chartadh taighe, gun bhualadh,
Gun atha, gun mhuileann Di-domhnuich.

Ge be chumadh an Domhnuch,
Bu chomhnard da-san 's bu bhuan,
Bho dhol fotha greine Di-Sathuirn
Gu eirigh greine Di-luain.

THE poem of the Lord's Day, O bright God,
Truth under the strength of Christ always.

On the Lord's Day Mary was born,
Mother of Christ of golden yellow hair,

On the Lord's Day Christ was born
As an honour to men.

The Lord's Day, the seventh day,
God ordained to take rest,
To keep the life everlasting,
Without taking use of ox or man,
Or of creature as Mary desired,
Without spinning thread of silk or of satin,
Without sewing, without embroidery either,
Without sowing, without harrowing, without reaping,
Without rowing, without games, without fishing,
Without going out to the hunting hill,
Without trimming arrows on the Lord's Day,
Without cleaning byre, without threshing corn,
Without kiln, without mill on the Lord's Day.

Whosoever would keep the Lord's Day,
Even would it be to him and lasting,
From setting of sun on Saturday
Till rising of sun on Monday.

Gheobhadh e feich ga chionn,
Toradh an deigh nan crann,
Iasg air abhuinn fior ghlan sala,
Sar iasg an ionnar gach abhuinn.

Uisg an Domhnuich blath mar mhil,
Ge be dh' oladh e mar dhibh
Gheobhadh e solas ga chion
Bho gach dolas a bhiodh na char.

Gul an Domhnuich gu ra-luath,
Bean ga dheanadh an an-uair;
Guileadh i gu moch Di-luain,
Ach na guileadh i uair 's an Domhnuch.

Fiodh an Domhnuich gu ra-luath,
Anns an linge mar is truagh,
Ge d' thuiteadh a cheann na ghual,
Bhiodh e gu Di-luain na chadal.
Mu thrath-nona Di-luain,
Eiridh am fiodh gu ra-luath,
'S air an dile mhor a muigh
Greas air sgeula mo chuimire.
Gun chnuasachd uan, meile, meinne no minsich

Nach buineadh dh' an Righ anns a bhlagh.
Is ann a nist bu choir a losgadh,
Gun eisdeachd ri gleadhraich nan gall,
No ri dall sgeileireachd choitchinn.

Gart a ghleidheadh air cnoc ard,
Leigh a thoir gu galar garga,
Bo chur gu tarbh treun na tana,
Falbh le beothach gu cuthaidh,

He would obtain recompense therefrom,
Produce after the ploughs,
Fish on the pure salt-water stream,
Fish excelling in every river confluence.

The water of the Lord's Day mild as honey,
Whoso would partake of it as drink
Would obtain health in consequence
From every disease afflicting him.

The weeping of the Lord's Day is out of place,
A woman doing it is untimely;
Let her weep betimes on Monday,
But not weep once on the Lord's Day.

The wood of the Lord's Day is too soon.
In the pool it is pitiful,
Though its head should fall in char,
It would till Monday be dormant.
About noon on the Monday,
The wood will arise very quickly,
And by the great flood without
Hasten the story of my trouble.
Without any searching for lamb, sheep, kid or goat
That would not belong to the King in the cause.
It is now it ought to be burnt,
Without listening to the clamour of the stranger,
Nor to the blind babbling of the public.

To keep corn on a high hillock,
To bring physician to a violent disease,
To send a cow to the potent bull of the herd,
To go with a beast to a cattle-fold,

Fada no fagasg anns a cheum,
Feumaidh gach creatair umhail.

Eathar a leigeil fo breid-shiuil bho thir,
Bho thir gu duthaich a h-aineoil.

Ge be mheoraicheadh mo dhuan
'S a ghabhadh e gach oidhche Luan,
Bhiodh rath Mhicheil air a cheann,
'S a chaoidh cha bu teann da irionn.

Far or near be the distance,
Every creature needs attention.
To allow a boat under her sail from land,
From land to the country of her unacquaintance.

Whoso would meditate my lay,
And say it every Monday eve,
The luck of Michael would be on his head,
And never would he see perdition.

DOIGHEAN EILE--

Abhuinn sleibh fior bhlasda,
A sior ialadh gu Iordan,
Is ra mhath chum i a cain,
Di-domhnuich ge lan a tuil.

Cha ruith braon ge glan a h-uisge,
An inne na Mara Ruaidh.

Fiodh an Domhnuich nis, mo nuar!
An inne na Mara Ruaidh
Ged thuiteadh an ruadh-cheann deth
Bhiodh e gu Di-luain na chadal.

Na fagairt mi ni air mo dheigh,
Greis thoir air sgeula mo chumraidh.

ALTERNATIVE VERSIONS--

Hill river is very palatable,
Ever meandering to Jordan,
Right well it retained its tribute
On the Lord's Day though great its flood.

No drop, though pure be its water,
Shall run in the channel of the Red Sea.

The wood of the Lord's Day now, alas!
In the channel of the Red Sea,
Though the red head should fall off
It would be till Monday asleep.

Let me not leave aught behind,
To talk a while of the redemption.

DUAN AN DOMHNAICH

HYMN OF THE SUNDAY

AN Domhnach naomha do Dhe
Tabhair do chre dh' an chinne-daon,
Do t' athair is do d' mhathair chaomh,
Thar gach aon 's gach ni 's an t-saoghal.

Na dean sainn air mhor no bheag,
Na dean tair air tais no truaigh,
Fiamh an uilc a d' choir na leig,
Na tabhair 's na toill masladh uair.

Na deich fana thug Dia duit,
Tuig gun dail iad agus dearbh,
Creid direach an Righ nan dul,
Cuir air chul uidh thoir a dhealbh.

Bi dileas da d' thighearna-cinn,
Bi dileas da d' righ 's gach eang,
Bi dileas duit fein a ris,
Dileas da d' Ard Righ thar gach dreang.

Na tabhair toi'eum do neach air bith,
An earail toi'eum a thoir ort fein,
'S ged shiubhladh tu cuan is cith,
Lean cas-cheum Aon-unga Dhe.

ON the holy Sunday of thy God
Give thou thine heart to all mankind,
To thy father and thy mother loving,
Beyond any person or thing in the world.

Do not covet large or small,
Do not despise weakling or poor,
Semblance of evil allow not near thee,
Never give nor earn thou shame.

The ten commands God gave thee,
Understand them early and prove,
Believe direct in the King of the elements,
Put behind thee ikon-worship.

Be faithful to thine over-lord,
Be true to thy king in every need,
Be true to thine own self besides,
True to thy High-King above all obstacles.

Do not thou malign any man,
Lest thou thyself maligned shouldst be,
And shouldst thou travel ocean and earth,
Follow the very step of God's Anointed.

DUAN NA DILINN

POEM OF THE FLOOD

DI-LUAIN thig an doireann trom,
A shileas am bith eutrom,
Bithidh sinn umhail gach greis,
Gach uile na dh' eisdeas.

Di-mairt thig an t-sian eile,
Cradh chridheach, cruaidh pheinneach,
A shileas na gruaidheana glana,
Frasa fala fiona.

Di-ciadain a sheideas gaoth,
Sguaba lom air shrath is raon,
Dortadh oiteag barra theann,
Beithir bheur 's reubadh bheann.

Di-ardaoin a shileas an cith,
Chuireas daoine 'n an dalla ruith,
Na 's luaithe na 'n duil air an fhiodh,
Mar bharr mhic-Muir air bhalla-chrith.

Di-haoine thig an coinneal dubh,
Is eitiche thainig fo'n t-saoghal;
Fagar an sluagh braon am beachd,
Fiar agus iasg fo'n aon leac.

Di-sathuirne thig am muir mor,

Ag iomairt air alt aibhne;
Bithidh gach uile mar a shnodh
Ag altachadh gu sliabh slighinn.

ON Monday will come the great storm
Which the airy firmament will pour,
We shall be obedient the while,
All who will hearken.

On Tuesday will come the other element,
Heart paining, hard piercing,
Wringing from pure pale cheeks
Blood, like showers of wine.

On Wednesday will blow the wind,
Sweeping bare strath and plain,
Showering gusts of galling grief,
Thunder bursts and rending hills.

On Thursday will pour the shower,
Driving people into blind flight,
Faster than the foliage on the trees,
Like the leaves of Mary's plant in terror trembling.

On Friday will come the dool cloud of darkness,
The direst dread that ever came over the world,
Leaving multitudes bereft of reason,
Grass and fish beneath the same flagstone.

On Saturday will come the great sea,
Rushing like a mighty river;
All will be at their best
Hastening to a hill of safety.

Di-domhnaich a dh' eireas mo Righ,
Lan feirge agus iminidh,
Ag eisdeachd ri searbh ghloir gach fir,
Crois dhearg air gach guala dheis.

On Sunday will arise my King,
Full of ire and tribulation,
Listening to the bitter talk of each man,
A red cross on each right shoulder.

III

OIBRE

LABOUR

BEANNACHADH BEOTHACHAIDH

BLESSING OF THE KINDLING

THE kindling of the fire is a work full of interest to the housewife. When 'lifting' the fire in the morning the woman prays, in an undertone, that the fire may be blessed to her and to her household, and to the glory of God who gave it. The people look upon fire as a miracle of Divine power provided for their good--to warm their bodies when they are cold, to cook their food when they are hungry, and to remind them that they too, like the fire, need constant renewal mentally and physically.

TOGAIDH mi mo theine an diugh,
An lathair ainghlean naomha neimh,
An lathair Airil is ailde cruth,
An lathair Uiril nan uile sgeimh,
Gun ghnu, gun tnu, gun fharmad.
Gun ghiomh, gun gheimh roimh neach fo'n ghrein,
Ach Naomh Mhac De da m' thearmad.
Gun ghnu, gun tnu, gun fharmad,
Gun ghiomh, gun gheimh, roimh neach fo'n ghrein,
Ach Naomh Mhac De da m' thearmad.

Dhe fadaidh fein na m' chridhe steach,
Aingheal ghraidh do m' choimhearsnach,
Do m' namh, do m' dhamh, do m' chairde,
Do 'n t-saoidh, do 'n daoidh, do 'n traille.
A Mhic na Moire min-ghile,
Bho 'n ni is isde crannchaire,
Gu ruig an t-Ainm is airde.
A Mhic na Moire min-ghile,
Bho 'n ni is isde crannchaire,
Gu ruig an t-Ainm is airde.

I WILL kindle my fire this morning
In presence of the holy angels of heaven,
In presence of Ariel of the loveliest form,
In presence of Uriel of the myriad charms,
Without malice, without jealousy, without envy,
Without fear, without terror of any one under the sun,
But the Holy Son of God to shield me.
Without malice, without jealousy, without envy,

131

Without fear, without terror of any one under the sun,
But the Holy Son of God to shield me.

God, kindle Thou in my heart within
A flame of love to my neighbour,
To my foe, to my friend, to my kindred all,
To the brave, to the knave, to the thrall,
O Son of the loveliest Mary,
From the lowliest thing that liveth,
To the Name that is highest of all.
O Son of the loveliest Mary,
From the lowliest thing that liveth,
To the Name that is highest of all.

TOGAIL AN TEINE

KINDLING THE FIRE

TOGAIDH mis an tula
Mar a thogadh Muire.
Cairn Bhride 's Mhuire
Air an tula 's air an lar,
'S air an fhardaich uile.

Co iad ri luim an lair?
Eoin, Peadail agus Pail.
Co iad ri bruaich mo leap?
Bride bhuidheach 's a Dalt.
Co iad ri fath mo shuain?
Muire ghraidh-gheal 's a h-Uan.
Co siud a tha 'n am theann?
Righ na grein e fein a th' ann,
Co siud ri cul mo chinn?
Mac nan dul gun tus, gun linn.

I WILL raise the hearth-fire
As Mary would.
The encirclement of Bride and of Mary
On the fire, and on the floor,
And on the household all.

Who are they on the bare floor?
John and Peter and Paul.
Who are they by my bed?
The lovely Bride and her Fosterling.
Who are those watching over my sleep?

The fair loving Mary and her Lamb.
Who is that anear me?
The King of the sun, He himself it is.
Who is that at the back of my head?
The Son of Life without beginning, without time.

SMALADH AN TEINE

SMOORING THE FIRE

PEAT is the fuel of the Highlands and Islands. Where wood is not obtainable the fire is kept in during the night. The process by which this is accomplished is called in Gaelic smaladh; in Scottish, smooring; and in English, smothering, or more correctly, subduing. The ceremony of smooring the fire is artistic and symbolic, and is performed with loving care. The embers are evenly spread on the hearth--which is generally in the middle of the floor--and formed into a circle. This circle is then divided into three equal sections, a small boss being left in the middle. A peat is laid between each section, each peat touching the boss, which forms a common centre. The first peat is laid down in name of the God of Life, the second in name of the God of Peace, the third in name of the God of Grace. The circle is then covered over with ashes sufficient to subdue but not to extinguish the fire, in name of the Three of Light. The heap slightly raised in the centre is called 'Tula nan Tri,' the Hearth of the Three. When the smooring operation is complete the woman closes her eyes, stretches her hand, and softly intones one of the many formulae current for these occasions.

Another way of keeping embers for morning use is to place them in a pit at night. The pit consists of a hole in the clay floor, generally under the dresser. The pit may be from half a foot to a foot in depth and diameter, with a flag fixed in the floor over the top. In the centre of this flag there is a hole by which the embers are put in and taken out. Another flag covers the hole to extinguish the fire at night, and to guard against accidents during the day. This extinguishing fire-pit is called 'slochd guail,' coke or coal-pit. This coke or charcoal is serviceable in kindling the fire.

AN Tri numh
A chumhnadh,
A chomhnadh,
A chomraig
An tula,
An taighe,
An teaghlaich,
An oidhche,
An nochd,
O! an oidhche,
An nochd,
Agus gach oidhche,
Gach aon oidhche.
Amen.

THE sacred Three

To save,
To shield,
To surround
The hearth,
The house,
The household,
This eve,
This night,
Oh! this eve,
This night,
And every night,
Each single night.
Amen.

SMALADH AN TEINE

SMOORING THE FIRE

CAIRIDH mi an tula,
Mar a chaireadh Muire,
Claim Bhride 's Mhuire,
Car an tula 's car an lair,
'S car an ardraich uile.

Co iad air lian a muigh?
Micheal grian-gheal mo luin.
Co iad air meadhon lair?
Eoin, Peadail, agus Pail.
Co iad ri bial mo stoc?
Moire ghrian-gheal 's a Mac.

Bial Dia dh' orduich,
Aingheal Dia bhoinich,
Aingheal geal an car an tealla,
Gon tig la geal gu beola.
Aingheal geal an car an tealla,
Gon tig la geal gu beola.

I WILL build the hearth,
As Mary would build it.
The encompassment of Bride and of Mary,
Guarding the hearth, guarding the floor,
Guarding the household all.

Who are they on the lawn without?
Michael the sun-radiant of my trust.

Who are they on the middle of the floor?
John and Peter and Paul.
Who are they by the front of my bed?
Sun-bright Mary and her Son.

The mouth of God ordained,
The angel of God proclaimed,
An angel white in charge of the hearth
Till white day shall come to the embers.
An angel white in charge of the hearth
Till white day shall come to the embers.

BEANNACHD SMALAIDH

BLESSING OF THE SMOORING

THA mi smaladh an teine,
Mar a smaladh Mac Moire;
Gu mu slan dh' an taigh 's dh' an teine,
Gu mu slan dh' an chuideachd uile.

Co siud shios air an lar?
Eoin agus Peadail agus Pal.
Co air am bheil an fhaire nochd?
Air Moire mhin-gheal 's air a Mac.

Beul De a thubhradh,
Aingheal De a labhradh,
Aingheal an dorus an taighe,
D'ar comhnadh 's d'ar gleidheadh
Gu 'n tig la geal am maireach.

O! ainghlean Aon Naomha Dhe
Da mo chaimhleachadh fein a nochd,
O! ainghlean Aon Unga Dhe,
Da mo chaim bho bheud 's bho lochd,
Da mo chaim bho bheud a nochd.

I AM smooring the fire
As the Son of Mary would smoor;
Blest be the house, blest be the fire,
Blest be the people all.

Who are those down on the floor?
John and Peter and Paul.
On whom is the vigil to-night?

On the fair gentle Mary and on her Son.

The mouth of God said,
The angel of God spake,
An angel in the door of the house,
To guard and to keep us all
Till comes daylight to-morrow.

Oh! may the angels of the Holy One of God
Environ me all this night,
Oh! may the angels of the Anointed One of God
Encompass me from harm and from evil,
Oh! encompass me from harm this night.

BEANNACHADH SMALAIDH

SMOORING BLESSING

SMALAIDH mis an tula
Mar a smaladh Muire;
Comraig Bhride 's Mhuire,
Air an tula 's air an lar,
'S air an fhardaich uile.

Co siud air liana mach?
Muire ghrian-gheal 's a Mac,
Bial Dia dh' iarradh, aingheal Dia labhradh;
Ainghle geallaidh faire an teallaidh,
Gu'n tig latha geal gu beallaidh.

I WILL smoor the hearth
As Mary would smoor;
The encompassment of Bride and of Mary,
On the fire and on the floor,
And on the household all.

Who is on the lawn without?
Fairest Mary and her Son,
The mouth of God ordained, the angel of God spoke;
Angels of promise watching the hearth,
Till white day comes to the fire.

AN COISRIGEADH SIOIL

THE CONSECRATION OF THE SEED

THE preparation of the seed-corn is of great importance to the people, who bestow much care on this work. Many ceremonies and proverbs are applied to seedtime and harvest.

The corn is prepared at certain seasons of the year, which are seldom deviated from. The rye is threshed to allow 'gaoth bhog nan Duldachd,' the soft wind of November and December, to winnow the seed; the oats to allow 'gaoth fhuar nam Faoilleach,' the cold winds of January and February, to winnow the seed; and the bere to allow 'gaoth gheur nam Mart,' the sharp winds of March and April, to winnow the seed. All these preparations are made to assist Nature in the coming Spring. Three days before being sown the seed is sprinkled with clear cold water, in the name of Father, and of Son, and of Spirit, the person sprinkling the seed walking sunwise the while.

The ritual is picturesque, and is performed with great care and solemnity and, like many of these ceremonies, is a combination of Paganism and Christianity. The moistening of the seed has the effect of hastening its growth when committed to the ground, which is generally begun on a Friday, that day being auspicious for all operations not necessitating the use of iron.

THEID mi mach a chur an t-sioil,
An ainm an Ti a thug da fas,
Cuirim m' aghaidh anns a ghaoith,
Is tilgim baslach caon an aird.
Ma thuiteas silc air lic luim,
Cha bhi fuinn aige gu fas;
Mheud 's a thuiteas anns an uir,
Bheir an druchd dha a bhi lan.

Di-aoine la nam buadh,
Thig dealt a nuas a chur failt
Air gach por a bha 'n an suain,
Bho na thainig fuachd gun bhaigh;
Friamhaichidh gach por 's an uir,
Mar a mhiannaich Righ nan dul,
Thig an fochann leis an druchd,
Gheobh e beatha bho 'n ghaoith chiuin.

Thig mi mu 'n cuairt le m' cheum,
Theid mi deiseil leis a ghrein,
An ainm Airil 's nan aingeal naodh,
An ainm Ghabril 's nan ostal caomh.

I WILL go out to sow the seed,
In name of Him who gave it growth;
I will place my front in the wind,
And throw a gracious handful on high.
Should a grain fall on a bare rock,
It shall have no soil in which to grow;
As much as falls into the earth,

The dew will make it to be full.

Friday, day auspicious,
The dew will come down to welcome
Every seed that lay in sleep
Since the coming of cold without mercy;
Every seed will take root in the earth,
As the King of the elements desired,
The braird will come forth with the dew,
It will inhale life from the soft wind.

I will come round with my step,
I will go rightways with the sun,
In name of Ariel and the angels nine,
In name of Gabriel and the Apostles kind.

Athair is Mac is Spiorad Naomh,
Bhi toir fas is toradh maoth
Do gach cail a ta 'n am raon,
Gon tar an latha caon.

La Fheill Micheil, la nam buadh,
Cuiridh mi mo chorran cuart
Bun an arbhair mar bu dual,
Togam an ceud bheum gu luath;
Cuirim e tri char mu 'n cuart
Mo cheann, 's mo rann ga luadh,
Mo chulaibh ris an airde tuath;
'S mo ghnuis ri grein ghil nam buadh.

Tilgim am beum fada bhuam,
Duinim mo dha shuil da uair,
Ma thuiteas e na aon dual
Bithidh mo chruachan biochar buan;
Cha tig Cailleach ri an-uair
Dh' iarraidh bonnach boise bhuainn,
Duair thig gaillionn garbh na gruaim
Cha bhi gainne oirnn no cruas.

Father, Son, and Spirit Holy,
Be giving growth and kindly substance
To every thing that is in my ground,
Till the day of gladness shall come.

The Feast day of Michael, day beneficent,
I will put my sickle round about

The root of my corn as was wont;
I will lift the first cut quickly;
I will put it three turns round
My head, saying my rune the while,
My back to the airt of the north;
My face to the fair sun of power.

I shall throw the handful far from me,
I shall close my two eyes twice,
Should it fall in one bunch
My stacks will be productive and lasting;
No Carlin will come with bad times
To ask a palm bannock from us,
What time rough storms come with frowns
Nor stint nor hardship shall be on us.

BEANNACHADH BUANA

REAPING BLESSING

THE day the people began to reap the corn was a day of commotion and ceremonial in the townland. The whole family repaired to the field dressed in their best attire to hail the God of the harvest.

Laying his bonnet on the ground, the father of the family took up his sickle, and facing the sun, he cut a handful of corn. Putting the handful of corn three times sunwise round his head, the man raised the 'Iolach Buana,' reaping salutation. The whole family took up the strain and praised the God of the harvest, who gave them corn and bread, food and flocks, wool and clothing, health and strength, and peace and plenty.

When the reaping was finished the people had a trial called 'cur nan corran,' casting the sickles, and 'deuchain chorran,' trial of hooks. This consisted, among other things, of throwing the sickles high up in the air, and observing how they came down, how each struck the earth, and how it lay on the ground. From these observations the people augured who was to remain single and who was to be married, who was to be sick and who was to die, before the next reaping came round.

DHE beannaich fein mo bhuain,
Gach imir, cluan, agus raon,
Gach corran cama, cuimir, cruaidh,
Gach dias is dual a theid 's an raoid,
Gach dias is dual a theid 's an raoid.

Beannaich gach murn agus mac,
Gach mnaoi agus miuchainn maoth,
Tiuir iad fo sgiath do neairt,
Is tearmaid ann an teach nan naomh,
Tearmaid ann an teach nan naomh.

Cuimrich gach mins, ciob, is uan,
Gach ni, agus mearc, is maon,
Cuartaich fein an treuid 's am buar,
Is cuallaich a chon buailidh chaon,
Cuallaich a chon buailidh chaon.

Air sgath Mhicheil mhil nam feachd,
Mhoire chneas-ghil leac nam buadh,
Bhride mhin-ghil ciabh nan cleachd,
Chaluim-chille nam feart 's nan tuam,
Chaluim-chille nam feart 's nan tuam.

GOD, bless Thou Thyself my reaping,
Each ridge, and plain, and field,
Each sickle curved, shapely, hard,
Each ear and handful in the sheaf,
Each ear and handful in the sheaf.

Bless each maiden and youth,
Each woman and tender youngling,
Safeguard them beneath Thy shield of strength,
And guard them in the house of the saints,
Guard them in the house of the saints.

Encompass each goat, sheep and lamb,
Each cow and horse, and store,
Surround Thou the Rocks and herds,
And tend them to a kindly fold,
Tend them to a kindly fold.

For the sake of Michael head of hosts,
Of Mary fair-skinned branch of grace,
Of Bride smooth-white of ringleted locks,
Of Columba of the graves and tombs,
Columba of the graves and tombs.

BEANNACHADH BUANA

REAPING BLESSING

DI-MAIRT feille ri eirigh greine,
Is cul na deise 's an aird an ear,
Theid mi mach le m' chorran fo m' sgeith,
Is buainidh mi am beum an ceud char.

140

Leigidh mi mo chorran sios
'S an dias biadhchar fo mo ghlac,
Togam suas mo shuil an aird,
Tionndam air mo shail gu grad,

Deiseil mar thriallas a ghrian
Bho 'n airde 'n ear gu ruig an iar,
Bho 'n airde tuath le gluasadh reidh,
Gu fior chre na h-airde deas.

Bheir mi cliu do Righ nan gras
Airson cinneas barr na h-uir,
Bheir e lon dhuinn fein 's dh' an al
Mar a bhairigeas e dhuinn.

Seumas is Eoin, Peadail is Pal,
Moire ghraidh-gheal lan soluis,
* * * * *

* * * * *
Oidhch Fheill-Micheil agus Nollaig,
Biasaidh sinn uile dhe 'n bhonnach.

ON Tuesday of the feast at the rise of the sun,
And the back of the ear of corn to the east,
I will go forth with my sickle under my arm,
And I will reap the cut the first act.

I will let my sickle down
While the fruitful ear is in my grasp,
I will raise mine eye upwards,
I will turn me on my heel quickly,

Rightway as travels the sun
From the airt of the east to the west,
From the airt of the north with motion calm
To the very core of the airt of the south.

I will give thanks to the King of grace
For the growing crops of the ground,
He will give food to ourselves and to the flocks
According as He disposeth to us.

James and John, Peter and Paul,
Mary beloved, the fullness of light,
* * * * *

* * * * *

On Michaelmas Eve and Christmas,
We will all taste of the bannock.

BEANNACHADH FUIRIRIDH

THE BLESSING OF THE PARCHING

WHEN it is necessary to provide a small quantity of meal hastily, ears of corn are plucked and placed in a net made of the tough roots of the yellow bedstraw, bent, or quicken grass, and hung above a slow smokeless fire. The bag is taken down now and again to turn the ears of corn. This net, however, can only be used for bere or barley; rye and oats, being more detachable, require the use of a pot or 'tarran' to dry them. This mode of drying corn is called 'fuirireadh,' parching, and the corn 'fuirireach,' parched. The meal ground from the grain is called 'min fhuiriridh,' parched meal. Bread made of meal thus prepared has a strong peaty flavour much relished by the people.

A LASAIR leith, chaol, chrom,
Tighinn a toll mhullach nam fod,
A lasair leumrach, leathann, theith,
Na teid le do chleid da m' choir.

Gabhail reidh, sheimh, shuairce,
Tighinn mu 'n cuart mo thetheann,
Teine cubhr, caon, cuana,
Nach dean scour, no smuar, no reubann.

Teasaich, cruadhaich mo shiol miamh,
Chon biadh dha mo leanu-beag,
An ainm Chriosda, Righ nan sian,
Thug duinn iodh, is iadh, is beannachd leis,
An ainm Chriosda, Righ nan sian,
Thug duinn iodh, is iadh, is beannachd leis.

THOU flame grey, slender, curved,
Coming from the top pore of the peat,
Thou flame of leaps, breadth, heat,
Come not nigh me with thy quips.

A burning steady, gentle, generous,
Coming round about my quicken roots,
A fire fragrant, fair, and peaceful,
Nor causes dust, nor grief, nor havoc.

Heat, parch my fat seed,
For food for my little child,

In name of Christ, King of the elements,
Who gave us corn and bread and blessing withal,
In name of Christ, King of the elements,
Who gave us corn and bread and blessing withal.

BEANNACHADH BRATHAIN

THE quern songs, like all the labour songs of the people, were composed in a measure suited to the special labour involved. The measure changed to suit the rhythmic motion of the body at work, at times slow, at times fast, as occasion required. I first saw the quern at work in October 1860 in the house of a cottar at Fearann-an-leatha, Skye. The cotter-woman procured some oats in the sheaf. Roughly evening the heads, and holding the corn in one hand and a rod in the other, she set fire to the ears. Then, holding the corn over an old partially-dressed sheep-skin, she switched off the grain. This is called 'gradanadh,' quickness, from the expert handling required in the operation. The whole straw of the sheaf was not burnt, only that part of the straw to which the grain was attached, the flame being kept from proceeding further. The straw was tied up and used for other purposes.

Having fanned the grain and swept the floor, the woman spread out the sheep-skin again and placed the quern thereon. She then sat down to grind, filling and relieving the quern with one hand and turning it with the other, singing the while to the accompaniment of the whirr! whirr! whirr! birr! birr! birr! of the revolving stone. Several strong sturdy boys in scant kilts, and sweet comely girls in nondescript frocks, sat round the peat fire enjoying it fully, and watching the work and listening to the song of their radiant mother. In a remarkably short space of time the grain from the field was converted into meal, and the meal into bannocks, which the unknown stranger was pressed to share. The bread was good and palatable, though with a slight taste of peat, which would probably become pleasant in time.

The second time I saw the quern at work was in January 1865, in the house of a crofter at Breubhaig, Barra, and it reminded me of Mungo Park's description of a similar scene in Africa. The quern was on the floor, with a well-worn cowhide under it. Two women sat opposite one another on the floor with the quern between them. The right leg of each was stretched out, while the knee of the other leg formed a sharp angle, with the foot resting against the knee joint of the straight leg. A fan containing bere lay beside the women, and from this one of them fed the quern, while the other relieved it of the constantly accumulating meal. Each woman held the 'sgonnan,' handle, with which they turned the quern, and as they turned they sang the Quern Blessing here given, to a very pretty air. Then they sang an impromptu song on the stranger, who was hungry and cold, and who was far from home and from the mother who loved him.

When mills were erected, the authorities destroyed the querns in order to compel the people to go to the mills and pay multure, mill dues. This wholesale and inconsiderate destruction of querns everywhere entailed untold hardships on thousands of people living in roadless districts and in distant isles without mills, especially during storms. Among other expedients to which the more remote people resorted was the searching of ancient ruins for the 'pollagan,' mortar mills, of former generations. The mortar is a still more primitive instrument for preparing corn than the quern. It is a block of stone about twenty-four inches by eighteen by eight. The centre and one end of this block are hollowed out to a breadth of about six or eight inches, and a depth of four or five, leaving three gradually sloping sides. The grain is placed in this scoop-like hollow and crushed with a stone. When sufficiently crushed, the meal is thrown out at the open end of the scoop, and fresh grain is put in to follow a similar process. When using the mortar, the woman is on her knees, unless the mortar is on a table.

The meal obtained by this process is called 'pronn, pronnt, pronntach, min phronntaidh,' bruised meal, to distinguish it from 'gradan, gradanach, min ghradain,' quick meal, 'min bhrath, min bhrathain,' quern meal, and 'min mhuille,' mill meal. The crushed meal of the primitive mortar is similar in character to the crushed meal of modern commerce.

The quern and mortar are still used in outlying districts of Scotland and Ireland, though isolatedly and sparingly.

[pp. <page 254>-5

BEANNACHADH BRATHAIN

THE QUERN BLESSING

OIDHCH Inid
Bi feoil againn,
'S bu choir 'uinn sin
Bu choir 'uinn sin.

Leth-cheann circe,
'S da ghreim eorna,
'S bu leoir 'uinn sin
Bu leoir 'uinn sin.

Bi bin againn,
Bi beoir againn,
Bi fion againn,
Bi roic againn.
Meilc is marrum,
Mil is bainne,
Sile fallain,
Meall dheth sin,
Meall dheth sin.

Bi cruit againn,
Bi clar againn,
Bi dus againn,
Bi das againn;
Bi saltair ghrinn,
Nan teuda binn,
'S hi fairchil, righ'nn

Nan dan againn,
Nan dan againn.

ON Ash Eve
We shall have flesh,
We should have that
We should have that.

The cheek of hen,
Two bits of barley,
That were enough
That were enough.

We shall have mead,
We shall have spruce,
We shall have wine,
We shall have feast.
We shall have sweetness and milk produce,
Honey and milk,
Wholesome ambrosia,
Abundance of that,
Abundance of that.

We shall have harp, (small?)
We shall have harp, (pedal?)
We shall have lute,
We shall have horn.
We shall have sweet psaltery
Of the melodious strings
And the regal lyre,
Of the songs we shall have,
Of the songs we shall have.

Bi Bride bhithe, bhana, leinn,
Bi Moire mhine mhathar, leinn.
Bi Micheal mil
Nan lanna liobh,
'S bi Righ nan righ,
'S bi Iosa Criosd
'S bith Spiorad sith
Nan grasa leinn,
Nan grasa leinn.

The calm fair Bride will be with us,
The gentle Mary mother will be with us.
Michael the chief

Of glancing glaves,
And the King of kings
And Jesus Christ,
And the Spirit of peace
And of grace will be with us,
Of grace will be with us.

CRONAN BLEOGHAIN

MILKING CROON

THE milking songs of the people are numerous and varied. They are sung to pretty airs, to please the cows and to induce them to give their milk, The cows become accustomed to these lilts and will not give their milk without them, nor, occasionally, without their favourite airs being sung to them. This fondness of Highland cows for music induces owners of large herds to secure milkmaids possessed of good voices and some 'go.' It is interesting and animating to see three or four comely girls among a fold of sixty, eighty, or a hundred picturesque Highland cows on meadow or mountain slope. The moaning and heaving of the sea afar, the swish of the wave on the shore, the carolling of the lark in the sky, the unbroken song of the mavis on the rock, the broken melody of the merle in the brake, the lowing of the kine without, the response of the calves within the fold, the singing of the milkmaids in unison with the movement of their hands, and of the soft sound of the snowy milk falling into the pail, the gilding of hill and dale, the glowing of the distant ocean beyond, as the sun sinks into the sea of golden glory, constitute a scene which the observer would not, if he could, forget.

THIG, a Bhreannain, o'n a chuan,
Thig, a Thorrainn, buadh nam fear,
Thig, a Mhicheil, mhil a nuas
'S dilinn domh-sa bua mo ghean.
Ho m' aghan, ho m' agh gaoil,
Ho m' aghan, ho m' agh gaoil,
M' aghan gradhach, bo gach airidh,
Sgath an Ard Righ gabh ri d' laogh.

Thig, a Chaluim chaoimh, o'n chro,
Thig, a Bhride mhor nam buar,
Thig, a Mhoire mhin, o'n neol,
'S dilinn domh-sa bo mo luaidh.
Ho m' aghan, ho m' agh gaoil.

Thig am fearan o'n a choill,
Thig an traill a druim nan stuagh,
Thig an sionn cha 'n ann am foill,
A chur aoibh air bo nam buadh.
Ho m' aghan, ho m' agh gaoil.

COME, Brendan, from the ocean,

Come, Ternan, most potent of men,
Come, Michael valiant, down
And propitiate to me the cow of my joy.
Ho my heifer, ho heifer of my love,
Ho my heifer, ho heifer of my love.
My beloved heifer, choice cow of every spieling,
For the sake of the High King take to thy calf.

Come, beloved Colum of the fold,
Come, great Bride of the flocks,
Come, fair Mary from the cloud,
And propitiate to me the cow of my love.
Ho my heifer, ho heifer of my love.

The stock-dove will come from the wood,
The tusk will come from the wave,
The fox will come but not with wiles,
To hail my cow of virtues.
Ho my heifer, ho heifer of my love.

CRONAN BLEOGHAIN

MILKING CROON

SIAN a chuir Moire nam buadh,
Moch is anamoch dol dachaidh is uath,
Buachaille Padruig, is banachaig Bride,
D' ur sion, d' ur dion, 's d' ur comhnadh.
Ho hi holigan, ho m' aighean,
Ho hi holigan, ho m' aighean,
Ho hi holigan, ho m' aighean,
Mo chrodh-laoigh air gach taobh an abhuinn.

Bith buarach chioba air m' aighean siocha,
Bith buarach shioda air m' aighean laoigh,
Bith buarach shugain air crodh na duthcha,
Ach buarach ur air m' aighean gaoil.
Ho hi holigan, ho m' aighean.

Fhaic thu bho ud air an lianu,
'S a laogh mear aic air a bialu,
Dean, a chaomhag, mar a rinn i chianu,
Thoir am bainne, a laoigh na Fiannaich.
Ho hi holigan, ho m' aighean.

THE charm placed of Mary of light,

Early and late going to and from home,
The herdsman Patrick and the milkmaid Bride,
Be saining you and saving you and shielding you.
Ho hi holigan, ho my heifer,
Ho hi holigan, ho my heifer,
Ho hi holigan, ho my heifer,
My calving kine on each side of the river.

A shackle of lint on my elfish heifer,
A shackle of silk on my heifer of calves,
A shackle of straw on the cows of the townland,
But a brand new shackle on my heifer beloved.
Ho hi holigan, ho my heifer.

Seest thou that cow on the plain,
With her frisky calf before her,
Do, thou lovable one, as she did erstwhile,
Give thou thy milk, O calf of 'Fiannach.'
Ho hi holigan, ho my heifer.

BEANNACHADH BLEOGHAIN

MILKING BLESSING

BHEIR Calum-cille dhi-se piseach,
Bheir Coibhi cinneil dhi-se fiar,
Bheir m' aghan ballaidh dhomh-s' am bainne
'S a laogh bainionn air a bial.
Ho! m' aghan, m' aghan, m' aghan,
Ho! m' aghan, caon, ciuin,
M' aghan caomh, caomh, gradhaidh,
Gur e gaol do mhathar thu.

Seall thu 'n druis ud thall a froineadh,
'S an druis eil air loin nan smiar,
Is ionann sin is m' aghan goirridh,
'S a laogh boirionn air a bial.
Ho! m' aghan,--

Bheir Bride bhith nan cire geala,
Li na h-eal am aghan gaoil,
'S bheir Muire mhin nam mire meala,
Dhi-se ceal nan cearca-fraoich,
Ho! m' aghan,--

COLUMBA will give to her progeny,

Coivi the propitious, will give to her grass,
My speckled heifer will give me her milk,
And her female calf before her.
Ho my heifer! heifer! heifer!
Ho my heifer! kindly, calm,
My heifer gentle, gentle, beloved,
Thou art the love of thy mother.

Seest yonder thriving bramble bush
And the other bush glossy with brambles,
Such like is my fox-coloured heifer,
And her female calf before her.
Ho my heifer!--

The calm Bride of the white combs
Will give to my loved heifer the lustre of the swan,
While the loving Mary, of the combs of honey.
Will give to her the mottle of the heather hen.
Ho my heifer!--

HO HOILIGEAN, HO M' AIGHEAN

HO HOILIGEAN, HO MY HEIFERS

EUDAIL thu 's thu dh'an chrodh mhara,
Chra chluasach, bheum chluasach, bheannach;
Chrathadh fual air cruach do sheanar,
'S cha tar thu uam-s' a Luan no Sha'urn.
Ho hoiligean, ho m' aighean!
Ho hoiligean, ho m' aighean!
Ho hoiligean, ho m' aighean!
Mo lochruidh chaomh gach taobh an abhuinn.

Eudail thu 's thu chrodh na tire.
Bheir thu marrum, bheir thu mis dhomh;
Bheir thu bainne barr na ciob dhomh,
'S cha b' e glaisle ghlas an t-siobain.
Ho hoiligean, ho m' aighean!

Eudail thu 's thu chrodh an t-saoghail,
Bheir thu bainne barr an fhraoich dhomh;
Cha bhainne glas air bhlas a chaorain,
Ach bainne meal 's e air gheal na faoileig.
Ho hoiligean, ho m' aighean!

Bheir Bride bhinn dhut linn is ograidh,

Bheir Moire mhin dhut li dha d' chomhdach,
Bheir Michael liobha dhut ri dha d' sheoladh,
'S bheir Iosda Criosda dhut sith is solas.
Ho hoiligean, ho m' aighean!

MY treasure thou, and thou art of the sea kine,
Red eared, notch eared, high horned;
Urine was sprinkled on the rump of thy grandsire,
And thou shalt not win from me on Monday nor Saturday.
Ho hoiligean, ho my heifers!
Ho hoiligean, ho my heifers!
Ho hoiligean, ho my heifers!
My kindly kine on each side of the stream.

My treasure thou, and thou art of the land trine,
Thou wilt give me milk produce, thou wilt give me dainty;
Thou wilt give me milk from the top of the club-moss,
And not the grey water of the sand-drift.
Ho hoiligean, ho my heifers!

My treasure thou, and thou art of the world's kine,
Thou wilt give me milk from the heather tops;
Not grey milk of the taste of the rowan berries,.
But honey milk and white as the sea-gull.
Ho hoiligean, ho my heifers!

The melodious Bride will give thee offspring and young,
The lovely Mary will give thee colour to cover thee,
The lustrous Michael will give thee a star to guide thee,
And Christ Jesu will give thee peace and joy.
Ho hoiligean, ho my heifers!

HO M' AGHAN!

HO, MY HEIFER!

OIDHCHE sin bha 'm Buachaill a muigh
Cha deacha buarach air boin,
Cha deacha geum a beul laoigh,
Caoineadh Buachaill a chruidh,
Caoineadh Buachaill a chruidh.

Ho m' aghan! ho m' aghan!
Ho m' aghan! m' aghan gaoil
Chridheag chridh, choir, ghradhaich,
Air sgath an Ard Righ gabh ri d' laogh.

Oidhche sin bha 'm Buachaill air chall,
Fhuaradh anns an Teampull e.
Righ na gile thighinn a nall!
Righ na greine nuas a neamh!
Righ na greine nuas a neamh!

THE night the Herdsman was out
No shackle went on a cow,
Lowing ceased not from the mouth of calf
Wailing the Herdsman of the flock,
Wailing the herdsman of the flock.

Ho my heifer! ho my heifer!
Ho my heifer! my heifer beloved!
My heartling heart, kind, fond,
For the sake of the High King take to thy calf.

The night the Herdsman was missing,
In the Temple He was found.
The King of the moon to come hither!
The King of the sun down from heaven!
King of the sun down from heaven!

THOIR AM BAINNE

GIVE THY MILK

THOIR am bainne, bho dhonn,
Ce 'n conn ma 'n ceillinn?
Laogh na ba ud braigh na beinge,
'S laogh mo ghraidh-sa air graisich eile.
O! ho! graisich eile.

Thoir am bainne, bho dhonn,
Moir am bainne, bho dhonn,
Thoir am bainne, bho dhonn,
Trom steilleach.

Ach gheobh mo ghaol-sa laoighean cais-fhionn,
Is buarach caon a theid caomh ma casan;
Cha bhuarach gaoisid, fraoich, no asgairt,
Ach buarach dhaor a bheir daoin a Sasgunn.
O! ho! a Sasgunn.

'S gheobh mo righinn-sa finn na maise

151

Buarach min a theid sliom ma casan;
Cha bhuarach cioba, lioin, no asgairt,
Ach buarach shiod thig a nios a Sasgunn.
O! ho! a Sasgunn.

'S gheobh mo chiall-sa fiar is fasga,
'S gheobh i aonach, fraoch, is machair,
'S gheobh i mislean, ciob, is fasbhuain,
'S gheobh i am fion thig 'o shian nan cas-bheann.
O! ho! nan cas-bheann.

GIVE thy milk, brown cow,
For what reason should I conceal?
The [skin of the] calf of yonder cow on the partition,
While the calf of my love is on another grange.
Oh! ho! another grange.

Give thy milk, brown cow,
Give thy milk, brown cow,
Give thy milk, brown cow,
Heavily flowing.

My beloved shall get white-bellied calves,
And a fetter fine that shall go kindly round her legs;
No fetter of hair, nor of heather, nor of lint refuse,
But a dear fetter that men bring from Saxon land.
Oh! ho! from Saxon land.

And my queen maiden of beauty shall get
A fetter smooth to go softly round her legs;
No fetter of cord, nor of lint, nor lint refuse,
But a fetter of silk up from Saxon land.
Oh! ho! from Saxon land.

My beloved shall get grass and shelter,
She shall get hill, heath, and plain,
She shall get meadow-grass, club-rush, and stubble,
And she shall get the wine that comes from the elements of the steep bens.
Oh! ho! the steep bens.

CRONAN BLEOGHAN

MILKING SONG

THIG, a Mhuire, 's bligh a bho,
Thig, a Bhride, 's comraig i,

Thig, a Chaluim-chille chaoimh,
'S iadh do dha laimh mu m' bhoin.
Ho m' aghan, ho m' agh gaoil,
Ho m' aghan, ho m' agh gaoil,
Ho m' aghan, ho m' agh gaoil,
M' aghan cri, coir, gradhach,
An sgath an Ard Righ gabh ri d' laogh.

Thig, a Mhuire, dh' fhios mo bho,
Thig, a Bhride mhor na loin,
Thig, a bhanachaig Iosda Criosda,
'S cur do lamh a nios fo m' bhoin.
Ho m' aghan, ho m' agh gaoil.

Bo lurach dhubh, bo na h-airidh,
Bo a bha-theach, mathair laogh,
Luban siomain air crodh na tire,
Buarach shiod air m' aighean gaoil.
Ho m' aghan, ho m' agh gaoil.

Mo bho dhubh, mo bho dhubh,
Is ionann galar dhomh-s' is dhuit,
Thus a caoidh do luran laoigh,
Mise mo mhac gaoil fo 'n mhuir,
M'aon mhac gaoil fo 'n mhuir.

COME, Mary, and milk my cow,
Come, Bride, and encompass her,
Come, Columba the benign,
And twine thine arms around my. cow.
Ho my heifer, ho my gentle heifer,
Ho my heifer, ho my gentle heifer,
Ho my heifer, ho my gentle heifer,
My heifer dear, generous and kind,
For the sake of the High King take to thy calf.

Come, Mary Virgin, to my cow,
Come, great Bride, the beauteous,
Come, thou milkmaid of Jesus Christ,
And place thine arms beneath my cow.
Ho my heifer, ho my gentle heifer.

Lovely black cow, pride of the ,
First cow of the byre, choice mother of calves,
Wisps of straw round the cows of the townland,
A shackle of silk on my heifer beloved.

Ho my heifer, ho my gentle heifer.

My black cow, my black cow,
A like sorrow afflicts me and thee,
Thou grieving for thy lovely calf,
I for my beloved son under the sea,
My beloved only son under the sea.

BEANNACHADH BUACHAILLEACHD

HERDING BLESSING

BEING a pastoral people, the Highlanders possess much pastoral poetry. The greater part of this is secular with fragments of sacred poetry interspersed. The herding runes are examples of these purely pastoral poems. They are sung by the people as they send their flocks to the pastures, or tend them on the hills, glens, or plains. The customs vary in details in different districts, but everywhere is the simple belief that the King of shepherds watches over men and flocks now as of old--'the same yesterday, to-day, and for ever.'

When a man has taken his herd to the pasture in the morning, and has got a knoll between himself and them, he bids, them a tender adieu, waving his hand, perhaps both hands, towards them, saying:--

'Buachailleachd Bride dh' an tan,
Buan is slan dh' an till sibh.

Munachas Mhuire Mhathar dhuibh,
Luth is lan gun till sibh.

The herding of Bride to the kine,
Whole and well may you return.

The prosperity of Mary Mother be yours,
Active and full may you return.

'Cumraig Chalum-chille ma'r casaibh,
Gu mu slan gun till sibh dachaidh.

'Micheal min-gheal righ nan aigheal
D'ur dion, 's d'ur gleidheadh's d'ur comhnadh.

'Comraig Dhe is Dhomhnach dhuibh
Gum faic mise no mo chroilean sibh.

Cobhair Choibhi dhuibh.

Siubhal coire, siubhal coille,
Siubhal comhnaird fada sola.
Buachailleachd mhin na Moire
Bhith mu'r cinn 's mu'r com 's mu'r cobhair.'

The safeguard of Columba round your feet,
Whole be your return home.

Be the bright Michael king of the angels
Protecting, and keeping, and saving you.

The guarding of God and the Lord be yours
Till I or mine shall see you again.

The help of Coivi to you.

Travelling coire, travelling copse,
Travelling meads long and grassy,
The herding of the fair Mary
Be about your head, your body, and aiding you.

When these patriarchal benedictions are intoned or chanted, and the music floats over moor and loch, the effect is charming to the ear of the listener.

COMRAIG Dhe is Dhomhnuich dhuibh.
Comraig Chriosd a chomhnuidh dhuibh,
Comraig Charmaig 's Chaluim-chille,
Comraig Chairbre, falbh 's a tilleadh,
Is comraig Airighil oirghil oirbh,
Comraig Airighil oirghil oirbh.

Comraig Bhride mhuime dhuibh,
Comraig Mhoire bhuidhe dhuibh,
Iosa Criosda, Mac na sithe,
Righ nan righre, muir is tire,
Is Spioraid siochaint, suthainn, dhuibh,
Spioraid siochaint, suthainn, dhuibh.

THE keeping of God and the Lord on you,
The keeping of Christ always on you,
The keeping of Carmac and of Columba on you,
The keeping of Cairbre on you going and coming,
And the keeping of Ariel the gold-bright on you,
The king of Ariel the gold-bright on you.

The keeping of Bride the foster-mother on you,

155

The keeping of Mary the yellow-haired on you,
Of Christ Jesus, the Son of peace,
The King of kings, land and sea,
And the peace-giving Spirit, everlasting, be yours,
The peace-giving Spirit, everlasting, be yours.

BEANNACHADH BUACHAILLEACHD

HERDING BLESSING

CUIRIDH mi an Di seo romham,
Mar a dh' orduich Righ an domhan,
Bride 'g an gleidheadh, 'g an coimhead, 's 'g an comhnadh,
Air bheann, air ghleann, air chomhnard,
Bride 'g an gleidheadh, 'g an coimhead, 's 'g an comhnadh,
Air bheann, air ghleann, air chomhnard.

Eirich, a Bhride mhin-gheal,
Glac do lion, do chir, agus t' fholt,
Bho rinn thu daibh eolas amhra,
'G an cumail bho chall is bho lochd,
Bho rinn thu daibh colas amhra,
'G an cumail bho chall is bho lochd.

Bho chreag, bho chathan, bho allt,
Bho chadha cam, bho mhille sluic,
Bho shaighde reang nam ban seanga sith,
Bho chridhe mhi-ruin, bho shuil an uilc,
Bho shaighde reang nam ban seanga sith,
Bho chridhe mhi-ruin, bho shuil an uilc.

Mhoire Mhathair, cuallaich an t-al gu leir,
Bhride nam basa mine, dion domh mo spreidh,
Chaluim chaoimh, a naoimh nan ioma buadh,
Comraig dhomh crodh an ail, bairig dhomh buar,
Chaluim chaoimh, a naoimh nan ioma buadh,
Comraig dhomh crodh an ail, bairig dhomh buar.

I WILL place this flock before me,
As was ordained of the King of the world,
Bride to keep them, to watch them, to tend them.
On ben, on glen, on plain,
Bride to keep them, to watch them, to tend them,
On ben, on glen, on plain.

Arise, thou Bride the gentle, the fair,

Take thou thy lint, thy comb, and thy hair,
Since thou to them madest the noble charm,
To keep them from straying, to save them from harm,
Since thou to them madest the noble charm,
To keep them from straying, to save them from harm.

From rocks, from drifts, from streams,
From crooked passes, from destructive pits,
From the straight arrows of the slender ban-shee,
From the heart of envy, from the eye of evil,
From the straight arrows of the slender ban-shee,
From the heart of envy, from the eye of evil.

Mary Mother, tend thou the offspring all,
Bride of the fair palms, guard thou my flocks,
Kindly Columba, thou saint of many powers,
Encompass thou the breeding cows, bestow on me herds,
Kindly Columba, thou saint of many powers,
Encompass thou the breeding cows, bestow on me herds.

BEANNACHADH BUACHAILLEACHD

HERDING BLESSING

SIUBHAL beinne, siubhal baile,
Siubhal featha fada, farsuinn,
Buachailleachd Mhic De mu'r casaibh,
Buan is reidh gun teid sibh dachaidh,
Buachailleachd Mhic De mu'r casaibh,
Buan is reidh gun teid sibh dachaidh.

Comraig Charmaig is Chaluim-chille
Bhith d' ar tearmad a falbh 's a tilleadh,
Agus banachaig nam basa mine,
Bride nan or chiabh donn,
Agus banachaig nam basa mine,
Bride nan or chiabh donn.

TRAVELLING moorland, travelling townland,
Travelling mossland long and wide,
Be the herding of God the Son about your feet,
Safe and whole may ye home return,
Be the herding of God the Son about your feet,
Safe and whole may ye home return.

The sanctuary of Carmac and of Columba

Be protecting you going and coining,
And of the milkmaid of the soft palms,
Bride of the clustering hair golden brown,
And of the milkmaid of the soft palms,
Bride of the clustering hair golden brown.

COMRAIG NAM BA

THE PROTECTION OF THE CATTLE

BLARAGAN reidh, fada, farsuinn,
Faileagan feile fo 'r casan,
Cairdeas Mhic De dh' ar toir dhachaidh
Gu faiche nam fuaran,
Faiche nam fuaran.

Gum bu duinte duibh gach slochd,
Gum bu sumhail duibh gach cnoc,
Gum bu clumhaidh duibh gach nochd,
Am fochar nam fuar-bheann,
Fochar ham fuar-bheann.

Comraig Pheadail agus Phoil,
Comraig Sheumais agus Eoin,
Comraig Bhride mhin 's Mhuir Oigh,
Dh' ar comhlach 's dh' ar cuallach,
O! comraig gach aon dh' an chomhl
Dh' ar comhnadh 's dh' ar cuanadh.

PASTURES smooth, long, and spreading,
Grassy meads aneath your feet,
The friendship of God the Son to bring you home
To the field of the fountains,
Field of the fountains.

Closed be every pit to you,
Smoothed be every knoll to you,
Cosy every exposure to you,
Beside the cold mountains,
Beside the cold mountains.

The care of Peter and of Paul,
The care of James and of John,
The care of Bride fair and of Mary Virgin,
To meet you and to tend you,
Oh! the care of all the band

To protect you and to strengthen you.

GLEIDHEADH TREUID

GUARDING THE FLOCKS

GUN gleidheadh Moire min an ciob,
Gun gleidheadh Bride bith an ciob,
Gun gleidheadh Calum-cille an ciob,
Gun gleidheadh Maol-ribhe an ciob,
Gun gleidheadh Carmag an ciob,
O'n mhi-chu 's o'n mharhh-chu.

Gun gleidheadh Odhran an crodh,
Gun gleidheadh Maodhan an crodh,
Gun gleidheadh Donnan an crodh,
Gun gleidheadh Moluag an crodh,
Gun gleidheadh Maolruan an crodh,
Am boglach 's an crualach.

Gun gleidheadh Spiorad foir an treud,
Gun gleidheadh Mac Moir Oigh an treud,
Gun gleidheadh Ti na gloir an treud,
Gun gleidheadh an Teoir an treud,
Bho reubain 's bho mhearchall,
Bho reubain 's bho mhearchall.

MAY Mary the mild keep the sheep,
May Bride the calm keep the sheep,
May Columba keep the sheep,
May Maolruba keep the sheep,
May Carmac keep the sheep,
From the fox and the wolf.

May Oran keep the kine,
May Modan keep the kine,
May Dorman keep the kine,
May Moluag keep the kine,
May Maolruan keep the kine,
On soft land and hard land.

May the Spirit of peace preserve the flocks,
May the Son of Mary Virgin preserve the flocks,
May the God of glory preserve the flocks,
May the Three preserve the flocks,
From wounding and from death-loss,

From wounding and from death-loss.

CRONAN CUALLAICH

A HERDING CROON

AN crodh an diugh a dol imirig,
Hill-i-ruin is o h-ug o,
Ho ro la ill o,
Hill-i-ruin is o h-ug o,
Dol a dh' itheadh feur na cille,
Hill-i-ruin is o h-ug o,
Am buachaille fein ann 'g an iomain,
Ho ro la ill o,
Hill-i-ruin is o h-ug o,
'G an cuallach, 'g an cuart, 'g an tilleadh,
Hill-i-ruin is o h-ug o,
Bride bhith-gheal bhi 'g am blighinn,
Hill-i-ruin is o h-ug o,
Muire mhin-gheal bhi 'g an glidheadh,
Hill-i-ruin is o h-ug o,
'S Iosa Criosda air chinn an slighe,
Iosa Criosda air chinn an slighe.
Hill-i-ruin is o h-ug o.

THE cattle are to-day going a-flitting,
Hill-i-ruin is o h-ug o,
Ho ro la ill o,
Hill-i-ruin is o h-ug o,
Going to eat the grass of the burial-place,
Hill-i-ruin is o h-ug o,
Their own herdsman there to tend them,
Ho ro la ill o,
Hill-i-ruin is o h-ug o,
Tending them, fending them, turning them,
Hill-i-ruin is o h-ug o,
Be the gentle Bride milking them,
Hill-i-ruin is o h-ug o,
Be the lovely Mary keeping them,
Hill i-ruin is o h-ug o,
And Jesu Christ at the end of their journey,
Jesu Christ at the end of their journey.
Hill-i-ruin is o h-ug o.

BEANNACHADH GUIR

HATCHING BLESSING

The reciter of this poem, Donald Maclean, was a native of the parish of Small Isles. He emigrated with many others to Canada. After an absence of many years he returned, as he said, 'Feuch am faighinn larach mo dha bhonn a bhothan, agus leathad mo dha shlinnein a dh' uaigh ann am fearann mo dhuthchais agus ann an uir m' aithriche'--' To see if I could get the site of my two soles of a bothy and the breadth of my two shoulders of a grave in the land of my heredity and in the lair of my fathers.' Not having obtained these in the land of his birth, Donald Maclean returned to the land of his adoption. Maclean heard this poem, and many other poems and tales, in Canada from a woman called 'Sorcha Chlann Radhail,' Clara Clanranald, beside whom he lived for sixteen years. When so many of the small crofts of Uist were converted into large farms, the people removed and not absorbed among the remaining crofters, emigrated to Nova Scotia, Prince Edward Island, and Cape Breton. Clara Clanranald's people had been evicted from Ormacleit, South Uist. She spoke so much of Uist and of the Clanranalds that she came to be known by the name of her loved chief.

When Donald Maclean left Canada, ten or twelve years ago, Clara was 102 years of age. She was still active and industrious, and in the possession of all her faculties, and of all her love for 'the old land.' When Maclean went to bid her good-bye she took his hand in her two hands, and looking him full in the face with her large lustrous blue eyes moist with tears, said:--

'Tha thu falbh a ghaoil a Dhomhnuill, agus Dia mor bhi eadar do dha shlinnein. Bu to fein an deagh nabaidh agus an caraide caomh. Ma 's a h-e agus gun ruig thu null fearann do dhuthchais agus duthaich do bhreith, agus gum feumair thu tilleadh a nall dh'an fhonn-sa rithist, tha mise cur mar bhoid agus mar bhriathar ort, agus mar naoi riaraiche nam bana-sith, thu dhol gu ruig Cladh Mhicheil ann an Ormacleit, an Uibhist, agus thu thoir as a sin thugam-sa deannan beag urach a churar air clar mo chridhe-sa la mo bhais.

'Agus Micheal caomh-gheal, cro-gheal, cra-gheal,
Ga do dhiona, ga do chaomhna, ga do charamh,
Le treun a laimhe, le nimh a ghaise,
Fo sgaile drilleanach a sgeith.'

'Thou art going away, beloved Donald, and may the great God be between thy two shoulders. Thou thyself welt the good neighbour and the kind friend. If it be that thou reach the land of thy heredity and the country of thy birth, and that thou shouldst have to come back again to the land of thine adoption, I place it upon thee as a vow and as a charge, and as the nine fulfilments of the fairy women, that thou go to the burial-place of Michael at Ormacleit in Uist, and bring to me from there a little earth that shall be placed upon the tablet of my heart the day that I die.

'And may Michael kind-white, strong-white, red-white,
Preserve thee, protect thee, provide for thee,
With the might of his hand, with the point of his spear,
Under the shade of his shimmering shield.'

EIRIDH mi moch maduinn Luan,
Gabhaidh mi mo rann 's mo dhuan,

Theid mi deiseil le mo chuaich,
Gu nead mo chearc le beachd na buaidh.

Cuiream mo lamh thoisg ri m' chich,
Mo lamb dheas ri taic mo chridh,
Iarram gliocas graidh an Ti,
Ta pailt an agh, an al 's an ni.

Duineam mo dha shuil air ball,
Mar dhallan-da ni snagan mall,
Sineam mo lamh chli a null
Gu nead mo chirc an taobh ud thall.

I WILL rise early on the morning of Monday,
I will sing my rune and rhyme,
I will go sunwise with my cog
To the nest of my hen with sure intent.

I will place my left hand to my breast,
My right hand to my heart,
I will seek the loving wisdom of Him
Abundant in grace, in broods, and in flocks.

I will close my two eyes quickly,
As in blind-man's buff moving slowly;
I will stretch my left hand over thither
To the nest of my hen on yonder side.

An ceud ugh a bheir mi m' cheann,
Cuiream tuathal e air mo cheann,
* * * *
* * * *

Togam mo lamh thoisg an suas,
Sineam i gun chlos gu luath,
Togam an da ugh an nuas,
Bithidh an uair sin tri 's a chuaich.

Sineam mo lamh dheas a ris,
Togam leath 's a ghreis a tri,
Iarram riaghladh air an Righ,
Bithidh, mo riar, a sia 's an linn.

Lamh mo thoisg an dara h-uair,
Togam ceithir leath an nuas,
An ainm Chriosda Righ nam buadh,

Bithidh an uair sin deich 's a chuaich.

An dorn deas is treasa coir,
Togam leis a dha fo m' mheoir,
Bithidh aig sgur mo ghur gun sgod,
Fo uchd na circe brice moir.

Cuiream suidhe air an da cheann,
Is mi mar bhalbhan balbh 's an am,
An ainm Chruithear mhuir is bheann,
An ainm gach naoimh is ostail ann.

An ainm Thrianailt uile naoimh,
An ainm Chalum-chille chaoimh,
Cuiream iad fo chirc Di-ardaoin,
Thig an t-alach aigh Di-aoin.

The first egg which I shall bring near me,
I will put it withershins round my head.
* * * *
* * * *

I will raise my left hand on high,
I will stretch it without halt quickly,
I will lift the two eggs down hither,
There shall be then three in the cog.

I will stretch my right hand again,
I will lift with it at the time three,
I will seek ruling from the King,
Then verily there shall be six in the clutch.

I will raise my left hand the second time,
I will lift four with it down,
In name of Christ, King of power,
There shall then be ten in the cog.

The right fist of strongest claim,
I will lift with it two in my fingers,
Thus at ceasing my brood will be complete,
Beneath the breast of the speckled big hen.

I will put soot on their two ends,
And I dumb as the dumb the while,
In name of Creator of sea and hill,
In name of saints and apostles all.

In name of the most Holy Trinity,
In name of Columba kindly,
I will set the eggs on Thursday,
The gladsome brood will come on Friday.

COMHARRACHADH NAN UAN

MARKING THE LAMBS

THE marking of the lambs is done on Thursday, being St Columba's Day. Upon no account would the people mark their lambs on Friday, or in any manner draw blood on that day. Nor till lately would they use iron in any form on Friday.

A blacksmith in Benbecula, a Protestant, an excellent man and an admirable tradesman, never opened his smithy on Friday. He maintained that 'that was the least he could do to honour his Master.'

When the lambs are marked, the people collect the bits taken out of their ears, and carefully bury them beyond the reach of beast or bird. They say that a plant, which they call 'gearradh-chluasach,' literally ear-cuts, ear-clips, grows from them. This plant is generally found growing where a carcase has been buried, and when ripe, it is cut, tied up in a bunch, and suspended from the 'casan ceanghail,' couple above the door of the lamb-cot, and dedicated to

'Moire mhin-gheal nan grasa buan,
Air shealbh chaorach air ghaol uan.'

The fair-white Mary of lasting graces,
For luck of sheep and love of lambs.

The marks made on the ears of sheep and lambs are varied and descriptive in name, as:--'barr,' 'beum,' 'cluigean,' 'cliopan,' 'cliopadh,' 'crocan,' 'corran,' 'duile,' 'meaghlan,' 'meangan,' 'sgolta,' 'slios,' 'snathad,' 'sulag,' 'toll.' These marks and their modifications are said to number over 250 in the island of Benbecula, in the island of North Uist over 480, and in the island of South Uist over 500. The people know all these marks and modifications at a glance.

When a man marries, it is considered a good omen of the union when the marks on his own sheep and those on the sheep brought him by his wife are nearly alike, and the necessary change easily effected.

'IARRATAS NA CAOIRE BIGE.

Na lom mo cheann,
'S na loisg mo chnamhan.'

THE REQUEST OF THE LITTLE SHEEP.

Do not clip my head,
And do not burn my bones.

The small native sheep have a long tuft of wool called 'sguman' coming down the face. They are hardy, picturesque little animals, almost wholly free from the innumerable diseases which the larger but softer breeds of sheep have brought in their train. The sheep is regarded with a veneration which is not extended to the cow or other animals.

BIDH mo sgian ur, geur, glan, gun mheirg,
Mo bhreacan fo m' ghlun le mo luirich dheirg,
Cuiream deiseil mo chleibh an ceud bheum gu sealbh,
An ath fhear na dheigh leis a ghrein mar ni falbh.

Uan firionn gun ghaoid, air aon dath, gun chearb,
Leig a mach ris an raon, fhuil chraobhach na tearb,
Ma mhaireas a chraobh air an fhraoch le barr dearg,
Bith mo shealbhan gun ghaoid fad 's nach caochail mi 'n t-ainm.

An Triuir ta shuas an Cathair nam buadh,
Bhi buachailleachd mo threuid is mo bhuair,
'G an iomachair ri teas, ri gaillinn 's ri fuachd,
Le beannachd nam buadh 'g an saodadh a nuas
Bho 'n tulaich ud shuas gu airidh.

MY knife will be new, keen, clean, without stain,
My plaid beneath my knee with my red robe,
I will put sunwise round my breast the first cut for luck,
The next one after that with the sun as it moves.

A male lamb without blemish, of one colour, without defect,
Allow thou out on the plain, nor his flowing blood check,
If the froth remains on the heather with red top,
My flock will be without flaw as long as I change not the name.

The Three who are above in the City of glory,
Be shepherding my flock and my kine,
Tending them duly in heat, in storm, and in cold,
With the blessing of power driving them down
From yonder height to the sheiling fold.

Ainm Airil is ailne snuadh,
Ainm Ghabril fadh an Uain,
Ainm Raphael flath nam buadh,
'G an cuartach is 'g an tearnadh.

Ainm Mhuiril is Mhuire Oigh,

Ainm Pheadail agus Phoil,
Ainm Sheumais agus Eoin,
Gach aingheal 's ostal air an toir,
'G an gleidheadh beo le 'n alach,
'G an gleidheadh beo le 'n alach.

The name of Ariel of beauteous bloom,
The name of Gabriel herald of the Lamb,
The name of Raphael prince of power,
Surrounding them and saving them.

The name of Muriel and of Mary Virgin,
The name of Peter and of Paul,
The name of James and of John,
Each angel and apostle on their track,
Keeping them alive and their progeny,
Keeping them alive and their progeny.

AM BEANNACHD LOMBAIDH

THE CLIPPING BLESSING

WHEN a man has shorn a sheep and has set it free, he waves his hand after it and says:--

FALBH lom 's thig molach,
Beir am boirionn Bealltain,
Bride mhin a bhi dha d' chonaill,
Moire gheal dha t' aurais,
Moire gheal dha t' aurais.

Micheal mil a bhi dha d' dhion
Bho 'n mhi-chu is bho 'n an-chu,
Bho 'n mhac-tir 's bho 'n mhadhan stig,
'S bho ianaibh ineach call-ghob,
Bho ianaibh ineach cam-ghob.

Go shorn and come woolly,
Bear the Beltane female lamb,
Be the lovely Bride thee endowing,
And the fair Mary thee sustaining,
The fair Mary sustaining thee.

Michael the chief be shielding thee
From the evil dog and from the fox,
From the wolf and from the sly bear,
And from the taloned birds of destructive bills,

From the taloned birds of hooked bills.

DUAN DEILBH

THE CHANT OF THE WARPING

DURING the winter months the women of Highland households are up late and early at 'calanas'--this comprehensive term embracing the whole process of wool-working from the raw material to the finished cloth. The process is an important factor in the internal economy of a Highland family. The industry of these women is wonderful, performed lovingly, uncomplainingly, day after day, year after year, till the sands of life run down. The life in a Highland home of the crofter class is well described in the following lines:--

'Air oidhche fhada gheamhraidh
Theid teanndadh ri gniamh,
A toir eolas do chloinn
Bith an seann duine liath,
An nighean a cardadh,
A mhathair a sniamh,
An t-iasgair le a shnathaid
A caramh a lian.'

In the long winter night
All are engaged,
Teaching the young
Is the grey-haired sage,
The daughter at her carding,
The mother at her wheel,
While the fisher mends his net
With his needle and his reel.

'Calanas' is an interesting process. The wool is carefully sorted and the coarser parts put aside. It is then washed and laid out to dry, and again examined and teased, and all lumps and refuse taken out.

If the wool is meant to be made into very fine cloth, it is drawn on combs of specially long teeth; if into ordinary cloth, it is carded on the cards without going through the combs. After carding, the wool is made into 'rolagan,' rowans, and spun into thread, which is arranged into hanks. At this stage the thread is generally dyed, although occasionally the wool is dyed after the teasing process and before being carded. The work of dyeing requires much care and knowledge and practical skill. It is done with native plants gathered with patient care from the rocks and hills, moors and fields and lakes, and with certain earths. When it is considered that a thorough knowledge of plants is necessary, their locality, their colouring properties, whether of root, stem, or leaf, and the stage of growth or decay, it will be understood that those who use them need much intelligence All Highland women are practical dyers, some more skilful than others. From infancy they are trained in 'calanas,' and in plants and dyeing; the whole clothing, including the blankets, of the household being dependent upon their skill and industry. Are there any other women in any class who can show such widespread skill and intelligence as these Highland women show in wool-working and dyeing operations? Home-made tartans and other fabrics, made many generations, sometimes centuries, ago, are not only wonderfully fine in texture, but all the different colours are remarkably bright and beautiful.

The Celts must have had an eye for colour in very early times. The Book of Kells is said by experts to be the most beautiful illuminated manuscript in the world. It is believed to have been written in the Columban monastery of Iona, and to have escaped the Norse destruction of mss. and been carried to the Columban monastery of Kells. Not only are the forms of the initial letters in the mss. marvellously intricate and artistic, but the different pigments used in colouring are still bright and beautiful and fresh, while the colouring of copies made during this century is already sickly and faded.

The pattern of the tartan or other cloth to be woven is first designed on a small piece of wood, the thread being placed on the wood according to the design proposed. This is called 'suidheachadh,' setting. It is a work that requires patient care and skill in order to bring out the pattern correctly. The Chant of the Warping is feelingly intoned by the women in warping the web. When a word or a phrase has struck their minds, they stop singing in order to emphasise the sentiment in a word or a phrase of their own, beseeching Mary's beloved Son to give them strength to observe His laws. These pious interjections and momentary stoppages may not add to the beauty of the singing, but they do to the picturesqueness.

DAORN nam buadh.
Gu deilbh 's gu luadh,
Bidh ceud gu leth dual
Ri aireamh.

Snath gorm gu math caol,
Dha gheala ri a thaobh,
Agus sgarlaid ri taobh
A mhadair.

THURSDAY of beneficence,
For warping and waulking,
An hundred and fifty strands there shall be
To number.

Blue thread, very fine,
Two of white by its side,
And scarlet by the side
Of the madder.

Bidh mo dheilbh gu math reidh,
Thoir do beannachd dhomh, Dhe,
Is do gach uile fo m' chleith
'S an fhardaich.

A Mhicheil, aingil nam buadh,
A Mhoire mhin-ghil tha shuas,
A Chriosd, a Bhuachaill an t-sluagh,
Dean bhur beannachd bi-bhuan
A bhairig.

Do gach neach laigheas sios,
An ainm Athar is Chriosd,
Agus Spiorad na siochaint
Ghrasmhor.

Crath a nuas oirnn mar dhriuchd,
Gliocas caon na ban chiuin,
Nach do dhibir riamh iul
An Ard Righ.

Cum air falbh gach droch shuil,
Gach uile mhuinntir droch ruin,
Coisrig cur agus dluth
Gach snathla.

Cur do ghairdean mu 'n cuairt,
Air gach te bhios ga luadh,
Agus dean a tearmad aig uair
A saruich.

Thoir domh subhailcean mor,
Mar bh' aig Muire ri a lo,
Chum 's gun sealbhaich mi gloir
An Ard Righ

My warp shall he very even,
Give to me Thy blessing, O God,
And to all who are beneath my roof
In the dwelling.

Michael, thou angel of power,
Mary fair, who art above,
Christ, Thou Shepherd of the people,
Do ye your eternal blessing
Bestow

On each one who shall lie down,
In name of the Father and of Christ,
And of the Spirit of peacefulness,
And of grace.

Sprinkle down on us like dew
The gracious wisdom of the mild woman.
Who neglected never the guidance
Of the High King.

Ward away every evil eye,
And all people of evil wishes,
Consecrate the woof and the warp
Of every thread.

Place Thou Thine arm around
Each woman who shall be waulking it,
And do Thou aid her in the hour
Of her need.

Give to me virtues abundant,
As Mary had in her day,
That I may possess the glory
Of the High King

Bho 'n 's tus a Dhe tha toir fas,
Do gach gne agus gnaths,
Thoir dhuinn olainn thar bharr
An fheuir ghlais.

Coisrig sealbh arms gach ait,
Le 'n uain bheaga bhinne bhath,
Is cuir an lionmhoireachd al
Ar treudais.

Chum 's gu 'm faigh sinn diubh cloimh,
Bainne sultmhor r' a ol,
Is nach hi gainn oirnn a chomhdach
Eirigh.

Since Thou, O God, it is who givest growth,
To each species and kind,
Give us wool from the surface
Of the green grass.

Consecrate the flock in every place,
With their little lambs melodious, innocent,
And increase the generations
Of our herds.

So that we may obtain from them wool,
And nourishing milk to drink,
And that no dearth may be ours
Of day clothing.

BEANNACHD BEAIRTE

LOOM BLESSING

FUIDHEAGAN no corr do shnath
Cha do chum 's cha chum mo lamh.

Gach dath a ta 's a bhogha-fhrois
Chaidh troimh mo mheoirean fo na chrois,

Geal is dubh, dearg is madar,
Uaine, ciar-ghlas, agus sgarlaid,

Gorm, is grisionn 's dath na caorach,
'S caoibean cha robh dhith air aodach.

Guidhim Bride bith na faolachd,
Guidhim Muire min na gaolachd,
Guidhim Iosa Criosd na daonnachd,
Gun mi fein dhol eug a 'n aonais,
Gun mi fein dhol eug a 'n aonais.

THRUMS nor odds of thread
My hand never kept, nor shall keep,

Every colour in the bow of the shower
Has gone through my fingers beneath the cross,

White and black, red and madder,
Green, dark grey, and scarlet,

Blue, and roan, and colour of the sheep,
And never a particle of cloth was wanting.

I beseech calm Bride the generous,
I beseech mild Mary the loving,
I beseech Christ Jesu the humane,
That I may not die without them,
That I may not die without them.

SUIDHEACHADH NA H-IOMAIRT

SETTING THE IOMAIRT

'IMIRT,' 'iomairt,' 'iumairt,' 'umairt' is cloth striped lengthwise, not crosswise. While the warp of the 'iomairt' is composed of stripes of various colours, the weft is confined to one--generally light blue, dark blue, or black. This cloth was confined to women's use, in the 'earasaid,' the 'tonnag,' the 'guaileachan,' and the petticoat. Setting the 'iomairt,' like setting other warp, and setting the eggs, and many other operations of the people, was done on Thursday, that being the day of St Columba. Framing the web is a work of much anxiety to the housewife, and she and her maidens are up very early to put the thread in order.

The thread of the 'iomairt,' like that of the tartan, was very fine, hard-spun and double twisted, rendering the cloth extremely durable.

AN dubh mu'n gheal,
An geal mu'n dubh,
An t-uain am meadhon an deirg,
An dearg am meadhon an duibh,

A n dubh am meadhon an deirg,
An dearg am meadhon a ghil,
An geal am meadhon an uaine,
An t-uaine am meadhon a ghil.

An geal am meadhon a ghuirm,
An gorm am meadhon na sgarlaid,
* * * *
* * * *

An sgarlaid ris a ghorm,
An gorm ris an sgarlaid,
An sgarlaid ris an dubh,
An dubh ris an sgarlaid.

Snathla ri da shnathla
Do dha dhath,
Da shnathla dhubh,
Ri aon snathla geal.

Seachd snathla ri coig,
Coig ri tri,
Tri ri dha,
Dha ri aon,
Anns gach oir.

THE black by the white,

172

The white by the black,
The green in the middle of the red,
The red in the middle of the black.

The black in the middle of the red,
The red in the middle of the white,
The white in the middle of the green,
The green in the middle of the white.

The white in the middle of the blue,
The blue in the middle of the scarlet,
* * * *
* * * *

The scarlet to the blue,
The blue to the scarlet,
The scarlet to the black,
The black to the scarlet.

A thread to two threads
Of two colours,
Two threads of black
To one thread of white.

Seven threads to five,
Five to three,
Three to two,
Two to one,
In each border.

BEANNACHADH GARMAIN

LOOM BLESSING

IN the Outer Isles women generally do the weaving, while in the Inner Isles and on the mainland it is usually done by men. In Uist, when the woman stops weaving on Saturday night she carefully ties up her loom and suspends the cross or crucifix above the sleay. This is for the purpose of keeping away the brownie, the banshee, the 'peallan,' and all evil spirits and malign influences from disarranging the thread and the loom. And all this is done with loving care and in good faith, and in prayer and purity of heart.

BEANNAICH, a Thriath nam flath fial,
Mo bheirt 's gach sian a to 'n am choir,
Beannaich, mi 'n am uile ghniomh
Dean mi tiaruinte ri m' bheo.

Bho gach gruagach is ban-shith,
Bho gach miorun agus bron,
Cuidich mi, a Chuidich-Thi,
Fad 's a bhios mi 'n tir nam beo.

An ainm Mhuire mhin nam feart,
Chalum-chille cheart nam buadh,
Coistrig ceithir phuist mo bheairt,
Gun am beairtich mi Di-luain.

A casachan, a slinn, 's a spal,
A h-iteachean, a snath, 's a gual,
A crann-aodaich, 's a crane-snath,
Fuidheagan is snath nan dual.

Gach aodach dubh, geal, is ban,
Grisionn, lachdunn, sgaireach, ruadh,
Thoir do bheannachd anns gach ait,
Air gach spal a theid fo dhual.

Mar sin bidh mo bheairt gun bheud,
Gu'n an eirich mi Di-luain;
Bheir Muire mhin-gheal dhomh dh' a speis,
'S cha bhi eis air nach faigh mi buaidh.

BLESS, O Chief of generous chiefs,
My loom and everything a-near me,
Bless me in my every action,
Make Thou me safe while I live.

From every brownie and fairy woman,
From every evil wish and sorrow,
Help me, O Thou helping Being,
As long as I shall be in the land of the living.

In name of Mary, mild of deeds,
In name of Columba, just and potent,
Consecrate the four posts of my loom,
Till I begin on Monday.

Her pedals, her sleay, and her shuttle,
Her reeds, her warp, and her cogs,
Her cloth-beam, and her thread-beam,
Thrums and the thread of the plies.

Every web, black, white, and fair,

Roan, dun, checked, and red,
Give Thy blessing everywhere,
On every shuttle passing under the thread.

Thus will my loom be unharmed,
Till I shall arise on Monday;
Beauteous Mary will give me of her hove,
And there shall be no obstruction I shall not overcome.

COISRIGEADH AN AODAICH

FORMERLY throughout the Highlands and Islands the cloth for the family was made at home. At present home-made clothing is chiefly made in the Islands, and even there to a lesser extent than formerly.

After the web of cloth is woven it is waulked, to thicken and strengthen and brighten it. The frame on which the cloth is waulked is a board some twelve to twenty-four feet long and about two feet broad, grooved lengthwise along its surface. The frame is called 'cleith,' wattle, and, 'cleith-luaidh,' waulking-wattle, probably from its having been originally constructed of wattle-work. The waulking-frame is raised upon trestles, while the waulking-women are ranged on seats on either side, about two feet of space being allowed to each woman. The web is unrolled and laid along the board. It is then saturated with ammonia, warm water, and soap-suds, and the women work it vigorously from side to side across the grooves of the frame, slowly moving it lengthwise also, that each part of the cloth may receive due attention. The lateral movement of the cloth is sunwise. Occasionally the waulking-board is laid on the ground instead of on trestles, and the women work the cloth with their feet instead of with their hands.

Generally the waulking-women are young maidens, a few married women of good voice being distributed among them. They sing as they work, one singing the song, the others the chorus. Their songs are varied, lively, and adapted to the class of work. Most of them are love-songs, with an occasional impromptu song on some passing event--perhaps on the casual stranger who has looked in, perhaps a wit combat between two of the girls about the real or supposed merits or demerits of their respective lovers. These wit combats are much enjoyed, being often clever, caustic, and apt.

A favourite subject at these waulkings is Prince Charlie, and a favourite song is 'Morag'--little Marion--the endearing term under which the Prince is veiled. The words of the song are vigorous and passionate, and the air stirring, while the subject is one to fire the hearts and imaginations of the people even at this distance of time, and notwithstanding the spoliations, oppressions, and butcheries inflicted on their fathers through their adherence to 'Morag.'

The song begins as follows:--

CHORUS. 'Agus ho Mhorag,
Ho ro na ho ro gheallaidh,
Agus ho Mhorag.

Mhorag chiatach a chul dualaich,
'S e do luaidh tha tighinn air m' aire.

And ho ro Morag,
Ho ro na ho ro darling,
And ho ro Morag,

Beauteous Morag of the clustering locks
To sing of thee is my intent.

Ma dh' imich thu null thar chuan
Gu mu luadh thig thu dachaidh.

Cuimhnich thoir leat bannal ghruagach,
A luaidheas an clo-ruadh gu daingean.'

If thou art gone beyond the sea,
Prithee hasten home to me.

Remember, bring a band of maidens,
Who will waulk the red cloth firmly.

When the women have waulked the cloth, they roll up the web and place it on end in the centre of the frame. They then turn it slowly and deliberately sunwise along the frame, saying with each turn of the web:

'Chan ath-aodach seo.
Chan fhaoigh seo.
Cha chuid cleir no sagairt seo.'

This is not second clothing.
This cloth is not thigged.
This is not the property of cleric or priest.

Another form is:--

'Roinn a h-aon, roinn a dha, roinn a
tri, roinn a ceithir, roinn a coig, roinn a
sia, roinn a seachd, roinn a seachd.

Division one, division two, division
three, division four, division five, division
six, division seven, division seven.

'Chan aodach seo do shagairt no chleir,
Ach 's aodach e do mo Dhomh'lan caomhach fein,

Do m' chombanach graidh 's do Iain an aigh,
'S do Mhuiril is aillidh sgeimh.'

This is not cloth for priest or cleric,
But it is cloth for my own little Donald of love,
For my companion beloved, for John of joy,
And for Muriel of loveliest hue.

Each member of the household for whom the cloth is intended is mentioned by name in the consecration. The cloth is then spat upon, and slowly reversed end by end in the name of Father and of Son and of Spirit till it stands again in the centre of the frame. The ceremony of consecrating the cloth is usually intoned, the women, hitherto gay and vivacious, now solemn and subdued, singing in unison. The woman who leads in the consecration is called 'coisreagan,' consecrator or celebrant. After the cloth is waulked and washed it is rolled up. This is called 'coilleachadh'--stretching,-- 'coillcachadh an aodaich'--stretching the cloth,--a process done with great care in order to secure equal tension throughout the web.

The operation of waulking is a singularly striking scene, and one which Highlanders cherish wherever situated.

[pp. <page 308>-9

COISRIGEADH AN AODAICH

THE CONSECRATION OF THE CLOTH

IS math a ghabhas mi mo rann,
A teurnadh le gleann;
Aon rann,
Da rann,
Tri rann,
Ceithir rann,
Coig rann,
Sia rann,
Seachd rann,
Seachd gu lath rann
Seachd gu lath rann.

Nar a gonar fear an eididh,
Nar a reubar e gu brath,
Cian theid e 'n cath no 'n comhrag,
Sgiath chomarach an Domhnach da,
Can theid e 'n cath no 'n comhrag,
Sgiath chomarach an Domhnach da.

Chan ath-aodach seo, 's chan fhaoigh e,

'S cha chuid cleir no sagairt e.

Biolair uaine ga buain fo
'S air a toir do mhnai gun fhiosd;
Lurg an fheidh an ceann an sgadain,
'S an caol chalp a bhradain bhric.

WELL can I say my rune,
Descending with the glen;
One rune,
Two runes,
Three runes,
Four runes,
Five runes,
Six runes.
Seven runes,
Seven and a half runes,
Seven and a half runes.

May the man of this clothing never be wounded,
May torn he never be;
What time he goes into battle or combat,
May the sanctuary shield of the Lord be his.
What time he goes into battle or combat,
May the sanctuary shield of the Lord be his.

This is not second clothing and it is not thigged,
Nor is it the right of sacristan or of priest.

Cresses green culled beneath a stone,
And given to a woman in secret.
The shank of the deer in the head of the herring,
And in the slender tail of the speckled salmon.

BEANNACHADH SEILG

HUNTING BLESSING

A YOUNG man was consecrated before he went out to hunt. Oil was put on his head, a bow was placed in his hand, and he was required to stand with bare feet on the bare grassless ground. The dedication of the young hunter was akin to those of the 'maor,' the judge, the chief, and the king, on installation. Many conditions were imposed on the young man, which he was required to observe throughout life. He was not to take life wantonly. He was not to kill a bird sitting, nor a beast lying down, and he was not to kill the mother of a brood, nor the mother of a suckling. Nor was he to kill an unfledged bird nor a suckling beast, unless it might be the young of a bird, or of a beast, of prey. It was at all times permissible and laudable to destroy certain clearly defined birds and beasts of prey and evil reptiles, with their young.

BHO m' leasraidh ghineadh thu a mhic,
Seolaim thu an t-iul tha ceart,
An ainm naomh nan aon ostal deug,
An ainm Mhic De chaidh a reubadh leat.

An ainm Sheumais, Pheadail, agus Phail,
Eoin bhaistidh, is Eoin ostail tha shuas,
Lucais leigh, agus Steafain a chraidh,
Mhuiril mhin, is Mhoire mathair Uain.

An ainm Phadra naoimh nam feart,
Agus Charmaig nan ceart 's nan tuam,
Chaluim chaoimh, 's Adhamhnain nan reachd,
Fhite bhith, is Bhride bhliochd is bhuar.

An ainm Mhicheil mil nan slogh,
An ainm Airil og nan snuadh,
An ainm Uiril nan ciabhan oir,
Agus Ghabrail fadh Oigh nam buadh.

An trath a dhuineas to do shuil,
Cha lub thu do ghlun 's cha ghluais,
Cha leon thu lach bhios air an t-snamh,
Chaoidh cha chreach thu h-alach uaip.

FROM my loins begotten wert thou, my son,
May I guide thee the way that is right,
In the holy name of the apostles eleven
In name of the Son of God torn of thee.

In name of James, and Peter, and Paul,
John the baptist, and John the apostle above,
Luke the physician, and Stephen the martyr,
Muriel the fair, and Mary mother of the Lamb.

In name of Patrick holy of the deeds,
And Carmac of the rights and tombs,
Columba beloved, and Adamnan of laws,
Fite calm, and Bride of the milk and kine.

In name of Michael chief of hosts,
In name of Ariel youth of lovely hues,
In name of Uriel of the golden locks,

And Gabriel seer of the Virgin of grace.

The time thou shalt have closed thine eye,
Thou shalt not bend thy knee nor move,
Thou shalt not wound the duck that is swimming,
Never shalt thou harry her of her young.

Eala bhan a ghlugaid bhinn,
Odhra sgaireach nan ciabh donn,
Cha ghear thu it as an druim,
Gu la-bhrath, air bharr nan tonn.

Air an ite bitheadh iad a ghnath
Mu 'n cuir thu lamhaidh ri do chluais,
Is bheir Moire mhin-gheal dhut dha gradh,
Is bheir Bride aluinn dhut dha buar.

Chan ith thu farasg no blianach,
No aon ian nach leag do lamh,
Bi-sa taingeil leis an aon-fhear,
Ge do robh a naodh air snamh.

Eala shith Bhride nan ni,
Lacha shith Mhoire na sith.

The white swan of the sweet gurgle,
The speckled dun of the brown tuft,
Thou shalt not cut a feather from their backs,
Till the doom-day, on the crest of the wave.

On the wing be they always
Ere thou place missile to thine ear,
And the fair Mary will give thee of her love,
And the lovely Bride will give thee of her trine.

Thou shalt not eat fallen fish nor fallen flesh,
Nor one bird that thy hand shall not bring down,
Be thou thankful for the one,
Though nine should be swimming.

The fairy swan of Bride of flocks,
The fairy duck of Mary of peace.

COISRIGEADH NA SEILG

CONSECRATING THE CHASE

THIS hymn was sung by the hunter when he went away in the morning, and when he had bathed his hands and face in the junction of the first three streams he met.

AN ainm na Trianailt, mar aon,
Ann am briathar, an gniomh 's an smaon,
Ta mi 'g ionn mo lamha fein,
Ann an sionn 's an sian nan speur.

A dubhradh nach till mi ri m' bheo
Gun iasgach, gun ianach ni 's mo,
Gun seing, gun sithinn nuas a beinn,
Gun sul, gun saill, a muigh a coill.

O Mhoire mhaoth-gheal, chaomh-gheal, ghradh-gheal,
Seachainn orm s' am bradan tarra-gheal marbh air sala,
Lach le h-alach nam b'e b'aill leat,
Nead ri beul an uisge far nach traigh e.

An liath-chearc air bharr nan stuc,
Is coileach-dubh an tuchain truim,
An deigh laighe luth na greine,
Seachainn, o seachainn orm fein an eisdeachd.

O Mhoire, mhathair chubhr mo Righ,
Crun-sa mi le crun do shith,
Cuir do bhrat rioghach oir dha m' dhion,
Is comhnuich mi le comhnadh Chriosd,
Comhnuich mi le comhnadh Chriosd.

IN name of the Holy Three-fold as one,
In word, in deed, and in thought,
I am bathing mine own hands,
In the light and in the elements of the sky.

Vowing that I shall never return in my life,
Without fishing, without fowling either,
Without game, without venison down from the hill,
Without fat, without blubber from out the copse.

O Mary tender-fair, gentle-fair, loving-fair,
Avoid thou to me the silvery salmon dead on the salt sea,
A duck with her brood an it please thee to show me,
A nest by the edge of the water where it does not dry.

The grey-hen on the crown of the knoll,

The black-cock of the hoarse croon,
After the strength of the sun has gone down,
Avoid, oh, avoid thou to me the hearing of them.

O Mary, fragrant mother of my King,
Crown thou me with the crown of thy peace,
Place thine own regal robe of gold to protect me,
And save me with the saving of Christ,
Save me with the saving of Christ.

ORA TURAIS

PRAYER FOR TRAVELLING

THIS hymn was sung by a pilgrim in setting out on his pilgrimage. The family and friends joined the traveller in singing the hymn and starting the journey, from which too frequently, for various causes, he never returned.

BITH a bhi na m' bhial,
Bladh a bhi na m' chainn,
Blath na siri na mo bhile,
Gun an tig mi nail.

An gaol thug Iosa Criosda
Bhi lionadh gach cridhe domh,
An gaol thug Iosa Criosda
Da m' lionadh air an son.

Siubhal choire, siubhal choille,
Siubhal fraoine fada, fas,
Moire mhin-gheal sior dha m' chobhair,
Am Buachaill Iosa m' dhion 's a char.
Moire mhin-gheal sior dha m' chobhair,
Am Buachaill Iosa m' dhion 's a chas.

LIFE be in my speech,
Sense in what I say,
The bloom of cherries on my lips,
Till I come back again.

The love Christ Jesus gave
Be filling every heart for me,
The love Christ Jesus gave
Filling me for every one.

Traversing corries, traversing forests,

Traversing valleys long and wild.
The fair white Mary still uphold me,
The Shepherd Jesu be my shield,
The fair white Mary still uphold me,
The Shepherd Jesu be my shield.

BEANNACHD IASGAICH

FISHING BLESSING

ON Christmas Day the young men of the townland go out to fish. All the fish they catch are sacred to the widows and the orphans and to the poor, and are distributed among them according to their necessities.

There is a tradition among the people of the Western Isles that Christ required Peter to row 707 strokes straight out from the shore when He commanded him to go and procure the fish containing the tribute-money. Following this tradition, the old men of Uist require the young men to row 707 strokes from the land before casting their lines on Christmas Day. And whatever fish they get are cordially given to the needy as a tribute in the name of Christ, King of the sea, and of Peter, king of fishermen. This is called 'dioladh deirc,' tribute-paying, 'deirce Pheadair,' Peter's tribute, 'dioladh Pheadail,' Peter's payment, and other terms. This tribute-paying on Christmas Day excites much emotional interest, and all try to enhance the tribute and in various ways to render the alms as substantial as possible.

The whiting and the haddock of the same size bear a strong resemblance to one another. There are differences, however. The haddock has a black spot on each side of its body above the pectoral fin, while the head of the whiting is more elongated than that of the haddock. Children and strangers are taught to differentiate between the two thus:--

'Ball dubh air an adaig,
Gob fad air a chuideig.'

A black spot of the haddock,
A long snout on the whiting.

The people of Uist say that the haddock was the fish in whose mouth Peter found the tribute-money, and that the two black spots are the marks left by Peter's fingers when he held the fish to extract the money from its mouth. The crew of young men who get most haddocks on Christmas Day are looked upon during the year as the real followers of the king of fishers. There is, therefore, considerable emulation among the different crews.

The haddock is called 'iasg Pheadail,' Peter's fish, and 'iasg Pheadair runaich,' the fish of loving Peter; and a family of birds 'peadaireach,' 'peitirich'--Peter-like, petrels, because in their flight they seem to be walking on the sea.

The tradition as to rowing 707 strokes is curious and interesting. The only other similar tradition which I know is of the wars between the Fomorians and the Milesians in Ireland. Both were invaders:--the Milesians earlier, the Fomorians later. When the Fomorians landed in Ireland the Milesians were already established, and the result was a long-continued war, till both sides were exhausted and tired of the strife. During a temporary truce it was agreed that the Fomorians should retire to the sea and row straight out 707 strokes from land, and if they succeeded in landing again they were to be allowed to remain and enjoy their hard-won honours. Whether for good or for ill to Ireland, the Fomorians effected a landing a second time, and settled in the south and west of the island.

The Irish were Pagan at the time, and the tradition of the 707 strokes being imposed by Christ on Peter must have been inserted in the Fomorian tradition after Ireland became Christian.

LA na soillse thainig oirnn,
Rugadh Criosda leis an Oigh.

'Na ainm-san cratham am burn
Air gach call a ta na m' churt.

A Righ nam feart 's nan neart tha shuas,
Do bheannachd iasgaich dort a nuas.

Suidhim sios le ramh 'na, m' ghlac,
Imirim a seachd ceud 's a seachd.

THE day of light has come upon us,
Christ is born of the Virgin.

In His name I sprinkle the water
Upon every thing within my court.

Thou King of deeds and powers above,
Thy fishing blessing pour down on us.

I will sit me down with an oar in my grasp,
I will row me seven hundred and seven [strokes].

Tilgidh mi mo dhubhan sios,
'S an ciad iasg a bheir mi nios,

An ainm Chriosda, Righ nan Sian,
Gheobh an deoir e mar a mhiann.

Is righ nan iasgair, Peadair treun,
Bheir e bheannachd dhomh na dheigh.

Airil, Gabril, agus Eoin,
Raphail baigheil, agus Poi,

Calum-cille caomh 's gach cas,
'S Muire mhin-gheal leis a ghras.

Siubhlaibh leinn gu iola cuain,
Ciuinibh dhuinne barr nan stuagh.

Righ nan righ ri crich ar cuart,
Sineadh saoghail is sonais buan.

Crun an Righ o'n Tri tha shuas,
Crois Chriosda d'ar dion a nuas.
Crun an Righ o'n Tri tha shuas,
Crois Chriosda d'ar dion a nuas.

I will cast down my hook,
The first fish which I bring up

In the name of Christ, King of the elements,
The poor shall have it at his wish.

And the king of fishers, the brave Peter,
He will after it give me his blessing.

Ariel, Gabriel, and John,
Raphael benign, and Paul,

Columba, tender in every distress,
And Mary fair, the endowed of grace.

Encompass ye us to the fishing-bank of ocean,
And still ye to us the crest of the waves.

Be the King of kings at the end of our course,
Of lengthened life and of lasting happiness.

Be the crown of the King from the Three on high,
Be the cross of Christ adown to shield us,
The crown of the King from the Three above,
The cross of Christ adown to shield us.

BEANNACHADH CUAIN

SEA prayers and sea hymns were common amongst the seafarers of the Western Islands. Probably these originated with the early Celtic missionaries, who constantly traversed in their frail skin coracles the storm-swept, strongly tidal seas of those Hebrid Isles, oft and oft sealing their devotion with their lives.

Before embarking on a journey the voyagers stood round their boat and prayed to the God of the elements for a peaceful voyage over the stormy sea. The steersman led the appeal, while the swish of the waves below, the sough of the sea beyond, and the sound of the wind around blended with the voices of the suppliants and lent dignity and solemnity to the scene.

There are many small oratories round the West Coast where chiefs and clansmen were wont to pray before and after voyaging. An interesting example of these is in the island of Grimisey, North Uist. The place is called Ceallan, cells, from 'ceall,' a cell. There were two oratories within two hundred yards of one another. One of the two has wholly disappeared, the other nearly. The ruin stands on a ridge near the end of the island looking out on the open bay of Ceallan and over the stormy Minch to the distant mountains of Mull and Morven. The oratory is known as 'Teampull Mhicheil,' the temple of St Michael. The structure was simple but beautiful, while the remains are interesting and touching from their historical associations. Tradition says that the oratory was built by 'Eibhric'--Euphemia or Amie, sole daughter and heiress of Ruaraidh, the son of Alan, High Chief of Lorn.

Amie, the daughter of Ruaraidh, married in 1337 John of Islay, Lord of the Isles. The two being related, they were granted a dispensation by Pope Benedict XII. The Lady Amie had three sons.

About the year 1358 John of Islay discarded Amie, and married Margaret, daughter of Robert Steward, and granddaughter of Robert Bruce. When the Lord of the Isles came south to celebrate his marriage with the Lady Margaret, one hundred and eight ships full of kinsmen and clansmen, chiefs and chieftains, came in his train. Such a sight had never been seen in Scotland before, and people came to the Clyde from long distances to see this large fleet. The power and influence indicated by this enormous retinue created much comment and envy among the nobles of the south and even at the Court.

The Lord of the Isles retained possession of the extensive territories of the Lady Amie, disposing of them afterwards to his several sons. The discarded lady took to a religions life, building and restoring oratories, churches, nunneries, monasteries, and castles throughout her ancestral lands. Saint Michael's Temple at Ceallan was one of these. In this little sanctuary built for the purpose the Lady Amie offered prayers and thanks before and after voyages to her kindred in Lorn.

John, Lord of the Isles, was a man of much munificence, like all those princely Macdonalds. He gave largely to the Church, earning for himself from the priests of the period the name of 'The Good John of Islay.' He was buried in Iona in the year 1386, in splendour and magnificence never surpassed, if ever equalled, in the case of the many kings of the five nationalities buried there.

About two years after his father's death, Ranald, the eldest surviving son of the Lady Amie, handed over the lordship of the Isles to Donald, eldest son of the Lady Margaret, who afterwards fought the battle of Harlaw. The ceremony of installing a Lord of the Isles usually took place at Loch Finlaggan in Islay, the principal seat of the Macdonalds, where the ruins of their castle, chapel, and other buildings are still to be seen, as well as the stone with the footmarks cut in it upon which the chief stood when, before the 'gentlemen of the Islands' and Highlands, he was proclaimed 'Macdonald' and 'High-prince of the seed of Conn.' But it was at Kildonan in the island of Eigg that, Ranald gave the sceptre into the hand of Donald, who thus became eighth Lord of the Isles. The account given of the ceremony by Hugh Macdonald, the Seanchie of Sleat, is interesting as representing the usual manner of installing a king, chief, or other dignitary among the Celts:--'At this the Bishop of Argyll, the Bishop of the Isles, and seven priests were sometimes present, but a Bishop was always present, with the chieftains of all the principal families and a Ruler of the Isles. There was a square stone seven or eight feet long, and the tract of a man's foot cut thereon, upon which he stood, denoting that he should walk in the footsteps and uprightness of his predecessors, and that he was installed by right in his possessions. He was clothed in a white habit to show his innocence and integrity of heart, that he would be a light to his people and maintain the true religion. The white apparel did afterwards belong to the poet by right. Then he was to receive a white rod in his hand intimating that he had power to rule, not with tyranny and partiality, but with discretion and sincerity. Then he received his forefathers' sword, or some other sword, signifying that his duty was to protect and defend them from their enemies in peace or war, as the obligations and customs of his predecessors were. The ceremony being over, mass was said after the blessing of the Bishop and seven priests, the people pouring their prayers for the success and prosperity of their new-created lord. When they were dismissed, the Lord of the Isles feasted them for a week thereafter, and gave liberally to the monks, poets, bards, and musicians. You may judge that they spent liberally without any exception of persons.' Other accounts differ but slightly from the above, as when Martin says that the young chief stood upon a cairn of stones, while his followers stood round him in a circle, his elevation signifying his authority over them, and their standing below their subjection to hint, also that immediately after the proclamation the chief druid or bard performed a rhetorical panegyric setting forth the ancient pedigree, valour, and liberality of the family as incentives to the young chieftain and fit for his imitation.' Martin speaks of this ceremony of installing a chief as prevalent in the eighteenth century.

[pp. <page 324>-5

BEANNACHADH CUAIN

THE OCEAN BLESSING

THI tha chomhnadh nan ard,
Tiuirich duinn do bheannachd aigh,
Iomchair leinn air bharr an t-sal,
Iomchair sinn gu cala tamh,
Beannaich ar sgioba agus bat,
Beannaich gach acair agus ramh,
Gach stadh is tarruinn agus rac,
Ar siuil-mhora ri crainn ard
Cum a Righ nan dul 'n an ait
Run 's gu 'n till sinn dachaidh slan;
Suidhidh mi fain air an stiuir,
Is e Mac De a bheir domh iuil,
Mar a thug e Chalum ciuin,

'N am dha stadh a chur ri siuil.

Mhuire, Bhride, Mhicheil, Phail,
Pheadair, Ghabriel, Eoin a ghraidh,
Doirtibh oirnn an driuchd o'n aird,
Bheireadh oirnn 's a chreideamh fas,
Daingnibh sinn 's a Charraig Ail,
Anns gach reachd a dhealbhas gradh,
Run 's gu 'n ruig sinn tir an aigh,
Am hi sith is seirc is baigh
Air an nochdadh duinn tre ghras;
Chaoidh chan fhaigh a chnoimh 'n ar dail,
Bithidh sinn tearuint ann gu brath,
Cha bhi sinn an geimhlibh bais,
Ge do tha sinn do shiol Adh.

O THOU who pervadest the heights,
Imprint on us Thy gracious blessing,
Carry us over the surface of the sea,
Carry us safely to a haven of peace,
Bless our boatmen and our boat,
Bless our anchors and our oars,
Each stay and halyard and traveller,
Our mainsails to our tall masts
Keep, O King of the elements, in their place
That we may return home in peace;
I myself will sit down at the helm,
It is God's own Son who will give me guidance,
As He gave to Columba the mild
What time he set stay to sails.

Mary, Bride, Michael, Paul,
Peter, Gabriel, John of love,
Pour ye down from above the dew
That would make our faith to grow,
Establish ye us in the Rock of rocks,
In every law that love exhibits,
That we may reach the land of glory,
Where peace and love and mercy reign,
All vouchsafed to us through grace;
Never shall the canker worm get near us,
We shall there be safe for ever,
We shall not be in the bonds of death
Though we are of the seed of Adam.

La Fheill Michell, La Fheill Mairt,

La Fheill Andrais, bann na baigh,
La Fheill Bride, la mo luaidh,
Tilg an nimhir sios an chuan,
Feuch an dean e slugadh suas;
La Fheill Paruig, la nam buadh,
Sorchair oirnn an stoirm o thuath,
Casg a fraoch, maol a gruam,
Diochd a gairge, marbh a fuachd.

La nan Tri Righrean shuas,
Ciuinich dhuinne barr nan stuadh,
La Bealltain thoir an driuchd,
La Fheill Sheathain thoir an ciuin,
La Fheill Moire mar nan char,
Seachainn oirnn an stoirm o 'n iar,
Gach la 's oidhche, gach stoirm is fiamh,
Bi thusa leinn, a Thriath nan triath,
Bi fein duinn ad chairt-iuil,
Biodh do lamh air failm ar stiuir,
Do lamh fein, a Dhe nan dul,
Moch is anamoch mar is iul,
Moch is anamoch mar is iul.

On the Feast Day of Michael, the Feast Day of Martin,
The Feast Day of Andrew, band of mercy,
The Feast Day of Bride, day of my choice,
Cast ye the serpent into the ocean,
So that the sea may swallow her up;
On the Feast Day of Patrick, day of power,
Reveal to us the storm from the north,
Quell its wrath and blunt its fury,
Lessen its fierceness, kill its cold.

On the Day of the Three Kings on high,
Subdue to us the crest of the waves,
On Beltane Day give us the dew,
On John's Day the gentle wind,
The Day of Mary the great of fame,
Ward off us the storm from the west;
Each day and night, storm and calm,
Be Thou with us, O Chief of chiefs,
Be Thou Thyself to us a compass-chart,
Be Thine hand on the helm of our rudder,
Thine own hand, Thou God of the elements,
Early and late as is becoming,
Early and late as is becoming.

BEANNACHADH CUAIN

OCEAN BLESSING

DHE, Athair uile-chumhachdaich, chaoimh,
Ios a Mhic nan deur agus na caoidh,
Le d' chomh-chomhnadh, O! a Spioraid Naoimh.

Thrithinn bhi-bheo, bhi-mhoir, bhi-bhuain,
Thug Clann Israil tri na Muir Ruaidh,
Is Ionah gu fonn a bronn miol-mhor a' chuain,

Thug Pol agus a chomhlain 's an long,
A doruinn na mara, a dolais nan tonn,
A stoirm a bha mor, a doinne bha trom.

Duair bhruchd an tuil air Muir Ghailili,
* * * * *
* * * * *

Shun agus saor agus naomhaich sinne,
Bi-sa, Righ nan dul, air ar stiuir ad shuidhe,
'S treoirich an sith sinn gu ceann-crich ar n-uidhe.

Le gaotha caona, caomha, coistre, cubhr,
Gun fhaobhadh, gun fhionnsadh, gun fhabhsadh,
Nach deanadh gniamh fabhtach dhuinn.

Iarramaid gach sian a Dhe,
A reir do rian 's do bhriathra fein.

GOD the Father all-powerful, benign,
Jesu the Son of tears and of sorrow,
With thy co-assistance, O! Holy Spirit.

The Three-One, ever-living, ever-mighty, everlasting,
Who brought the Children of Israel through the Red Sea,
And Jonah to land from the belly of the great creature of the ocean,

Who brought Paul and his companions in the ship,
From the torment of the sea, from the dolour of the waves,
From the gale that was great, from the storm that was heavy.

When the storm poured on the Sea of Galilee,
* * * * *

Sain us and shield and sanctify us,
Be Thou, King of the elements, seated at our helm,
And lead us in peace to the end of our journey.

With winds mild, kindly, benign, pleasant.
Without swirl, without whirl, without eddy,
That would do no harmful deed to us.

We ask all things of Thee, O God,
According to Thine own will and word.

RIAGHLAIR NAN SIAN

RULER OF THE ELEMENTS

CLANN Israil is Dia da 'n gabhail,
Troimh 'n Mhuir Ruaidh fhuair iad rathad,
Is ann a fhuair iad casg am pathaidh,
An creag nach d' fhaodadh le saor a shnaidheadh.

Co iad air faim mo stiuir
Deanamh falbh da m' iubhraich shoir?
Peadail, Pal, is Eoin mo ruin,
Triuir da 'n talmaich fiu is foir.

Co 'n croil an coir mo stiuir?
Peadail, Poil, is Eoin Baistidh,
Criosda na shuidh air mo stiuir,
Deanamh iuil da 'n ghaoith a deas.

Co da 'n criothnaich guth na gaoith?
Co da 'n caonaich caol is cuan?
Iosa Criosda, Triath gach naoimh,
Mac Moire, Friamh nam buadh,
Mac Moire, Friamh nam buadh.

THE Children of Israel, God taking them,
Through the Red Sea obtained a path,
They obtained the quenching of their thirst
From a rock that might not by craftsman be hewn.

Who are they on the tiller of my rudder,
Giving speed to my east bound barge?
Peter and Paul and John the beloved,

Three to whom laud and obeisance are due.

Who are the group near to my helm?
Peter and Paul and John the Baptist;
Christ is sitting on my helm,
Making guidance to the wind from the south.

To whom does tremble the voice of the wind?
To whom become tranquil strait and ocean?
To Jesus Christ, Chief of each saint,
Son of Mary, Root of victory,
Son of Mary, Root of victory.

URNUIGH MHARA

SEA PRAYER

STIURADAIR

Beannaicht an long.

HELMSMAN

Blest be the boat.

SGIOBA

Beannaicheadh Dia an t-Athair i.

CREW

God the Father bless her.

STIURADAIR

Beannaicht an long.

HELMSMAN

Blest be the boat.

SGIOBA

Beannaicheadh Dia am Mac i.

CREW

God the Son bless her.

STIURADAIR

Beannaicht an long.

HELMSMAN

Blest be the boat.

SGIOBA

Beannaicheadh Dia an Spiorad i.

CREW

God the Spirit bless her.

UILE

Dia an t-Athair,
Dia am Mac,
Dia an Spiorad,
Beannaicheadh an long.

ALL

God the Father,
God the Son,
God the Spirit,
Bless the boat.

STIURADAIR

Ciod is eagal duibh
Is Dia an t-Athair leibh?

HELMSMAN

What can befall you
And God the Father with you?

SGIOBA

Cha 'n eagal duinn ni.

CREW

No harm can befall us.

STIURADAIR

Ciad is eagal duibh
Is Dia am Mac leibh?

HELMSMAN

What can befall you
And God the Son with you?

SGIOBA

Cha 'n eagal duinn ni.

CREW

No harm can befall us.

STIURADAIR

Ciod is eagal duibh
Is Dia an Spiorad leibh?

HELMSMAN

What can befall you
And God the Spirit with you?

SGIOBA

Cha 'n eagal duinn ni.

CREW

No harm can befall us.

UILE

Dia an t-Athair,
Dia am Mac,
Dia an Spiorad,

Leinn gu sior.

ALL

God the Father,
God the Son,
God the Spirit,
With us eternally.

STIURADAIR

Ciod is fath bhur curam
Is Ti nan dul os bhur cinn?

HELMSMAN

What can cause you anxiety
And the God of the elements over you?

SGIOBA

Cha churam dhuinn ni.

CREW

No anxiety can be ours.

STIURADAIR

Ciod is fath bhur curam
Is Righ nan dul os bhur cinn?

HELMSMAN

What can cause you anxiety
And the King of the elements over you?

SGIOBA

Cha churam dhuinn ni.

CREW

No anxiety can be ours.

STIURADAIR

Ciod is fath bhur curam
Is Spiorad nan dul os bhur cinn?

HELMSMAN

What can cause you anxiety
And the Spirit of the elements over you

SGIOBA

Cha churam dhuinn ni.

CREW

No anxiety can be ours.

UILE

Ti nan dui,
Righ nan dul,
Spiorad nan dul,
Dluth os ar cinn,
Suthainn sior.

ALL

The God of the elements,
The King of the elements,
The Spirit of the elements,
Close over us,
Ever eternally.

IV

UIBE

INCANTATIONS

EOLAS NA RUAIDH

CHARM FOR ROSE

WHEN this charm is applied, the point of a knife or a needle, or the tongue of a brooch or of some other sharp instrument, is pointed threateningly at the part affected. The part is then spat upon and crossed three times in the names of the three Persons of the Trinity, whether it be the breast of a woman or the udder of a cow. The legend says that Mary and Jesus were walking together when Mary took rose (erysipelas) in her breast, and she said to Jesus:--

AIC, a Mhic 's a Chriosda,
Cioch do Mhathar air at;
Thoir-sa fois dh' an chich,
Cuir-s' an crion an t-at;
Thoir-sa fois dh' an chich,
Cuir-s' an crion an t-at.

Faic fein i, Righinn,
'S tu a rug am Mac,
Cuir-sa casgadh air a chich,
Cuir-sa crionadh air an at;
Cuir-sa casgadh air a chich,
Cuir-sa crionadh air an at.

Faic thus i, Iosda,
Is tu Righ nan dul;
Cuir-sa casgadh air a chich,
Cuir-sa crionadh air an uth;
Cuir-sa casgadh air a chich,
Cuir-sa crionadh air an uth.

Chithim, thubhairt Criosda,
Is nithim mar is fiu,
Bheirim fois dh' an chich,
'S bheirim sith dh' an uth;
Bheirim fois dh' an chich,
'S bheirim sith dh' an uth.

BEHOLD, Son and Christ,
The breast of Thy Mother swollen;

Give Thou peace to the breast,
Subdue Thou the swelling;
Give Thou peace to the breast,
Subdue Thou the swelling.

Behold it thyself, Queen,
Since of thee the Son was born,
Appease thou the breast,
Subdue thou the swelling;
Appease thou the breast,
Subdue thou the swelling.

See Thou it, Jesu,
Since Thou art King of life;
Appease Thou the breast,
Subdue Thou the udder;
Appease Thou the breast,
Subdue Thou the udder.

I behold, said Christ,
And I do as is meet,
I give ease to the breast,
And rest to the udder;
I give ease to the breast,
And rest to the udder.

EOLAS NA RUAIDH

CHARM FOR ROSE

A RUADH ghaothar, atar, aogail,
Fag an taobh agus an tac sin,
Sin an carr 's an lar,
Agus fag a chioch.

Seall, a Chriosd, a bhean
Agus a cioch air at,
Seall fein i, Mhuire,
'S tu rug am Mac.

A ruadh ghaothar, aogar, iota,
Fag a chioch agus am bac,
Agus sin a mach,
Slan gu robh dh' an chich,
Crion gu robh dh' an at.

Teich a bhradag ruadh,
Teich gu luath a bhradag,
At a bha 's a chich,
Fag a charr 's a chioch,
Agus sin a mach.

THOU rose windy, swelling, deadly,
Leave that part and spot,
There is the udder in the ground,
And leave the breast.

See, Christ, the woman
And her breast swollen,
See her thyself, Mary,
It was thou didst bear the Son.

Thou rose windy, deadly, thirsty,
Leave the breast and the spot,
And take thyself off;
Healed be the breast,
Withered be the swelling.

Flee thieving red one,
Flee quickly thieving one,
Swelling that was in the breast,
Leave the udder and the breast,
And flee hence.

EOLAS NA RU

CHARM FOR ROSE

A RU eugail, aogail, atail,
Fag uth na ba caisne,
Fag uth na ba cait-cinn,
Fag, fag a phait sin,
Agus tar pait eil ort.

A ru rag, rudaidh,
Our an uth a mhairt,
Fag an t-at 's an t-utha,
Teich gu grunn na claiche.

Cuirim ru ri clach,
Cuirim clach ri lar,
Cuirim bainne an uth,

Cuirim sugh an ar.

THOU rose deathly, deadly, swollen,
Leave the udder of the white-footed cow,
Leave the udder of the spotted cow,
Leave, leave that swelling,
And betake thyself to other swelling.

Thou rose thrawn, obstinate,
Surly in the udder of the cow,
Leave thou the swelling and the udder,
Flee to the bottom of the stone.

I place the rose to the stone,
I place the stone to the earth,
I place milk in the udder,
I place substance in the kidney.

EOLAS AT CIOCH

CHARM FOR SWOLLEN BREAST

EOLAS a rinn Gille-Caluim
A dh' aona bho na caillich,
Air ruaidh, air chruaidh, air chradh,
Air at, air pat, air mam,
Air dhair, air chairr, air bhleoghan,
Air tri corracha crith,
Air tri corracha cnamh,
Air tri corracha creothail,
Na ob e do bhruid,
Na diult e do mhne,
Na tar e 's an Domhnach.
Eolas a rinn Fionn fial,
Da dhearbh phiuthair,
Air ruaidh, air chruaidh,
Air at ciche.

THE charm made by Gillecaluim,
On the one cow of the carlin,
For rose, for hardness, for pain,
For swelling, for lump, for growth,
For uzzening, for udder, for milking,
For the three 'corracha crith,'
For the three 'corracha cnamh,'
For the three 'corracha creothail,'

Do not deny it to beast,
Do not refuse it to wife,
Do not withhold it on Sunday.
The charm made of generous Fionn,
To his very sister,
For rose, for hardness,
For swelling of breast.

EOLAS AN DEIDIDH

TOOTHACHE CHARM

THE teeth of ancient human skeletons found in stone coffins and other enclosures, and without enclosures, are usually good and complete. This is in marked contrast to the teeth of modern human remains, which are generally much impaired if not wholly absent. But there must have been toothache and even artificial teeth in ancient times, as indicated by the mummies in Egypt and the toothache charms and toothache wells in the Highlands. One toothache charm and one toothache well must suffice to illustrate this. The toothache well is in the island of North Uist. It is situated 195 feet above the sea, at the foot of a hill 757 feet high, and nearly three miles in the moorland from the nearest townland.

The place is called 'Cuidh-airidh,' shieling fold, while the well is variously known as 'Tobar Chuidh-airidh,' well of the shieling fold, 'Tobar an deididh,' well of the toothache, 'Tobar na cnoidh,' well of the worm, and 'Tobar cnuimh fhiacail,' well of the tooth worm, from a belief that toothache is caused by a worm in the tooth.

The general name of the well is 'Tobar Chuidh-airidh,' well of the shieling fold, to distinguish it from other healing wells throughout the Isles. The pilgrim suffering from toothache must not speak, nor eat, nor drink, after beginning the pilgrimage till after three draughts of the well of Cuidh-airidh are drunk in name of God, and in name of Christ, and in name of Spirit.

Some persons profess to derive no relief, some profess to derive partial relief, and some profess to derive complete relief from toothache after drinking the water of the well of Cuidh-airidh.

OB a chuir Bride bhoidheach
Romh ordag Mathar De,
Air mhir, air lion, air chorcraich,
Air chnoidh, air ghoimh, air dheud.

A chnoidh a rinn domh deistinn,
Air deudach mo chinn,
Ifrinn teann da m' dheud,
Deud ifrinn da mo theinn.

* * * *

Deud ifrinn da mo theann;

Am fad 's is maireann mi-fein
Gu mair mo dheud am cheann.

DOIGHEAN EILE--
Air mhir, air chir, air chnodaich.
Air mhuir, air chuan, air chorsa.
Air li, air lionn, air liogradh.

THE incantation put by lovely Bride
Before the thumb of the Mother of God,
On lint, on wort, on hemp,
For worm, for venom, for teeth.

The worm that tortured me,
In the teeth of my head,
Hell hard by my teeth,
The teeth of hell distressing me.

* * * *
The teeth of hell close to me;
As long as I myself shall last
May my teeth last in my head.

VARIANTS--
On lint, on comb, on agony.
On sea, on ocean, on coast.
On water, on lakes, on marshes.

EOLAS NA BUDHA

CHARM FOR JAUNDICE

THE following scene was described to me by Angus MacEachain, herdsman, Staonabrig, South Uist, one of the chief actors in the episode.

The daughter of a farmer in the neighbourhood was ill with jaundice. The doctor of the parish was attending her, but she was becoming worse instead of better, and her end seemed near. Her distressed parents sent for 'Aonas nan gisrean,' Angus of the exorcisms, and he came. The man examined the girl and announced that she was possessed of the demon of the jaundice, but that he would expel the demon and cure the girl. He requested the mother to put on a big fire, the sisters to bring a tub of clear cold water, and the father to bring the plough irons, evil spirits being unable to withstand iron. All this was promptly done. The exorcist placed the plough irons in the fire, displaying much solicitude that they should be red-hot. The room was darkened and the eyes of the patient were bandaged that the eyes of the body might be subjective to the eyes of the mind. Directed by the exorcist, the mother and sisters placed the back of the girl to the front of the bed, and laying it bare left the room, the man securing the door after them. Making a clanging noise with the plough irons as if to drive away the jaundice demon, the man replaced the share in the fire and put the coulter in the water. Then pretending to take the red-hot share out of the fire, he took up the icy-cold coulter and placed it along the spine of the patient, loudly commanding the demon to depart. The girl screamed in evident agony, calling on the Mother of Christ and on the Foster-mother of Christ, and on her own mother, to come and rescue her from the brutal treatment of black Angus the father of evil, the brother of demons, and to see how her blood was flowing in streams and her flesh was burnt off her back, laying her backbone bare. While loudly calling to the jaundice demon to depart, the expert exorcist threw the red-hot share into the tub of water, adding to the already abundant noise in the room. Against the remonstrances of the father, who said that Angus knew what he was about, the mother and sisters burst open the door, calling on Mary Mother to rescue the maltreated girl, and on Calumcille to redress her wrongs.

'Whether the cure was due to her simple faith in the exorcist or to the shock to her nervous system I do not know,' continued the narrator, 'but in a few days the girl was up and about. She is grateful, but shy of me ever since, probably remembering the hard things she said. She will always believe that I exercised some occult power over the jaundice demon. The case of this girl was as bad as any I have seen. She had been an attractive, comely girl, with a winning expression and a clear complexion, but she had become yellow-black instead of rosy-red.'

Angus MacEachain told of this and similar cases with much humour, but without a smile on his lips, though his eyes sparkled, and his countenance glowed with evident appreciation of the scenes.

AIR bhuidhe, air dhuibhe, air arnach,
Air a ghalar-dhearg, air a ghalar-shearg,
Air a ghalar-tholl, air a ghalar-lom,
Air a ghalar-dhonn, air a ghalar-bhonn,
'S air Bach galar a dh' f haodadh
A bhi an aorabh ba
No an sgath gamhna.

FOR the jaundice, for the spaul, for the bloody flux,
For the red disease, for the withering disease,
For the bot disease, for the skin disease,
For the brown disease, for the foot disease,
And for every disease that might be
In the constitution of cow
Or adhering to stirk.

EOLAS SGIUCHA FEITHE

CHARM FOR A BURSTING VEIN

RANN a rinn ban-naomh Bride
Dh' an mharaiche chrubach,
Air ghlun, air lug, air chuagas,
Air na naodh galara gith, air na tri galara cuara,

Na ob e do bhruid, na diult e do mhne.

Chaidh Criosd air each,
Bhrist each a chas,
Chaidh Criosd a bhan,
Rinn e slan a chas.

Mar a shlanuich Criosd sin,
Gun slanuich Criosd seo,
Agus na 's mo na seo,
Ma 's e thoil a dheanamh.

An t-eolas a rinn Calum-cille,
Air eorlain a ghlinne,
Do sgocha feithe, do leum cnamha--
Tha thu tinn an diugh, bithidh thu slan am maireach.

THE rune made by the holy maiden Bride
To the lame mariner,
For knee, for crookedness, for crippleness,
For the nine painful diseases, for the three venomous diseases,
Refuse it not to beast, deny it not to dame.

Christ went on a horse,
A horse broke his leg,
Christ went down,
He made whole the leg.

As Christ made whole that,
May Christ make whole this,
And more than this,
If it be His will so to do.

The charm made by Columba,
On the bottom of the glen,
For bursting of vein, for dislocation of bone--
Thou art ill to-day, thou shalt be well to-morrow.

EOLAS SGOCHA FEITH

CHARM FOR BURSTING VEIN

PAIDIR Moire a h-aon,
Paidir Moire a dha,
Paidir Moire a tri,
Paidir Moire a ceithir,

Paidir Moire a coig,
Paidir Moire a sia,
Paidir Moire a seachd,
Seachd paidriche Moire gu brath
Eadar cradh agus ceart,
Eadar bonn agus braigh,
Eadar slan agus feart.

Chaidh Criosd air as,
Sgiuch a cas,
Thainig e bhan
Shlanuich e cas;
Mar a shlanuich e sin
Gun slanuich e seo,
Agus na 's mo na seo
Ma 's e thoil a dheanamh.

ROSARY of Mary, one,
Rosary of Mary, two,
Rosary of Mary, three,
Rosary of Mary, four,
Rosary of Mary, five,
Rosary of Mary, six,
Rosary of Mary, seven,
Seven Rosaries of Mary ever
Between pain and ease,
Between sole and summit,
Between health and grave

Christ went on an ass,
She sprained her foot,
He came down
And healed her foot;
As He healed that
May He heal this,
And greater than this,
If it be His will to do.

EOLAS AN T-SNIAMH

CHARM OF THE SPRAIN

CHAR Bride mach
Maduinn mhoch,
Le caraid each;
Bhris each a chas,

Le uinich och,
Bha sid mu seach,
Chuir i cnamh ri cnamh,
Chuir i feoil ri feoil,
Chuir i feithe ri feithe,
Chuir i cuisle ri cuisle;
Mar a leighis ise sin
Gun leighis mise seo.

BRIDE went out
In the morning early,
With a pair of horses;
One broke his leg,
With much ado,
That was apart,
She put bone to bone,
She put flesh to flesh,
She put sinew to sinew,
She put vein to vein;
As she healed that
May I heal this.

EOLAS AN T-SNIAMH

CHARM FOR SPRAIN

CHAIDH Criosda ri croich,
Sgiuch cas eich;
Thainig Criosda ri lar,
Shlanaich a chas.

Mar a shlanaich sin
Gun slanaich seo,
Ma 's e thoil a dheanamh,
A uchd Ti nan dul,
Agus Triuir na Trianaid,
Ti nan dul,
Triuir na Trianaid.

CHRIST went on the cross,
Sprained the leg of a horse;
Christ came to the ground,
Whole became the leg.

As that was made whole
May this become whole,

If His will be so to do,
Through the bosom of the God of life,
And of the Three of the Trinity,
The God of life,
The Three of Trinity.

EOLAS AN T-SNIAMH

CHARM FOR SPRAIN

CHAIDH Criosd a mach
Maduinn moch,
Fhuair e cas nan each
'Nan spruilleach bog;
Chuir e smior ri smior,
Chuir e smuais ri smuais,
Chuir e cnaimh ri cnaimh,
Chuir e streabhon ri streabhon,
Chuir e feith ri feith,
Chuir e fuil ri fuil,
Chuir e creais ri creais,
Chuir e feoil ri feoil,
Chuir e saill ri saill,
Chuir e craicionn ri craicionn,
Chuir e flonn ri flonn,
Chuir e blath ri blath,
Chuir e fuar ri fuar;
Mar a leighis Righ nam buadh sin
Is dual gun leighis e seo,
Ma 's e thoil fein a dheanamh.
A uchd Ti nan dul,
Agus Tiur na Trianaid.

CHRIST went out
In the morning early,
He found the legs of the horses
In fragments soft;
He put marrow to marrow,
He put pith to pith,
He put bone to bone,
He put membrane to membrane,
He put tendon to tendon,
He put blood to blood,
He put tallow to tallow,
He put flesh to flesh,
He put fat to fat,

He put skin to skin,
He put hair to hair,
He put warm to warm,
He put cool to cool,
As the King of power healed that
It is in His nature to heal this,
If it be His own will to do it.
Through the bosom of the Being of life,
And of the Three of the Trinity.

FATH-FITH

'FATH-FITH' and 'fith-fath' are interchangeable terms and indiscriminately used. They are applied to the occult power which rendered a person invisible to mortal eyes and which transformed one object into another. Men and women were made invisible, or men were transformed into horses, bulls, or stags, while women were transformed into cats, hares, or hinds. These transmutations were sometimes voluntary, sometimes involuntary. The 'fith-fath' was especially serviceable to hunters, warriors, and travellers, rendering them invisible or unrecognisable to enemies and to animals.

Fionn had a fairy sweetheart, a daughter of the people of the mounds, but Fionn forsook her and married a daughter of the sons of men. The fairy was angry at the slight put upon her, and she placed the wife of Fionn under the 'fith-fath' spell in the form of a hind of the hill. The wife of Fionn bore a son in the island of Sanndraigh in Loch-nan-ceall in Arasaig. The mother possessed so much of the nature of the hind that she licked the temple of the child when he was born, but she possessed so much of the nature of the woman that she only gave one lick. But hair like the hair of a fawn grew on the part of the temple of the child which the tongue of the hind-mother had touched. And because of this patch of fawn's hair on his temple the child was called 'Oisein,' the fawn. While still a boy Ossian followed Fionn and the Feinne to the hunting-hill to chase the mountain deer. In the midst of the chase a magic mist darker than night came down upon the hunters, blinding them from one another and from their surroundings--no one knew where was another or where he was himself. Hunt-wandering came over Ossian, and he wandered wearily alone, and at last found himself in a deep green glen surrounded by high blue hills. As he walked along he saw a timid hind browsing in a green corrie before him. And Ossian thought to himself that he had never seen a creature so lovely as this timid hind, and he stood gazing upon her with joy. But the spirit of the hunt was strong upon Ossian, and the blood of the hunter was hot in his veins, and he drew his spear to throw it at the hind. The hind turned and looked at Ossian and gazed upon him with her full wistful grey eyes, more lovely and alluring than the blue eyes of love. 'Do not hurt me, Ossian,' said the hind; 'I am thy mother under the "fith-fath," in the form of a hind abroad and in the form of a woman at home. Thou art hungry and thirsty and weary. Come thou home with me, thou fawn of my heart.' And Ossian accompanied the hind step by step till they reached a rock in the base of the hill. The hind opened a leaf in a door in the rock where no door seemed to be, and she went in, and Ossian went in after her. She closed the door-leaf in the rock and there was no appearance of a door. And the graceful hind became transformed into a beautiful woman, like the lovely woman of the green kirtle and the locks of gold. There was light in the bower in the bosom of the ben like the light of 'trath-nona la leth an t-samhraidh'--noontide on midsummer day. Nor was it the light of the sun, nor was it the light of the moon, nor was it the light of the star of guidance. His mother prepared food and drink and music for Ossian. And she placed food in a place of eating for him, and she placed drink in a place of drinking for him, and she placed music in a place of hearing for him. Ossian took of the food and of the drink and of the music till he was full satisfied--his seven full satiations. After feasting, Ossian said to his mother, 'I am going, mother, to see what Fionn and the Feinne are doing in the hunting-hill.' And his mother placed her arm around his neck and kissed Ossian with the three kisses of a mother, and then she opened the door-leaf in the door of the bower and allowed him out. When she closed it there was no appearance of a door in the rock.

Ossian had been feasting on food and drink and music in the bower with his mother for the space of three days, as he thought, but he had been in the bower for the space of three years instead. And he made a song, the first song he made, warning his mother against the men and the hounds of the Feinne.

In his Leabhar Na Feinne Iain Campbell of Islay says that he had received fourteen versions of this song of Ossian. Six of these had been sent to him by the present writer. One of these versions was obtained from Oirig Nic Iain--Effric or Effie Mac Iain--lineally descended, she said, from Alexander Mac Iain, chief of the massacred Macdonalds of Glencoe.

Effric Mac Iain was not tall, but she was very beautiful, intelligent, and pleasant. I obtained a silver brooch from her which, she said, had come down like herself through the generations from the massacred chief of Glencoe. The brooch is circular and beautifully chased, though much worn.

'SANAS OISEIN D'A MHATHAIR

'MA 's tu mo mhathair 's gur a fiadh thu,
Bheir mi hoirion ho a hau,
Eirich mu 'n eirich grian ort.
Bheir mi hoirion ho a hau,
Eho hir ir i-ibhag o,
Na hao hi ho a ro hau.

Ma 's tu mo mhathair 's gur a fiadh thu,
Siubhail sliabh mu 'n tig an teasach.

Ma 's tu mo mhathair 's gur a fiadh thu,
Faicill ort romh fhearaibh Fianna.

Ma 's tu mo mhathair 's gur a fiadh thu,
Faicill ort romh chonaibh Fianna.

Ma theid thu do choiribh dona,
Faicill ort romh ghniamh nan conu,
Conaibh conachar, conaibh confhach,
Is iad air mhire-chatha romhad.

OSSIAN'S WARNING TO HIS MOTHER

IF thou be my mother and thou a deer,

Arise ere the sun arises on thee.

If thou be my mother and thou a deer,
Travel the hills ere the heat of the hunt.

If thou be my mother and thou a deer,
Beware thou the men of the Feinne.

If thou be my mother and thou a deer,
Beware thou the hounds of the Feinne.

If thou shouldst go to hurtful corries,
Beware thou the deeds of the hounds,
Hounds of uproar and hounds of rage,
And they in battle-fury before thee.

Seachainn Caoilte, seachainn Luath,
Seachainn Bruchag dhubh nam bruach,
Seachainn saigh an earbail dhuibh,
Bran mac Buidheig, namh nam fiadh,
Agus Geolaidh dian nan damh.

Ma theid thu do ghleannaibh iosal,
Faicill ort romh chlanna Baoisge,
Clanna Baoisge 's an cuid con,
Da chiad diag a dh' aireamh fhear,
A lann fein an laimh gach laoich,
A chu fein an deigh gach fir,
Is iad air eil aig Leide mac Liannain,
Is fearan beag ri sgath creaige,
Is da chu dhiag air lothain aige,
Is eagal air nach tig thige.

Avoid 'Caoilte,' avoid 'Luath,
Avoid black 'Bruchag' of the banks,
Avoid the bitch of the black tail,
'Bran' son of 'Buidheag,' foe of deer,
And little 'Geolaidh' keen of stags.

Shouldst thou go to low glens,
Beware thou of the 'Baoisge' Clan,

The 'Baoisge' Clan and their hounds,
Twelve hundred of numbered men,
His own blade in each hero's hand,
His own hound after each man,
And they on the thong of 'Lide' son of 'Liannan,'
And a little manikin in shade of a rock,
While twelve dogs he has on leash,
And he fears the hunt will not come to him.

Ma theid thu do bheannaibh mora,
Faicill ort romh Chlanna Morna,
Clanna Morna 's an cuid con,
Da chiad diag a dh' aireamh fhear
A lann fein an laimh gach laoich.

Ma theid thu do bheannaibh arda,
Faicill ort romh Chlanna Gaisge,
Clanna Gaisge 's an cuid con,
Da chiad diag a dh' aireamh fhear,
A lann fein an laimh gach laoich.

Ma theid thu gu fairir frithe,
Faicill ort romh Chlanna Frithir,
Clanna Frithir 's an cuid con,
Da chiad diag a dh' aireamh fhear,
A lann fein an laimh gach laoich.'

Shouldst thou go to the great bens,
Beware thou of the 'Morni' Clan,
The 'Morni' Clan and their hounds,
Twelve hundred of numbered men,
His own blade in each hero's hand.

Shouldst thou go to the high bens,
Beware thou of the 'Gaisge' Clan,
The 'Gaisge' Clan and their hounds,
Twelve hundred of numbered men,
His own blade in each hero's hand.

Shouldst thou go to the haze-land forest,
Beware thou of the 'Frithir' Clan,
The 'Frithir' Clan and their hounds,
Twelve hundred of numbered men,
His own blade in each hero's hand.

FATH fith

Ni mi ort,
Le Muire na frithe,
Le Bride na brot,
Bho chire, bho ruta,
Bho mhise, bho bhoc,
Bho shionn, 's bho mhac-tire,
Bho chrain, 's bho thorc,
Bho chu, 's bho chat,
Bho mhaghan masaich,
Bho chu fasaich,
Bho scan foirir,
Bho bho, bho mharc,
Bho tharbh, bho earc,
Bho mhurn, bho mhac,
Bho iantaidh an adhar,
Bho shnagaidh na talmha,
Bho iasgaidh na mara,
'S bho shiantaidh na gailbhe.

FATH fith
Will I make on thee,
By Mary of the augury,
By Bride of the corslet,
From sheep, from ram,
From goat, from buck,
From fox, from wolf,
From sow, from boar,
From dog, from cat,
From hipped-bear,
From wilderness-dog,
From watchful 'scan,'
From cow, from horse,
From bull, from heifer,
From daughter, from son,
From the birds of the air,
From the creeping things of the earth,
From the fishes of the sea,
From the imps of the storm.

SIAN A BHEATHA BHUAN

'SIAN' or 'seun' is occult agency, supernatural power used to ward away injury, and to protect invisibly. Belief in the charm was common, and examples of its efficacy are frequently told. A woman at Bearnasdale, in Skye, put such a charm on Macleod of Bearnaray, Harris, when on his way to join Prince Charlie in 1745. At Culloden the bullets showered upon him like hail, but they had no effect. When all was lost, Macleod threw off his coat to facilitate his flight. His faithful foster-brother

Murdoch Macaskail was close behind him and took up the coat. When examined it was found to be riddled with bullet-holes. But not one of these bullets had hurt Macleod!

A woman at Bornish, South Uist, put a charm on Allan Macdonald of Clanranald when he was leaving to join the Earl of Mar at Perth in 1715. But Clanranald took a lad away against the will of his mother, who lived at Staonabrig, South Uist. The woman implored Clanranald to leave her only son, and she a widow, but he would not. Then she vowed that 'Ailean Beag,' Little Allan, as Clanranald was called, would never return. She baked two bannocks, a little bannock and a big bannock, and asked her son whether he would have the little bannock with his mother's blessing, or the big one with her cursing. The lad said that he would have the little bannock with his mother's blessing. So she gave him the little bannock and her blessing and also a crooked sixpence, saying, 'Here, my son, is a sixpence seven times cursed. Use it in battle against Little Allan and earn the blessing of thy mother, or refrain and earn her cursing.' At the battle of Sheriffmuir blows and bullets were showering on Allan of Clanranald, but he heeded them not, and for every blow he got he gave three. When the strife was hottest and the contest doubtful, the son of the widow of Staonabrig remembered his mother's injunction, and that it was better to fight with her blessing than fall with her cursing, and he put the crooked sixpence in his gun. He aimed, and Clanranald fell. His people crowded round Clanranald weeping and wailing like children. But Glengarry called out, 'An diugh gu aichbheil, am maireach gu bron,'--'To-day for revenge, to-morrow for weeping,' and the Macdonalds renewed the fight. Thirsting for revenge they fell upon the English division of Argyll's army, cutting it to pieces and routing it for several miles.

When Clanranald's foster-father was asked whom he wept and watched, his only reply was, 'Bu duine an de e'--'He was a man yesterday.'

Allan Macdonald of Clanranald was called 'Ailean Beag,' Little Allan, in contradistinction to some of his predecessors who had been exceptionally big men. If apparently short of stature, he was exceedingly broad and powerful, active, gallant of bearing, and greatly beloved by his people.

After the failure of Dundee in 1689 Clanranald lived in France for several years. There he made the acquaintance of Penelope, daughter of Colonel Mackenzie, governor of Tangiers under Charles II. Clanranald married Penelope Mackenzie and brought her home. He also brought a French architect, French masons, and French freestone to build a new house at Ormacleit. The house took seven years in building and was occupied for seven years. On the night of the battle of Sheriffmuir, when its owner was killed, the house was burnt to the ground through the kitchen chimney taking fire. Some days previously Lady Clanranald had told some guests that she had had a vision that her eyes melted away in scalding water and that her heart burned up like a live coal, and she feared some dire double disaster was to befall her.

'Tota mhor Ormacleit'--the great ruins of Ormacleit, stand high and picturesque on the monotonous far-reaching machairs of the Atlantic side of South Uist. The gables are high-pointed, and the wings being at right angles to the main building, the ruins show to admirable advantage in the long level landscape.

The freestone forming the corners, doors, and windows is of peculiar hardness, and of a blue tint.

The farm of Ormacleit had been tenanted during many years by Mr John Maclellan, whose wife was Miss Penelope Macdonald, a kinswoman of Flora Macdonald and of her chief Clanranald. Mrs Maclellan was a lady of great beauty, excellence, historical knowledge, and good sense. She had the happiness, a few years before she died, of handing to her chief and relative, Admiral Sir Reginald Macdonald of Clanranald, some jewellery that had been found in the ruins of the castle. The jewellery in all probability had been the property of Penelope Mackenzie, the lady of the gallant Clanranald of the '15, and for whom Penelope Macdonald had been named.

[pp. <page 28>-31.

SIAN A BHEATHA BHUAN

CHARM OF THE LASTING LIFE

CUIRIM an seun air do chom,
Agus air do shealbhachd,
Seun Dhe nan dul
Chum do thearmaid.

An seun a chuir Bride nan ni
Mu mhuineal min Dhornghil,
An seun a chuir Moire mu Mac,
Eadar bonn agus broghaid,
Eadar cioch agus glun,
Eadar cul agus broth,
Eadar braigh agus bonn,
Eadar suil agus folt.

Cliar Mhicheil air do thaobh,
Sgiath Mhicheil air do shlinnean,
Ni bheil eadar neamh is lar
Na bheir buaidh air Righ nan gras.

Cha reub lainn thu,
Cha mhill muir thu,
Cha teum mnaoi thu,
Cha treann duin thu.

Brat Chriosda fein umad,
Sgath Chriosda fein tharad,
Bho mhullach do chinn
Gu buinn do chas.

I PLACE the charm on thy body,
And on thy prosperity,
The charm of the God of life

For thy protection.

The charm that Bride of the kine
Put round the fair neck of Dornghil,
The charm that Mary put about her Son,
Between sole and throat,
Between pap and knee,
Between back and breast,
Between chest and sole,
Between eye and hair.

The host of Michael on thy side,
The shield of Michael on thy shoulder,
There is not between heaven and earth
That can overcome the King of grace.

No spear shall rive thee,
No sea shall drown thee,
No woman shall wile thee,
No man shall wound thee.

The mantle of Christ Himself about thee,
The shadow of Christ Himself above thee,
From the crown of thy head
To the soles of thy feet.

Ta seun De ort a nis,
Cha teid gu brath ort ailis.

Theid thu mach an ainm do Righ,
Thig thu steach an ainm do Phriomh,
Is le Dia nan dul thu nis gu h-uilidh,
Agus leis na Cumhachdan comhla.

Cuirim an seun seo moch Di-luain,
An ceum cruaidh, druiseach, droigheach,
Falbh a mach 's an seun mu d' chom,
Is na biodh bonn eagail ort.

Diridh tu cirein nan stuc,
Dionar tu a thaobh do chuil,
Is tu an eala chiuin 's a bhlar,
Cumhnar tu am measg nan ar,
Seasaidh tu troimh choig ceud,
Is bidh t'eircirich an sas.

Seun De umad!
Feun De tharad!

The charm of God is on thee now,
Thou shalt never know disgrace.

Thou shalt go forth in name of thy King,
Thou shalt come in in name of thy Chief,
To the God of life thou now belongest wholly,
And to all the Powers together.

I place this charm early on Monday,
In passage hard, brambly, thorny,
Go thou out and the charm about thy body,
And be not the least fear upon thee.

Thou shalt ascend the crest of the hill,
Protected thou shalt be behind thee,
Thou art the calm swan in battle,
Preserved thou shalt be amidst the slaughter,
Stand thou canst against five hundred,
And thine oppressors shall be seized.

The charm of God about thee!
The arm of God above thee!

SIAN A BHEATHA BHUAN

THE CHARM OF THE LASTING LIFE

CUIRIM sian a bheatha bhuan,
Mu 'r crodh luath, leathann, lan,
An creagan air an laigh an spreidh,
Gun eirich iad beo slan.

A nuas le buaidh 's le beannachd,
A suas le luaths 's le leannachd,
Gun ghnu, gun tnu, gun fharmad,
Gun suil bhig, gun suil mhoir,
Gun suil choig an dearmaid.

Sughaidh mise seo, sughadh feith farmaid
Air ceannard an tighe 's air teaghlaich a bhaile,
Gun eirich gach droch-bhuil, 's gach droch-bhuaidh
Bu dhualta dhuibh-se dhaibh-san.

Ma mhallaich teanga duibh,
Bheannaich cridhe duibh;
Ma ghonaich suil duibh,
Shonaich run duibh.

Tionndanam is teanndanam,
Culionn cruaidh is creanndagaich
Air an caoire boirionn 's air an laoighe firionn,
Fad nan naodh 's nan naodh fichead bliadhna.

I WILL place the charm of the lasting life,
Upon your cattle active, broad, and full,
The knoll upon which the herds shall lie down,
That they may rise from it whole and well.

Down with success, and with blessing,
Up with activity and following,
Without envy, without malice, without ill-will,
Without small eye, without large eye,
Without the five eyes of neglect.

I will suck this, the sucking of envious vein
On the head of the house, and the townland families,
That every evil trait, and every evil tendency
Inherent in you shall cleave to them.

If tongue cursed you,
A heart blessed you;
If eye blighted you,
A wish prospered you.

A hurly-burlying, a topsy-turvying,
A hard hollying and a wan withering
To their female sheep and to their male calves,
For the nine and the nine score years.

SIAN BRIDE

ST BRIDE'S CHARM

SIAN a chuir Bride nam buadh,
M'a mise, m'a cire, m'a buar,
M'a capuill, m'a cathmhil, m'a cual,
Moch is anamach dol dachaidh is uaith.

Gan cumail bho chreagan, bho chleitean,

Bho ladhara 's bho adhaircean a cheile,
Bho iana na Creige Ruaidh,
Is bho Luath na Feinne.

Bho lannaire liath Creag Duilionn,
Bho iolaire riabhach Beinn-Ard,
Bho sheobhag luth Torr-an-Duin,
Is fitheach dur Creag-a-Bhaird.

Bho mhada-ruadh nan cuireid,
Bho mhada-ulai a Mhaim,
Bho thaghan tocaidh na tuide,
'S bho mhaghan udail a mhais.

* * * * *
* * * * *
Bho gach ceithir-chasach spuireach,
Agus guireach da sgiath.

THE charm put by Bride the beneficent,
On her goats, on her sheep, on her kine,
On her horses, on her chargers, on her herds,
Early and late going home, and from home.

To keep them from rocks and ridges,
From the heels and the horns of one another
From the birds of the Red Rock,
And from Luath of the Feinne.

From the blue peregrine hawk of Creag Duilion,
From the brindled eagle of Ben-Ard,
From the swift hawk of Tordun,
From the surly raven of Bard's Creag.

From the fox of the wiles,
From the wolf of the Mam,
From the foul-smelling fumart,
And from the restless great-hipped bear.

* * * * *
* * * * *
From every hoofed of four feet,
And from every hatched of two wings.

SIAN

SAIN

SIAN a chuir Moir air a Mac,
Sian romh mharbhadh, sian romh lot,
Sian eadar cioch agus glun,
Sian eadar glun agus lorc,
Sian nan tri sian,
Sian nan coig sian,
Sian nan seachd sian,
Eadar barr do chinn
Agus bonn do chos.
Sian nan seachd paidir, a h-aon,
Sian nan seachd paidir, a dha,
Sian nan seachd paidir, a tri,
Sian nan seachd paidir, a ceithir,
Sian nan seachd paidir, a coig,
Sian nan seachd paidir, a sia,
Sian nan seachd paidir, a seachd
Ort a nis.
Bho chlaban do bhathas,
Gu dathas do bhonn,
Ga d' chumail o d' chul,
Ga d' chumhn o t' aghaidh.

Clogad slainne mu d' cheann,
Cearcul comhnant mu d' bhraigh,
Uchd-eididh an t-sagairt mu d' bhrollach,
Ga d' dhion an cogadh 's an comhrag nan namh.

Ma's ruaig dhuit, oig, o thaobh do chuil,
Buaidh na h-Oigh ga do chomhnadh dluth,
Sear no siar, siar no sear,
Tuath no deas, deas no tuath.

THE sain put by Mary on her Son,
Sain from death, sain from wound,
Sain from breast to knee,
Sain from knee to foot,
Sain of the three sains,
Sain of the five sains,
Sain of the seven sains,
From the crown of thy head
To the soles of thy feet.
Sain of the seven paters, one,
Sain of the seven paters, two,
Sain of the seven paters, three,

219

Sain of the seven paters, four,
Sain of the seven paters, five,
Sain of the seven paters, six,
Sain of the seven paters, seven
Upon thee now.
From the edge of thy brow,
To thy coloured soles,
To preserve thee from behind,
To sustain thee in front.

Be the helmet of salvation about thine head,
Be the corslet of the covenant about thy throat,
Be the breastplate of the priest upon thy breast,
To shield thee in the battle and combat of thine enemies.

If pursued, oh youth, from behind thy back,
The power of the Virgin be close to succour thee,
East or west, west or east,
North or south, south or north.

EOLAS GRADHAICH

LOVE CHARM

THE people quote many proverbs relating to love and to love charms. 'Is leth-aoin an caothach agus an gaol,'--Twins are lunacy and love. 'Is ionann an galar gaoil agus an galar caothaich,'--Alike the complaint of love and the complaint of madness. 'Duinidh gaol mile suil ach duisgidh cuig mile farmaid,'--Love will close a thousand eyes but waken five thousand jealousies.

The lucky bones are the joint of the big toe of the right foot and the nail-joints of the left foot of an old man. These are said to be the first part of the human body to decay.

CHAN eolas gradhach duit
Uisge thraghadh tromh shop,
Ach gradh an fhir [te] thig riut,
Le bhlaths a tharsainn ort.

Eirich moth 's an Domhnach,
Gu leac comhnard pleatach
Beir leat currachd sagart,
Agus puball beannach.

Tog sid air do ghualainn
Ann an sluasaid mhaide,
Faigh naoi gasa roinnich
Air an gearradh le tuaigh,

Tri cnamhan seann-duine,
Air an tarruinn a uaigh,
Loisg iad air teine crionaich,
Is dean gu leir 'n an luath.

Crath an dearbh bhrollach do leannain,
An aghaidh gath gaoth tuath,
'S theid mis an rath, 's am baran duit,
Nach falbh am fear [bean] sin uat.

IT is not love knowledge to thee
To draw water through a reed,
But the love of him [her] thou choosest,
With his warmth to draw to thee.

Arise thou early on the day of the Lord,
To the broad flat flag
Take with thee the biretta of a priest, [fox-glove (?)
And the pinnacled canopy. [butter-bur (?)

Lift them on thy shoulder
In a wooden shovel,
Get thee nine stems of ferns
Cut with an axe,

The three bones of an old man,
That have been drawn from the grave,
Burn them on a fire of faggots,
And make them all into ashes.

Shake it in the very breast of thy lover,
Against the sting of the north wind,
And I will pledge, and warrant thee,
That man [woman] will never leave thee.

EOLAS GRADHAIDH

LOVE CHARM

EOLAS gradhaidh dut,
Uisge thraghadh thromh shop,
Blaths an fhir [te] thig riut,
Le ghradh a tharsainn ort.

Eirich moch Di-domhnaich,

Gu lic chomhnard chladaich
Beir leat beannach pubaill,
Agus currachd sagairt.

Deannan beag a ghriosaich
An iochdar do bhadain,
Dolman corr a ghruaigean
Ann an sluasaid mhaide.

Tri cnamhan seann-duine,
An deigh an creann a uaigh,
Naoi goisne reann-roinnich,
An deigh an treann le tuaigh.

Loisg iad air teine crionaich
Is dean gu leir diubh luath;
Crath am brollach broth do leannain,
An aghaidh gath gaoth tuath.

Rach ruaig rath an alachd,
Car nan coig cuart,
'S bheirim brath is baran duit
Nach falbh am fear [bean] sin uat.

A LOVE charm for thee,
Water drawn through a straw,
The warmth of him [her] thou lovest,
With love to draw on thee.

Arise betimes on Lord's day,
To the flat rock of the shore
Take with thee the pointed canopy, [butter-bur (?)
And the cap of a priest. [fox-glove (?)

A small quantity of embers
In the skirt of thy kirtle,
A special handful of sea-weed
In a wooden shovel.

Three bones of an old man,
Newly torn from the grave,
Nine stalks of royal fern,
Newly trimmed with an axe.

Burn them on a fire of faggots
And make them all into ashes;

Sprinkle in the fleshy breast of thy lover,
Against the venom of the north wind.

Go round the 'rath' of procreation,
The circuit of the five turns,
And I will vow and warrant thee
That man [woman] shall never leave thee.

CRONACHDUINN SUIL

THWARTING THE EVIL EYE

THE results of the evil eye appear in yawning and vomiting and in a general disturbance of the system. The countenance assumes an appearance grim, gruesome, and repulsive--'greann, greisne, grannda.'

This formula for removing the effects of the evil eye is handed down from male to female, from female to male, and is efficacious only when thus transmitted. Before pronouncing it over the particular case of sickness, the operator proceeds to a stream, where the living and the dead alike pass, and lifts water, in name of the Holy Trinity, into a wooden ladle. In no case is the ladle of metal. On returning, a wife's gold ring, a piece of gold, of silver, and of copper, are put in the ladle. The sign of the holy cross is then made, and this rhyme is repeated in a slow recitative manner--the name of the person or animal under treatment being mentioned towards the end. In the case of an animal a woollen thread, generally of the natural colour of the sheep, is tied round the tail. The consecrated water is then given as a draught, and sprinkled over the head and backbone. In the case of a cow the horns and the space between the horns are carefully anointed.

The remnant of the water, no drop of which must have reached the ground previously, is poured over a corner stone, threshold flag, or other immovable stone or rock, which is said to split if the sickness be severe. Experts profess to distinguish whether it be a man or a woman who has laid the evil eye:--if a man, the copper adheres to the bottom of the upturned ladle, significant of the 'iomadh car,' many turns in a man's dark wily heart; if a woman, only the silver and gold adhere, the heart of a woman being to that of man--not in this case, 'as moonlight unto sunlight and as water unto wine'--but as gold and silver to copper and brass. Old women in the Highlands say that if men's hearts were laid bare they would be found to contain many more twists and turns and wiles than those of women.

CO a thilleas cronachduinn suil?
Tillidh mise tha mi 'n duil,
Ann an ainm Righ nan dul.
Tri seachd gairmeachdain co ceart,
Labhair Criosd an dorusd na cathrach;
Paidir Moire a h-aon,
Paidir Righ a dha,
Paidir Moire a tri,
Paidir Righ a ceithir,
Paidir Moire a coig,

Paidir Righ a sia,
Paidir Moire a seachd;
Tillidh seachd paidrichean Moire
Cronachduinn suil,
Co dhiubh bhitheas e air duine no air bruid,
Air mart no air earc;
Thusa bhi na d' h-ioma shlainte nochd,
[An t-ainm]
An ainm an Athar, a Mhic, 's an Spioraid Naoimh. Amen.

WHO shall thwart the evil eye?
I shall thwart it, methinks,
In name of the King of life.
Three seven commands so potent,
Spake Christ in the door of the city;
Pater Mary one,
Pater King two,
Pater Mary three,
Pater King four,
Pater Mary five,
Pater King six,
Pater Mary seven;
Seven pater Maries will thwart
The evil eye,
Whether it be on man or on beast,
On horse or on cow;
Be thou in thy full health this night,
[The name]
In name of the Father, the Son, and the Holy Spirit. Amen.

EOLAS A BHEUM SHULA

EXORCISM OF THE EYE

SALTRAIM air an t-suil,
Mar a shaltrais lach air luin,
Mar a shaltrais eal air burn,
Mar a shaltrais each air uir,
Mar a shaltrais earc air iuc,
Mar a shaltrais feachd nan dul,
Mar a shaltrais feachd nan dul.

Ta neart gaoith agam air,
Ta neart fraoich agam air,
Ta neart teine agam air,
Ta neart torruinn agam air,

Ta neart dealain agam air,
Ta neart gaillinn agam air,
Ta neart gile agam air,
Ta neart greine agam air,
Ta neart nan reul agam air,
Ta neart nan speur agam air,
Ta neart nan neamh
Is nan ce agam air,
Neart nan neamh
Is nan ce agam air.

Trian air na clacha glasa dheth,
Trian air na beanna casa dheth,
Trian air na h-easa brasa dheth,

I TRAMPLE upon the eye,
As tramples the duck upon the lake,
As tramples the swan upon the water,
As tramples the horse upon the plain,
As tramples the cow upon the 'iuc,'
As tramples the host of the elements,
As tramples the host of the elements.

Power of wind I have over it,
Power of wrath I have over it,
Power of fire I have over it,
Power of thunder I have over it,
Power of lightning I have over it,
Power of storms I have over it,
Power of moon I have over it,
Power of sun I have over it,
Power of stars I have over it,
Power of firmament I have over it,
Power of the heavens
And of the worlds I have over it,
Power of the heavens
And of the worlds I have over it.

A portion of it upon the grey stones, [third
A portion of it upon the steep hills,
A portion of it upon the fast falls,

Trian air na liana maiseach dheth,
'S trian air a mhuir mhoir shalach,
'S i fein asair is fearr gu ghiulan,
A mhuir mhor shalach,

Asair is fearr gu ghiulan.

An ainm Tri nan Dul,
An ainm nan Tri Numh,
An ainm nan uile Run,
Agus nan Cursa comhla.

A portion of it upon the fair meads,
And a portion upon the great salt sea,
She herself is the best instrument to carry it,
The great salt sea,
The best instrument to carry it.

In name of the Three of Life,
In name of the Sacred Three,
In name of all the Secret Ones,
And of the Powers together.

CRONACHDAIN SUIL

COUNTERACTING THE EVIL EYE

CHURNAICH suil thu,
Thurmaich bial thu,
Runaich cridh thu,
Smunaich miann thu.

Ceathrar a rinn du-sa trasd,
Fear agus bean,
Mac agus murn;
Triuir cuiream riu 'g an casg,
Athair,
Mac,
Spiorad Numh.

Cuiream fianuis chon Moire,
Mathair-chobhair an t-sluaigh,
Cuiream fianuis chon Bride,
Muime Chriosda nam buadh,
Cuiream fianuis chon Chaluim,
Ostal oirthir is chuain,
'S cuiream fianuis chon flathas,
Chon gach naoimh is gach aingil tha shuas.

Ma's e fear a rinn do lochd,
Le droch shuil,

Le droch run,
Le droch ruam,

AN eye covered thee,
A mouth spoke thee,
A heart envied thee,
A mind desired thee.

Four made thee thy cross, [? have done thee harm
Man and wife,
Youth and maid;
Three will I send to thwart them,
Father,
Son,
Spirit Holy.

I appeal to Mary,
Aidful mother of men,
I appeal to Bride,
Foster-mother of Christ omnipotent,
I appeal to Columba,
Apostle of shore and sea,
And I appeal to heaven,
To all saints and angels that be above.

If it be a man that has done thee harm,
With evil eye,
With evil wish,
With evil passion,

Gun tilg thu dhiot gach olc,
Gach mug,
Gach gnug,
Gach gruam,
'S gum bi thu gu math gu brath,
Ri linn an snathle seo
Dhol a d' dhail mu'n cuart,
An onair De agus Ios,
Agus Spioraid ioic bhi-bhuain.

Mayest thou cast off each ill,
Every malignity,
Every malice,
Every harassment,
And mayest thou be well for ever,
While this thread

Goes round thee,
In honour of God and of Jesus,
And of the Spirit of balm everlasting.

UIBE RI SHUL

SPELL FOR EVIL EYE

UIBE gheal chuir Muire mhin,
A nail air allt, air muir, 's air tir,
Air bhrig, 's air ghat fharmaid,
Air mhac armaid,
Air fiacaill coin-ghiorr,
Air siadhadh coin-ghearr,
Air tri chorracha-cri,
Air tri chorracha cnamh,
Air tri chorracha creothail,
'S air lion leothair lair. [? leobhar

Ge be co rinn dut an t-suil,
Gun laigh i air fein,
Gun laigh i air a thur,
Gun laigh i air a spreidh,
Gun laigh i air a shult,
Gun laigh i air a shaill,
Gun laigh i air a chuid,
Gun laigh i air a chlainn,
Gun laigh i air a bhean,
Gun laigh i air a loinn.

Clomhaidh mise an t-suil,
Somhaidh mise an t-suil,
Imirichidh mi 'n t-suil,
A thri feithean feiche,
'S teang eug an iomalain.
Tri maighdeana beaga caomh,
A rugadh 's an aon oidhche ri Criosd,
Ma's beo dh'an triuir sin air an oidhche nochd,
Beo bhith d' ire-sa, bheothaich bhochd.

THE fair spell that lovely Mary sent,
Over stream, over sea, over land,
Against incantations, against withering glance,
Against inimical power,
Against the teeth of wolf,
Against the testicles of wolf,

Against the three crooked cranes,
Against the three crooked bones,
Against the three crooked 'creothail,'
And against lint 'leothair' of the ground. [? long lint

Whoso made to thee the eye,'
May it lie upon himself,
May it lie upon his house,
May it lie upon his flocks,
May it lie upon his substance,
May it lie upon his fatness,
May it lie upon his means,
May it lie upon his children,
May it lie upon his wife,
May it lie upon his descendants.

I will subdue the eye,
I will suppress the eye,
And I will banish the eye,
The three arteries inviting (?),
And the tongue of death completely.
Three lovely little maidens,
Born the same night with Christ,
If alive be these three to-night,
Life be anear thee, poor beast.

OBI RI SHUIL

CHARM FOR THE EYE

CUIRIM an obi seo ri m' shuil,
Mar a dh' orduich Ti nan dul,
A uchd Pheadail, a uchd Phoil,
An treas ob is fearr fo'n ghrein.

Sil, a Mhoire, sil, a Bhride,
Sil, a Phadra, righ nan reachd,
Sil, a Chalum-chille chaoimh,
Sil, a Chiarain naoimh nam feart.

Air bhuadh larach, air chruadh lamha,
An cath tearmaid, an cath farmaid,
Air gach mac da math d' an teid,
Bidh Mac De leis an treuin armachd.

A uchd Athar,

A uchd Mic,
A uchd Spioraid Naoimh.
Amen.

I PLACE this charm to mine eye,
As the King of life ordained,
From the bosom of Peter and Paul,
The third best amulet under the sun.

Pour Mary, pour Bride,
Pour Patrick, king of laws,
Pour Columba the kindly,
Pour Ciaran, saint of power.

For victory in battle, for hardness of hand,
In battle of defence, in battle of offence,
On every son with whom it shall go well,
The Son of God will be with him in full armour.

From the bosom of Father,
From the bosom of Son,
From the bosom of Holy Spirit.
Amen.

EOIR BEUM SULA

CHARM FOR THE EVIL EYE

GE be co rinn duit an t-suil,
Gun curn i air fein,
Gun curn i air a thur,
Gun curn i air a spreidh,
Air a chaillich mhungaich,
Air a chaillaich mhiongaich,
Air a chaillaich mhangaich,
'S air a chaillich gheur-luirg,
A dh' eirich 's a mhaduinn,
'S a suil 'n a seilbh,
'S a seilbh 'n a seoin,
Nar a leatha a buaile fein,
Nar a leatha leth a deoin,
A chuid nach ith na fithich di,
Gun ith na h-eoin.

Ceathrar a rinn duit an t-suil,
Fear agus bean, mac agus mum;

230

Triuir a thilgeas diot an tnu,
Athair agus Mac, agus Spiorad Numh.

Mar a thog Criosd am meas,
Thar bharra nam preas,
Gun ann a thogas e dhiot-s' a nis
Gach cnid, gach tnu, gach farmad,
O'n la'n diugh gu la deireannach do shaoghail.

WHOSO laid on thee the eye,
May it lie upon himself,
May it lie upon his house,
May it lie upon his flocks,
On the shuffling carlin,
On the sour-faced carlin,
On the bounding carlin,
On the sharp-shanked carlin,
Who arose in the morning,
With her eye on her flocks,
With her flocks in her 'seoin,'
May she never own a fold,
May she never have half her desires,
The part of her which the ravens do not eat,
May the birds devour.

Four made to thee the eye,
Man and dame, youth and maid;
Three who will cast off thee the envy,
The Father, the Son, and the Holy Spirit.

As Christ lifted the fruit,
From the branches of the bushes,
May He now lift off thee
Every ailment, every envy, every jealousy,
From this day forth till the last day of thy life.

EOLAS

CHARM

PEADAIR is Seumas is Eoin,
Triuir is binne beuis an gloir,
Dh' eirich a dheanamh na h-eoir,
Romh mhor dhorus na Cathrach,
Ri glun deas De a Mhic.

Air na feara fur-shuileach,
Air na bana bur-shuileach,
Air na siocharra seanga sith,
Air na saighde siubhlach sibheideach.

Dithis a rinn dut dibhidh sul,
Fear agus bean le nimh agus tnu,
Triuir a chuirim an urra riu,
Athair, agus Mac, agus Spiorad Numh.

Ceithir ghalara fichead an aorabh duine 's bruid,
Dia d' an sgrid, Dia d' an sgroid, Dia d' an sgruid,
A t' fhuil, a t' fheoil a d' chnamha cubhra caoin,
O'n la'n duigh 's gach la thig, gun tig la crich do shaoghail.

PETER and James and John,
The three of sweetest virtues in glory,
Who arose to make the charm,
Before the great door of the City,
By the right knee of God the Son.

Against the keen-eyed men,
Against the peering-eyed women,
Against the slim, slender, fairy-darts,
Against the swift arrows of furies.

Two made to thee the withered eye,
Man and woman with venom and envy,
Three whom I will set against them,
Father, Son, and Spirit Holy.

Four and twenty diseases in the constitution of man and beast,
God scrape them, God search them, God cleanse them,
From out thy blood, from out thy flesh, from out thy fragrant bones,
From this day and each day that comes, till thy day on earth be done.

MALLACHD

A MALEDICTION

THAINIG dithis a mach
A Cathrach Neobh,
Fear agus bean,
A dheanadh nan oisnean.

Mallaich dha na beana bur-shuileach,

Mallaich dha na feara fur-shuileach,
Mallaich dha na ceithir saighde, guineach, guid,
Dh' fhaodadh a bhi 'n aorabh duine 's bruid.

THERE came two out
From the City of Heaven,
A man and a woman,
To make the 'oisnean.'

Curses on the blear-eyed women,
Curses on the sharp-eyed men,
Curses on the four venomous arrows of disease,
That may be in the constitution of man and beast.

EOLAS A BHEIM SHUIL

SPELL OF THE EVIL EYE

THE following fragment was copied from an old manuscript and sent to me by the Rev. Angus Macdonald, Killearnan, Black Isle. The reciter's name is given as 'Anna Chaimbeul'--Ann Campbell.

SALTRUIGHIDH mis air an t-suil,
Mar a shaltruigheas eal air tigh nocht, [traigh?
Ta neart gaoithe agam air,
Ta neart greine agam air,
Ta neart Mhic Righ Neamh
Agus talmhainn agam air,
Trian air na clacha glasa,

* * * *
'S trian air a mhuir mhoir,
Is i fein acfhuinn is fearr 'g a ghiulan.

TRAMPLE I upon the eye,
As tramples the swan on a bare house, [strand?
Power of wind I have over it,
The power of the Son of the King of Heaven
And of earth I have over it,
A portion of it on the grey stones, [third

* * * *
And a portion on the great sea,
She herself is the instrument most able to bear it.

OBI NAN SUL

233

INCANTATION FOR THE EYE

OBI nan geur shul,
Obi nan reul-iul,
Obi Re nan uile re,
Obi Dhe nan dul,
Obi Re nan uile re,
Obi Dhe nan dul.

Obi Bhride nan ciabh oir,
Obi Mhoire mhin-ghil Oigh,
Obi Bheus nan uile bheus,
Obi Dhe na gloir,
Obi Bheus nan uile bheus,
Obi Dhe na gloir.

Obi Pheadail agus Phail,
Obi Airil 's Eoin a ghraidh,
Obi Dhe nan uile dhe,
Obi Dhe nan gras,
Obi Dhe nan uile dhe,
Obi Dhe nan gras.

Feill Mhairi, Feill Dhe,
Feill shagart agus chleir,
Feill Chriosd, Righ nam feart,
Dhiongaich anns a ghrein a neart,
Feill Chriosd, Righ nam feart,
Dhiongaich anns a ghrein a neart.

INCANTATION of the seeing eye,
Incantation of the guiding star,
Incantation of the King of all kings,
Incantation of the God of life,
Incantation of the King of all kings,
Incantation of the God of life.

Incantation of Bride of the locks of gold,
Incantation of the beauteous Mary Virgin,
Incantation of the Virtue of all virtues,
Incantation of the God of glory,
Incantation of the Virtue of all virtues,
Incantation of the God of glory.

Incantation of Peter and of Paul,
Incantation of Ariel and John of love,

Incantation of the God of all gods,
Incantation of the God of grace,
Incantation of the God of all gods,
Incantation of the God of grace.

Feast of Mary, Feast of God,
Feast of cleric and of priest,
Feast of Christ, Prince of power,
Who established the sun with strength,
Feast of Christ, Prince of power,
Who endowed the sun with strength.

OBA RI SHUL

SPELL OF THE EYE

CUIRIM an oba seo ri m' shuil,
Mar a dh' orduich Righ nan dul,
Oba Pheadail, oba Phoil,
Oba Sheumais, oba Eoin,
Oba Chaluim-chille chaoimh,
Oba Phadra sar gach naoimh,
Oba Bhride bhith nam ba,
Oba Mhoire mhin nan agh,
Oba tromla, oba treuid,
Oba lomra, oba spreidh,
Oba nolla, oba ni,
Oba sona, oba sith,
Oba troga, oba treuin,
An treas oba is fearr fo'n ghrein,
Oba bhuadha nan Tri Bhuadh,
Athar, Mic, Spioraid buan.

I PLACE this spell to mine eye,
As the Ring of life ordained,
Spell of Peter, spell of Paul,
Spell of James, spell of John,
Spell of Columba benign,
Spell of Patrick, chief of saints,
Spell of Bride, tranquil of the kine,
Spell of Mary, lovely of the joys,
Spell of cows, spell of herds,
Spell of sheep, spell of flocks,
Spell of greatness, spell of means,
Spell of joy, spell of peace,
Spell of war, spell of the brave,

The third best spell under the sun,
The powerful spell of the Three Powers,
Father, Son, Spirit everlasting.

OBA RI SUL

SPELL OF THE EYE

OBA mho-ghil,
A chuir Moir Oighe,
Chon ighinn Dorail,
Nan or-bhi cuach,
A nall air mor-thir,
A nall air oir-thir,
A nall air log-thir,
A nall air cuan,
Chon casga sula,
Chon casga dula,
Chon casga tnutha,
Chon casga fuatha,
Chon tilleadh breotaich,
Chon tilleadh greotaich,
Chon tilleadh sreotaich,
Chon tilleadh ruaidh.

THE spell fair-white,
Sent of Mary Virgin,
To the daughter of Dorail,
Of the golden-yellow hair,
Hither on main-land,
Hither on coast-land,
Hither on lake-land,
Hither on ocean,
To thwart eye,
To thwart net,
To thwart envy,
To thwart hate.
To repel 'breotaich,'
To repel 'greotaich,'
To repel 'sreotaich,'
To repel rose.

OB RI SHUL

SPELL OF THE EYE

OB a chuir Moire mhor-gheal
Gu Bride mhin-gheal,
Air muir, air tir, air li, 's rachd fharmaid,
Air fiacail coin-ghiorr, 's air siadha coin-ghearr.

Ge be co leag ort an t-suil,
Gum much i air fein,
Gum much i air a thur,
Gum much i air a spreidh.

Clomhadh mis an t-suil,
Somhadh mis an t-suil,
Tri teanga tur nan iomlan,
Am feithean a chridhe,
An eibhlean imileig.

A uchd Athar,
A uchd Mic,
A uchd Spioraid Naoimh.

THE spell the great white Mary sent
To Bride the lovely fair,
For sea, for land, for water, and for withering glance,
For teeth of wolf, for testicle of wolf.

Whoso laid on thee the eye,
May it oppress himself,
May it oppress his house,
May it oppress his flocks.

Let me subdue the eye,
Let me avert the eye,
The three complete tongues of fullness,
In the arteries of the heart,
In the vitals of the navel.

From the bosom of Father,
From the bosom of Son,
From the bosom of Holy Spirit.

EOLAS A CHRONACHAIDH

SPELL OF THE COUNTERACTING

BUAINIDH mi a chathair aigh
A bhuain Criosd le leth-laimh.

Thainig Ard Righ nan aingeal
Le ghradh 's le fhath os mo chionn.

Thainig Iosa Criosda steach
Le bliochd, le blachd, le barr,
Le laoigh bhoirionn, le ais.

Air suil bhig, air suil mhoir,
Air uachdar cuid Chriosd.

An ainm Ti nan dul
Cum rium do ghras,
Crun Righ nan aingeal,
Bainne chur an uth 's an ar,
Le laoigh bhoirionn, le al.

Gun robh agaibh fad nan seachd bliadhna
Gun chall laogh, gun chall bainne,
Gun chall maona no caomh charaid.

I WILL pluck the gracious yarrow
That Christ plucked with His one hand.

The High King of the angels
Came with His love and His countenance above me.

Jesus Christ came hitherward
With milk, with substance, with produce,
With female calves, with milk product.

On small eye, on large eye,
Over Christ's property.

In name of the Being of life
Supply me with Thy grace,
The crown of the King of the angels
To put milk in udder and gland,
With female calves, with progeny.

May you have the length of seven years
Without loss of calf, without loss of milk,
Without loss of means or of dear friends.

CUNNTAS AN T-SLEAMHNAIN

THE COUNTING OF THE STYE

THE exorcism of the stye is variously called 'Cunntas an t-Sleamhnain'--Counting of the Stye, 'Bolas an t-Sleamhnain'--Exorcism of the Stye, and 'Eoir an t-Sleamhnain'--Charm of the Stye.

When making the charm the exorcist holds some sharp-pointed instrument, preferably a nail, or the tongue of a brooch or buckle, between the thumb and forefinger of the right hand. With each question the operator makes a feint with the instrument at the stye, going perilously near the eye. The sensation caused by the thrusting is extremely painful to the sufferer and even to the observer.

The reciter assured the writer that a cure immediately follows the operation. Possibly the thrusting acts upon the nervous system of the patient.

Ordinarily the exorcist omits mentioning the word 'sleamhnan' after the first two times, abbreviating thus:--

'C'uim an tainig a dha an seo
Gun a tri an seo?'

Why came the two here
Without the three here?

After the incantation the Lord's Prayer is intoned, and the following is repeated:

'Paidir a h-aon,
Paidir a dha,
Paidir a tri,
Paidir a ceithir,
Paidir a coig,
Paidir a sia,
Paidir a seachd,
Paidir a h-ochd,
Paidir a naodh,
Paidir a h-aon
'S a h-ochd,
Paidir Chriosda chaoimh
Ort an oidhche nochd,
Paidir Tri nan dul
Air a shuil gun lochd.'

Pater one,
Pater two,
Pater three,
Pater four,
Pater five,
Pater six,

Pater seven,
Pater eight,
Pater nine,
Pater one
And eight,
Pater of Christ the kindly
Be upon thee to-night,
Pater of the Three of life
Upon thine eye without harm.

This seems to indicate that the Lord's Prayer was originally repeated nine times.

C'UIM an tainig an aon sleamhnan,
Gun an da shleamhnan an seo?
C'uim an tainig an da shleamhnan,
Gun na tri sleamhnain an seo?
C'uim an tainig na tri sleamhnain,
Gun na ceithir sleamhnain an seo?
C'uim an tainig na ceithir sleamhnain,
Gun na coig sleamhnain an seo?
C'uim an tainig na coig sleamhnain,
Gun na sia sleamhnain an seo?
C'uim an tainig na sia sleamhnain,
Gun na seachd sleamhnain an seo?
C'uim an tainig na seachd sleamhnain,
Gun na h-ochd sleamhnain an seo?
C'uim an tainig na h-ochd sleamhnain,
Gun na naodh sleamhnain an seo?
C'uim an tainig a naodh,
No aon idir an seo?

WHY came the one stye,
Without the two styes here?
Why came the two styes,
Without the three styes here?
Why came the three styes,
Without the four styes here?
Why came the four styes,
Without the five styes here?
Why came the five styes,
Without the six styes here?
Why came the six styes,
Without the seven styes here?
Why came the seven styes,
Without the eight styes here?
Why came the eight styes,

Without the nine styes here?
Why came the nine,
Or one at all here?

AM FIONN-FAOILIDH

THE 'FIONN-FAOILIDH'

CUIREAM fionn-faoilidh umam,
A thraoghadh feirge falamh,
A chumail rium mo chliu,
Fad 's a bhios mi biu air talamh.

O Mhicheil! glac mo lamh,
Liobh rium cairdeas De,
Ma tha mi-run no di-run air mo namh,
Criosd a bhi eadar mis is e,
O, Criosd eadar mis is e!

Ma tha mi-run no di-run air mo sgath,
Criosd a bhi eadar mis is e,
O, Criosd eadar mis is e!

I PLACE the 'fionn-faoilidh' on me,
To drain wrath empty,
To preserve to me my fame,
While I shall live on earth.

O Michael! grasp my hand,
Vouchsafe to me the love of God,
If there be ill-will or ill-wish in mine enemy,
Christ be between me and him,
Oh, Christ between me and him!

If there be ill-will or ill-wish concerning me,
Christ be between me and it,
Oh, Christ between me and it!

EOLAS TNU

ENVY SPELL

THESE lines were obtained in Tiree from a woman known as 'Nic 'aldomhnuich, the daughter of Maoldomhnuich, rendered 'Ludovic.' This woman had known many such runes, but was forgetting them.

241

MaolDomhnuich is one of the many personal names originating in the Celtic Church, now rare elsewhere, but still current in the Western Isles. Some of these names with their meanings are interesting. MaolDomhnuich means 'the tonsured of the Lord,' MaolCiaran 'the tonsured of Ciaran,' MaolPadruig 'the tonsured of Patrick,' MaolCalum 'the tonsured of Columba,' MaolMicheil 'the tonsured of Michael,' MaolBride 'the tonsured of Bride,' MaolMoire 'the tonsured of Mary.' MaolIosa, 'the tonsured of Jesus,' is the Malise and Malsie of Sir Walter Scott, and the Malisu of the Earls of Strathearn. A precipitous island near the east entrance to Macneilltown, Barra, is called 'Maoldomhnuich' from an anchorite of the name who lived there and whose cell is still to be seen. The island is also called 'Eilean nam fiadh,' isle of the deer, from the ancient Macneills of Barra having had deer there.

There is hardly an island however remote, or an ocean-girt rock however precipitous, throughout the stormy Hebrid seas, that does not show touching traces of the courage and devotion of these self-denying anchorites.

The writer often took pleasure in visiting these almost inaccessible rocks and tracing their cells.

GE be co rinn duit an tnu,
Fear dubh, no bean fionn,
Triuir cuirim riu ga chasg--
Spiorad Numh, Athair, Mac.

WHOSO made to thee the envy,
Swarthy man or woman fair,
Three I will send to thwart it--
Holy Spirit, Father, Son.

AN DEARG CHASACHAN

THE RED-STALK

BUAINIDH mi an dearg-chasachan aic,
An lion a bhuain Bride mhin tromh glaic,
Air buaidh shlainte, air buaidh chairdeas
Air buaidh thoileachais,
Air buaidh droch run, air buaidh droch shul,
Air buaidh chronachais.
Air buaidh droch bheud, air buaidh droch bheus,
Air buaidh ghonachais,
Air buaidh droch sgeul, air buaidh droch bheul,
Air buaidh shonachais--
Air buaidh shonachais.

PLUCK will I the little red-stalk of surety,
The lint the lovely Bride drew through her palm,
For success of health, for success of friendship,

For success of joyousness,
For overcoming of evil mind, for overcoming of evil eye,
For overcoming of bewitchment,
For overcoming of evil deed, for overcoming of evil conduct,
For overcoming of malediction,
For overcoming of evil news, for overcoming of evil words,
For success of blissfulness--
For success of blissfulness.

AN EIDHEANN-MU-CHRANN

THE TREE-ENTWINING IVY

BUAINIDH mis an eidheann-mu-chrann,
Mar a bhuain Moire le a leth-laimh,
Mar a dh' orduich Righ nan dul,
Bainne chur an uth 's an ar,
Le laoigh bhreaca, bhoirionn, bhailgneach,
Mar a thubhradh anns an dailgneachd,
Air an laraich seo gu ceann la 's bliadhna,
A uchd Dia nan dul 's nan cursa comhla.

I WILL pluck the tree-entwining ivy,
As Mary plucked with her one hand,
As the King of life has ordained,
To put milk in udder and gland,
With speckled fair female calves,
As was spoken in the prophecy,
On this foundation for a year and a day,
Through the bosom of the God of life, and of all the powers.

EOLAS AN TORRANAIN

THE figwort is known as 'farach dubh,' 'farach donn,' 'farum,' 'forum,' 'fothlus,' 'fotlus,' 'lus nan cnapan,' 'lus nan clugan,' 'clugan,' 'cluganach,' 'lus an torranain,' 'torranach,' and 'torranan.' The names are descriptive:--'farach dubh'--black mallet, 'farach donn'--brown mallet; 'farum' and 'forum' are probably forms of 'farach.' 'Fothlus' and 'fotlus'--crumbs, refuse, scrofulous, 'lus nan clugan'--plant of the clusters, 'lus an torranain'--plant of the thunderer. Probably 'tarrann,' 'torrann,' 'torranan,' 'tarranan,' are variants of Taranis, the name of the thunder god of the Gauls.

On the mainland the figwort is known for its medicinal properties, and in the islands for its magical powers. On the mainland the leaf of the plant is applied to cuts and bruises, and the tuber to sores and tumours. In the islands the plant was placed on the cow fetter, under the milk boyne, and over the byre door, to ensure milk in the cows.

Having intoned the incantation of the 'torranan,' the reciter said--'The "torranan" is a blessed plant. It grows in sight of the sea. Its root is a cluster of four bulbs like the four teats of a cow. The stalk of the plant is as long as the arm, and the bloom is as large as the breast of a woman, and as pure white as the driven snow of the hill. It is full of the milk of grace and goodness and of the gift of peace and power, and fills with the filling and ebbs with the ebbing tide. It is therefore meet to cull the plant with the flow and not with the ebb of the restless sea. If I had the "torranan" it would ensure to me abundant milk in my cow all the year. Poor as I am, I would rather than a Saxon pound that I had the blessed "torranan." I went away to John the son of Fearachar, who knows every plant that comes through the ground, to see if he would get me the "torranan" of power. But John's wife said "No," and that I was only an "oinig," a silly woman. The jade!'

John Beaton, known as John, son of Fearachar, son of John, son of 'Niall Dotair,' Neil the Doctor, was a shepherd by occupation but a botanist by instinct. He knew Gaelic only, and he knew no letters, but probably he knew more about plants and plant habitats and characteristics than any other man in Scotland. He lived in close communion with Nature, and loved plants as he loved his children--with a warm abiding love which no poverty could cool and no age could dim. A Gaelic proverb says:--'Bu dual da sin'--that was hereditary to him: and:--'Sgoiltidh an dualchas a chreig'--heredity will cleave the rock;

and again:--'Theid dualchas an aghaigh nan creag'--heredity will go against the rocks. John Beaton was a striking confirmation of these sayings, being descended from a long line of botanists and botanical doctors who left their impress on the minds and on the language of their fellow-countrymen. He was descended from the Beatons of Skye, who were descended from the Beatons of Islay. They in turn were descended from the Beatons of Mull, who are said to have come down from Beatan, the medical missionary of the Columban Church of Iona. These Beatons produced many eminent men, among them James Beaton, Archbishop of Glasgow, and his still greater nephew David, the Cardinal Archbishop of St Andrews, and, through the Barons Livingstone of Bachuill, Lismore, David Livingstone, physician, missionary, traveller and explorer. Mary Beaton, mentioned in the song of the Queen's Four Maries, was also of these Beatons:

'Last night there were four Maries,
This night there shall be but three;
There was Marie Beaton and Marie Seaton
And Marie Carmichael and me.'

[paragraph continues] The people of Mull say that this Mary Beaton was of the Mull family, but the distinguished scholar, the late Hector Maclean, and other Islay men, claimed that she was of the Islay Beatons. The Beatons were hereditary 'leighean,' physicians, to the Lords of the Isles and to other great insular and mainland chiefs. They were also physicians to the Kings of Scotland, whom they visited periodically. Payments for some of these visits are recorded in the Exchequer Rolls.

The Beatons left many MSS. on medicine and on medicinal plants. Some of these are in the Advocates' Library, some are in private possession, and many are known to have been lost. Some of the most beautiful sculptured stones in Iona, Mull, Islay, and elsewhere, are over the tombs of Beatons.

244

Several of the Beatons of Mull and Islay went to Paris and other Continental cities to complete their medical and theological studies. Some of these remained abroad and rose to positions of distinction. The name is still to be met with in France in the French form of Bethune. One of the Beatons on returning to Scotland retained that form of the name. He settled in Fife. A descendant of his settled in Skye as leech to Macleod of Macleod, founding the Skye branch of the family. One of this family was known as 'Fearachar Leigh,' 'Fearachar Lighiche,' Farquhar the Physician. He held the small estate of Husabost, near the mouth of Dunvegan Loch, for his services. He had a medical MS. valued at sixty milch cows; and so careful was he of this manuscript, that when he himself came up to Dunvegan by boat he sent a trusted man-servant on horse-back round by land with the manuscript. John Beaton, the shepherd of Uist, was descended from this 'Fearachar Leigh.'

John Beaton was too old and too rheumatic to move from home, but he

described the 'torranan,' its flower, leaf, stalk, and root, and its situation in Benmore, to his son and the writer, with marvellous fullness and accuracy, though he had not been to Benmore nor seen the 'torranan' for many years previously. He said that there were only two plants of it there, and that these were near one another on Benmore and overlooking the sea. He explained the various medicinal uses of the plant, but smiled at its alleged magical powers.

This was in 1877. John Beaton died in 1881, aged 92, one of nature's scientists and of nature's gentlemen. In 1896 his son, Fearachar, sent me the two plants from Benmore in South Uist. One of them I gave to Professor Bayley Balfour of the University of Edinburgh, who kindly identified the plant for me.

The following tradition is current in Uist:--The Pope sent Torranan to teach the people of Ireland the way of salvation. But the people of Ireland would not receive Torranan, whom they beat and maltreated in various ways. Torranan prayed to God to deliver him from the Irish, and shook the dust of Ireland off his feet. He betook himself to his coracle and turned it sun-wise, in name of God, and in name of Christ, and in name of Spirit, praying the 'Teora Naomh,' Holy Three, to send him when and where and whichever way they listed and had work for him to do--but not again to Ireland. The man was driven about hither and thither on the wild waves in his frail coracle no one knows how long or how far. But an Eye was on his prow, and a Hand was on his helm and the tide, and the wind, and the waves combined to take him into the little creek of Cailigeo in Benbecula.

The Island of Benbecula is situated between the islands of South Uist and North Uist, its axis being at right angles to the axis of these islands--one end on the Minch, the other on the Atlantic. It is fordable on both sides when the tide is out, hence the Gaelic name 'Beinn-nam-faoghla'--ben of the fords. The hill indicated in the name is near the centre of the island and nearly in a direct line between the fords. It is called 'Ruaidhbhal,' 'Ruaival'--red hill, from the Gaelic 'ruadh'--red, and the Norse 'fell' a hill. Ruaival is the only hill in Benbecula. It is cone-shaped, flat and level on the top, and 409 feet in height. The sloping sides are flushed with heather, while the flat summit is green and grassy. The summit commands an extraordinary view of fords and channels, islands, peninsulas and mainlands, seas and lakes, and of moors and machairs broken up and dotted over in the most marvellous manner with shallow pools, tarns, and lakes scattered broadcast beyond count, beyond number. Probably the world does not contain anything more disorderly than the distribution of land and water in and around Benbecula.

When Torranan was ascending the round red hill of Ruaival to survey his surroundings and to ascertain his whereabouts, his breast was sore from thirst, for he had had no water to drink since leaving Ireland. And Torranan prayed to God for water to quench his thirst, and lo! the red rock before him rent

asunder, and from the fissure a clear rill of cold water issued. Torranan thus pre-experienced the truth of Goethe's words:--

'At his appointed time revolving,
The sun these shades of night dispels,
The rock, its rugged breast dissolving,
Gives up to earth its hidden wells.'

The water was fair to see and pleasing to taste, and Torranan drank his 'seachd sath'--seven satiations, and he blessed the rill from the rent rock and called it 'Gamhnach'--farrow cow. 'Agus ghuidh Torranan air Dia mor nan dul nach d'reathadh a Ghamhnach gu brath an diosg'--'And Torranan beseeched the great God of the elements that the "Gamhnach" might never go dry.' And ever since then all pilgrims who go to the 'Gamhnach' and drink of the rill give a choice green leaf to the 'farrow cow' in memory of its refreshing drink to the holy man who came to teach the people of 'Innis Cat'-- Isle of the Caty--the way of salvation.

The man rejected of the people of Ireland became the accepted missionary of the people of Uist. He wished to build his prayer-house on 'Cnoc Feannaig,' the knoll of the hooded crow, within sight and hearing of the wild waves of Cailigeo where he had been driven ashore from his perilous voyage. Accordingly he began to gather stones to build himself a prayer-house on the knoll. But the stones that Torranan collected on the knoll during the day, the spirits transferred by night to the island in the lake adjoining. After a time Torranan gave up the unequal contest, saying that it was not meet for him to set his will against the will of God as revealed by His angels. Then Torranan built his prayer-house on the little island within hearing but not within seeing of the green seas and white waves of Cailigeo. And when the house was made Torranan dedicated the labour of his hands and the subject of his prayers to God and to Columba.

The lake containing the islet on which the seafarer built his oratory is now lowered, and what was formerly an island is now a peninsula jutting into the lake. The oratory said to have been built by Torranan is a ruin. The ruin shows an extension of the original building. This extension is said to have been made by Amie, daughter of Ruairi mac Allan, High Chief of Lorn, and wife of John of Islay, Lord of the Isles. Shell lime is used in the extension ascribed to the Lady Amie, but not in the original structure ascribed to Torranan. Captain Thomas, R.N., to whom the antiquities and archaeology of the Outer Hebrides owe much, said that the part of the church ascribed to Torranan might well belong to the Columban period. The Columban churches are believed to have been usually constructed of wattles. But there were no wattles nor wood of any kind in Uist so late as Columba's time. Consequently, in this and similar situations the Columban brethren and followers had to depart from their usual practice, and build of stone.

The lake containing the peninsula on which Torranan built his prayer-house, dedicated to Columba, is called 'Loch Chaluim-chille'--Columba's Loch. It only

covers an area of some few acres and is of no great depth. Cairns and crosses studded the many knolls and hillocks surrounding the lake. But no trace of cairn nor of cross now remains. These pious offerings of a grateful people and of a bygone age to the memory of the saint have been secularised and utilised in making roads and in building culverts.

A religious house was afterwards built on Cnoc Feannaig, where Torranan had wished to build his prayer-house. It is now, and has been for centuries, a dwelling-house, and is probably the oldest inhabited house in Scotland.

Torranan is represented on the West in the island of 'Tarransey,' Tarran's island. In this small rocky glaciated island of the Atlantic there were two small churches, of which nothing now remains but the foundations, with a small burying-ground attached to each. The churches are beautifully situated on the sea-shore near one another, and look across to the ice-rounded mountains of Harris and Uist, while in the far-away blue distance are seen the serrated calcined hills of Skye. One of these simple churches with its burying-ground was dedicated to Saint Tarran and called 'Teampull Tharrain'--the Temple of Tarran, and 'Cladh Tharrain'--the burial-place of Tarran. The other church and burying-ground were dedicated to Saint Ce, or Keith, and were called 'Teampull Che'--the Temple of Ce, and 'Cladh Che'--the burial-place of Ce. The temple and burying-ground of Tarran were exclusively for the use of women, while the temple and burying-ground of Ce were exclusively for the use of men. This rule could not be violated with impunity. If the body of a man were buried in St Tarran's, or the body of a woman in St Ce's, the guardian spirits of the temples and burying-grounds thrust forth the obtruded corpse during the night, and it was found in the morning lying stiff and stark above-ground. In North Uist there is a tall obelisk called 'Clach Che'--the stone of Ce. Saint Ce is represented on the East by 'Beinn Che'--Benachie, the hill of Ce, 'Innis Che'--Inchkeith, the island of Ce, and 'Dail Che'--Dalkeith, the plain of Ce.

Palladius is the name usually assigned to the missionary sent by the Pope to the Irish and rejected by them. Skene thinks that Ternan was a disciple of Palladius, with whom he is confounded. 'Ternan was buried at Liconium or My Toren of Tulach Fortchirn, in Ui Felmada, and Druim Cliab in Cairbre.' Skene thinks that Liconium was the old name of Banchory-Ternan on the river Dee in Aberdeenshire.

The feast of St Ternan is the 12th of June. Like St Brendan of Clonfert, St Ternan was a seafarer, visiting many countries. He is spoken of as 'Torranan buan bannach darler lethan longach'-- 'Torranan lasting, deedful, over a wide shipful sea.' Many popular stories and distinctive names attach to him.

The plant named after him is popularly supposed to grow only near the sea which Torranan loved. The small rill from which Torranan obtained a drink is named 'Gamhnach,' farrow cow--a cow that does not carry a calf, but which

gives milk of good quality and continuous but small in quantity. At present the blade of any grass or the leaf of any plant is given to the 'Gamhnach' in offering. Probably it was permissible for pilgrims who came to drink the water and to worship the 'Gamhnach,' to offer only the leaf of the 'torranan' to the rill. Another curious thing is that two streams into which the 'Gamhnach' runs are called 'na Deathachan,' the Dees, and that two lakes into which these streams flow are called 'Loch nan Deathachan fo dheas,' the Loch of the Dees to the south, and 'Loch nan Deathachan fo thuath,' Loch of the Dees to the north. 'Dee' and 'Deathachan' are plurals of 'dia,' god. Were these rivers worshipped as gods?

St Ternan forms a connecting-link between the Dees of Benbecula and the Dee of Aberdeen.

[pp. <page 84>-85

EOLAS AN TORRANAIN

THE CHARM OF THE FIGWORT

BUAINIDH mi an torranan,
Le toradh mara 's tir,
Lus nan agh 's nan sonas e,
Lus a bhainne mhi.

Mar a dh' orduich Righ nan righ,
Brigh a chur an cich 's an carr,
'S mar a dh' orduich Ti nan dul,
Sugh a chur an uth 's an ar,
Le bliochd, le blachd, le bladh,
Le cobhan, le omhan, 's le ais,
Le laoigh bhoirionn, bhreac,
Gun laoigh fhirionn ac,
Le al, le agh, le toradh,
Le gradh, le baigh, le sonadh,

Gun fear mi-run,
Gun bhean mi-shul,
Gun ghnu, gun tnu, gun toirinn,
Gun mhaghan masach,
Gun chu fasaich,
Gun scan foirinn
Dh' fhaighinn greim air a chugain
Anns an teid seo,
Torranan nan sionn,
Toradh ga chur ann,
Le al, le agh, le sonas.

I WILL pluck the figwort,
With the fruitage of sea and land,
The plant of joy and gladness,
The plant of rich milk.

As the King of kings ordained,
To put milk in pap and gland,
As the Being of life ordained,
To place substance in udder and kidney,
With milk, with milkiness, with butter milk,
With produce, with whisked whey, with milk-product,
With speckled female calves,
Without male calves,
With progeny, with joy, with fruitage,
With love, with charity, with bounty,

Without man of evil wish,
Without woman of evil eye,
Without malice, without envy, without 'toirinn,'
Without hipped bear,
Without wilderness dog,
Without 'scan foirinn,'
Obtaining hold of the rich dainty
Into which this shall go.
Figwort of bright lights,
Fruitage to place therein,
With fruit, with grace, with joyance.

AN TORRANAN

THE FIGWORT

BUAINIDH mi an torranan,
Le toradh mara 's tir,
Ri lionadh gun traghadh,
Le d' laimh, a Mhoire mhin.

Calum caomh da m' sheoladh,
Odhran naomh da m' dhion,
'S Bride nam ban buadhach
Cur bhuadh anns an ni.

Mar a dh' orduich Righ nan righ,
Bainne chur an cich 's an carr,
Mar a dh' orduich Ri nan dul,
Sugh a chur an uth 's an ar.

Ann an uth bruc,
Ann an uth brac,
Ann an uth murc,

Ann an uth marc.

Ann an uth urc,
Ann an uth arc,
An uth gobhar, othasg, agus caora,
Maoiseach, agus mart.

I WILL pluck the figwort,
With the fullness of sea and land,
At the flow, not the ebb of the tide,
By thine hand, gentle Mary.

The kindly Colum directing me,
The holy Oran protecting me,
Whilst Bride of women beneficent
Shall put fruitage in the kine.

As the King of kings ordained,
To put milk in breast and gland,
As the Being of life ordained,
To put sap in udder and teat.

In udder of badger,
In udder of reindeer,
In udder of sow (?),
In udder of mare.

In udder of sow (?),
In udder of heifer,
In udder of goat, ewe, and sheep,
Of roe, and of cow.

Le bliochd, le blachd, le bladh,
Le bair, le dair, le toradh,
Le laoigh bhoirionn, bharr,
Le al, le agh, le sonadh.

Gun fear mi-ruin,
Gun bhean mi-shuil,
Gun ghnu, gun tnu,
Gun aon donadh.

An ainm nan ostal deug, [da
An ainm Mathar De,
An ainm Chriosda fein,
Agus Phadruig.

With milk, with cream, with substance,
With rutting, with begetting, with fruitfulness,
With female calves excelling,
With progeny, with joyance, with blessing.

Without man of evil wish,
Without woman of evil eye,
Without malice, without envy,
Without one evil.

In name of the apostles twelve,
In name of the Mother of God,
In name of Christ Himself,
And of Patrick.

EOLAS AN TORRANAIN

THE CHARM OF THE FIGWORT

BUAINIDH mi an torranan,
Le mile beannachd, le mile buaidh,
Bride bhith dha chonall dhomh,
Moire mhin dha thoradh dhomh,
Moire mhor, Mathair chobhair an t-sluaigh.

Thainig na naoi sonais,
Le na naoi marannan,
A bhuain an torranain,
Le mile beannachd, le mile buaidh--
Le mile beannachd, le mile buaidh.

Lamh Chriosda liom,
Fath Chriosda rium,
Sgath Chriosda tharam,
Tha mo lus allail an allos a bhuain--
Tha mo lus allail an allos a bhuain.

An ainm Athar ais,
An ainm Criosda Phais,
An ainm Spiorad grais,
An agallaich mo bhais,
Nach fag mi gu Luan--
An agallaich mo bhais,
Nach fag mi gu Luan.

I WILL cull the figwort,
Of thousand blessings, of thousand virtues,
The calm Bride endowing it to me,
The fair Mary enriching it to me,
The great Mary, aid-Mother of the people.

Came the nine joys,
With the nine waves,
To cull the figwort,
Of thousand blessings, of thousand virtues--
Of thousand blessings, of thousand virtues.

The arm of Christ about me,
The face of Christ before me,
The shade of Christ over me,
My noble plant is being culled--
My noble plant is being culled.

In name of the Father of wisdom,
In name of the Christ of Pasch,
In name of the Spirit of grace,
Who in the struggles of my death,
Will not leave me till Doom
Who in the struggles of my death,
Will not leave me till Doom.

AN EARNAID SHITH

THE FAIRY WORT

BUAINIDH mi an earnaid,
Le earlaid a bruth,
Chur barrlait air gach ainreit,
Fad 's is earnaid i.

Earnaid shith, earnaid shith,
Mo niarach an neach dh' am bi,
Ni bheil ni mu iadhadh grein,
Nach bheil di-se le buaidh reidh.

Buainidh mi a chraobh urramach
Bhuain Moire mhor, Mathair chobhair an t-sluaigh,
Chur dhiom gach sgeula sguana, sgulanach,
Dim-bith, dim-baigh, dim-buaidh,
Fuailisg, guailisg, duailisg, doilisg,
Gun teid mi dh' an fhuar lic fo'n talamh.

PLUCK will I the fairy wort,
With expectation from the fairy bower,
To overcome every oppression,
As long as it be fairy wort.

Fairy wort, fairy wort,
I envy the one who has thee,
There is nothing the sun encircles,
But is to her a sure victory.

Pluck will I mine honoured plant
Plucked by the great Mary, helpful Mother of the people,
To cast off me every tale of scandal and flippancy,
Ill-life, ill-love, ill-luck,
Hatred, falsity, fraud and vexation,
Till I go in the cold grave beneath the sod.

EARR THALMHAINN

THE YARROW

BUAINIDH mi an earr reidh,
Gum bu cheinide mo chruth,
Gum bu bhlathaide mo bheuil,
Gum bu gheinide mo ghuth.
Biodh mo ghuth mar ghath na grein,
Biodh mo bheuil mar ein nan subh.

Gum bu h-eilean mi air muir,
Gum bu tulach mi air tir,
Gum bu reuil mi ri ra dorcha,
Gum bu lorg mi dhuine cli,
Leonaidh mi a h-uile duine,
Cha leoin duine mi.

I WILL pluck the yarrow fair,
That more benign shall be my face,
That more warm shall be my lips,
That more chaste shall be my speech,
Be my speech the beams of the sun,
Be my lips the sap of the strawberry.

May I be an isle in the sea,
May I be a hill on the shore,
May I be a star in waning of the moon,

May I be a staff to the weak,
Wound can I every man,
Wound can no man me.

AN EARR-THALMHAINN

THE YARROW

BUAINIDH mi an earr reidh,
Gum bu treuinide mo bhas,
Gum bu bhlathaide mo bheuil,
Gum bu ceumaide mo chas;
Gum bu h-eilean mi air muir,
Gum bu carraig mi air tir,
Leonar liom gach duine,
Cha leon duine mi.

I WILL pluck the yarrow fair,
That more brave shall be my hand,
That more warm shall be my lips,
That more swift shall be my foot;
May I an island be at sea,
May I a rock be on land,
That I can afflict any man,
No man can afflict me.

ACHLASAN CHALUIM-CHILLE

SAINT JOHN'S WORT

SAINT JOHN'S wort is known by various names, all significant of the position of the plant in the minds of the people:--'achlasan Chaluim-chille,' armpit package of Columba; 'caod Chaluim-chile,' hail of Columba; 'seun Chaluim-chille,' charm of Columba; 'seud Chaluim chille,' jewel of Columba; 'allus Chaluim-chille,' glory of Columba; 'alla Mhoire,' noble plant of Mary; 'alla-bhi,' 'alla-bhuidhe,' noble yellow plant. Possibly these are pre-Christian terms to which are added the endearing names of Mary and Columba.

Saint John's wort is one of the few plants still cherished by the people to ward away second-sight, enchantment, witchcraft, evil eye, and death, and to ensure peace and plenty in the house, increase and prosperity in the fold, and growth and fruition in the field. The plant is secretly secured in the bodices of the women and in the vests of the men, under the left armpit. Saint John's wort, however, is effective only when the plant is accidentally found.

When this occurs the joy of the finder is great, and gratefully expressed:--

'Achlasan Chaluim-chille,

Gun sireadh, gun iarraidh!
Dheoin Dhia agus Chriosda
Am bliadhna chan fhaigheas bas.'

Saint John's wort, Saint John's wort,
Without search, without seeking!
Please God and Christ Jesu
This year I shall not die.

[paragraph continues] It is specially prized when found in the fold of the flocks, auguring peace and prosperity to the herds throughout the year. The person who discovers it says:--

'Alla bhi, alla bhi,
Mo niarach a neach dh' am bi,
An ti a gheobh an cro an ail,
Cha bhi gu brath gun ni.'

Saint John's wort, Saint John's wort,
Happy those who have thee,
Whoso gets thee in the herd's fold,
Shall never be without kine.

[paragraph continues] There is a tradition among the people that Saint Columba carried the plant on his person because of his love and admiration for him who went about preaching Christ, and baptizing the converted, clothed in a garment of camel's hair and fed upon locusts and wild honey.

BUAINIDH mise m' achlasan,
Mar achan ri mo Righ,
Chosga fuath nam fear fala,
Chosga meanm nam ban bith.

Buainidh mise m' achlasan,
Mar achan ri mo Righ,
Gur liom-sa buaidh an achlasain
Thar gach neach a chi.

Buainidh mise m' achlasan,
Mar achan ris an Tri,
An sgath Triura nan Bras,
Agus Moire Mathair Ios.

I WILL cull my plantlet,
As a prayer to my King,
To quiet the wrath of men of blood,
To check the wiles of wanton women.

I will cull my plantlet,
As a prayer to my King,
That mine may be its power
Over all I see.

I will cull my plantlet,
As a prayer to the Three,
Beneath the shade of the Triune of grace,
And of Mary the Mother of Jesu.

ACHLASAN CHALUIM-CHILLE

ST COLUMBA'S PLANT

BUAINIDH mi mo choinneachan,
Mar choinneamh ri mo naomh,
Chasga fuath nam fear foille,
Agus boile nam ban baoth.

Buainidh mi m' achlasan,
Mar achainidh ri m' Righ,
Gur liom-sa buaidh an achlasain,
Thar gach neach a chi.

Buainim an duille gu h-ard,
Mar a dh' orduich an t-Ard Righ,
An ainm Tri Naomh nan agh,
Agus Moire, Mathair Chriosd.

I WILL pluck what I meet,
As in communion with my saint,
To stop the wiles of wily men,
And the arts of foolish women.

I will pluck my Columba plant,
As a prayer to my King,
That mine be the power of Columba's plant,
Over every one I see.

I will pluck the leaf above,
As ordained of the High King,
In name of the Three of glory,
And of Mary, Mother of Christ.

ACHLASAN CHALUIM-CHILLE

ST COLUMBA'S PLANT

ACHLASAIN Chaluim-chille,
Gun sireadh, gun iarraidh,
Achlasain Chaluim-chille,
Fo m' righe gu siorruidh!

Air shealbh dhaona,
Air shealbh mhaona,
Air shealbh mhianna,
Air shealbh chaora,
Air shealbh mhaosa,
Air shealbh iana,
Air shealbh raona,
Air shealbh mhaora,
Air shealbh iasga,
Air shealbh bhliochd is bhuar,
Air shealbh shliochd is shluagh,
Air shealbh bhlar is bhuadh,
Air tir, air lir, air cuan,
Trid an Tri ta shuas,
Trid an Tri ta nuns,
Trid an Tri ta buan,
Achlasain Chaluim-chille,
Ta mis a nis da d' bhuain,
Ta mis a nis da d' bhuain.

PLANTLET of Columba,
Without seeking, without searching,
Plantlet of Columba,
Under my arm for ever!

For luck of men,
For luck of means,
For luck of wish (?),
For luck of sheep,
For luck of goats,
For luck of birds,
For luck of fields,
For luck of shell-fish,
For luck of fish,
For luck of produce and kine,
For luck of progeny and people,
For luck of battle and victory,
On land, on sea, on ocean,
Through the Three on high,

257

Through the Three a-nigh,
Through the Three eternal,
Plantlet of Columba,
I cull thee now,
I cull thee now.

EALA-BHI, EALA-BHI

SAINT JOHN'S WORT

EALA-BHI, eala-bhi,
Mo niarach neach aig am bi,
Buaineam thu le mo lamh dheas,
Teasdam thu le mo lamh chli,
Ga ba co a gheabh thu 'n cro an ail,
Cha bhi e gu brath gun ni.

SAINT JOHN'S wort, Saint John's wort,
My envy whosoever has thee,
I will pluck thee with my right hand,
I will preserve thee with my left hand,
Whoso findeth thee in the cattle fold,
Shall never be without kine.

AN CRITHIONN

THE ASPEN

THE people of Uist say 'gu bheil an crithionn crion air a chroiseadh tri turais'--that the hateful aspen is banned three times. The aspen is banned the first time because it haughtily held up its head while all the other trees of the forest bowed their heads lowly down as the King of all created things was being led to Calvary. And the aspen is banned the second time because it was chosen by the enemies of Christ for the cross upon which to crucify the Saviour of mankind. And the aspen is banned the third time because [here the reciter's memory failed him]. Hence the ever-tremulous, ever-quivering, ever-quaking motion of the guilty hateful aspen even in the stillest air.

Clods and stones and other missiles, as well as curses, are hurled at the aspen by the people. The reciter, a man of much natural intelligence, said that he always took of his bonnet and cursed the hateful aspen in all sincerity wherever he saw it. No crofter in Uist would use aspen about his plough or about his harrows, or about his farming implements of any kind. Nor would a fisherman use aspen about his boat or about his creels or about any fishing-gear whatsoever.

MALLACHD ort, a chrithinn chrann!
Ort a chrochtadh nigh nam beann,
'S na bhualtadh tarrann gun lann,
'S bha 'n sparradh cheusda sin gle theann--

Bha 'n sparradh cheusda sin gle theann.

Mallachd ort, a chrithinn chruaidh!
Ort a chrochtadh Righ nam buadh,
Iobairt Firinn, Uan gun truaill,
Is fhuil na taosg a taom' a nuas--
Fhuil na taosg a taom' a nuas.

Mallachd ort, a chrithinn chrin!
Ort a chrochtadh Righ nan righ,
Is mallaichte gach suil a chi,
Mar mallaich i thu, a chrithinn chrin--
Mar mallaich i thu, a chrithinn chrin!

MALISON be on thee, O aspen tree!
On thee was crucified the King of the mountains,
In whom were driven the nails without clench,
And that driving crucifying was exceeding sore--
That driving crucifying was exceeding sore.

Malison be on thee, O aspen hard!
On thee was crucified the King of glory,
Sacrifice of Truth, Lamb without blemish,
His blood in streams down pouring--
His blood in streams down pouring.

Malison be on thee, O aspen cursed!
On thee was crucified the King of kings,
And malison be on the eye that seeth thee,
If it maledict thee not, thou aspen cursed--
If it maledict thee not, thou aspen cursed!

SEAMARAG NAM BUADH

SHAMROCK OF LUCK

SOME of the people say that the four-leaved shamrock is the shamrock of luck. Others maintain that the shamrock of luck is the five-leaved shamrock. This is a very rare plant and much prized when found.

The shamrock of luck must be found, like many of the other propitious plants, 'gun sireadh, gun iarraidh'--without searching, without seeking. When thus discovered the lucky shamrock is warmly cherished and preserved as an invincible talisman.

'Seamarag nan buadh,' shamrock of luck, is often lovingly called 'seamarag nam buadh agus nam beannachd,' shamrock of luck and of blessing.

It is also called 'seamarag nan each,' horse shamrock, 'seamarag nan searrach,' foal shamrock, 'seamarag an deocain,' shamrock of the 'deocan,' 'seamarag an deocadain,' shamrock of the 'deocadan,' and simply 'deocan' and 'deocadan.'

Immediately after birth the foal throws up a pale soft substance resembling a sponge or the seed-cells of the cod. This sponge-like substance coughed up by the newly-born foal is variously called 'deocan, deocadan, deocardan.' The people bury this in the ground, believing that the lucky shamrock grows from it as the nettles grow from human remains, whether buried in the pure shelly sand on the sea-shore or in the pure peat moss on the mountain-side.

A SHEAMARAG nam buadh,
A fas fo bhruaich
Air na sheas Moire shuairce,
Mathair De.

Tha na seachd sonais,
Gun sgath donais
Ort, a mhoth-ghil
Nan gath grein--

Sonas slainte,
Sonas chairde,
Sonas taine,
Sonas treuid,
Sonas mhac, is
Mhurn mhin-gheal,
Sonas siocha,
Sonas De!

Ceithir dhuilleagan na luirge dirich, [coig
Na luirge dirich a friamh nam meanglan ceud,
A sheamarag gheallaidh La Fheill Moire,
Buaidh is beannachd thu gash re.

THOU shamrock of good omens,
Beneath the bank growing
Whereon stood the gracious Mary,
The Mother of God.

The seven joys are,
Without evil traces,
On thee, peerless one
Of the sunbeams--

Joy of health,

Joy of friends,
Joy of kine,
Joy of sheep,
Joy of sons, and
Daughters fair,
Joy of peace,
Joy of God!

The four leaves of the straight stem, [five
Of the straight stem from the root of the hundred rootlets,
Thou shamrock of promise on Mary's Day,
Bounty and blessing thou art at all times.

SEAMARAG NAM BUADH

THE SHAMROCK OF POWER

A SHEAMARAG nan duilleag,
A sheamarag nam buadh,
A sheamarag nan duilleag,
Bha aig Muire fo bhruaich,
A sheamarag mo ghraidh,
Is ailinde snuadh,
B' e mo mhiann anns a bhas,
Thu bhi fas air m' uaigh,
B' e mo mhiann anns a bhas,
Thu bhi fas air m' uaigh.

THOU shamrock of foliage,
Thou shamrock of power,
Thou shamrock of foliage,
Which Mary had under the bank,
Thou shamrock of my love,
Of most beauteous hue,
I would choose thee in death,
To grow on my grave,
I would choose thee in death,
To grow on my grave.

AM MOTHAN

THE 'MOTHAN'

THE 'mothan' (bog-violet?) is one of the most prized plants in the occult science of the people. It is used in promoting and conserving the happiness of the people, in securing love, in ensuring life, in bringing good, and in warding away evil.

When the 'mothan' is used as a love-philtre, the woman who gives it goes upon her left knee and plucks nine roots of the plant and knots them together, forming them into a 'cuach'--ring. The woman places the ring in the mouth of the girl for whom it is made, in name of the King of the sun, and of the moon, and of the stars, and in name of the Holy Three. When the girl meets her lover or a man whom she loves and whose love she desires to secure, she puts the ring in her mouth. And should the man kiss the girl while the 'mothan' is in her mouth becomes henceforth her bondsman, bound to her everlastingly in cords infinitely finer than the gossamer net of the spider, and infinitely stronger than the adamant chain of the giant.

The 'mothan' is placed under parturient women to ensure delivery, and it is carried by wayfarers to safeguard them on their journeys. It is sewn by women in their bodice, and by men in their vest under the left arm.

An old woman in Benbecula said:--'Thug mi am mothan beannaichte do Ruaraidh ruadh mac Raoghail Leothasaich as a Cheann-a-deas agus e air a thuras do Loch-nam-madadh, dol ga fhiachain air bialabh an t-siorram agus fhuair e dheth ge do bha e co ciontach 's a chionta ri mac peacaich'--'I gave the blessed "mothan" to red Roderick son of Ranald of Lewis from the South-end (of Uist), and he on his journey to Lochmaddy to be tried before the sheriff, and he got off although he was as guilty of the guilt as the son of a sinner.' 'Ach a Chairistine carson a thug sibh am mothan dh'an duine agus fios agaibh gun robh e ciontach? Saoilidh mi fein nach robh e ceart dhuibh a dhol ga dheanamh'--'But, Christina, why did you give the "mothan" to the man when you knew that he was guilty? I think myself it was not right of you to go and do it!' 'O bhidh 's aodaich! a ghraidhean mo chridhe agus a ghaoilean mo dhaoine, cha b' urra dhomh fhein dhol ga dhiultadh. Bhoinich e orm, agus bhochain e orm, agus bhoidich a orm, agus chuir e rud am laimh, agus O! a Righ na gile 's na greine, agus nan corracha ceuta, curra, de b' urra dhomh fhein a gh' radh no dheanamh agus an duine dona na dhubh-eigin na dheargtheinn agus na chruaidh-chas'--'O food and clothing! thou dear one of my heart, and thou loved one of my people, I could not myself go and refuse him. He beseeched to me, and he swelled to me, and he vowed to me, and he placed a thing in my hand, and oh! King of the moon, and of the sun, and of the beautiful, sublime stars, what could I myself say or do, and the bad man in his black trouble, in his red difficulty, and in his hard plight!' I remembered Bacon and was silent.

To drink the milk of an animal that ate the 'mothan' ensures immunity from harm. If a man makes a miraculous escape it is said of him, 'Dh' of e bainne na bo ba a dh' ith am mothan'--'He drank the milk of the guileless cow that ate the "mothan."'

I am not sure what the plant is--perhaps the bog-violet.

BUAINIDH mi am mothan suairce,
Mar a bhuain nigh buadhach domhan;
An ainm Athar, agus Mic, agus Spioraid buan,
Bride agus Moire, agus Micheal romham.

Mi anns a bhlar ghabhaidh dhearg,
Anns an traoghar gach fraoch is fearg,
Aobhar gach sonais, agus gach solais,

Sgiath an Domhnaich dha m' dhion.

I WILL pluck the gracious 'mothan,'
As plucked the victorious King of the universe;
In name of Father and of Son and of Spirit everlasting,
Bride, and Mary, and Michael, before me.

I in the field of red conflict,
In which every wrath and fury are quelled,
The cause of all joy and gladness,
The shield of the Lord protecting me.

AM MOTHAN

THE 'MOTHAN'

BUAINIDH mi am mothan,
Luibh nan naodh alt,
Buainidh agus boinichidh,
Do Bhride bhorr 's dh' a Dalt.

Buainidh mi am mothan,
A dh' orduich Righ nam feart,
Buainidh agus boinichidh,
Do Mhoire mhor 's dh' a Mac.

Buainidh mi am mothan,
A dh' orduich Righ nan dul,
Bheir buaidh air gach foirneart,
Is ob air obi shul.

PLUCK will I the 'mothan,'
Plant of the nine joints,
Pluck will I and vow me,
To noble Bride and her Fosterling.

Pluck will I the 'mothan,'
As ordained of the King of power,
Pluck will I and vow me,
To great Mary and her Son.

Pluck will I the 'mothan,'
As ordained of the King of life,
To overcome all oppression,
And the spell of evil eye.

AM MOTHAN

THE 'MOTHAN'

BUAINIDH mis am mothan suairce,
An luibh is luachmhoire 's an tom,
Dulagan nan seachd sagart,
'S an agallaich a ta n' an com.

* * * *
* * * *
Gur liom an ciall 's an codhail,
Fad 's a bhios am mothan liom.

I WILL pluck the gracious 'mothan,'
Plant most precious in the field,
That mine be the holiness of the seven priests,
And the eloquence that is within them.

* * * *
* * * *
That mine be their wisdom and their counsel,
While the 'mothan' is mine.

CEUS-CHRANN NAM BUADH

THE PASSION-FLOWER OF VIRTUES

A CHEUS-CHRANN chaomh nam buadh,
A naomhaich fuil naomh an Uain,
Mac Moire min, Dalta Bride nam buar,
Mac Moire mor, Mathair chobhair an t-sluaigh.

Ni bheil tur, no tir,
Ni bheil cith, no cuan,
Ni bheil lod, no li,
Ni bheil frith, no fruan,
Nach bheil domh-sa reidh,
Le comhnadh ceus nam buadh,
Nach bheil domh-sa reidh,
Le comhnadh ceus nam buadh.

Thou passion-flower of virtues beloved,
Sanctified by the holy blood of the Lamb,
Son of Mary fair, Foster Son of Bride of kine,
Son of Mary great, helpful Mother of the people.

There is no earth, no land,
There is no lake, no ocean,
There is no pool, no water,
There is no forest, no steep,
That is not to me full safe,
By the protection of the passion-flower of virtues,
But is to me full safe,
By the protection of the passion-flower of virtues.

GARBHAG AN T-SLEIBH

THE CLUB-MOSS

GARBHAG an t-sleibh air mo shiubhal,
Chan eirich domh beud no pudhar;
Cha mharbh garmaisg, cha dearg iubhar mi,
Cha riab grianuisg no glaislig uidhir mi.

THE club-moss is on my person,
No harm nor mishap can me befall;
No sprite shall slay me, no arrow shall wound me,
No fay nor dun water-nymph shall tear me.

AN DEARG-BHASACH

THE RED-PALMED

CRIOSD ag imeachd le ostail,
'S a briste tosd thubhairt e--
'Ciod e ainm na lusa seo?'
'Is e ainm na lusa seo
An dearg-bhasach, [chasach
Bos deas De a Mhic
Agus a chos chli.'

CHRIST walking with His apostles,
And breaking silence He said
'What is the name of this plant?'
'The name of this plant is
The red-palmed, [stalked
The right palm of God the Son
And His left foot.'

A CHLOIMH CHAT

265

THE CATKIN WOOL

BUAINIDH mi a chloimh chat,
Mar a bhuain Mathair Chriosda tromh glac,
Air bhuaidh, air bhuar, air bhleoghann,
Air chual, 's air thoradh na tana,
Gun chall uan, gun chall caora,
Gun chall maosa, gun chall lara,
Gun chall bo, gun chall laogha,
Gun chall maona, gun chall carda,
A uchd Ti nan dui,
'S nan cursa comhla.

I WILL pluck the catkin wool,
As plucked the Mother of Christ through her palm,
For luck, for kine, for milking,
For herds, for increase, for cattle,
Without loss of lamb, without loss of sheep,
Without loss of goat, without loss of mare,
Without loss of cow, without loss of calf,
Without loss of means, without loss of friends,
From the bosom of the God of life,
And the courses together.

A CHLOIMH CHAT

THE CATKIN WOOL

BUAINIDH mi fhin a chloimh chat,
An lion a bhuain Bride mhin tromh glac,
Air bhuaidh, air bhuar, air thoradh,
Air dhair, air chairr, air bhleoghann,
Air laoigh bhoineann bhailgionn,
Mar a thubhradh anns an deailgne.

PLUCK will I myself the catkin wool,
The lint the lovely Bride culled through her palm,
For success, for cattle, for increase,
For pairing, for uddering, for milking,
For female calves, white bellied,
As was spoken in the prophecy.

EOLAS A BHUN DEIRG

INCANTATION OF THE RED WATER

IN making the incantation of the red water, the exorcist forms her two palms into a basin. She places this basin under the urine of the cow or other animal affected, and throws the urine into water, preferably running water, to carry away the demon of the complaint. Having washed her hands in clean cold water, the woman forms them into a trumpet. She then faces the rising sun, and intones the incantation through the trumpet as loudly as she can.

AN ainm Athar caoimh,
An ainm Mic na caoidh,
An ainm Spioraid Naoimh.
Amen.

Muir mor, muir ruadh,
Neart mara, neart cuain,
Naoi tobraiche Mhic-a-Lir,
Cobhair ort a shil,
Casg a chur air t-fhuil,
Ruith a chur air t-fhual.
[An t-ainm.]

IN name of the Father of love,
In name of the Son of sorrow,
In name of the Sacred Spirit.
Amen.

Great wave, red wave,
Strength of sea, strength of ocean,
The nine wells of Mac-Lir,
Help on thee to pour,
Put stop to thy blood,
Put flood to thy urine.
[The name.]

EOLAS BUN DEIRG

RED WATER CHARM

TA mis a nis air leirg,
Traogh' fraoich is feirg,
Deanamh eolas a bhun deirg,
Dh' an bho bhailg dhuibh.

Air bhliochd, air bhlachd, air bhlath,
Air omhan agus ais,
Air slaman agus slaig,
Air im, air cais, air gruth.

Air aghar agus agh,
Air damhair agus dair,
Air taghar agus tan,
Air rathaich agus ruth.

Naoi tobraiche Mhic-an-Lir,
Cobhair ort a shil,
Casg a chur air t-fhuil,
Ruith a chur air t-fhual,
A bho bhuar, dhubh.

Muir mor,
Eas ruadh,
Casg fuil,
Ruith fual.

I AM now on the plain,
Reducing wrath and fury,
Making the charm of the red water,
To the beauteous black cow.

For milk, for milk substance, for milk produce,
For whisked whey, for milk riches,
For curdled milk, for milk plenty,
For butter, for cheese, for curds.

For progeny and prosperity,
For rutting time and rutting,
For desire and kine,
For passion and prosperity.

The nine wells of Mac-Lir,
Relief on thee to pour,
Put stop to thy blood,
Put run to thy urine,
Thou cow of cows, black cow.

Great sea,
Red cascade,
Stop blood,
Flow urine.

EOLAS A GHALAR FHUAIL

THE GRAVEL CHARM

EOLAS ta agam air a ghalar fhuail,
Air a ghalar a ta buan;
Eolas ta agam air a ghalar dhearg,
Air a ghalar a ta garg.

Mar a ruitheas abhuinn fhuar,
Mar a mheileas muileann luath,
Fhir a dh'orduich tir is muir,
Casg air fhuil, ruith air fhual.

An ainm Athar, agus Mic,
An ainm Spioraid Naoimh.

I HAVE a charm for the gravel disease,
For the disease that is perverse
I have a charm for the red disease,
For the disease that is irritating.

As runs a river cold,
As grinds a rapid mill,
Thou who didst ordain land and sea,
Cease the blood and let flow the urine.

In name of Father, and of Son,
In name of Holy Spirit.

AN STRINGLEIN

THE STRANGLES

'EACH 's an stringlein,'
Orsa Calum-cille.

'Tillidh mis e,'
Thubhairt Criosd.

'Moch Di-domhnaich?'
Orsa Calum-cille.

'Romh eirigh ghreine,'
Thubhairt Criosd.

'Tri postachan anns an tobar,'
Orsa Calum-cille.

'Togaidh mis iad,'

Thubhairt Criosd.

'An leighis sin e?'
Ors Eoin Baistidh.

'Barantaich e,'
Thubhairt Criosd.

'A HORSE in strangles,'
Quoth Columba.

'I will turn it,'
Said Christ.

'On Sunday morning? '
Quoth Columba.

'Ere rise of sun,'
Said Christ.

'Three pillars in the well,'
Quoth Columba.

'I will lift them,'
Said Christ.

'Will that heal him?'
Quoth John the Baptist.

'Assuredly,'
Said Christ.

SIAN SIONNAICH

THE SPELL OF THE FOX

THE fox was the plague of the people of the Highlands, killing their sheep as the wolf killed their cattle, and as the foumart killed their fowls. From the wildness of the land and the sparseness of the people, the Highlands were the natural habitat of beasts and birds of prey and other noxious creatures, which took the people much time and trouble to subdue.

Much could be written of the intelligence of the fox. One of the tales illustrating this intelligence is known as 'Sionnach na Maoile'--the Fox of the Mull [of Kintire]. This fox never committed destruction near his home--always going considerable distances to make his raids, sometimes ten or twenty miles. He caused much injury to the sheep that he attacked, and to the dogs that chased him.

When pressed, the fox leaped over a certain precipice and the dogs leaped over after him. The dogs were found dead on the rocks below, but not the fox, who in due time turned up as before.

Nothing could be seen from above nor from below the precipice to account for the immunity of the fox. No shelf or ledge could be seen whereon the fox could leap, and the people were puzzled. But the fox-hunter was not satisfied, and procuring ropes, he went down the precipice and examined it carefully. He found a sapling mountain ash growing out of the rock, and marked as if to distinguish it from the saplings of ordinary ash, bramble, plane, and other woods which were growing in the neighbourhood. And he found that by bending the marked mountain ash to a certain degree from its perpendicular and at a certain angle to the plane of the precipice, it touched a narrow thread-like sinuous ledge that might yield a precarious footing to a cat, to a marten, or possibly to a fox. This ledge led away to other ledges up and down the cliff. The fox-hunter cut the marked sapling, securing it, however, in its place. When the next havoc of the sheep had occurred, and the next pursuit of the fox had followed, the fox was found dead at the foot of the precipice, the marked mountain ash in his mouth! Choosing the tough mountain ash sapling in preference to the other less tough saplings showed sagacity, leaping from the precipice and seizing the sapling in mid-air to arrest his fall showed courage, and taking the precipice at an angle by which to get the sapling to land him in the only possible spot showed intelligence of a high order in the fox. The scene of this story has ever since been called 'Creag an t-Sionnaich'--precipice of the fox.

The conduct of this fox gave rise to many sayings of the people, 'Co carrach ri sionnach ruadh Maol Chinntire,'--as crafty as the red fox of the Mull of Kintire. 'Co seolta ri sionnach na Maoile,'--as cunning as the fox of the Mull. 'Co siogada sinn seanarach ri sionnach na Maoile,'--as great-great-great-grandfatherish as the fox of the Mull. 'Bheir e leis a chreaig sibh mar a thug an sionnach na todhlairean,'--He will lead you over the cliff as the fox led the hounds.

BIODH sian a choin-choille,
Mu chasaibh an t-sionnaich,
Mu mhiann, mu ghoile,
Mu shlugaid a ghionaich,
Mu chorr fhiacail chorraich,
Mu chorran a mhionaich.

Biodh sian an Domhnaich mu chaorail,
Sian Chriosda chaoimh-ghil, chaoin-ghil,
Sian Mhoire mhin-ghil, mhaoth-ghil,
Romh chona, romh iana, romh dhaonail,
Romh chona shithil, romh chona shaoghail,
Far an t-saoghail a bhos, far an t-saoghail thall.

BE the spell of the wood dog,
On the feet of the fox,
On his heart, on his liver,
On his gullet of greediness,
On his surpassing pointed teeth,
On the bend of his stomach.

Be the charm of the Lord upon the sheep-kind,
The charm of Christ kindly-white, mild-white,
The charm of Mary lovely-fair, tender-fair,
Against dogs, against birds, against man-kind,
Against fairy dogs, against world dogs,
Of the world hither, of the world thither.

ORA CUITHE

PRAYER OF THE CATTLE-FOLD

CUIREAM tan a steach
Air bhearn nan speach,
Air ghuth mairbh,
Air ghuth tairbh,
Air ghuth dair,
Air ghuth na ba ceire
Cionnara, ceannara, cairr,
Clach mhor bhun sgonnaig
Gun faothachadh, gun lomadh,
Na taodaiche tromaidh
Bhi slaodadh ri dronnaig bhur tairr,
Gon tig latha geal am mair.

An t-Athair, am Mac, an Spiorad Naomh,
D'ar caomhnadh, d'ar comhnadh, 's d'ar tilleadh,
Gun comhlaich mise no mo dhuine sibh.

I DRIVE the kine within
The gateway of the herds,
On voice of the dead,
On voice of bull,
On voice of pairing,
On voice of grayling cow
White-headed, strong-headed, of udder.
Be the big stone of the base of the couple
Without ceasing, without decreasing,
As a full-weighted tether
Trailing from the hunch of your rump,
Till bright daylight comes in to-morrow.

The Father, the Son, the Holy Spirit,
Save you, and shield you, and tend you,
Till I or mine shall meet you again.

FEITH MHOIRE

THE DITCH OF MARY

FLAT moorland is generally intersected with innumerable veins, channels, and ditches. Sometimes these are serious obstacles to cattle, more especially to cows, which are accurate judges. When a cow hesitates to cross, the person driving her throws a stalk or a twig into the ditch before the unwilling animal and sings the 'Feith Mhoire,' Vein of Mary, to encourage her to cross, and to assure her that a safe bridge is before her. The stalk may be of any corn or grass except the reed, and the twig of any wood except the wild fig, the aspen, and the thorn. All these are forbidden, or 'crossed' as the people say, because of their ungracious conduct to the Gracious One. The reed is 'crossed' because it carried the sponge dipped in vinegar; the fig-tree because of its inhospitality; the aspen because it held up its head haughtily, proud that the cross was made of its wood, when all the trees of the forest--all save the aspen alone--bowed their heads in reverence to the King of glory passing by on the way to Calvary; and the thorn-tree because of its prickly pride in having been made into a crown for the King of kings. Notwithstanding, however, the wand of safety and the hymn of the herdsman, a cow driven against her will sometimes sinks into the ditch while crossing. This may necessitate the assistance of neighbours to extricate her from her helpless position. Hence the proverb:--'Is e fear na bo fein theid 's an fheith an tos'--It is the man of the cow himself who shall go into the ditch first. The practice of throwing down the wand and repeating the hymn gave rise to a proverb among the more sceptical of the people:--'Cha dean thu feith Mhoire orm-s' idir a mhicean'--Thou wilt not make a 'vein of Mary' upon me at all, sonnie.

FEITH Mhoire,
Feith Mhoire;
Casa curra,
Casa curra;
Feith Mhoire,
Feith Mhoire;
Casa curra fothaibh,
Drochaid urra romhaibh.

Chuir Moire gas ann,
Chuir Bride bas ann,
Chuir Calum cas ann,
Chuir Padra clach fhuar.

Feith Mhoire,
Feith Mhoire;
Casa curra,
Casa curra;
Feith Mhoire,
Feith Mhoire;
Casa curra fothaibh,
Drochaid urra romhaibh.

DITCH of Mary,
Ditch of Mary;
Heron legs,
Heron legs;
Ditch of Mary,
Ditch of Mary;
Heron legs under you,
Bridge of warranty before you.

Mary placed a wand in it,
Bride placed a hand in it,
Columba placed a foot in it,
Patrick placed a cold stone.

Ditch of Mary,
Ditch of Mary;
Heron legs,
Heron legs;
Ditch of Mary,
Ditch of Mary;
Heron legs under you,
Bridge of warranty before you.

Chuir Muiril mirr ann,
Chuir Uiril mil ann,
Chuir Muirinn fion ann,
'S chuir Micheal ann buadh.

Feith Mhoire,
Feith Mhoire;
Casa curra,
Casa curra;
Feith Mhoire,
Feith Mhoire;
Casa curra fodhaibh,
Drochaid urra romhaibh.

Muirel placed myrrh in it,
Uriel placed honey in it,
Muirinn placed wine in it,
And Michael placed in it power.

Ditch of Mary,
Ditch of Mary;
Heron legs,
Heron legs;

Ditch of Mary,
Ditch of Mary;
Heron legs under you,
Bridge of warranty before you.

AN EILID

THE HIND

BHA Peadail is Pol a dol seachad,
Is eilid 's an ro a cur laoigh;
'Tha eilid a breith,' osa Peadail;
'Chi mi gu bheil,' osa Pol.

'Mar a thuiteas a duille bho 'n chraoibh,
Gun ann a thuiteadh a seile gu lar,
An ainm Athar an aigh agus Mhic an aoibh,
Agus Spiorad a ghliocais ghraidh;
Athar an aigh agus Mhic an aoibh,
Agus Spioraid a ghliocais ghraidh.'

PETER and Paul were passing by,
While a hind in the path was bearing a fawn;
'A hind is bearing there,' said Peter;
'I see it is so,' said Paul.

'As her foliage falls from the tree,
So may her placenta fall to the ground,
In name of the Father of love and of the Son of grace,
And of the Spirit of loving wisdom;
Father of love and Son of grace,
And Spirit of loving wisdom.'

CALUM-CILLE, PEADAIL, AGUS POL

COLUMBA, PETER, AND PAUL

LA domh 's mi dol dh' an Roimh,
Thachair orm Calum-cille, Peadail, agus Pol,
Is e comhradh a bh' aca 's a thachair bhi 'n am beul,
Laoigh bheura, bhoirionn, bhailgionn,
Mar thubhradh anns an dailgionn,
Air an laraich seo gu ceann la 's bliadhna,
A uchd Dia nan dul is nan uile bhuadh,
Triath nan triath 's nan Cumhachdan siorruidh shuas.

A DAY as I was going to Rome,
I forgathered with Columba, Peter, and Paul,
The talk that they had and that happened in their mouths,
Was loud-lunged, white-bellied, female calves,
As was spoken in the prophecy,
On this foundation for a year and a day,
Through the bosom of the God of life and all the hosts,
Chief of chiefs and of the everlasting Powers above.

EOLAS A MHEIRBHEIN

THE INDIGESTION SPELL

EOLAS a rinn Calum,
Dh' aona bho caillich,
Air a chraillich, air a ghaillich,
Air a bholg, air a cholg,
Air a mheirbhein;

Air a ghalar ghir,
Air a ghalar chir,
Air a ghalar mhir,
Air a ghalar tolg,
Air an tairbhein;

Air a ghalar chil,
Air a ghalar mhil,
Air a ghalar lioil,
Air a ghalar dhearg,
Air a mhearchann;

Sgoiltidh mi an crailleach,
Sgoiltidh mi an gailleach,
Sgoiltidh mi am bolg,
Sgoiltidh mi an colg,
Agus marbhaidh mi am meirbhein;

Sgoiltidh mi an gir,
Sgoiltidh mi an cir,
Sgoiltidh mi am mir,
Sgoiltidh mi an tolg,
Agus falbhaidh an tairbhein;

Sgoiltidh mi an cil,
Sgoiltidh mi am mil,
Sgoiltidh mi an lioil,

Sgoiltidh mi an dearg,
Is seargaidh am mearchann.

THE spell made of Columba,
To the one cow of the woman,
For the 'crailleach,' for the gum disease,
For the bag, for the 'colg,'
For the indigestion (?);

For the flux disease,
For the cud disease,
For the 'mir' disease,
For the 'tolg' disease,
For the surfeit (?);

For the 'cil' disease,
For the 'mil' disease,
For the water disease,
For the red disease,
For the madness (?);

I will cleave the 'crailleach,'
I will cleave the gum disease,
I will cleave the bag,
I will cleave the 'colg,'
And I will kill the indigestion (?);

I will cleave the flux,
I will cleave the cud,
I will cleave the 'mir,'
I will cleave the 'tolg,'
And drive away the surfeit (?);

I will cleave the 'cil,'
I will cleave the 'mil,'
I will cleave the water,
I will cleave the red,
And wither will the madness (?).

EOLAS CHNAMH CHIR

CUD CHEWING CHARM

THIS incantation is said over an animal suffering from surfeit. It is repeated three times, representing the Three Persons of the Trinity. If the surfeit is from eating too much grass or from drinking too much water, the cow or other animal affected begins to chew the cud on being appealed to. If the animal does not begin to chew the cud, the cause of swelling must be sought for otherwise, and the appropriate incantation applied.

dh' ith thu fiar nan naodh beann,
Nan naodh meall, nan naodh toman,
Ma dh' ol thu sian nan naodh steallt,
Nan naodh allt, nan naodh lodan,
A Ghruaigein thruaigh na maodail cruaidh,
Cnamh, a luaidh, do chir.
A Ghruaigein thruaigh na maodail cruaidh,
Cnamh, a luaidh, do chir.

IF thou hast eaten the grass of the nine bens,
Of the nine fells, of the nine hillocks,
If thou hast drunk the water of the nine falls,
Of the nine streams, of the nine lakelets,
Poor 'Gruaigein' of the hard paunch,
Loved one, chew thou thy cud.
Poor 'Gruaigein' of the hard paunch,
Loved one, chew thou thy cud.

EOLAS A CHRANNACHAIN

EOLAS A CHRANNACHAIN

AN evil eye or an evil spirit is powerless across water, especially across a running stream or a tidal water.

'Sir Eoghan Dubh Lochiall'--Black Sir Ewen Cameron of Lochiel, was at feud with Mackintosh of Moy about lands in Lochaber. 'Gormshul mhor na Moighe'--great Gormul of Moy, the celebrated witch, wished to destroy Lochiel, the foe of her chief and of her race. But, though she nursed her wrath and pursued her course day and night, she could not accomplish her purpose, as running water lay between herself and the object of her hatred. Lochiel knew this, and, although brave to recklessness, he prudently kept out of the way of the witch-woman. But on one occasion when Lochiel was returning from a conference at Inverness, great Gormul saw him far away on the blue horizon; but, if far away was he, not long was she in reaching him:--

GORMSHUL--
'Ceum ann, eudail Eoghain.'

LOCHIALL--
'Ceum ann thu fhein, a chailleach,
'S ma 's a h-eudar an ceum a ghabhail,
Ceum a bharrachd aig Eoghan.'

GORMUL--

278

'Step on, beloved Ewen.'

LOCHIALL--
'Step on thou thyself, carlin,
And if it be necessary to take the step,
A step beyond thee for Ewen.'

[paragraph continues] Sir Ewen Cameron was one of the bravest men in Albain, and one of the best walkers in Gaeldom. Many a brave Saxon man he met without quailing, and many a hero he laid low, but this froward woman was trying him severely, and he was anxious to be rid of her with the least delay of time and the least betrayal of fear. The witch-woman observed this; and the more desperately he pressed on space, the more she pressed on him, while she herself appeared to be only making 'cas ceum coilich feasgar fann foghair agus a sgroban lan'--the footstep of a cock on a gentle autumn eve when his crop is full.

GORMSHUL--
'Ceum ann, eudail Eoghain,
'S a Righ Goileam 's a Righ Geigean!
Is fhada fhein o'n latha sin!'

GORMUL--
'Step on, thou beloved Ewen,
And oh! King Goileam and King Geigean!
Long indeed since that day!'

LOCHIALL--
'Ceum ann thu fhein, a chailleach,
'S ma 's a h-eudar an ceum a ghabhail,
Ceum a bharrachd aig Eoghan.'

LOCHIEL--
'Step on thou thyself, carlin,
And if the step must be taken,
A step beyond thee for Ewen.'

[paragraph continues] Remembering that occult power could not operate across running water, Lochiel suddenly swerved aside to the first stream he saw and plunged into it. The witch, chagrined at the escape of the prey she had thought safe, immediately called after him:--

GORMSHUL--
'Durachd mo chridhe dhut,
A ghradh nam fear, a Lochiall.'

LOCHIALL--
'Durachd do chridhe, chailleach,
Dh'an chlaich ghlais ud thall.'

GORMUL--
'The wish of mine heart to thee,
Thou best-beloved of men, Lochiel.'

LOCHIEL--
'The wish of thine heart, carlin,
Be upon yonder grey stone.'

[paragraph continues] The pillared grey stone on the bank of the river to which Lochiel pointed with his sword rent from top to base! Gallant courtier though he was, Sir Ewen Cameron waited to show but scant courtesy to great Gormul of Moy.

The influence of an evil spirit commanded by an evil mind is believed to retard or wholly to prevent butter from coming upon the cream in the churn. This evil influence was used by one woman against another in order to spirit away the butter from her neighbour's churn to her own churn. This, however, could only be done if no stream ran between the two women. A fire for kindling carried across a stream, however small, loses its occult power and is ineffective in spiriting away milk, cream, butter, or other milk product.

The following story was told me in 1870 by Mor Macneill, cottar, Glen, Barra. Sometimes the substance is spirited out of the milk, nothing being left but the semblance. On one occasion a household in Skye were at the peat-moss making peats, none remaining at home but the housewife and a tailor who was making clothes for the father and the sons of the house.

The housewife was up in the 'ben' churning, and the tailor was down in the 'butt' sewing. He sat on the meal-girnel, cross-legged, after the manner of tailors. Presently a neighbour woman came in and asked for a kindling for her fire. She took the kindling and went her way. When she went out, the tailor leaped down, and taking a live cinder from the fire, placed it in the water-stoup below the dresser, and with a bound was back again cross-legged on the meal-girnel sewing away as before. In a little while the woman came back saying that she failed to kindle her fire, and asked for another kindling, which she took. The tailor leapt down again and took another live cinder out of the fire and put it in the water-stoup below the dresser, and, with a spring to the meal-girnel, resumed his work. The woman came a third time saying that she had failed to

kindle her fire, and for the third time she took a kindling and went her way. As soon as she had left, the tailor leapt down, and taking a live cinder from the fire, placed it in the water-stoup as he had done before, and then springing to the top of the meal-girnel sat cross-legged sewing as if nothing unusual had occurred.

Towards evening the housewife came down in sore distress, saying--'O Mary and Son, am I not the sorely shamed woman, churning away at that churn the live-long day till my spirit is broken and my arms are weary, and that I have utterly failed to bring butter on the churn after all! O Mary! Mary, fair

[paragraph continues] Mother of grace! what shall I do when the people come home? I shall never hear the end of this churning till the day of my death!' 'Place thine hand in the water-stoup below the

280

dresser and see if thy butter be there,' said the tailor. And with that the woman placed her hand in the water-stoup as directed, and three successive times, and each time brought up a large lump of butter as fresh and fair and fragrant as the beauteous butter-cups in their prime. The clever tailor had counteracted the machinations of the greedy neighbour woman by placing the live cinders in the water-stoup.

'

EOLAS A CHRANNACHAIN

CHARM OF THE CHURN

THIG na saor, thig;
Thig na daor, thig;
Thig na caor, thig;
Thig na maor, thig;
Thig na faor, thig;
Thig na baor, thig;
Thig na gaor, thig;
Thig na caoch, thig;
Thig na caon, thig;
Thig na caomh, thig;
Thig na gaol, thig;
Thig na claon, thig;
Thig fear a churraig bhuidhe,
Chuireas am muighe na ruith.

Thig na saora.
Thig na daora,
Thig na caora,
Thig na maora,
Thig na faora,
Thig na baora,
Thig na gaora,
Thig na caocha,

COME will the free, come;
Come will the bond, come;
Come will the bells, come;
Come will the maers, come;
Come will the blade, come;
Come will the sharp, come;
Come will the hounds, come;
Come will the wild, come;
Come will the mild, come;
Come will the kind, come;

Come will the loving, come;
Come will the squint, come;
Come will he of the yellow cap,
That will set the churn a-running.

The free will come,
The bond will come,
The bells will come,
The maers will come,
The blades will come,
The sharp will come,
The hounds will come,
The wild will come,

Thig na caona,
Thig na caomha,
Thig na gaola,
Thig na claona,
Thig loma lan na cruinne,
Chur a mhuighe na ruith;
Thig Calum caomh na uidheam,
'S thig Bride bhuidhe chruidh.

Tha glug a seo,
Tha glag a seo,
Tha glag a seo,
Tha glug a seo,
Tha slug a seo,
Tha slag a seo,
Tha slag a seo,
Tha slug a seo,
Tha seilcheag mhor bhog a seo,
Tha brigh gach te dhe'n chrodh a seo,
Tha rud is foir na mil is beoir,
Tha bocan buidhe nodh a seo.

Tha rud is fearr na choir a seo,
Tha dorn an t-sagairt mhoir a seo,
Tha rud is fearr na chairbh a seo,
Tha ceann an duine mhairbh a seo,
Tha rud is fearr na fion a seo,
Tha lan cuman Cairistine
Do mhiala boga bine seo,
Do mhiala boga bine seo.

Thig, a chuinneag, thig;

Thig, a chuinneag, thig;

The mild will come,
The kind will come,
The loving will come,
The devious will come,
The brim-full of the globe will come,
To set the churn a-running;
The kindly Columba will come in his array;
And the golden-haired Bride of the kine.

A splash is here,
A plash is here,
A plash is here,
A splash is here,
A crash is here,
A squash is here,
A squash is here,
A crash is here,
A big soft snail is here,
The sap of each of the cows is here,
A thing better than honey and spruce,
A bogle yellow and fresh is here.

A thing better than right is here,
The fist of the big priest is here,
A thing better than the carcase is here,
The head of the dead man is here,
A thing better than wine is here,
The full of the cog of Caristine
Of live things soft and fair are here,
Of live things soft and fair are here.

Come, thou churn, come;
Come, thou churn, come;

Thig, a bhitheag; thig, a bheathag;
Thig, a chuinneag, thig;
Thig, a chuinneag, thig;
Thig, a chuthag; thig, a cheathag;
Thig, a chuinneag, thig;
Thig, a chuinneag, thig;
Thig an fhosgag a adhar,
'S thig cailleag a chinn-duibh.

Thig, a chuinneag, thig;

Thig, a chuinneag, thig;
Thig an ion, thig an smeol,
'S thig an ceol as a bhrugh;
Thig, a chuinneag, thig;
Thig, a chuinneag, thig;
Thig, a chait chaothaich,
Chur faoch air do ruch;
Thig, a chuinneag, thig;
Thig, a chuinneag, thig.

Thig, a mhaduidh, 's caisg do phathadh;
Thig, a chuinneag, thig;
Thig, a chuinneag, thig;
Thig, a bhuichd; thig, a nuichd;
Thig, a chuinneag, thig;
Thig, a chuinneag, thig;
Thig, a dhiola-deirce
Is deistiniche ruichd;
Thig, a chuinneag, thig;
Thig, a chuinneag, thig;
Thig, gach creutair acrach,
Is dioil tart do chuirp.

Come, thou life; (?) come, thou breath; (?)
Come, thou churn, come;
Come, thou churn, come;
Come, thou cuckoo; come, thou jackdaw;
Come, thou churn, come;
Come, thou churn, come;
Come will the little lark from the sky,
Come will the little carlin of the black-cap.

Come, thou churn, come;
Come, thou churn, come;
Come will the merle, come will the mavis,
Come will the music from the bower;
Come, thou churn, come;
Come, thou churn, come;
Come, thou wild cat,
To ease thy throat;
Come, thou churn, come;
Come, thou churn, come.

Come, thou hound, and quench thy thirst;
Come, thou churn, come;
Come, thou churn, come;

Come, thou poor; come, thou naked;
Come, thou churn, come;
Come, thou churn, come;
Come, ye alms-deserver
Of most distressful moan;
Come, thou churn, come;
Come, thou churn, come;
Come, each hungry creature,
And satisfy the thirst of thy body.

Thig, a chuinneag, thig;
Thig, a chuinneag, thig;
'S e Dia duileach a chuir oirnn,
'S chan ora caillich le luibh.
Thig, a chuinneag, thig;
Thig, a chuinneag, thig;
Thig, a Mhuire mhin-ghil,
Is dilimich mo chuid;
Thig, a chuinneag, thig;
Thig, a chuinneag, thig;
Thig, a Bhride bhith-ghil,
Is coistrig brigh mo chruidh.

Thig, a chuinneag, thig;
Thig, a chuinneag, thig;
Am maistreadh rinn Moire,
Air astradh a ghlinne,
A lughdachadh a boinne,
A mheudachadh a h-ime;
Blathach gu dorn,
Im gu uileann;
Thig, a chuinneag, thig;
Thig, a chuinneag, thig.

Come, thou churn, come;
Come, thou churn, come;
It is the God of the elements who bestowed on us,
And not the charm of a carlin with plant.
Come, thou churn, come;
Come, thou churn, come;
Come, thou fair-white Mary,
And endow to me my means;
Come, thou churn, come;
Come, thou churn, come;
Come, thou beauteous Bride,
And bless the substance of my kine.

Come, thou churn, come;
Come, thou churn, come;
The churning made of Mary,
In the fastness of the glen,
To decrease her milk,
To increase her butter;
Butter-milk to wrist,
Butter to elbow;
Come, thou churn, come;
Come, thou churn, come.

AN EOIR A CHUIR MOIRE

THE CHARM SENT OF MARY

EOIR a chuir Moir Oighe,
Dh' an chaillich bha chomhnuidh
Air orrlain a ghlinne,
Air fireacha fuara--
Air orrlain a ghlinne,
Air fireacha fuara.

Chuir i eoir ri stile,
Chon meudach a h-ime,
Chon lughdach a bainne,
Chon tachradh a tuara--
Chon meudach a h-ime,
Chon lughdach a bainne,
Chon tachradh a tuara.

THE charm sent of Mary Virgin,
To the nun who was dwelling
On the floor of the glen,
On the cold high moors--
On the floor of the glen,
On the cold high moors.

She put spell to saliva,
To increase her butter,
To decrease her milk,
To make plentiful her food--
To increase her butter,
To decrease her milk,
To make plentiful her food.

[The nun referred to is Brigit, of whom Broccan's Hymn says, 'She was not a milkmaid of a mountain-side; she wrought in the midst of a plain.' The second stanza is an echo of one of the miracles attributed to her in the same hymn; 'when the first dairying was sent with the first butter in a hamper, it kept not from bounty to her guests, their attachment was not diminished,' explained further as follows: 'Brigit serving a certain wizard was wont to give away much butter in charity. This displeased the wizard and his wife, who came on her without notice. Brigit had only a small churning ready and she repeated this stave--"My store-room, a store-room of fair God, a store-room which my King has blessed, a store-room with somewhat therein.

"'May Mary's Son, my friend, come to bless my store-room which my King has blessed, a store-room with somewhat therein.

"'May Mary's Son, my friend, come to bless my store-room. The Prince of the world to the border may there be plenty with Him.

"'O my Prince, who hast power over all these things! Bless, O God--a cry unforbidden--with thy right hand this store-room."

'She brought a half churning to the wizard's wife. "That is good to fill a big hamper!" said the wizard's wife. "Fill ye your hamper," said Brigit, "and God will put somewhat therein." She still kept going into her kitchen and bringing half a making thereout and singing a stave of these staves as she went back. If the hampers which the men of Munster possessed had been given to her she would have filled them all. The wizard and his wife marvelled at the miracle which they beheld. Then said the wizard to Brigit: "This butter and the kine which thou hast milked, I offer to thee; and thou shalt not be serving me but serve the Lord." Said Brigit: "Take thou the kine, but give me my mother's freedom. Said the wizard: "Behold thy mother and the kine; and whatsoever thou shalt say, that will I do." Then Brigit dealt out the kine to the poor and the needy; and the wizard was baptized and "he was full of faith."'

See Broccan's Hymn, told at greater length in the note. Thesaurus Palaeohibernicus, vol. ii., p. 331, etc. Also Lismore Lives, p. 186-7; compare also pp. <page 18>-19, <page 34>-35, <page 150>-151, <page 158>-159 of this volume with incidents in the Life of St Brigit as recorded in the above books.

ULC A DHEAN MO LOCHD

THE WICKED WHO WOULD ME HARM

THIS and other poems were obtained from Isabella Chisholm, a travelling tinker. Though old, Isabella Chisholm was still tall and straight, fine-featured, and fresh-complexioned. She was endowed with personal attraction, mental ability, and astute diplomacy of no common order. Her father, John Chisholm, is said to have been a 'pious, prayerful man'--terms not usually applied to his class. Isabella Chisholm had none of the swarthy skin and far-away look of the ordinary gipsy. But she had the gipsy habits and the gipsy language, variously called 'Cant,' 'Shelta,' 'Romany,' with rich fluent Gaelic and English. She had many curious spells, runes, and hymns, that would have enriched Gaelic literature, and many rare words and phrases and expressions that would have improved the Gaelic dictionary.

ULC a dhean mo lochd

Gun gabh e 'n galar gluc gloc,
Guirneanach, gioirneanach, guairneach,
Gaornanach, garnanach, gruam.

Gum bu cruaidhe c na chlach,
Gum bu duibhe e na 'n gual,
Gum bu luaithe e na 'n lach,
Gum bu truime e na 'n luaidh.

Gum bu gointe, gointe, geuire, gairbhe, guiniche e,
Na'n cuilionn cruaidh cnea-chridheach,
Gum bu gairge e na'n salann sion, sionn, searbh, sailte,
Seachd seachd uair.

A turabal a null,
A tarabal a nall,
A treosdail a sios,
A dreochail a suas,

A breochail a muigh,
A geochail a staigh,
Dol a mach minic,
Tighinn a steach ainmic.

THE wicked who would do me harm
May he take the [throat] disease,
Globularly, spirally, circularly,
Fluxy, pellety, horny-grim.

Be it harder than the stone,
Be it blacker than the coal,
Be it swifter than the duck,
Be it heavier than the lead.

Be it fiercer, fiercer, sharper, harsher, more malignant,
Than the hard, wound-quivering holly,
Be it sourer than the sained, lustrous, bitter, salt salt,
Seven seven times.

Oscillating thither,
Undulating hither,
Staggering downwards,
Floundering upwards.

Drivelling outwards,
Snivelling inwards,

Oft hurrying out,
Seldom coming in.

Sop an luib gach laimhe,
Cas an cois gach cailbhe,
Lurg am bun gach ursann,
Sput ga chur 's ga chairbinn.

Gearrach fhala le cridhe, le crutha, le cnamha,
Le gruthan, le sgumhan, le sgamha,
Agus sgrudadh cuisil, ugan is arna,
Dha mo luchd-tair agus tuaileis.

An ainm Dhia nam feart,
A shiab uam gach olc,
'S a dhion mi le neart,
Bho lion mo luchd-freachd
Agus fuathachd.

A wisp the portion of each hand,
A foot in the base of each pillar,
A leg the prop of each jamb,
A flux driving and dragging him.

A dysentery of blood from heart, from form, from bones,
From the liver, from the lobe, from the lungs,
And a searching of veins, of throat, and of kidneys,
To my contemners and traducers.

In name of the God of might,
Who warded from me every evil,
And who shielded me in strength,
From the net of my breakers
And destroyers.

FRITH MHOIRE

AUGURY OF MARY

THE 'frith,' augury, was a species of divination enabling the 'frithir,' augurer, to see into the unseen. This divination was made to ascertain the position and condition of the absent and the lost, and was applied to man and beast. The augury was made on the first Monday of the quarter and immediately before sunrise. The augurer, fasting, and with bare feet, bare head, and closed eyes, went to the doorstep and placed a hand on each jamb. Mentally beseeching the God of the unseen to show him his quest and to grant him his augury, the augurer opened his eyes and looked steadfastly straight in front of him. From the nature and position of the objects within his sight, he drew his conclusions.

Many men in the Highlands and Islands were famed augurers, and many stories, realistic, romantic, and extremely curious, are still told of their divinations.

The people say that the Virgin made an augury when Christ was missing, and that it was by means of this augury that Mary and Joseph ascertained that Christ was in the Temple disputing with the doctors. Hence this divination is called 'frith Mhoire,'--the augury of Mary; and 'frithireachd Mhoire,'--the auguration of Mary.

The 'frith' of the Celt is akin to the 'frett' of the Norseman. Probably the surnames Freer, Frere, are modifications of 'frithir,' augurer. Persons bearing this name claim that their progenitors were astrologers to the kings of Scotland.

DIA faram, Dia fodham,
Dia romham, Dia am dheoghainn,
Mis air do shlighe Dhia,
Thus, a Dhia, air mo luirg.

Frith rinn Muire d'a Mac,
Iobair Bride ri a glac,
Am fac thu i, a Righ nan dul?--
Ursa Righ nan dul gum fac.

Frith Muire da muirichinn fein,
Trath dha bhi re ri cuairt,
Fios firinn gun fios breuige,
Gum faic mi fein na bheil uam.

Mac Muire min-ghil, Righ nan dul,
A shulachadh domh-s' na bheil uam,
Le gras nach falnaich, mu m' choinneamh,
Gu brath nach smalaich 's nach doillich.

GOD over me, God under me,
God before me, God behind me,
I on Thy path, O God,
Thou, O God, in my steps.

The augury made of Mary to her Son,
The offering made of Bride through her palm,
Sawest Thou it, King of life?--
Said the King of life that He saw.

The augury made by Mary for her own offspring,
When He was for a space amissing,
Knowledge of truth, not knowledge of falsehood,

That I shall truly see all my quest.

Son of beauteous Mary, King of life,
Give Thou me eyes to see all my quest,
With grace that shall never fail, before me,
That shall never quench nor dim.

V

MEASGAIN

MISCELLANEOUS

CIAD MIARAIL CHRIOSD

THE FIRST MIRACLE OF CHRIST

THIS poem was obtained in 1891 from Malcolm Macmillan, crofter, Grimnis, Benbecula. Macmillan was then an old man. He heard this and many other poems when a boy from old people who, when evicted in Uist, emigrated to Prince Edward's Island, Nova Scotia, Cape Breton, and other parts of the Canadian Dominion, and to Australia. These old people took great quantities of traditional Gaelic lore with them to their new homes, some of which still lingers among their descendants. Many original and translated songs of the Highlands and Islands are sung among these settlers, whose hearts still yearn towards their motherland.

CHAIDH Eosai is Mairi
Chon aireamh a suas,
'S chaidh eoin an geall caithream
Ann an caille nan cuach.

Bha 'n dithis a siubhal slighe,
Gon a ranuig iad coille tiugh,
Is anns a choille bha miosan
Bha co dearg ris na subh.

Sin an t-am an robh ise torrach,
Anns an robh i giulan nigh nan gras,
Is ghabh i miann air na miosan
Bha air sliosrach an aigh.

Is labhair Mairi ri Eosai,
Le guth malda, miamh,
'Tabhair miosan domh, Eosai,
Gon caisg mi mo mhiann.'

Is labhair Eosai ri Mairi,
'S an cradh cruaidh na chom,
'Bheir mi 'uit miosan, a Mhairi,
Ach co is athair dha d' throm?'

JOSEPH and Mary went
To the numbering up,
And the birds began chorusing

In the woods of the turtle-doves.

The two were walking the way,
Till they reached a thick wood,
And in the wood there was fruit
Which was as red as the rasp.

That was the time when she was great,
That she was carrying the King of grace,
And she took a desire for the fruit
That was growing on the gracious slope.

Then spoke Mary to Joseph,
In a voice low and sweet,
'Give to me of the fruit, Joseph,
That I may quench my desire.'

And Joseph spoke to Mary,
And the hard pain in his breast,
'I will give thee of the fruit, Mary,
But who is the father of thy burthen?'

Sin 'd uair labhair an Leanabh,
A mach as a bru,
'Lub a sios gach geug aluinn,
Gon caisg mo Mhathair a ruth.'

'S o 'n mheanglan is airde,
Chon a mheanglan is isde,
Lub iad a sios gon a glun,
'S ghabh Mairi dhe na miosan
Ann am fearann fiosraidh a ruin.

An sin thuirt Eosai ri Mairi,
'S e lan aithreachais trom,
'Is ann air a ghiulan a tasa,
Righ na glorach 's nan grasa.
Beannaicht thu, Mhairi,
Measg mnai gach fonn.
Beannaicht thu, Mhairi,
Measg mnai gach fonn.'

Then it was that the Babe spoke,
From out of her womb,
'Bend ye down every beautiful bough,
That my Mother may quench her desire.'

And from the bough that was highest,
To the bough that was lowest,
They all bent down to her knee,
And Mary partook of the fruit
In her loved land of prophecy.

Then Joseph said to Mary,
And he full of heavy contrition,
'It is carrying Him thou art,
The King of glory and of grace.
Blessed art thou, Mary,
Among the women of all lands.
Blessed art thou, Mary,
Among the women of all lands.'

AN OIGH AGUS AN LEANABH

THE VIRGIN AND CHILD

CHUNNACAS an Oigh a teachd,
Criosda gu h-og na h-uchd,
Ainghle a lubadh dhaibh umhlachd,
Righ nan dul a dubhradh gur ceart.

An Oigh is or-dhealta cleachd,
An t-Ios is ro ghile na 'n sneachd,
Searapha ciuil a seinn an cliu,
Righ nan dul a dubhradh gur ceart.

THE Virgin was seen approaching,
Christ so young on her breast,
Angels making them obeisance,
The King of glory saying it is just.

The Virgin of gold-bedewed locks,
The Jesu whiter than snow,
Seraphs of song singing their praise,
The King of glory saying it is just.

DIA NA GILE

GOD OF THE MOON

DIA na gile, Dia na greine,
Dia na cruinne, Dia nan reula,

Dia nan dile, tir, is neamha,
Dh' orduich dhuinne Righ na feile.

'S i Moire mhin chaidh air a glun,
'S e Ti nan dul a chaidh na h-uchd,
Chaidh durch is diuir a chur air chul,
'S chaidh reul an iuil an aird gu much.

Dh' fhoillsich fearann, dh' fhoillsich fonn,
Dh' fhoillsich doltrom agus struth,
Leagadh bron is thogadh fonn,
Chaidh ceol air bonn le clar is cruth.

GOD of the moon, God of the sun,
God of the globe, God of the stars,
God of the waters, the land, and the skies,
Who ordained to us the King of promise.

It was Mary fair who went upon her knee,
It was the King of life who went upon her lap,
Darkness and tears were set behind,
And the star of guidance went up early.

Illumed the land, illumed the world,
Illumed doldrum and current,
Grief was laid and joy was raised,
Music was set up with harp and pedal-harp.

DIA NA GILE, DIA NA GREINE

GOD OF THE MOON, GOD OF THE SUN

DIA na gile, Dia na greine,
Dh' orduich dhuinne Mac na meine.
Muire min gheal air a glun,
Criosda nigh nan dul 'n a h-uchd.
Is mise an cleireach stucanach,
Dol timcheall nan clach stacanach,
Is leir dhomh tulach, is leir dhomh traigh,
Is leir dhomh ainghlean air an t-snamh,
Is leir dhomh calpa cuimir, cruinn,
A tighinn air tir le cairdeas duinn.

GOD of the moon, God of the sun,
Who ordained to us the Son of mercy.
The fair Mary upon her knee,

Christ the King of life in her lap.
I am the cleric established,
Going round the founded stones,
I behold mansions, I behold shores,
I behold angels floating,
I behold the shapely rounded column
Coming landwards in friendship to us.

TEARUINTEACHD NAM FIAL

SAFETY OF THE GENEROUS

THIS verse, the only verse of the poem he could remember, was obtained from John Kane, a native of Ireland. John Kane had many traditional stories of Saint Columba showing that he 'being dead yet speaketh.' These stories were vivid and graphic, the probable and improbable, possible and impossible, blending and diffusing throughout.

DEIR Calum-cille ruinn,
Dh' ifrinn gu brath nach tar am fial;
Ach luchd na meirle 's luchd nam mionn,
Caillidh siad an coir air Dia.

COLUMBA tells to us, that
To hell the generous shall never go;
But those who steal and those who swear,
They shall lose their right to God.

COISTRIG MATHAR

MOTHER'S CONSECRATION

THE following lines are whispered by mothers into the ears of sons and daughters when leaving their homes in the Outer Isles for the towns of the south and for foreign lands. Probably they are the last accents of the mother's voice--heard in the far-away home among the hills clothed with mist or on the machair washed by the sea--that linger on the Gaelic ear as it sinks in the sleep that knows no waking.

AN Dia mor bhi eadar do dha shlinnein,
Ga do chomhnadh a falbh 's a tilleadh,
Mac Moire Oighe bhi an coir do chridhe,
'S an Spiorad foirfe bhi ort a sileadh--
O, an Spiorad foirfe bhi ort a sileadh!
[Aoidh [Una
[Thorcuil [Shorcha
[Thascail [Shlainte.

BE the great God between thy two shoulders,
To protect thee in thy going and in thy coming,
Be the Son of Mary Virgin near thine heart,
And be the perfect Spirit upon thee pouring--
Oh, the perfect Spirit upon thee pouring!
[Aodh [Una
[Torquil [Light
[Tascal [Health.

AM FEAR A CHEUSADH

HE WHO WAS CRUCIFIED

THE two following poems were got in Kintail. They are obscure in themselves, and the dialect of Kintail in which they were recited increases their obscurity. The reciters repeated them as one poem, but were uncertain whether they were one or two poems.

FHIR a chruchadh air a chribh,
Fhir a chiosadh le minn an t-sluaigh, [binn
Nis bho dh' f has mi aosda, liath,
Gabh ri m' fhaosaid, a Dhia! truais.

Chan ioghnadh domh is mor mo lochd,
Is mi an clab-goileam bochd bua'all,
Ri m' oige gun robh mi baoth,
Ri m' aois gu bheil mi truagh.

Seal mu'n taine Mac De,
Bha 'n ce na lodruich dhuibh,
Gun ri, gun ro, gun re,
Gun chro, gun chre, gun chruth.

Shoillsich fearann, shoillsich fonn,
Shoillsich an trom fhairge ghlas,
Shoillsich an cruinne ce gu leir,
Ri linn Mhic De tigh'nn gu teach.

Sin 'd uair labhair Moire nan gras,
An Oigh bhaigheil a bha ghnath glic,
'D uair thug Eosai dhi-se ghradh,
Bu mhiann leis bhi 'n a lathair tric.

THOU who wert hanged upon the tree,
And wert crucified by the condemnation of the people,
Now that I am grown old and grey,
Take to my confession-prayer, O God! pity.

No wonder to me great is my wickedness,
I am a poor clattering cymbal,
In my youth I was profane,
In my age I am forlorn.

A time ere came the Son of God,
The earth was a black morass,
Without star, without sun, without moon,
Without body, without heart, without form.

Illumined plains, illumined hills,
Illumined the great green sea,
Illumined the whole globe together,
When the Son of God came to earth.

Then it was that spoke the Mary of grace,
The Virgin always most kindly and wise,
When Joseph gave to her his love,
He desired to be often in her presence.

Bha cumhnant eadar Eos agus Oigh,
Ann an ordugh dligheach ceart,
Gum biodh cuis ga cur air doigh
Le seula Righ Mor nam feart.

Chair iad leis gu Teampull De,
Far an robh a chleir a steach;
Mar a dh' orduich an t-Ard High Mor,
Phos iad mu'n taine mach.

Thainig aingeal na dheigh:--
'Eosai, ciod e 'n gleus a th' ort?'
'Fhuair mi boirionnach bho 'n chleir,
Cha dual domh fein a bhi ceart.'

'Eosai, fuirich ri do cheil,
Chan nodaidh dhuit beud a radh,
Gur h-e th' agad an Oigh ghlan,
Air nach deachaidh le fear lamh.'

'Ciamar a chreideas mi sin uat?
Agam fein, mo nuar! tha fios--
'D uair a laigh mi sios ri gual'
Bha leanabh beo a briosg fo crios.'

299

A compact there was between Joseph and Virgin,
In order well-becoming and just,
That the compact might be confirmed
By the seal of the Great King of virtues.

They went with him to the Temple of God,
Where the clerics sat within;
As ordained of the Great High King,
They married ere they came out.

An angel came afterwards:
'Joseph, why excited thou?'
'I got a woman from the clerics,
It is not natural for me to be calm.'

'Joseph, abide thou by thy reason,
Not enlightened of thee to find fault,
What thou hast gotten is a virgin pure,
On whom man never put hand.'

'How can I believe that from thee?
I myself, my grief! have knowledge--
When I laid me down by her shoulder
A living child beneath her girdle throbbed.'

AN COILEACH SIN

THAT COCK

SIN 'd uair labhair a bhean bhorb--
'Is iad na coirb a rinn mo chreach,
Cuir am breugaire sios fo lorg,
'S bidh do bheatha nios dha m' theach.

An coileach sin agad 's a phoit,
Air a phronnadh cho broit ri cal,
Cha teid am breugadair an sloc
Gon an goir e air an sparr.'

Chair an coileach air an sparr,
Chairich e dha sgiath r'a chorp,
Ghoir e ann gu blasdar, binn,
Is thainig mo Righ bho 'n chroibh.

An dream nach miannach le Dia
Luchd nam breug is luchd nam mionn;

B' annsa leis an urnuigh fhior
Is li nan rosg a ruith gu teann.

IT was then spoke the rude woman--
'It was the wicked who made my ruin,
Drive the liar down below the beam,
And thou shalt be welcome to my house.

That cock thou hast in the pot,
Chopped as broken as the kail,
The liar shall not go to the pit
Till he shall crow upon the spar.'

The cock went upon the spar,
He placed his two wings to his body,
He crew sweetly, melodiously,
And my King came from the tree.

The people not liked of God
Are those who lie and those who swear;
Rather would He have the genuine prayer
And water from the eyelids flowing swiftly.

MANAIDH

OMENS

THE people believed in omens of birds and beasts, fishes and insects, and of men and women. These omens were innumerable, and a few only can be mentioned.

The fisher would deem it a bad omen to meet a red-haired woman when on his way to fish; and were the woman defective in mind or body, probably the man would return home muttering strong adjectives beneath his breath. On the other hand, it was lucky for a girl to find the red hair of a woman in the nest of certain birds, particularly in the nest of the wheatear.

'Gruag ruadh boirionnaich,
Fiasag liath firionnaich,
Ruth agus rath na leirist
Gheobh an nead a chlacharain.'
[bhigirein

The red hair of a woman,
The grey beard of a man,
Are love and luck to the sloven
Who gets them in the nest of the
wheatear. [tit.

MOCH maduinn Luan,
Chualas meaghal uan,

Agus meigead eunaraig,
Seimh am shuidhe crom,

Agus cuthag liath-ghorm,
'S gun am biadh am bhronn.

Feasgar finidh Mhart,
Chunnas air lic mhin,
Seilicheag shlim, bhan,

Agus an clacharan fionn
Air barr a gharraidh toll,

Searrach seann larach
Spagail 's a chula rium.

Dh' aithnich mi fein 'n an deigh
Nach eireadh a bhliadhna liom.

EARLY on the morning of Monday,
I heard the bleating of a lamb,

And the kid-like cry of snipe,
While gently sitting bent,

And the grey-blue cuckoo,
And no food on my stomach.

On the fair evening of Tuesday,
I saw on the smooth stone,
The snail slimy, pale,

And the ashy wheatear
On the top of the dyke of holes,

The foal of the old mare
Of sprauchly gait and its back to me.

And I knew from these
That the year would not go well with me.

MOCH LA LUAN CASG

302

EARLY EASTER MONDAY

MOCH La Luan Casg,
Chunna mi air sal
Lach is eala bhan
A snamh le cheile.

Chuala mi Di-mart
Eunarag nan trath,
Meannanaich 's an ard
'S ag eigheach.

Di-ciadain bha mi
Buain na feamain-chir,
Is chunna mi na tri
Ri eirigh.

Dh' aithnich mi air ball
Gun robh an imirig ann,
Beannachd nach biodh ann
An deigh sin.

Comraig Bhride bhith,
Comraig Mhoire mhin,
Comraig Mhicheil mhil,
Dhomh fhi' 's dha m' eudail,
Dhomh fhi' 's dha m' eudail.

EARLY on the day of Easter Monday,
I saw on the brine
A duck and a white swan
Swim together.

I heard on Tuesday
The snipe of the seasons,
Bleating on high
And calling.

On Wednesday I had been
Cutting the channelled fucus,
And then saw I the three
Arising.

I knew immediately
That a flitting there was,

Blessing there would not be
After that.

The girth of Bride calm,
The girth of Mary mild,
The girth of Michael strong,
Upon me and mine,
Upon me and mine.

MANADH NAN EALA

OMEN OF THE SWANS

CHUALA mi guth binn nan eala,
Ann an dealachadh nan trath,
Glugalaich air sgiathaibh siubhlach,
Cur nan cura dhiubh gu h-ard.

Ghrad sheas mi, cha d' rinn mi gluasad,
Suil dh'an tug mi bhuam co bha
Deanamh iuil air an toiseach?
Righinn an t-sonais an eala bhan.

Bha seo air feasgar Di-aona,
Bha mo smaontan air Di-mart--
Chaill mi mo chuid 's mo dhaona
Bliadhn o'n Aona sin gu brath.

Ma chi thu eala air Di-aona,
Moch 's a mhaduinn fhaoilidh, agh,
Bidh cinneas air do chuid 's do dhaona,
Do bhuar cha chaochail a ghnath.

I HEARD the sweet voice of the swans,
At the parting of night and day,
Gurgling on the wings of travelling,
Pouring forth their strength on high.

I quickly stood me, nor made I move,
A look which I gave from me forth
Who should be guiding in front?
The queen of luck, the white swan.

This was on the evening of Friday,
My thoughts were of the Tuesday--
I lost my means and my kinsfolk

A year from that Friday for ever.

Shouldst thou see a swan on Friday,
In the joyous morning dawn,
There shall be increase on thy means and thy kin,
Nor shall thy flocks be always dying.

MANAIDH

OMENS

CHUALA mi chuthag 's gun bhiadh am bhroinn,
Chuala mi am fearan am barr a chroinn,
Chuala mi 'n suaircean shuas anns a choill,
'S chuala mi nualla cumhachag na h-oidhche.

Chunna mi 'n t-uan 's a chula rium,
Chunna mi 'n t-seiliche air lic luim,
Chunna mi 'n searrach le thulachain rium,
Chunna mi an clachran air gharadh tuill,
An eunarag 's mi 'm shuidhe cruinn,
'S dh' aithnich mi fhe' nach teidheadh
A bhliadhna lion.

I HEARD the cuckoo with no food in my stomach,
I heard the stock-dove on the top of the tree,
I heard the sweet singer in the copse beyond,
And I heard the screech of the owl of the night.

I saw the lamb with his back to me,
I saw the snail on the bare flag-stone,
I saw the foal with his rump to me,
I saw the wheatear on a dyke of holes,
I saw the snipe while sitting bent,
And I foresaw that the year would not
Go well with me.

AN TUIS

THE INCENSE

RI la do shlainte,
Cha dean thu crabhadh,
Cha tabhair thu taine,
'S cha tar thu tuis;

305

Ceann an ardain,
Cridhe na gabhachd,
Beul gun fhaigheam,
'S cha nar leat cuis.

Ach thig do gheamhradh,
Is cruas do theanndachd,
Is bidh do cheann mar
Am meall 's an uir;

Do luth air failing,
Do chruth air fhagail,
Is tu na do thraill,
Air do dha ghlun.

IN the day of thy health,
Thou wilt not give devotion,
Thou wilt not give kine,
Nor wilt thou offer incense;

Head of haughtiness,
Heart of greediness,
Mouth unhemmed,
Nor ashamed art thou.

But thy winter will come,
And the hardness of thy distress,
And thy head shall be as
The clod in the earth

Thy strength having failed,
Thine aspect having gone,
And thou a thrall,
On thy two knees.

DUAN NAN DAOL

THERE are many curious legends and beliefs current in the Isles about the 'cearr-dubhan,' or sacred beetle. When his enemies were in search of Christ to put Him to death, they met the sacred beetle and the gravedigger beetle out on a foraging expedition in search of food for their families. The Jews asked the beetles if they had seen Christ passing that way. Proud to be asked, and anxious to conciliate the great people, the gravedigger promptly and volubly replied: 'Yes, yes! He passed here yesterday evening, when I and the people of the townland were digging a grave and burying the body of a field-mouse that had come to an untimely end.' 'You lie! you lie!' said the sacred beetle; 'it was a year ago yesterday that Christ the Son passed here, when my children and I were searching for food, after the king's horse had passed.'

Because of his ready officiousness against Christ, the gravedigger is always killed when seen; while for his desire to shield Christ, the sacred beetle is spared, but because he told a lie he is always turned on his back. The sacred beetle is covered with a strong integument like a knight encased in armour. Consequently he is unable to resume his position, and he struggles continually, waving his feet in the effort to touch something which will assist him to rise. It is unlawful to pass by the sacred beetle without putting him on his back, but should he succeed in righting himself, it is unlawful to molest him further.

In some places the gravedigger is killed because otherwise he will profane the grave of the grandmother of the person who passes him by.

The following somewhat similar legend is also current in Uist:--

The anti-Christians were pursuing Christ, wishing to kill Him. Christ came to a townland where a crofter was winnowing corn on the hillock. The good crofter placed Christ under the heap of grain to conceal Him from his enemies. The crofter went into the barn to bring out more grain to place over Christ to hide Him more effectually. In his absence the fowls attacked the heap of corn under which Christ was hidden. They were round the heap and over the heap--hens and ducks feeding as rapidly as they could. The ducks contented themselves with eating and tramping the corn. Not so the hens: they scattered the corn about with their feet as they ate, so that the hidden Christ was exposed to view when the crofter returned. In consequence of this disservice to Christ in His distress, it was left as a heritage to the hen and to her seed for ever that she should be sever-toed; that she should be confined to land; that

she should dislike hail, rain, sleet, and snow; that she should dread thunder and lightning; that dust, not water, should be her bath; that she should have no oil with which to annoint herself and preen her feathers; and finally, that she should have only one life and only one joy in life--the joy of land.

And because the duck contented herself with eating the corn without exposing the person of Christ, it was left to her and her descendants ever more that she should be web-footed, and not be confined to land; that she should rejoice in hail and rain and sleet and snow; that she should rejoice in thunder and lightning; that water not dust should be her bath; that she should have oil with which to anoint herself and preen her feathers; that she should have three lives and three joys--the joy of earth, the joy of air, and the joy of water; nay, a fourth life and a fourth joy--the joy of under the water; that she should be most dressed when the hen was most draggled; that she should be most joyous when the hen was most miserable; that she should be most hopeful when the hen was in most despair; that she should be most happy when the hen was in most dread; that she should dance with joy when the hen quaked with fear. When the hen hears thunder she trembles as the aspen and hurries home in terror, screaming and screeching the while. Hence the saying--

'Tha do chridh air chrith
Mar chirc ri torruinn.'

Thine heart is quivering
Like a hen in thunder.

The converse is true of the duck. When she hears thunder she rejoices and dances to her own 'port-a-bial'--mouth music. This gave rise to the saying--

'Is coltach thu ri tunnaig
'S a fiughair ri torruinn.'

Thou art like a duck
Expectant of thunder.

[pp. <page 190>-191

DUAN NAN DAOL

POEM OF THE BEETLES

TRATH bha Ti nan dul fo choill,
Agus daoibhidh air a dheigh,
De thuirt daolaire na doill,
Ris an daol 's an dealan-de?

'Am facas seach an diugh no 'n raoir,
Mac mo ghaoil-sa--Mac De?'
'Chunnas, chunnas,' os an daol,
'Mac na saorsa seach an de.'

'Cearr! cearr! cearr thu fhe,'
Os an cearr-dubhan feach;
'A bhliadhna mhor chon an de
Chaidh Mac De seach.'

WHEN the Being of glory was in retreat,
And wicked men in pursuit of Him,
What said the groveller of blindness,
To the beetle and the butterfly?

'Saw ye passing to-day or yestreen,
The Son of my love--the Son of God?'
'We saw, we saw,' said the black beetle,
'The Son of freedom pass yesterday.'

'Wrong! wrong! wrong art thou,'
Said the sacred beetle earthy;
'A big year it was yestreen
Since the Son of God passed.'

DUAN NAN DAOL

POEM OF THE BEETLES

D UAIR bha Criosda fo choill,
Agus naimhdean air a dheigh,
Is e thuirt faochaire na foill,
Ris an daol 's an dealan-de--

'Am facas seach an diugh no 'n raoir,
Mac mo ghaol-sa, Mac De?'
'Chunna, chunna,' ors an daol,
'Mac na saorsa seach an de.'

'Breug! breug! breug!'
Orsa cearran cre nan each,
'A bhliadhna mhor chon an de,
Chaidh Mac De seach.'

WHEN Christ was under the wood,
And enemies were pursuing Him,
The crooked one of deception,
Said to the black beetle and the butterfly

'Saw ye pass to-day or yesterday,
The Son of my love, the Son of God?'
'We saw! we saw!' said the black beetle,
'The Son of redemption pass yesterday.'

'False! false! false!'
Said the little clay beetle of horses,
'A full year yesterday,
The Son of God went by.'

DUAN AN DAOIL

POEM OF THE BEETLE

A DHAOLAG, a dhaolag,
An cuimhne leat an la 'n de?
A dhaolag, a dhaolag,
An cuimhne leat an la 'n de?
A dhaolag, a dhaolag,
An cuimhne leat an la 'n de
Chaidh Mac De seachad?

LITTLE beetle, little beetle,
Rememberest thou yesterday?
Little beetle, little beetle,
Rememberest thou yesterday?
Little beetle, little beetle,
Rememberest thou yesterday
The Son of God went by?

TALADH

LULLABY

THE swan is a favourite bird and of good omen. To hear it in the morning fasting--especially on a Tuesday morning--is much to be desired. To see seven, or a multiple of seven, swans on the wing ensures peace and prosperity for seven, or a multiple of seven years.

In windy, snowy, or wet weather swans fly low, but in calm, bright, or frosty weather they fly high; but even when the birds are only specks in the distant blue lift above, their soft, silvery, flute-like notes penetrate to earth below. Swans are said to be ill-used religious ladies under enchantment, driven from their homes and forced to wander, and to dwell where most kindly treated and where least molested. They are therefore regarded with loving pity and veneration, and the man who would injure a swan would thereby hurt the feelings of the community.

A woman found a wounded swan on a frozen lake near her house, and took it home, where she set the broken wing, dressed the bleeding feet, and fed the starving bird with lintseed and water. The woman had an ailing child, and as the wounds of the swan healed the health of the child improved, and the woman believed that her treatment of the swan caused the recovery of her child, and she rejoiced accordingly and composed the following lullaby to her restored child:--

EALA bhan thu,
Hu hi! ho ho!

'S truagh do charamh,
Hu hi! ho ho!

'S truagh mar tha thu,
Hu hi! ho ho!

'S t-fhuil a t' fhagail,
Hu hi! ho ho!
Hu hi! ho ho!

Eala bhan thu,
Hu hi! ho ho!

Cian o d' chairdiu,

Hu hi! ho ho!

Bean do mhanrain,
Hu hi! ho ho!

THOU white swan,
Hu hi! ho ho!

Sad thy condition,
Hu hi! ho ho!

Pitiful thy state,
Hu hi! ho ho!

Thy blood flowing,
Hu hi! ho ho!
Hu hi! ho ho!

Thou white swan,
Hu hi! ho ho!

Far from thy friends,
Hu hi! ho ho!

Dame of thy converse,
Hu hi! ho ho!

Fan am nabachd,
Hu hi! ho ho!
Hu hi! ho ho!

Leigh an aigh thu,
Hu hi! ho ho!

Sian mo phaisdean,
Hu hi! ho ho!

Dion o 'n bhas e,
Hu hi! ho ho!

Greas gu slaint e,
Hu hi! ho ho!

Mar is ail leat,
Hu hi! ho ho!
Hu hi! hi ho!

Pian is anradh
Hu hi! ho ho!

Dh' fhear do sharuich,
Hu hi! ho ho!
Hu hi! hi ho!

Mile failt ort,
Hu hi! ho ho!

Buan is slan thu,
Hu hi! ho ho!

Linn an aigh dhut,
Hu hi! ho ho!

Remain near me,
Hi hi! ho ho!
Hu hi! ho ho!

Leech of gladness thou,
Hu hi! ho ho!

Sain my little child,
Hu hi! ho ho!

Shield him from death,
Hu hi! ho ho!

Hasten him to health,
Hu hi! ho ho!

As thou desirest,
Hu hi! ho ho!
Hu hi! hi ho!

Pain and sorrow
Hu hi! ho ho!

To thine injurer,
Hu hi! ho ho!
Hu hi! hi ho!

A thousand welcomes to thee,
Hu hi! ho ho!

Life and health be thine,
Hu hi! ho ho!

The age of joy be thine,
Hu hi! ho ho!

Anns gach aite,
Hu hi! ho ho!
Hu hi! hi ho!

* * * *

Furt is fas dha,
Hi hi! ho ho!

Neart is nas dha,
Hu hi! ho ho!

Buadh na larach,
Hu hi! ho ho!

Anns gach ait dha,
Hu hi! ho ho!
Hu hi! hi ho!

Moire Mhathair,
Hu hi! ho ho!

Mhin ghil aluinn,
Hu hi! ho ho!

Bhi da d' bhriodal,
Hu hi! ho ho!

Bhi dha d' mhanran,
Hu hi! ho ho!

Bhi dha d' lithiu,
Hu hi! ho ho!

Bhi dha d' arach,
Hu hi! ho ho!

In every place,
Hu hi! ho ho!

Hu hi! hi ho!

* * * *

Peace and growth to him,
Hu hi! ho ho!

Strength and worth to him,
Hu hi! ho ho!

Victory of place,
Hu hi! ho ho!

Everywhere to him,
Hu hi! ho ho!
Hu hi! hi ho!

The Mary Mother,
Hu hi! ho ho!

Fair white lovely,
Hu hi! ho ho!

Be fondling thee,
Hu hi! ho ho!

Be dandling thee,
Hu hi! ho ho!

Be bathing thee,
Hu hi! ho ho!

Be rearing thee,
Hu hi! ho ho!

Bhi dha d' dhion
Hu hi! ho ho!

Bho lion do namhu;
Hu hi! ho ho!
Hu hi! ho ho!

Bhi dha d' bheadru,
Hu hi! ho ho!

Bhi dha d' naisdiu,

Hu hi! ho ho!

Bhi dha d' lionu
Hu hi! ho ho!

Leis na grasu;
Hu hi! ho ho!
Hu hi! hi ho!

Gaol do mhathar thu,
Hu hi! ho ho!

Gaol a graidh thu,
Hu hi! ho ho!

Gaol nan ainghlean thu,
Hu hi! ho ho!

Ann am Paras!
Hu hi! ho ho!
Hu hi! hi ho!

Be shielding thee
Hu hi! ho ho!

From the net of thine enemy;
Hu hi! ho ho!
Hu hi! ho ho!

Be caressing thee,
Hu hi! ho ho!

Be guarding thee,
Hu hi! ho ho!

Be filling thee
Hu hi! ho ho!

With the graces;
Hu hi! ho ho!
Hu hi! hi ho!

The love of thy mother, thou,
Hu hi! ho ho!

The love of her love, thou,

Hu hi! ho ho!

The love of the angels, thou,
Hu hi! ho ho!

In Paradise!
Hu hi! ho ho!
Hu hi! hi ho!

BAN-TIGHEARNA BHINN

THE MELODIOUS LADY-LORD

THERE were many religious houses throughout the Isles. Two of these were in Benbecula--one at 'Baile-mhanaich,' Monk's-town, and one at 'Baile-nan-cailleach,' Nuns'-town. These houses were attached to Iona, and were ruled and occupied by members of the first families of the Western Isles. Probably their insularity secured them from dissolution at the time of the Reformation, for these communities lingered long after the Reformation, and ceased to exist simply through natural decay.

It is said that two nuns had been visiting a sick woman. When returning home from the moorland to the townland, they heard the shrill voice of a child and the soft voice of a woman. The nuns groped their way down the rugged rocks, and there found a woman soothing a child in her arms. They were the only two saved from a wreck--the two frailest in the ship. The nuns took them home to Nunton. The woman was an Irish princess and a nun, and the child an Irish prince, against whose life a usurper to the throne had conceived a plot. The holy princess fled with the child-prince, intending to take him for safety to Scandinavia. The two nuns are said to have composed the two following poems.

One version of the story says that the child grew up and succeeded to the throne in Ireland; another that he died in the North Sea, and that he was buried in North Ronaldsay, Orkney.

During the three centuries of the Norse occupation there was much cordial communication between Scotland and Ireland, and much, but not cordial communication between Ireland and Scandinavia. Norsemen infested the east of Ireland and west of Scotland. There were plots and counterplots and wars innumerable between invaders and invaded, the ends of the beam ascending and descending in sore quick succession. Ultimately the Irish succeeded in inflicting a crushing defeat on the Scandinavians at the battle of Clontarf.

Clontarf is situated on Dublin Bay, a few miles below the city. It is a low-lying plain of much extent and great fertility. In the adjoining sea is a spit or bar emitting curious sounds during certain conditions of tide and wind. The sounds resemble the bellowing of a bull, and hence the name 'Cluain tarbh,' Clontarf, the plain of bulls.

The famous battle of Clontarf was fought on Good Friday, 23rd April, 1014. The Irish were led by their celebrated warrior-king, Brian Boroimhe, monarch of all Ireland, and the Danes by their Celto-Danish Prince, Earl Sigurd. There was indescribable havoc on both sides. The slaughter, as seen from the walls of Dublin, is described as resembling the work of mad reapers in a field of corn. Earl Sigurd fell. This was foretold him by his mother, Audna, daughter of Carroll, King of Ireland, when she gave him the 'Raven Banner of Battle' at Skidda-myre, now Skidden, in Caithness. Audna told Sigurd that the Raven Banner would always bring victory to the owner, but death to the bearer. At the battle of Clontarf every man who took up the Raven Banner fell. At last no one would take it up. Seeing this, Sigurd himself seized the banner, saying, "'Tis meetest that the beggar himself should bear his bag.' Immediately thereafter Sigurd fell, and with him the Norse power in Ireland. The victorious Irish slaughtered the defeated Danes with all the concentrated hate of three centuries of cruel wrong. The fall of Earl Sigurd was made known to his friends in the North through the fore-knowledge of the Valkymar, the twelve weird sisters of Northern Mythology, of whom Gray sings in his 'Fatal Sisters.'

CO i bhain-tighearna bhinn,
An bun an tuim,
Am beul an tuim?

Chan alca, [fhalc
Cha lacha,
Chan eala,
'S chan aonar i.

WHO is she the melodious lady-lord,
At the base of the knoll,
At the mouth of the wave?

Not the ale,
Not the duck,
Not the swan,
And not alone is she.

Co i bhain-tighearna bhinn,
Am bun an tuim,
Am beul an tuim?

Chan fhosga,
Cha lona,
Cha smeorach,
Air gheuig i.

Co i bhain-tighearna bhinn,
Am bun an tuim,
Am beul an tuim?

❊ ❊ ❊ ❊
❊ ❊ ❊ ❊
Cha tarman tuirim
An t-sleibh i.

317

Co i bhain-tighearna bhinn,
Am bun an tuim,
Am beul an tuim?

Cha bhreac air a bhuinne,
Cha mhoineis na tuinne,
Cha mhuirghin-mhuire
Na Ceit i.

Co i bhain-tighearna bhinn,
Am bun an tuim,
Am beul an tuim?

Cha bhainisg na cuigeil,
Chan ainnir na fuiril,
Cha bhainnireach bhuidhe
Na spreidh i.

Who is she the melodious lady-lord,
At the base of the knoll,
At the mouth of the wave?

Not the lark,
Not the merle,
Not the mavis,
On the bough is she.

Who is she the melodious lady-lord,
At the base of the knoll,
At the mouth of the wave?

* * * *
* * * *
Not the murmuring ptarmigan
Of the hill is she.

Who is she the melodious lady-lord,
At the base of the knoll,
At the mouth of the wave?

Not the grilse of the stream,
Not the seal of the wave,
Not the sea maiden
Of May is she.

Who is she the melodious lady-lord,

At the base of the knoll,
At the mouth of the wave?

Not the dame of the distaff,
Not the damsel of the lyre,
Not the golden-haired maid
Of the flocks is she.

Co i bhain-tighearna bhinn,
Am bun an tuim,
Am beul an tuim?

Bain-tighearna bhinn,
Bhaindidh mhin,

Ighinn righ,
Ogha righ,
Iar-ogh righ,
Ion-ogh righ,
Dubh-ogh righ,
Bean righ,
Mathair righ,
Muime righ,
I taladh righ,
Is e fo breid aic.

A Eirinn a shiubhail i,
Gu Lochlann tha fiughair aic,
An Trianaid bhi siubhal leath
H-uile taobh a theid i--
H-uile taobh a theid i.

Who is she the melodious lady-lord,
At the base of the knoll,
At the mouth of the wave?

Melodious lady-lord,
God-like in loveliness,

Daughter of a king,
Granddaughter of a king,
Great-granddaughter of a king,
Great-great-granddaughter of a king,
Great-great-great-granddaughter of a king,
Wife of a king,
Mother of a king,

Foster-mother of a king,
She lullabying a king,
And he under her plaid.

From Erin she travelled,
For Lochlann is bound,
May the Trinity travel with her
Whithersoever she goes--
Whithersoever she goes.

RIGHINN NAM BUADH

QUEEN OF GRACE

IS min a has,
Is fin a cas,
Is caomh a cruth,
Is caoin a guth,
Is binn a cainn,
Is grinn a meinn,
Is blath sealladh a sul,
Is tlath meaghail a gnuis,
'S a brollach graidh-gheal a snamh 'n a com
Mar chra-fhaoileag air bharr nan tonn.

Is naomhar an oigh is or-dhealta cul,
Le maotharan og am bonn nan stuc,
Gun lon dhaibh le cheil fo chorr nan speur,
Gun sgoth fo 'n ghrein bho 'n namhaid.

Ta sgiath Mhic De da comhdach,
Ta ciall Mhic De da seoladh,
Ta briathar Mhic De mar bhiadh di fein,
Ta reul 'n a leirsinn mhoir di.

Ta duibhre na h-oidhche dhi mar shoillse an lo,
Ta an lo dhi a ghnath 'n a sholas,
Ta Moir oigh nan gras 's a h-uile h-ait,
Le na seachd graidh 'g a comhnadh,
Na seachd graidh 'g a comhnadh.

SMOOTH her hand,
Fair her foot,
Graceful her form,
Winsome her voice,
Gentle her speech,

Stately her mien,
Warm the look of her eye,
Mild the expression of her face,
While her lovely white breast heaves on her bosom
Like the black-headed sea-gull on the gently heaving wave.

Holy is the virgin of gold-mist hair,
With tenderest babe at the base of the bens,
No food for either of them under the arch of the sky,
No shelter under the sun to shield them from the foe.

The shield of the Son of God covers her,
The inspiration of the Son of God guides her,
The word of the Son of God is food to her,
His star is a bright revealing light to her.

The darkness of night is to her as the brightness of day,
The day to her gaze is always a joy,
While the Mary of grace is in every place,
With the seven beatitudes compassing her,
The seven beatitudes compassing her.

CILL-MOLUAG

KILLMOLUAG

A curious ceremony was current in the Island of Lismore. When several boys gathered together, two boys seized a third by the head and heels, and swaying him from side to side sang an eerie chant over him.

UILL! hill! uill! O!
Co chill an teid seo?

FIRST BOY

UILL! hill! uill! O!
In what kill shall this go?

Cill-Moluag an Lios-mor,
Far an cinn na cnoimheagan!

Uill! hill! uill! O!
Co chill an teid seo?

Cill-Moluag an Lios-mor,
Loisealam na greine.

Uill! hill! uill! O!
Co chill an teid seo?

Cill-Moluag an Lios-mor,
Boid nach dean e eiridh!

SECOND BOY

In Killmoluag of Lismore,
Where the maggots grow!

Uill! hill! uill! O!
In what kill shall this go?

In Killmoluag of Lismore,
Fairest 'neath the sun.

Uill! hill! uill! O!
In what kill shall this go?

In Killmoluag of Lismore,
I vow he shall not rise!

After more questions and more answers, the boy was carried round in procession sunwise to a wailing march, in which all the boys joined. The boy was then laid upon a rock or knoll for an altar. After more singing and more ceremonial the victim was laid in some convenient hollow for a grave, to the music of another eerie lament and the laughter of the boys. The writer was an actor in this boyish drama, but what the drama represented he does not know.

AM BREID

'AM BREID,' the kertch or coif, was a square of linen formed into a cap and donned by a woman on the morning after her marriage. It was the sign of wifehood as the 'stiom,' snood, was the emblem of maidenhood. The linen of the kertch was pure white and very fine. The square was arranged into three angles symbolic of the Trinity, under whose guidance the young wife was to walk. From this it is called 'currachd tri-chearnach'--three-cornered cap. The kertch was fastened to the hair with cords of silk or pins of silver or of gold. It is said to have been very becoming and picturesque. It is mentioned in many of the sayings of the people as:--'breid ban'--white kertch; 'breid cuailean'--hair kertch; 'breid beannach'--pinnacled kertch; 'breid an crannaig'--kertch on props; 'breid cuimir nan crun,' the shapely coif of the crowns; and 'breid cuimir nan tri crun'--the shapely coif of the three crowns. It is also spoken of in many songs.

'Nar a faicear ort breid
La feille no clachain,
'S nar a faicear do chlann

Doi gu teampull baistidh.'

'Na 'm faighinn dhomh fein
Thu le beannachd na cleire,
Gur a mis a bhitheadh reidh
Ri bhi faicinn do bhreid
An ceud Domhnach.'

'A cul dualach, camlach, cuachach,
Ann an sguaib aig m' eudail,
'S ge boidheach e 's an stiom a suas
Cha mheas an cuailean breid e.'

'Gur a math thig breid ban
Air a charamh beannach dhut,
Agus staoise dh' an t-sioda mhin,
'G a theannadh ort.'

Never on thee be seen kertch
Upon feast-day or church-day,
And never be seen thy children
Going to the temple of baptism.

Were I to obtain to myself
Thee with the blessing of the clerics,
It is I who would be joyous
At seeing on thee thy kertch
The first Sunday.

Her hair in coils, curled, curved,
And in clustered folds has my beloved,
And though beautiful it seems within the snood,
It would not look worse beneath the kertch.

Well becomes thee the white kertch,
Placed pinnacle-wise,
And cords of the fine silk
Binding it upon thee.

[paragraph continues] The song from which this last verse is quoted had curious wanderings and narrow escapes--from Lochaber to Lahore, from Lahore to Lochalsh, and from Lochalsh to Skye and Uist. It was taken down at Howmore, South Uist, from Peggie Macaulay, better known as Peggie Robertson and 'Peigi Sgiathanach'--Skye

[paragraph continues] Peggie. She came from 'Sleibhte riabhach nam ban boidheach,'--brindled Sleat of the beautiful women, and well upheld the reputation of her native place, for she was a tall, straight, comely brunette, with beautiful brown eyes and hair 'like raven's plumage, smoothed on snow.' She had accompanied her master and mistress, Captain and Mrs Macdonald, Knock, Skye, on a visit to Sir John Macrae, Airdantouil, Lochalsh. Sir John was famed for his symmetry, bravery, and accomplishments. He inherited the musical talents of the Macleods of Raarsey, and could play a phenomenal number of musical instruments. He was wont to say that there was no music for the house equal to Highland music, nor instrument for the field equal to the Highland bagpipe. Sir John had been military attache to his cousin, the Marquis of Hastings, when he was Governor-General of India. From Sir John Macrae, Peggie Macaulay heard the words of this song and an account of how he got them. Sir John said that when in India he was sent with despatches to a distant fort. As he was nearing the gate under cover of night, he was surprised to hear a Gaelic song once heard in childhood and often sought since. When he reined in his horse to listen, the sentry stopped his song and challenged. The answer was given in Gaelic, and the sentry was surprised in his turn. Macrae was just in time to rouse the Governor from his fancied security and to lead the garrison to repel an attack, in which the singer Eoghan Cameron fell after killing seven sepoys single-handed.

Sir John Macrae died soon after Peggie Macaulay heard him singing the song, and she died soon after the song was taken down from her dictation by the present writer. Sir John Macrae called this song, 'treas taladh na h-Alba,'--the third lullaby of Alban, and as sung by bright Peggie Robertson it merited praise.

[pp. <page 214>-215

AM BREID

THE KERTCH

MILE failte dhut fo d' bhreid,
Ri do re gu robh thu slan,
Luth is laithean dhut le sith,
Do pharas le do ni bhi fas.

An tus do chomh-ruith is tu og,
An tus do lo iarr Ti nan dul,
Cha churam dha nach toir e ceart
Gach foil is feart a bhios 'nad run.

An coron-ceile a chuir thu suas,
Is tric a fhuair e buaidh do mhnai;
Bi-sa subhailc ach bi suairc,
Bi-sa stuam an lid 's an laimh.

Bi-sa fialaidh ach bi glic,
Bi-sa misneachail ach stold,
Bi-sa bruithneach ach bi balbh,
Bi-sa caimeineach ach coir.

Na dean criontaireachd an toirt,
Na dean brosg ach na bi fuar,
Na labhair fos air neach ge h-olc,
Ma labhrar ort na toir-sa fuath.

Bi-sa gleidhteach air h-ainm,
Bi-sa sgeimineach ach suairc,
Lamh Dhe biodh air h-eilm,
An deilbh, an gniamh 's an smuain.

Na bi gearanach fo d' chrois,
Siubhail socair fo chopan lan,
A chaoidh dh'an olc na toir-sa speis,
'S le do bhreid dhut ceud mile failt!

A THOUSAND hails to thee beneath thy kertch,
During thy course mayest thou be whole,
Strength and days be thine in peace,
Thy paradise with thy means increase.

In beginning thy dual race, and thou young,
In beginning thy course, seek thou the God of life,
Fear not but He will rightly rule
Thine every secret need and prayer.

This spousal crown thou now hast donned,
Full oft has gotten grace to woman,
Be thou virtuous, but be gracious,
Be thou pure in word and hand.

Be thou hospitable, yet be wise,
Be thou courageous, but be calm,
Be thou frank, but be reserved,
Be thou exact, yet generous.

Be not miserly in giving,
Do not flatter, yet be not cold,
Speak not ill of man, though ill he be,
If spoken of, show not resentment.

Be thou careful of thy name,
Be thou dignified yet kind,
The hand of God be on thine helm,
In inception, in act, and in thought.

Be not querulous beneath thy cross,

Walk thou warily when thy cup is full,
Never to evil give thou countenance,
And with thy kertch, to thee a hundred thousand hails!

FUIGHEAL

FRAGMENT

MAR a bha,
Mar a tha,
Mar a bhitheas
Gu brath,
A Thrithinn
Nan gras!
Ri traghadh,
'S ri lionadh!
A Thrithinn
Nan gras!
Ri traghadh,
'S ri lionadh!

As it was,
As it is,
As it shall be
Evermore,
O Thou Triune
Of grace!
With the ebb,
With the flow,
O Thou Triune
Of grace!
With the ebb,
With the flow.

Made in the USA
Lexington, KY
20 June 2016